To Day

I hope you enjoy the read. All the best

GENESIS

BY

EDWARD JOHNS

GW00496569

ACKNOWLEDGMENTS

The author wishes to thank Captain John Ward for his help in offering advice and technical assistance regarding all aspects of commercial flying and commercial flight training; Captain George Carnell for his insight into the area of firearms and ballistics of which the author knew very little and anybody else who helped to guide and point me in the right direction.

Edward Johns
http;//edwardjohns.net

1

He could hear their dogs clearly now: before it was just an annoying, rough noise battering his senses, and he tried to fool himself with a convincing argument that it could have been anybody's dogs out here in these woods, especially at this time of year, but no here they were loud and clear, as if someone was standing beside him clanging an enormous bell announcing their imminent arrival. And he knew it was their dogs.

His heart began to race, and it started a chain reaction of panic that rose exponentially with every bark and howl emanating from the hounds.

Control, that's what was needed now, self-control, controlled breathing, controlled relaxation and a controlled heartbeat. It was what his cardiologist had prescribed as a helpful preventative measure once he'd recovered fully from his heart attack, that and a glass of red wine with his evening meal. He had been lucky that particular day: by some quirk of fate he was visiting a friend in hospital, who had nearly died of a heart attack themselves while out on the golf course, when he felt a searing pain in the chest like somebody was clamping it in a vice and slowly turning the handle tighter and tighter.

He tried in vain to regulate his breathing, just as the DVD given to him demonstrated, but it was proving to be a thankless task: this physical exertion was not conducive to relaxation and meditation.

Voices, he could clearly discern voices intermingling with the incessant noise from those damned dogs, but these were voices he knew all too well.

'Damn them!' he cussed. 'Damn them all to hell!'

He knew his time was short and more importantly so did they. He swore an oath there and then that he would never go quietly, not as long as he could draw a breath.

'You thought you could get one over on and steal from old Jack Hennessey did you!' he hissed between gasps. This outburst brought about an unexpected and immediately perceptible increase in decibels from his pursuers.

'We'll see you assholes, we'll see who is the smarter!' And Jack Hennessey steeled himself to push on with even greater resolve. He accepted the risks and even embraced them, and when the first tell-tale symptoms reared their ugly heads he simple shrugged them off with another, 'We'll see assholes!'

The sharpness of the pain along with the shortness of breath bothered him but a little in the big scheme of things; they wanted what was his, what he had earned with honesty and good old fashioned hard graft, and he was not about to give it up to a bunch of money grabbing bastards whose only saving grace, it appeared, was their penchant for not staying in one place for any great length of time.

The hounds were gaining on him, and were now close enough as to make it possible to differentiate each dog's subtle tones from one another. He recognised old Jasper and vowed to break the bloody animal's neck.

Hennessey clutched his chest as he slowly and explicably ventured towards a dead-end for which he had no possible means of escape. He started to pray that God would delay any triumph long enough for him to stick it to these fucking shitheads once and for all. Then it suddenly occurred to him in his hour of need that he had never been the most pious of individuals and any attempt to pray would ultimately be considered by the big man upstairs as nothing short of hypocrisy on a grand scale, but pray he did and with all the sincerity he could muster, intermingled with several apologies for the increase in the level of his profanity.

The sun shone through the high, dense foliage that sat on the Western edge of Starr Mountain, sitting in the Southeast corner of McMinn County, Tennessee.

'Assholes!' he muttered again.

The undulating ground began to rise hindering his forward progress, for although he had traversed it many times, it was now proving ideal for the big man to make life excruciatingly painful for him.

'If this doesn't finish me off, nothing will!'

Sadly for him it did not, and added to that, he had the unenviable pleasure of witnessing the hounds sprint through the undergrowth below him, howling to their master's orders now that their prey was well within their grasp.

'Keep on coming boys!' he said confidently, jogging with one hand resting on his chest in a pitiful display of defence against any attack that may grip him.

One of the Boyd clan's voices punctuated the howls of the dogs.

'Asshole!' repeated Hennessey.

The strain clearly evident in the dogs' howling, denoting their effort whilst racing up the incline in order to catch the old man, made him laugh.

'If you damn animals can't catch a seventy-year-old man with a dodgy ticker, then you ain't worth shit!'

Hennessey laughed again, strained and clambered his way through a large row of bushes surrounding a group of trees; they seemed to him to be acting as sentries for whatever treasure these majestic giants of the forest were guarding from the brute of a destroyer, namely man, then he stumbled and fell headfirst into the dirt some thirty yards shy of the bushes and became immediately aware that he was not alone. The heavy breathing of one of the hounds filled his senses, as he hit the deck. Instinctively he lashed out and his yelping pursuer backed off.

'Hold him down Bessie!' shouted one of them, who thankfully for him, was out of sight.

'This ain't your day, Bessie.' And he kicked the mutt straight in the face, scrambling her brains, rendering her nigh on unconscious.

The effort to get to his feet was the final straw for his poor, worn out heart; his breath was laboured, his head was spinning, causing him to crash headlong into the bushes, which had the added advantage of hiding him from the nearest Boyd. His wheezing came to his aid in drowning out the advancing enemy, and it helped relax his troubled soul, but it was nothing short of a miracle that they didn't find him straight off, either that or just plain stupidity, he couldn't rightly tell with this lot. Here he lay for what seemed like an age struggling for breath. Hennessey felt like he had drunk a litre of bourbon. That would have finished him off no problem with an added element of pleasure to boot.

Jack Hennessey's head began to clear just in time for him to witness Jake Boyd's flushed red, pocked marked face fill his view of the beautiful Tennessee woodland. The chase had taken much out him and he was feeling every day of his thirty years.

'Mr Hennessey.'

'Mr Boyd.'

'You've given us a right run for our money!'

'Shame it has to end, eh? And I was having so much fun.'

'You know we never take no for an answer.'

'No! How about fuck you?'

'Mr Hennessey, me and my brothers have been more than patient with you and been more than generous in our offer.'

'So what part didn't you understand? Was it the fuck you part?'

'No, is not a word that appears in our vocabulary, especially with people who we place demands upon!'

'No, you don't say!' wheezed Hennessey. His head began to spin widely out of control.

'You run well for a worn out old man.'

'Obviously not well enough, as I'm talking to a prick like you!'

Jake Boyd knelt down beside the ailing old man and began to get the first inkling that time was seriously starting to run out for the old timer.

'You don't look too hot?'

'Like you care!'

'I have to thank you for giving the dogs a good run out this morning, with the exception of Bessie of course, but I'm sure she'd like to thank you later when she pisses all over your corpse.'

'Shame I couldn't give them all the Bessie treatment!'

Jake's younger brother Carl appeared and squatted down beside his kin.

'Is he dead yet?'

'Not quite brain-ache!' Hennessey struggled out.

'Go ahead Hennessey and stop wasting our time. Just die!' Carl said before going back to see to the dogs. 'I won't forget Bessie!' he added without looking back.

'Your brother's not the sharpest pencil in the box.'

'He's honest! What you see is what you get with him.' Jake eased his head forward until he was inches from Hennessey's: he liked this technique as it always emphasised his point and displayed an element of solidarity with his brother.

'That'll be shit then!'

'Don't push me Hennessey!'

'Oh, I am sorry, have I touched a nerve with you Boyds?'

'You just carry on kidding yourself that it will make your final moments memorable, and maybe justify your pathetic excuse for a life.'

'You won't get shit!'

'I'm going to see the next sunrise, and you're not!'

Hennessey could sense another attack coming on and deep in his heart knew that this or the next was going to be the last, for with every passing minute he was struggling against nature and God's will to force valuable air into his lungs.

'I've had a good run for my money. I got no complaints!'

Jake rose slowly and purposefully to his feet. He stood nearly six feet, had the build of an ageing linebacker, but appeared smaller because he walked with a slight stoop. He wore his dark hair slicked back, which gave him the look of a sleazy drug dealer, and the broken nose acquired during one too many bar fights only added to the misconception. Jake glanced quickly over his shoulder to ascertain the whereabouts of his two brothers; Rudy had yet to show his face, but he could hear his voice talking to the hounds.

'Rudy,' said Hennessey quietly, shocking the older Boyd that the man lying prostrate on the ground before him in his final death throes, should know that he was thinking of his brother, 'is a right prick!'

If anything was guaranteed to shake the elder Boyd sibling back to the here and now then that comment was it.

'Sorry?' He regretted the reply the split second he uttered the word.

'Your younger brother is a useless, worthless, no good prick!'

Jake had foolishly left himself open to this second, stinging repost and it angered his own blown up feeling of self-importance.

'My brother is not, as you like to put it, the sharpest button in the box-'

'Pencil!'

'Sorry?' Jake said, not hiding his displeasure at being interrupted.

'Pencil! Not the sharpest pencil in the box!' Hennessey said a second time, laughing whilst deliberately over pronouncing the word pencil.

Jake refused to rise to the bait being dangled in front of his nose by this wheezing, ashen faced old man. 'You shouldn't insult a man's family. A man's family honour is sacrosanct when it comes to the opinion of strangers.'

'But I'm not a stranger you moron!' Hennessey said, trying to get comfortable, but he was prevented from rising from his seated position by Jake laying his sizeable paw on his shoulder. 'I'm the guy you're trying to steal from!'

'People say it's best you pay the dying their due respects,' Jake said studying the tops of the trees. 'Aaaah! It should be a hell of a nice day tomorrow.' He lowered his gaze to the dying man. 'Shame you won't see it.'

Hennessey failed to focus on him. He became aware that they were not alone: Carl's and Rudy's dulcet tones punctuated any remaining consciousness he managed to salvage.

'He still alive?' Carl said with a hint of incredulity.

'He's a strong old brute!' added Rudy.

Hennessey dearly wanted to give the three of them one more put down, but his head was spinning at such a rate that it was only matched in its severity by the heaving of his chest for every available ounce of oxygen.

'At least this will save us a bullet and a very uncomfortable and awkward police enquiry,' Carl said turning away from Hennessey's last few minutes.

'Sheriff Poulsen's an idiot at the best of times!'

Jake's curt remark regarding the Sheriff made Hennessey smile: it was true, Sheriff Poulsen could give the impression of being permanently stuck behind the eight ball at times, but it added humour to his final minutes to hear somebody else share the same thoughts about the local law enforcement.

'Glad to see your last moments are amusing you Hennessey!' Rudy added.

It was always easy to tell the youngest, Rudy, apart from his brothers by his slightly squeaky voice, which caused much mirth around the town, and was the spark which indubitable set off his infamous temper.

'No, I just couldn't think of a bigger bunch of fucking dickheads with which to gratefully kiss this God forsaken life a fond farewell!'

Rudy delivered a sharp right kick to Hennessey's ribs before Jake had any chance to react or attempt to talk him out of it.

'You idiot!' shouted Jake confronting his younger sibling and setting off the dogs.

'Told you!' laughed Hennessey between wheezes.

'Why?'

'Because they will find the body with your size nine boot print all over it!'

'Oh!'

'Yes!'

'We better dispose of the body then!'

'No Rudy, as discussed,' Jake said turning his attention back to Hennessey. 'And I want to enjoy what's coming to me for a long, long time to come!'

'Oh!' Rudy repeated.

'Moron!' mumbled Hennessey.

'You can shut up........dead man!'

'Is that the best you got "Shut up dead man"?'

Hennessey grabbed his chest; the searing pain shot through his upper body. He gasped valiantly for breath, but it was to no avail, his body shuddered one last time under the strain to maintain life and he keeled over, sighing as he did so.

'Is he dead?' asked Rudy.

'If he ain't he's doin' a damn fine job of acting like a corpse!' replied Jake.

Carl stood over Jack for a few seconds, grunted his approval at their quarry finally having died then went back to his beloved dogs.

He and Rudy were not only the youngest of the three brothers, but in fact were twins: Carl was born exactly three minutes before Rudy and that is where any similarity between the two men ended: he was short, dark and stocky after their father Jessie; Rudy was tall, fair, lithe and athletic and as long as he didn't open his mouth could charm any girl, bar the locals, he met with his flashing smile. It wound the hell out of his twin that Rudy always had the means to get the girl, but never the talent to keep them.

'We should leave him as he is,' Rudy said, waiting expectantly for a nod of approval from his older brother.

Jake paused giving his younger sibling's suggestion some serious thought. 'Yep, I can't think of anything better, and it will look as though he went for a walk in the woods and just sat down to die.'

2

A small bead of sweat began its slow, methodical journey, traversing the back of one Captain Harry Travers: a stocky, ex-rugby player of around six feet in height with dark hair, brown eyes, thirty-five years of age, single and a professional airline pilot with over twelve years commercial flying experience and known to a few close friends and family simply as 'H'. The cause was the one most singular experience he personally hated about his job, others loved it, but he most certainly didn't and it wasn't anybody's fault: it certainly wasn't the Training Captain's fault; it wasn't the Training Department's fault; the Airline sure as hell didn't set these tests on purpose. He just hated waking up on the morning of his simulator detail feeling like he was going to throw up due to nervous tension, but for all his dislike for this biannual revalidation he could see the worthwhile benefit from it all. Pilots, he argued, whenever the subject came up at dinner parties, are the most regulated body of professionals on earth bar none; doctors aren't regulated as much, nor are barristers, lawyers, dentists or politicians, but pilots continually have to jump through hoops to prove their worth, but as soon as anything goes wrong who's automatically to blame? The most dangerous part of his day, he would say to any nervous flyer, was the drive to work.

The Training Captain taking today's detail was Captain Harvey Lyons, who had been training just as long as Harry had been flying, so there wasn't much he hadn't seen and this guaranteed a day with no hidden extras, but did little to alleviate the nervous tension gripping his insides. His first officer was twenty-three year old Curtis Traherne.

The perspiration finally ran its course descending to the base of his back followed by more emanating from the palms of his hands. He released a blast of cold air from the ventilation duct positioned to the left of the side-stick on this Airbus A320 simulator. The job has its moments, he thought, but kept it to himself; the last thing he needed was an ambitious first officer being tipped off to his less than desirable level of comfort. Harry glanced down at his Navigation Display to read off the instantaneous wind readout: 0 head, 28 left glowed in green back at him. He could clearly make put the PAPI lights through the artificially engineered inclement weather. Position Approach Path Indicators were made up of four lights designed to guide pilots down a nominated flight path: four reds you are too low; four whites you are too high; two white, two red is perfect.

'Two whites, two reds seen,' Curtis interposed.

'Thanks,' he replied.

He'd managed so far to keep the jet on that perfect three-degree glide path with the number one, left-hand, engine shut down due to an in-flight fire, but the closer the moment of truth came the quicker he could sense his breathing increase. Don't fuck it up, his subconscious cried, don't fuck it up. Harry smiled.

'Five hundred!' claimed the electronic voice, which took its reading directly off the radio altimeter. Harry consciously slowed his breathing and increased his scan rate in order to land at his designate touchdown point. Through the corner of his eye Curtis began to fidget. He blocked it out.

It would now only be a matter of minutes to touchdown, so Harry fed the vertical speed indicator into his scan to gauge the aircraft's rate of descent over the runway threshold, and quietly prayed he wouldn't fuck it up.

'One hundred!' said the voice.

Harry broke off his scan and now concentrated on his touchdown point.

'Fifty!' He braced himself, and mentally prepared for the landing.

'Thirty!' Harry began his flare to arrest the aircraft's rate of descent.

'Twenty!' Travers smoothly closed the thrust lever on the right-hand engine whilst simultaneously correcting any crab effect, the crosswind had caused, by using the appropriate rudder input.

'Ten!'

A second later the jet's main wheels kissed the runway and he applied full reverse on the good engine, as he gently lowered the nose-wheel onto the runway. The aircraft's auto-brake system now kicked in and they started to slow.

Traherne backed him up by confirming all the retardation devices were in working order. As their forward speed reduced and approached seventy knots, Curtis confirmed the speed. Idle reverse was selected. A couple of seconds passed before Harry applied manual braking until the jet came to a halt. Reverse thrust was safely stowed once they reached taxi speed.

Captain Lyons now took over and began to reposition the jet in preparation for the next part of their simulator detail. Nothing was said at this point and Harry took a moment to recompose. Curtis remained mute. The one single instruction that he adhered to at all times was: "To fly the simulator, as you would the aircraft", and he was satisfied he'd done just that.

'Well?' asked Lyons. 'How do you think that went?'

Travers saw where this was leading and was not going to give away any ammunition which could be fired back at him, so he simply replied: 'Okay.'

'You wouldn't have done anything different then?'

'No, not really, but I appreciate there is always room for improvement.'

Harry could feel himself beginning to perspire again, and then quickly and quietly chastised his lack of self-control. You're a professional, behave like one.

Lyons turned his attention to the man in the right-hand seat: 'Curtis, what would you have done in that situation?'

Oh, here we go, he thought, and braced for the points score.

'I wouldn't have done anything differently Captain Lyons,' came the shock response. 'With my limited experience I thought Harry handled it really well!'

Well fuck me, thought Harry, as he studied Curtis Traherne closely, finding himself trying to figure the kid out: here he was hearing stories, drifting down the proverbial grapevine, regarding Curtis' determination to "Get one over", as one put it, yet when an ideal situation lands smack bang in his lap, he let it pass him by. Why?

'Good!' said Lyons sharply, without giving anything away. 'It's time for a coffee break, tea break, whatever break you want and when we return it's your turn Curtis.'

Captain Lyons repositioned the simulator during the fifteen minute recess while Harry and his partner went to get coffees from the cafeteria. Before Travers could say anything, and cut off any chance of a serious piss-take, Curtis bought the drinks. The talk, once all three had sat down and started to sip their hot beverages, invariably turned to the running of the company.

'Bunch of incompetent wankers!' stated Travers. 'There's no way you can explain away such an astronomical debt mountain!'

'That's a bit harsh!' countered Lyons

'Bloody incompetents, I would have fired the lot of them a long time ago! What I want to know is how they kept their jobs for so long? Because if I had flown the jet the way they ran this company I'd have been out on my ear years ago!'

'You need to look at all the positives Harry,' Lyons said, taking too big a sip of his coffee.

'Which are?'

'In the present climate you should be grateful to still have a job!'

It was all Travers could do not to choke on his drink.

'I'm with Harry on this. My CV is already doing the rounds,' stated Curtis.

He definitely choked now.

'I thought a young lad like you would want to stay now that you've started to get yourself settled,' Lyons said inquisitively.

'I borrowed a lot of money, and contrary to popular belief along with other stories doing the rounds, my family aren't filthy rich, so I can ill afford to be out of work.'

'Stories?' quizzed Lyons.

'Apparently I'm a "Points scorer"!'

'I take it that's a no then?'

'Damn right!'

'You got anything lined up?' asked Harry.

Curtis denied wholeheartedly, with a face any professional poker player would have been proud of, that he had anything in the pipeline, but Harry knew he was being bullshitted so just let it go. He'd have done the same.

'I think you should reconsider any move, Curtis,' started Lyons. 'The airline will not always be in such a precarious position: we've now got new management in, who are turning this company around, and a couple of years down the road you'll have that extra, invaluable experience which, if your sims are okay, will put you in the frame for a possible command.'

It was good, sound, solid advice and Harry just nodded in agreement giving his partner a sideways look as he did so. Suddenly, he wasn't such a bad guy after all. Even Harvey was okay right now after his mini speech.

The short recess soon evaporated and they returned to the "Box", their affectionate term for the simulator, for Curtis to fly his exercise.

* * *

Harry dumped the large green bag containing the company manuals on the floor, once they had reached the debriefing room following Curtis' session in the "Box", which had flown by with him putting in an accomplished performance: his handling of all his single engine work was well above the required standard bearing in mind his level of experience. Harry offered to do the polite thing and supply the refreshments.

He passed Curtis in the corridor and gave a knowing nod, Harry could see the guy was about to get himself worked up and wanted him to know that he had done alright, and not to give himself such a hard time.

The briefing was, as expected, thorough but fair with all the relevant points covered with a couple of recommendations; Harry knew all too well that you're never too old to learn in aviation and Captain Lyons furnished them with plenty of food for thought. He spent the time it took him to reach his classic blue Porsche 924, with smart brown leather interior, in self-chastisement for any thoughts he had of Curtis: it was a terrible habit of his and he knew it, of allowing any preconceived ideas to influence his thinking.

'Nice car Harry!' called out Curtis, who had followed him outside.

Harry stopped, turned and waited politely for the young man to catch up. 'Restored it myself; I found it in a barn where it had sat for fourteen years.'

'I've always wanted to restore a classic car.'

'You should. You're never too old to start. Just find a car you love.'

'I don't go along with all these people who believe the 924 is not a real Porsche.'

The two men approached the shiny blue Porsche with admiring glances. Before Curtis could say another word Harry offered him a lift and, as no transport had been arranged, he gratefully accepted.

It was normally, on a good day, a fifteen to twenty minute drive from the training facility in Cheadle to the hotel situated at Manchester Airport via the two motorways M60 and M56; Harry wasted no time in opening up the taps on the two litre, Bosch K-Jetronic fuel injected classic once the freedom of the motorway was at his disposal.

The 924 purred as they swiftly and effortlessly accelerated through fifty to eighty miles an hour. Harry kept it at eighty. The car hugged the M60 motorway, itching to be let loose, to break free of the constraints being imposed upon its desire to rip up the road by a proud and occasionally law abiding owner. The talk inevitable turned to the car.

'I've promised myself a fast, noisy toy one day.'

'Do it sooner rather than later; all too quickly you find time marches by and the moment is gone forever.'

No sooner had Harry finished passing on one of his few pearls of wisdom than a metallic green Mazda screamed past, horn blaring accompanied with a generous two fingered salute emanating from the passengers' side window.

'You can't stand for that Harry!'

'Fuck no!' This was the red flag to the bull, and any and all constraints were abandoned. Travers unleashed the beast upon its prey.

The green Mazda was quickly held at station, and the two of them were thankful that the roads for once were reasonably quiet. Then slowly, but surely they began to reel them in. The driver of the Mazda knew early on of the Porsche's intentions, as any and all lane changes were not pre-empted by the required visual indication.

'He's going to exit at the last minute!' Harry said calmly.

'I reckon so,' Curtis replied eagerly, whilst checking his side mirror for any sign of the law.

The Mazda veered sharply, recklessly, into the middle lane in an effort to undertake a red Rover then swung back into the outside lane. Harry held the middle lane: unnecessary lane changing would cost them time and he was not left waiting to be proved right. Three further abrupt changes meant the Porsche was now no more than three car lengths behind.

'You weren't in a hurry to get back to your hotel were you?' Harry politely enquired.

He pulled closer to the Mazda.

'Fuck no!'

Signs for the M56 turn off indicated that it was only a few miles further up the motorway and Harry was beginning to get bored of this game of cat and mouse. It was time to put these upstarts in their place and he closed the gap to half a car length. A quick glance to the right, a half smile, and his right foot hit the floor about the same time as a lone finger salute embedded itself in the memory of the green Mazda's occupants. Within seconds Harry pulled out a gap until any hope of retaliation was a forlorn hope or just plain foolhardy. Harry exited the motorway to find the most expeditious route back to the airport.

'You want to stay at mine tonight?' Harry asked, slowing for traffic.

'Sure.'

'We'll get a ruby and a few beers.'

'Great.'

'Unless of course you have some studying time planned.'

'My liver can take anything you care to throw at it!'

'That's settled then.'

Harry lived alone in a three story, terraced house in Heald Green situated a little over two miles from the airport: he had bought the property when he first joined JaguAir twelve years ago, and enjoyed the place so much that when the opportunity arose to move, once his personal circumstances improved quite considerably, he declined and instead bought another place three houses down and rented it out to cabin crew.

His normal watering hole was Jack's Bar on Outwood Road, approximately a ten minute walk from his front door; when he first moved there he knew nobody or anywhere else to go and to his intense delight they served a mean pint of his favourite beer: Boddingtons. Recently the bar had been taken over by Steve, an old friend of his, which made the experience even more enjoyable. The icing on the cake was a superb Indian takeaway next door.

With the Porsche safely parked in the driveway, the two men quickly attacked the small walk standing between them and their liquid refreshment, and before any clock could strike another hour off the day the creamy brown beer tickled their taste buds.

Travers, as was his want when out and about partaking of any pleasures that took his fancy, put his mobile phone on vibrate and now that vibration interrupted his personal time causing him to momentarily abandon a half-finished pint. He took the call in the car park to guarantee privacy. The number was blocked.

'Hello,' he said cautiously.

An American voice came over broken and almost incomprehensible.

'Hello,' he said again, slightly louder.

The American's voice remained broken, but he could make out certain words: two guys named Will and Jack. The delicate connection finally gave out.

Harry stared at his mobile like a complete idiot, which he had only recently acquired as part of an upgrade.

'Piece of crap!' he said furiously, as he seriously contemplated throwing the upgrade in the nearest bin.

The piece of crap burst into life.

'Hello!' This time he shouted.

'Is this Mister Harry Travers?'

'It is!' he replied rather too abruptly.

'My name is Anton Jeffries.'

'I've never heard of you. What do you want?'

'I was your late uncle's lawyer.'

'My late uncle?' Travers asked incredulously.

'Mister Jack Hennessy, ' Jeffries said very deliberately, 'was your mother's cousin, and unfortunately I have to be the bearer of bad news: he died a little while ago of a heart attack. He did have a history of heart disease.'

'Right,' Harry interposed.

'The reason for the call is to inform you that Jack Hennessey has named you his only heir.'

Harry was stunned to silence.

'Mister Travers?'

'I'm still here.'

'I know this is a lot for you to take on right now, and if it would be more convenient I will call back at a later time.'

'How did you get my number by the way?'

'Your uncle had it.'

'Okay. Text your number and I'll call you later.'

Jeffries agreed and hung up.

Within a couple of minutes Harry had the number. He stood and contemplated ringing straight away, but a half empty pint of beer was calling him from the bar, and he needed valuable time to digest this news.

Once back inside Curtis took the liberty of ordering another round.

'Not bad news I hope,' he said, as Harry took hold of his half empty glass.

His mind was racing and Curtis' polite enquiry caught him momentarily off guard. He took time to compose himself: 'No, no, it was something unexpected.' He downed his half pint in a matter of seconds then without any hesitation attacked the next.

'Wow! It must have come as a real shock. Either that or I'm going to struggle to keep up!'

'Yeah, wow!'

Curtis took a stab in the dark: 'You got an inheritance?'

'I don't rightly know.'

'How much?'

'Like a complete idiot I never asked!' Harry shrugged his shoulders as he spoke, chastising himself for failing to ask the logical question.

'You could be a millionaire!'

The thought that he could be among the rich and elite, plus move in privileged circles, only added undue stress to the situation.

'Millionaire!' he said slowly, and very deliberately.

'You got to call Harry and find out,' Curtis added smiling. 'I won't be able to sleep soundly until you do!'

'I hate it when other people are always right, and there's no mute button to keep them quiet.'

'It's not easy being right all the time.'

'You're damn right there!'

Travers finished off his remaining beer and immediately ordered another round. His mind was made up. It's not that he was being blasé about the whole affair, but just a matter of economics: it was cheaper to make the call from the house.

* * *

Armed with sustenance for the night, the new found friends entered Travers' house and made for the first floor.

Harry picked up the house phone, which sat on a small table, turned on the TV and headed for the kitchen to dish up the evening's delight. He dialled the number Jeffries gave him.

'Mister Jeffries.'

'Mister Travers.'

'My uncle-'

'You want to know what he left you?'

'Basically, yes.'

'I'm surprised you didn't ask earlier.'

'Yeah, thanks for that.'

'Everything, Mister Travers, he left you everything.'

'Which is what exactly?'

'A fine two-story, five bedroom house which sits serenely on the outskirts of Athens, Tennessee.'

Harry dished up tea, jamming the phone under his chin in order to continue the conversation, took a huge mouthful of Indian takeaway and digested not only the food, but a fine two-story, five bedroom house.

'Mister Travers?'

'I'm still here. Was there anything else?'

'In addition there is a little short of one hundred thousand dollars in cash. That's about the size of it, if you pardon the pun.'

'I can't see what I'm going to do with all that from over on this side of the pond, although the money will definitely come in handy, so my first inclination will be to sell. What's the current value of the house?'

'I will make some enquiries on your behalf Mister Travers, but I'm afraid I will need to see you in order to settle all the relevant legalities.'

'That's not a problem. I'm due a holiday.'

From his end of the line Harry heard Jeffries' cell-phone spring into life. 'I've got to take this call Mister Travers, just let me know when you have your travel plans.'

'Will do.'

Once Jeffries had hung up Harry wasted no time in joining Curtis.

'Well?' asked Curtis.

'None the wiser!' It was prudent to keep it under his hat for now.

Harry handed over the food.

* * *

Travers prided himself on being an appalling early riser and on this bright, sunlit morning failed to disappoint. The annoying, constant buzzing of his bedside alarm clock pierced his very subconscious, severely testing any early morning patience. The poor alarm received a hefty blow. Silence once again reigned supreme. He rolled onto his back and glanced over at the clock's led display: it displayed 05:00. 'Fuck!'

From the next room he could hear Curtis' alarm go off, followed by his muffled, dulcet tones, as his feet hit the floor: 'Fuck!'

Harry laughed and slipped into his robe. 'You're getting too old for this shit, Travers!'

He was finding that his feet were stiff and sore every morning, and the first few steps were used to loosen his ageing muscles. Forty was a bummer of an age: his head hurt; his feet hurt and what he needed more than anything right now was coffee, even though every ounce of intelligence, and no little experience, was shouting out to him that possible dehydration was not going to be solved by the world's second worst diuretic.

Harry opened his bedroom door to be met by Curtis looking like he'd just lost a fight with a hair dryer.

'You slept well!'

'Does it show?'

'Coffee?'

'Black and strong.'

'Your order is my command.'

Ten minutes later the two reconvened in the kitchen and Harry handed him a mug of strong, black coffee before rustling up breakfast.

'Eggs and bacon okay?'

'This time of the morning?'

'Got to start the day right.'

'Get much studying done?'

'Curtis, you are taking the piss!'

'Yeah, right. I know you tucked into the books for an hour or so before lights out.'

Harry stayed mute.

'I spent a couple of hours going over today.'

'I figured you would so I did fuck all!' Harry said smiling.

'If there's one thing I've learnt Harry, is that nobody goes into a simulator unprepared, yet most will tell you they've done fuck all!'

'Yep!'

Harry dished up breakfast.

'And then everything miraculously goes okay!'

'I'd like to say something profound right now, but it would sound crass.'

Once breakfast was finished they dumped the crockery in the sink, dressed and were out of the house in plenty of time to make their check-in time for day two.

* * *

Captain Lyons sat finishing the last of the vending machine coffee, wishing he was back at home with his pregnant wife, when the arrival of the two men broke his train of thought.

'Morning gentlemen.'

'Good morning,' Curtis replied. 'Coffee?'

With the answer from both sides in the affirmative, he left to procure three hot drinks.

Day two turned out to be a breeze: the Low Visibility training, which allows the crew to practice autolands, go-arounds and aborted take-offs in reduced visibility conditions, plus the Line Orientated Flight Training or LOFT exercise, a simulator scenario designed specifically to aid and improve flight crews efficiency in the use of abnormal and emergency procedures during a simulated line flight, were handled very professionally by both men with any technical issues that arose during their four hour stint being dealt with correctly and in the right order, which resulted in both men receiving a good write up with little or no debrief afterwards.

'Well the bank manager will be happy for another six months,' Curtis said on reaching the car park.

'One thing about Harvey Lyons is he doesn't suffer fools, so if he says you did well, you did and with your level of experience-'

'I was told a sim with him was "death by debrief"!'

'Just goes to show you never can tell.'

Harry offered to give him a lift to the airport; saving the company a taxi fare was how he put it.

Once again the two men boarded the Porsche and headed off.

As soon as Curtis was safely deposited at the correct terminal, and they had swapped the obligatory phone numbers, swearing to keep in touch, Harry made a beeline for his solicitor: Marvin Schular.

3

Schular, as always, when Harry turned up was seated behind his desk writing notes so fast that it was a minor miracle he was ever able to decipher any of it afterwards.

'Morning Harry,' he said without visibly acknowledging his entrance.

'Does my aftershave smell that bad?'

'No, just you!' Schular added, finally deigning to lift his head off the page.

'Fuck you!'

'No, fuck you!'

'No, no, fuck you!'

'This joke could just run and run.'

'Explain to me again why I hire you?'

'Because I'm the best!'

'You are such an arrogant arsehole!'

'No, no, I'm just that good.'

Probably the single, most important reason Harry kept Marvin on as his legal counsel entered the room with no small amount of flounce: Elizabeth Ryan was a curvy, thirty-one year old with dark hair, green eyes and tall with a five feet eight inches frame that exuded sex appeal from every pore.

'Morning Harry.'

'Morning Liz.'

'What brings your desperate arse to our doorstep?' Liz purred, giving him a seductive sideways glance.

'You say the nicest things,' he replied taking a seat opposite Schular.

'You just bring it out of me.'

She deposited a batch of papers on her boss' desk, paused long enough so that Harry could admire her for a second, but only a second, then swung her hips all the way back out into the reception area.

'You know she fancies you, always has!'

'The lady has taste.'

'For an intelligent man you're such an idiot! Now why are you here?'

'I've come into an inheritance from an uncle I never knew I had.'

'Really?' Marvin put the pen down and gave Harry his fullest attention.

'He died recently, and I was, am, his nearest relative.'

'How are you related to him?'

'He's my mother's cousin.....I think.'

Schular stood, turned his attention back to the correspondence on his desk then went to pour two whiskies from a small bar standing quietly, and unassumingly, in the far right hand corner of his office.

'So what exactly is your inheritance worth? He said on his return, handing Harry his drink.

'Still waiting on that one.'

'What's he left you?'

'A fine two-story, five bedroom house,' Harry said, swirling his whiskey around the bottom of the glass, 'which sits on the outskirts of Athens, Tennessee plus about one hundred thousand dollars.'

'Wow!' Schular replied while sitting back behind his desk and sipping his triple distilled Bushmills. 'Not forgetting the contents of the house. You looking to emigrate?'

'No, I'm looking to sell once I can find out its true value.'

'You want me to make some enquiries?'

'Just don't want to be ripped off!'

'I'm only here to serve.'

'Now I definitely know why I retain your services.'

The two men enjoyed their whiskies in silence.

'If you're not going to show any interest in my Liz,' started Schular, smiling confidently, 'then you wouldn't take offence if I did?'

'How long have you fancied your own secretary?'

'Since always!'

'And you need me for what?' Harry said finishing his drink.

'Not to do anything and ignore that walking sex bomb out there!'

'But how often am I here? I'm not going to get in your way!'

'You're still an obstacle whether here or not. We got a deal?'

'Easier said than done!'

'We're not all Harry Travers!'

'Damn right!'

'So?'

'I'll keep out of your way Marvin, at least until I get this bloody inheritance sorted out, then if you've been blown out she's fair game for the old Harry Travers' charm.'

'Deal!'

Harry placed his empty glass on Marvin's desk, stood, and after a few short but polite pleasantries, which included Schular promising to find out the value of the house, he departed.

'Leaving already Harry?' Elizabeth cooed as he vacated the office.

'I'm afraid so; I'd love to stay, but I don't think my blood pressure or liver could take either of you for any great length of time!'

She laughed and flashed those beautiful green eyes at him.

Damn, he thought, but a promise is a promise.

The day had threatened persistent rain, but here at a little past three in the afternoon the clouds had begun to break letting the sunshine through and promise a pleasant and warm late afternoon.

What should he do? He found himself getting annoyed for not having made any plans for the rest of the day, but any ready made arrangements would have been blown out of the water and thrown onto chaos by his recent news, and so he was left with the only possible alternative to wasting the time away: Jack's Bar.

With the Porsche parked safely, and the short, but annoying walk negotiated, it always seemed to get longer and longer the more times he took it, he entered the welcome and familiar surroundings of his favourite watering hole.

'You're early!' The dulcet tones belonged to Steve: his friend was a few years older than him at fifty, kept his dark hair cut short, was always well turned out and could deliver a stinging repost whenever required.

'It's never too early!' Harry replied, smiling that knowing, welcoming smile of someone who knew that a session was imminent; the one thing you could guarantee with Steve was you never drank alone.

'You know the secret to being a good landlord?' Steve opened with, as Harry strode up to the bar.

'Don't drink the profits!'

'That's me failed then!' Steve handed him his beer.

Harry admired the clear brown liquid and smooth white head of a true Boddingtons pint. 'Not to fuck up pulling my pint?'

'Nice try!'

A few of the afternoon drinkers started to laugh. Harry took a huge first hit and wiped the excess beer off his lips: 'I give up! Put me out of my misery.'

'To know your customers!'

'You read that somewhere?'

'Yeah, in this,' Steve produced a small booklet from underneath the bar. 'It says here that a good landlord should understand and appreciate his regular customers whilst creating a desirable ambience to attract new ones.'

'And your point is?'

'I've been given this challenge: to sell more of the less than popular offerings like Pimm's and Cinzano in order to win some holiday.'

'You don't strike me as a Pimm's man!'

'I can be an anything you want kind of man, especially when it comes to promotions and restocking!'

'Well, you can restock this then.' Harry finished off what was left of his beer and handed his friend the empty glass.

It took less than a minute for the pint to be pulled and Harry to take his first sip.

'Well that clearly shows what a great landlord you are: you didn't fuck up pulling my pint.'

'I aim to please.' Steve pulled one for himself.

'Drinking the profits again I see!' shouted one of a group of regulars from across the saloon bar.

'Shit landlord!' laughed another.

'It's a good job I like you lot!'

'Someone's got to put a roof over your head!'

'Just drink up and shut up!'

The two friends polished off a few more beers, swapped yarns neither had heard before, and raised many a laugh until Susie, a local lady Steve had hired to tend the bar, turned up to start her shift leaving them free to attack the profits.

Harry started to get that buzzing sensation in his ears when he was at that point of no return during a drinking session. His mobile phone again burst into life. A quick check revealed Anton Jeffries.

'I got to take this!' Harry said heading for the door.

'Which ex is it this time?'

'Not anyone you know and if you did they're not your type.'

'Oh, I don't know!'

'Trust me on this one!' Harry said sliding out of the door.

A sudden change in conditions, added to a sharp intake of breath, made him lightheaded, but he still managed to gather his senses in time to answer the call before his answer machine kicked in.

The upshot was to ascertain his travel itinerary, and where and when he was going to land in the U.S

Harry paused to take stock. This was new territory to him: somebody placing demands on his free time. He was uncomfortable in its surroundings plus Jeffries was beginning to display rather impatient traits and playing up to one of his many pet hates: that of being hurried into making any kind of decision, unless of course it was a dire emergency and this definitely was not one of those.

'Give me a couple of days and I'll have them.'

This placated Jeffries for the time being. The telephone conversation was ended abruptly leaving the distinct impression that the man was in too much of a hurry to get off the phone.

Harry took a large lungful of crisp clean air and then spent the next five minutes coughing. The question of his fitness arose followed by that hollow promise to join a gym and lose weight: during his last medical the examiner told him he was class one obese with a BMI of nearly 27.0. What a load of crap, he thought at the time, but three days later after a weekend of excess with friends, which included parties on Friday and Saturday, his trousers were definitely tighter.

Hitching up those offending trousers, he re-entered the bar.

'That didn't take long!' One of the locals said rather too loudly for his liking, obviously trying to get a laugh. 'Does she still love you?' A few more people had entered the bar and they all joined in the mirth. Harry smiled.

'If you can't take a joke then you shouldn't have joined,' he said quietly.

Steve returned from the cellar after replacing a barrel, and the two friends resumed from where they had left off.

* * *

Jeffries stood and paced around his office: this was the first setback and he was not comfortable with setbacks. 'Just be patient,' he whispered, hoping it would have the desired effect of calming his agitated nerves, but he knew what the response would be once he'd informed them that Travers had not yet arranged any flights over.

'It has only been a day, give the man a chance!' he blurted out, and found comfort with a defence that he knew would silence any rising doubts.

* * *

Harry opened one bleary eye and immediately realised he had been snoring his head off by the revolting taste in the back of his throat, which was compounded by the serious aftertaste of last night's takeaway. Far off in some distant part of the room his phone called out to him, and although he appreciated he was duty bound to answer, lay motionless on the bed willing the ringing to stop. Four more rings and his prayers were answered.

The morning was but a blur spent nursing the mother of all hangovers, but still at regular intervals he wondered who had been foolish enough to call him at such an ungodly hour. Any use of the call back system revealed a withheld number. His roster after his two day simulator detail was quiet until the day after tomorrow, and he was left struggling to fill the next forty-eight hours with anything worthwhile. The phone rang again. This time he took the call.

'Hello?'

It was Jeffries.

'Bugger me,' Harry murmured, 'this guy's got the patience of a peanut!'

'Harry, I hope you don't mind me calling you Harry?'

He just managed to get out an answer that he wasn't fussed one way or the other before Jeffries continued with his side of the conversation; the upshot was he had arranged for Harry to view his uncle's property the day after his arrival. Jeffries was very careful not to mention flights, instead he promised to e-mail his address and any other information that Harry would need for his trip.

Travers quickly rattled off his e-mail address then cussed as he hung up. His head throbbed. Self-inflicted punishment was not new to him, but when it was incorporated with obligations it made life nothing short of murder. And now this man knew his home number: his uncle was a real piece of work.

Breakfast was by-passed and after a very brief and rewarding phone call to his immediate manager, who reassured him a week's leave at such a short notice to deal with a family bereavement was okay, he left the house and began the twenty minute walk to the local travel agents. His choices were either British Airways or Delta, the two main operators to Atlanta via London Heathrow from which he could get his connection to Athens, Tennessee. Delta Air Lines DL 29 won the day due to its schedule fitting in better with his itinerary.

'Better call him,' Travers said reluctantly whilst strolling out of the travel agents and only narrowly avoided being run over by a guy on a bike. He sent him on his way with a volley of expletives. Dialling out on his mobile he became aware of the disapproving stares of two elderly ladies. He shrugged his shoulders, looked up the road at the erratic cyclist and let rip once more.

Once back at the house and the annoying chore of informing Jeffries of his travel plans was out of the way, with him receiving his instructions on where to go once in Atlanta, Harry packed a bag.

For an airline pilot Harry hated airports, primarily because they had become so bloody commercial and for him taken some of the fun out of flying, but his connecting flight to Heathrow a couple of days later, thankfully for him, was mercilessly painless. Even London Gatwick had changed from when he was a lad: he remembered fondly standing on the spectator gallery with all the spotters holding their scanners, watching, documenting all the departures and arrivals and taking in that wonderful smell of jet fuel; this alone ignited his passion for flying and afterwards wondering through the South Terminal he would look up and stare at the departures board imagining all those exotic destinations listed. When studying Gatwick's North Terminal with all its lettered zones it didn't quite have the same appeal or invoke the response as when he was a kid, but then again nothing really could and so with a heavy heart, yearning for times gone by, he checked in at Terminal 3, Heathrow.

The constant chimes and announcements reverberated around and through the throngs of duty free shoppers, but Travers had only one thing on his mind in the short time available and that was bottle of his favourite tipple: Jack Daniels. For someone working in the business he was guilty of always pushing his luck when it came to boarding: familiarity had definitely grown a small amount of contempt and now armed with his duty free Harry answered the announcement requesting his presence and beckoning him forward towards his fate and whatever destiny awaited him. He knew one thing for sure; he would not waste his time, but instead try and enjoy every second, all things considered. Nor would he be travelling anything other than at least business class; he was a bachelor, had no girlfriend, owned a smart car, but any spare money was to be spent on making his life as comfortable as possible, and there was no better way to express his personal philosophy than to travel business or first class.

With his seat nicely reclined and the flight in its infancy, Harry settled back and sipped his opening Jack Daniels. Life was good: he had a week off work for bereavement, was due a holiday and here was the ideal situation to take one, albeit tinged with a little sadness, but he hadn't known his uncle and this kind of acted as a form of safety blanket for his emotions, not that he was the crying type.

A stewardess came to take his meal order and as always he chose the chicken, but only after the obligatory top up. She's a looker, he thought, as the beautifully formed hour glass figure with blonde hair floated up the aisle towards the forward galley. Suddenly a ten and a half hour flight wasn't long enough. Five minutes later Harry was sipping a second JD and it rapidly caused the day to creep up on him.

Dinner when it arrived was delicious and he gratefully washed it down with a few glasses of white wine. He lined up two movies off the In-Flight Entertainment and again remarked that ten and a half hours was definitely not long enough. The two movies took a large chunk out of the flight time until he was left with an hour or so before his arrival into Atlanta. He was more tired than he realized because his short power nap was disturbed by the stunning blonde asking him to adjust his seat. He tried in vain to wake himself up. Harry knew that patience would be required in order to get through US Immigration unscathed, and he prayed he wouldn't get stuck behind the one stroppy passenger guaranteed to annoy them and add another couple of hours to his trip. He needn't have worried, for it took less than an hour to clear Immigration, collect his bag and walk at a brisk pace over to the taxi rank. He wasted no time hailing a cab and set off for Fulton County Airport, also known as Charlie Brown Field, as per his itinerary sent by the lawyer.

* * *

The cool refreshing breeze generated by the air conditioning unit was a welcome respite from the stifling Georgia heat, and he collapsed into one of the courtesy chairs supplied for the benefit of waiting passengers in the general aviation terminal. The journey was starting to take its toll and for the first time since leaving home he questioned the sagacity of the venture. Looking around the sumptuous waiting area he remarked that the tidiness and cleanliness put most of the commercial airport terminals back home to shame, and this thought alone made him more determined than ever to get his business over with. Out of the corner of his eye he spotted a coffee machine and went in search of a brew.

'Mister Travers?' A voice dripping in a Tennessee drawl interrupted him quenching his thirst.

Harry nearly spilt the hot vending machine coffee, but he managed to compose himself sufficiently to take a sip and answered: 'That's me!'

The voice belonged to a tall, athletic, lean looking man, who Harry put at about thirty years of age, with thinning brown hair, who went by the name of Tommy Shearen. Tommy looked at the Englishman quizzically.

'Are you Mister Harry Travers?'

'Yes, yes I am,' Harry said backing it up with a nod. 'And you are?'

The tall, lean man with the Tennessee drawl smiled: 'Tommy Shearen.' He held out his hand for him to take.

Harry did the polite thing and accepted an overly firm handshake.

'Going to have to get used to that accent, we don't often hear your brand of English where I come from.'

'And where's that?' Harry asked before quickly finishing his coffee.

'Up in the mountains.'

Hillbilly, he thought, and probably up there making moonshine along with anything else he can that's remotely illegal.

'What do you do up there in the mountains?'

'Fix airplanes, fix anything really that will make me a quick buck.'

He wasn't expecting that: first impressions had fooled him again.

'What do you do, Mister Travers?'

'Call me Harry.'

'What do you do, Harry?'

Harry was extremely reluctant to give away any information to a complete stranger, and had learnt long ago not to divulge to anybody his true occupation if ever he wanted a quiet life.

'I'm in aluminium tubing!'

'Cool!'

'Yeah, cool!'

'Is that all your luggage?'

'I like to travel light.'

Tommy went to take the bag, but Harry politely informed him that it wasn't necessary.

'Oh, I am sorry. I'm being rude and forgetting my manners!'

For all his misgivings, when it came to strangers, Harry was taking a liking to this man from the mountains.

The two men promptly proceeded out onto the general aviation apron towards a twin engine Piper Seneca. Tommy began to fill Harry in on why the machine was in his possession: he had just completed an engine change on the number two engine and needed to take it for a test flight.

Fantastic Harry wondered, as he trod over to the aircraft then concluded, to put his mind at rest more than anything, that whatever this small twin could throw at them they would be able to handle it with little or no bother.

Throughout it all Tommy never stopped talking about anything of any importance that happened around his county. Harry was definitely beginning to like this stranger.

Once they were settled inside the Seneca's cockpit Harry felt right at home as Tommy fired up both engines, and in what seemed like no time at all they had taxi clearance and were airborne, and still Tommy hadn't stopped talking: he had a story for every occasion. Never trust a man who doesn't drink or talk his father had told him, and he was right. They finally reached cruising altitude of three thousand feet when the idea hit Harry squarely between the eyes.

'Do you know why I'm here Tommy?'

'No.'

'Did Jeffries send you?'

'Sure did. He just rang me up out of the blue offering me a whole bunch of money to come down here and pick you up.'

'And he told you nothing about me?'

'Should he?'

'Did you know a man called Jack Hennessey?'

'You mean "Mad Jack Hennessey"? I sure did. He was a good friend of mine and helped me out of many a fix!'

'I'm his nephew!'

'No, shit!'

'Yes, shit!'

Tommy beamed back a huge smile.

Harry could always tell when somebody was being truly sincere.

'Anything you want to know just ask.'

'Thank you.'

'You're obviously here to.......you know, clear up the necessary?'

'I'm afraid so.'

'Shame what happened to him!'

'Yeah, can you spread any more light on that?'

Harry loathed for Tommy to suspect that Jeffries would keep anything from him, but past experience had taught him to keep people at arms-length until he had all the facts at his disposal: here it had started with the call to his house and grown steadily from there, gnawing away at his insides.

'What do you know?' asked Tommy.

'That it was very sad.'

'And weird!'

'Yeah, weird.'

'And they still haven't found the poor bastard's body!'

Harry shook his head. This was new.

'They had to get a court order to pronounce him dead, which is why you're here I reckon.'

'I reckon so!' Why wasn't he told this by the lawyer?

'Sad, you're damn right there, sad, sad, sad!'

'Are they still looking?'

'Don't rightly know now that he's legally dead! You need to talk to the County Sheriff, Sheriff Poulsen.'

He was starting to paint a picture of Mister Jeffries.

Tommy looked sideways at him still grinning from ear to ear like a Cheshire cat, and it was now that he truly began to appreciate the man's flying skills: the Seneca flew like it was on rails.

'Then I kind of think I'm going need your help!'

'Anytime, you only have to ask.'

Yep, he was going to get to like Tommy. The rest of the flight to Athens, Tennessee was spent detailing dealings and adventures Tommy had over the years with "Mad Jack Hennessey".

'Shame you're not named after your uncle, then you'd be the second Jack from your family I'd know!'

'In a way I am: my middle name is Jack.'

Until this very moment that thought had never occurred to him; his parents were no longer around, they had both died within six months of each other three years ago, and him being an only child, there was no one to confirm it.

'Would be cool if you were.'

'He sounds a bit of a rebel!'

'Yeah, one thing you need to know though.'

'What's that?' Harry sensed impending doom.

'Sheriff Poulsen hated your uncle with a vengeance!'

'Why?'

'They had a serious run-in a few years back when Poulsen was running for re-election: your uncle levelled some accusations at him regarding his competence, which as you can gather went down well!'

'Let me guess, Sheriff Poulsen holds a grudge.'

'Wouldn't you?'

'And I bet my uncle lapped it up!'

'He regretted it afterwards.'

'But if he's that bad why did he get voted in?'

'He's not! And nobody of any value ran against him anyway.'

'That'll do it!'

'Your uncle just loved getting under certain people's skin, especially when they represented authority.'

Tommy was the perfect host, taking time to point out a few well known landmarks, including a number of power stations which, according to him, had saved his life on more than one occasion when up in poor visibility, and then before he knew it they slowly started their descent into McMinn County Airport.

Twenty minutes later, after a blissfully uneventful landing, they taxied onto an apron outside a modern looking red brick terminal.

'You can see where the money's gone!' Harry said admiringly, thinking once again of some of the sorry looking terminals back home.

'Yep, can't fault them for that!'

As soon as Tommy shut down both engines and completed all his checks, Harry wasted not a second unloading his one and only bag before both went in search of his transport for the next part of the journey.

'I'll be seeing you,' Tommy said as they both entered the bright, airy terminal.

Harry was informed by a bored, elderly woman sitting behind the information desk that a hire car was waiting for him outside with the address of Anton Jeffries' law practice inside it. Tommy surreptitiously slipped a piece of paper into his back pocket. Harry made no attempt to acknowledge the present and simply thanked him for a nice flight and wished him a safe onward journey.

The hire car, if you can call it that, was a white Volkswagen Scirocco with "stick shift". The woman paid particular attention to the fact that Travers' car was not an automatic and was he okay to drive it, but also took great pleasure in informing him that it had satnav in case he should have any difficulty with the Tennessee roads.

The driver's seat was boiling hot and the steering wheel nearly scolded his hands due to the rising temperatures, so he decided it was prudent to fire her up and run the air conditioning for a few minutes. It did give him the opportunity to have a look around.

At the south end of the field sat several hangars; the doors were closed so Harry could only guess what treats lay parked up inside, but going by the business jets on the apron there could be any number of goodies waiting to be discovered.

After ten minutes he checked the steering wheel. Harry was impatient to be on his way, and found to his delight that the air conditioning had done its job. With the satnav loaded with Jeffries' address he hit the road.

County Road 552 from the airport led Harry directly towards the David W Lillard Memorial Highway and then South White Street for a near straight drive to Athens. The car for all its faults, age being one of them, drove like a dream and the smoothness of the road surface made him feel sorry that the drive should have to end after what seemed like five minutes when in fact once he'd checked his watch was over twenty.

Jeffries for all his grandeur had an office which sat on West Madison Avenue right next door to a dentist practice. Well at least I can get me teeth fixed if nothing else, he thought, as he entered the reception area and stood in front of an oak door with frosted glass bearing the man's name. Three quick raps and Harry ventured inside on hearing the familiar voice.

He found a fit looking, mid-forties man in a shirt and tie with piercing, interrogating brown eyes, a long thin face, still carrying a full head of medium brown hair, on the phone and clearly in the middle of an argument. Jeffries waved a hand at him to help himself to some coffee. Harry was knackered and a strong coffee was now a necessity rather than a pleasure. He put Jeffries at around five feet ten inches.

'So Harry,' the lawyer started, once he'd hung up, 'you found us alright?'

'Piece of cake!'

'Good. I suppose you want to know where you'll be sleeping tonight?'

'The thought had occurred to me,' Harry said sipping his freshly made coffee.

Harry sat down at the precise time Jeffries did the exact opposite and stood, making his way around the front of the desk to shake his hand and to formally introduce himself. Harry felt obliged to rise to his feet and offered his, and then sat back down once the niceties were over. Jeffries returned to his desk and leant against it. 'My secretary, who is out at the moment, has booked you into the Oakridge Motel; it is south of here in Etowah. You can always move after you've been here a couple of days, if you're not happy.'

'Sure.'

'What do you think of my other car?'

'Drives well!'

'Thought it best to save a few dollars and lend it to you for the duration.'

'That's very kind of you.'

'Think nothing of it.'

The lawyer began to pace slowly around the room clearly searching for the right words to say; normally this would have annoyed the hell out of Harry, but by now he was so tired he just didn't give a damn.

'Let me tell you about your uncle.'

'Yeah, you have the advantage over me there.' It was a lie.

Jeffries stopped pacing and leant back against his desk. 'He was a difficult man,' he started. 'Someone who, I'm afraid to say rubbed a lot of people up the wrong way.'

Sheriff Poulsen sprang to mind. Harry kept a respectable silence.

'So you need to be very careful where you mention his name!'

The first thing I'm going to do, he thought, looking straight at the lawyer, trying to gauge his true intentions, is ask all the relevant people about my uncle: if he wasn't being openly lied to then he was beginning to experience that uncomfortable sensation of being taken for a complete fool.

'My uncle made some enemies then?'

'In all the wrong places, Harry.'

Harry smiled: he was taking a liking to this rogue of an uncle, who he knew next to nothing about.

'You obviously want to know how he died?'

'That would help.' Harry finished his coffee.

'It's not something that I felt appropriate to discuss over the phone, you understand.'

'I appreciate your concern, but exactly how did my uncle meet his maker?'

Jeffries pulled himself slowly off his desk, straightened up and started to pace the room again.

He's going to bloody bullshit me, Harry realised from the outset; the effrontery of the man. The pacing around the room is for show and to gain a few valuable seconds while he thinks up a believable lie, but why? Why leave him, a complete stranger, feeling decidedly uncomfortable? Harry may have a bad habit of judging people, on rare occasions it must be said, but here he was not wrong. Jeffries was his uncle's lawyer and should be anything but reticent regarding his uncle. The man was only passing on information he thought Harry should know.

'We'll need to speak to the sheriff to get the official line,' Jeffries finally said.

He was suddenly eager to get out of Jeffries' office before he said something he would later come to regret, and rose sharply to his feet: it was best to go along with this facade for the time being and play the ignorant foreigner and let this run its natural course. 'You can tell me everything tomorrow.'

'Of course, Harry!'

Jeffries collected his car keys and gave him instructions to follow before joking that he hoped Harry had the skill to keep up.

Travers was too exhausted to bother entering into any form of banter and instead felt unwanted pangs of guilt for harbouring these distasteful feelings towards the lawyer. All the way back to the cars Jeffries friendly goaded him, as to his skills behind the wheel, but Harry simply smiled and walked at a sedate pace over to the Scirocco.

Jeffries fired up his newly cleaned, metallic red Dodge Charger SXT, leaned out of the driver's window and gave it one last try to extract a reaction out of this Englishman.

Harry stopped a few paces short of the Scirocco, smiled at the man and for the first time since leaving the office seriously considered taking him up on his challenge.

'How far is to the motel?'

'Not far enough for you my friend!' The lawyer sneered, now that he finally received the reaction he so desperately sought. The thought of competition stirred his blood.

The two men made themselves comfortable before the disturbing thought occurred to Harry that maybe the lawyer had deliberately forced him into this race, and somehow scuppered the Volkswagen while they were in his office. He tried to gauge the American's thoughts by looking him straight in the eye during yet another bout of banter. Harry was none the wiser, so gunned the Scirocco into life and reversed out of his parking slot. Jeffries followed suit.

'Gonna show you what real driving looks like Harry!' shouted Jeffries, who then wheel spun out towards the open road. Harry erred on the side of caution until he could get a feel of the ambient conditions, and it was a good job he did for at that exact moment Sheriff Poulsen arrived and only a last minute hard right turn by Jeffries averted imminent disaster. Harry laughed. He could see the

Sheriff was less than amused with the reckless driving and he re-parked the Scirocco.

'Mister Travers.' asked the Sheriff, as the two men met halfway between their respective vehicles.

They shared an unblinking, firm handshake. Harry put the Sheriff in his early forties, a shade over six foot and could have been Burt Reynolds' twin such was the likeness between the man and one of his heroes.

'I have informed my client, as to the current state of affairs regarding your investigation,' added Jeffries, who wasted no time joining the two men.

'Did you now!'

Exactly, thought Harry, sensing a subtle shift in Jeffries.

'Well Mister Travers, what would you like to know?'

It was an opening question one would dream of hearing, but again he felt all too strongly that relevant, pertinent information would be purposefully withheld. Jeffries omitting to mention the court order was a prime example.

'As much as you can tell me.'

'Shall we go inside? It's better than discussing it out here.'

Harry couldn't argue with that.

Jeffries was naturally reluctant to make the return journey to his office.

Sheriff Poulsen led the way. Harry brought up the rear.

The office seemed cooler the second time around and the sudden change in temperature produced another bout of tiredness; he was now starting to flag and losing patience with the whole affair.

'Mister Travers,' started the Sheriff, as soon as Jeffries had shut his office door; Harry noticed that he was so keen to enter into a confab with him that any common courtesies were abandoned.

'What?' Harry tried hard to hide his rising contempt.

Sheriff Poulsen turned sharply to face him, exuding aggression: the abruptness of the reply had caught him off guard and he paused to take stock of this foreigner.

'Where will you be staying tonight?'

'The Oakridge Motel,' butted in Jeffries.

'Nice! And for how long?'

'Just as long as I'm needed here, Sheriff!' Harry knew this would rile the man, but he found himself unable to check his impulses. He could see Jeffries out of the corner of his eye shift his weight from one foot to another in nervous anticipation.

'Be a short stay then!' answered Poulsen equally as abruptly.

'So, tell me about my uncle?' Harry wanted to sleep, wanted a bed and so cut to the chase.

'Anything in particular you wanted to know?'

'How did he die?'

'We don't rightly know! Although I suspect it was a heart attack: your uncle had a history of heart disease. We found evidence he had been out in the woods by Starr Mountain, which we believe was just prior to his demise. Why? We don't know. But we discovered no body, and after sufficient time had elapsed he was pronounced dead in absentia: a court order was applied for and granted to pronounce him legally dead. We had no way of knowing his next of kin until his will was read.

Jeffries was conspicuous by his silence.

'Do you suspect foul play?'

'No!'

Harry was not so much surprised by the Sheriff's confidence in a steadfast denial of foul play, but more by the total apathy he displayed.

'No!' The Sheriff reiterated.

'Short, sweet and to the point!'

'Mister Travers, your uncle had a very bad habit of going, how do you say, walkabout. He was warned on numerous occasions by Doctor Adams to take it easy, but as always he ignored every piece of sensible advice he was ever given because he knew best. I suspect he went out on walkabout, had no medication with him, and suffered a fatal heart attack. As for his body, it could be laying anywhere or it was taken by another of the forest's inhabitants. We may never know the answer to that one.'

'Will you keep looking?'

'We are not obliged to look any further Mister Travers now that your uncle has been officially declared dead, and as I have limited resources available to me there is little I can do even if I wanted to.

Harry nodded, remembering Tommy's words of warning regarding this man and his uncle.

'Here's my card Mister Travers.' The Sheriff handed him a small white card; policemen with business cards was something he found strange, but today he was happy to accept it when realizing the lawyer had not offered his. He saw one on the man's desk and helped himself.

For all the cloak and dagger of not wanting to discuss his uncle's demise in public, the meeting was over in what seemed a matter of minutes and Harry once again found himself in the car park and boarded the Scirocco. The Sheriff had already departed and a clearly subdued Jeffries waited patiently for him at the entrance to the road.

I hope he's not still up for that bloody challenge, he thought, as Jeffries pulled away. Harry stayed two car lengths back.

The American drove at a sedate pace all the way to the Oakridge Motel, just off the David W Lillard Memorial Highway: the single story, sky blue walled, red tiled building was typical of those motels he had seen in the movies, and it made him recollect a few of his favourites, as he pulled up outside the main entrance. His head began to throb: he needed a bed, a soft white pillow and he prayed his guide would not stay long. His luck was in.

The reception area stank of fresh pizza. His stomach grumbled right on cue when an unshaven, elderly man wearing baggy jeans with an AC/DC t-shirt advertising one of his favourite albums of theirs from the seventies: 'Dirty Deeds Done Dirt Cheap', answered the buzzer his opening of the main entrance door had caused to go off.

'How long?' asked the man, who Harry put at mid to late fifties.

'Sorry?'

'How long do you want a room?'

'Do I not have a reservation?'

The man laughed out loud then shouted back to his wife not to eat all the pizza.

'I take that as a no then?'

'You can take it any way you want buddy!'

'A week, I need a room for a week!'

The man's whole demeanour changed on hearing that this foreigner would want one of his prized rooms for seven whole days: 'That'll be forty dollars a night!'

'Fine,' answered Harry. 'Does that include breakfast?'

This time the man nearly choked: 'You can take that as a no!'

'Would I be right in my understanding that there is no room service in your fine establishment?' Harry knew the answer even before he finished asking the question.

'You would, but don't fret yourself young fella, 'cos there's a cafe over the ways next to the launderette,' he said waving a hand in the general direction of the cafe that Harry clocked on the way in. 'We do though have a right nice ice machine!'

Oh goody! The idea of having to trot across the road at all hours of the day for ham and eggs followed by a service wash filled him with unending joy.

The man slid Harry a key to room 217 and requested the register be signed, which Harry did in a flash before witnessing the t-shirt slide back into the recess of the living quarters leaving him to find his room and get some much needed rest.

Room 217 proved easy to find, plus as an added bonus there by the side of the phone, which looked about thirty years old, was a menu and the number of a local pizza joint.

The bag be-damned, he was starving, and by the time his case was open on the bed ready to be unloaded, his order for a twelve inch pepperoni and mushroom pizza was in. The idea of food perked him up.

Twenty long minutes later his taste buds were satiated by slice after slice of delicious pizza; he struggled to recollect ever having tasted one as good and life suddenly didn't seem so bad after all. The only thing missing from this picture was beer and that small omission was soon rectified by a brief visit to a seven eleven about half a mile up the road.

4

His neck was locked solid; Harry woke in the same position he remembered being in whilst watching baseball on the TV. In front of him lay the pizza box balancing on the end of the bed, protecting the last three slices, to his right were the four remaining cans littering the duvet. Outside it was dark and the clock by the bed read 03:30.

'Damn!' he whispered.

The three slices and four beers were consumed with equal relish and Harry strode around the room wide awake. This was one of the downsides of long haul travelling: the time it took for your body clock to catch up. He toyed with the idea of going for a walk, but quickly dismissed it.

An hour passed before the beer kicked in and he thankfully fell asleep.

A thunderous knocking on the door woke him with a start and he cussed for falling asleep a second time fully clothed; his light brown chinos and black golf polo shirt had definitely taken a beating. Even his brown leather loafers were beginning to complain.

'Damn!'

The warm, dry Tennessee air hit his face and the bright sunlight caused him to squint, as he pulled the door open with a hard swing to the right. The t-shirt stood hand on hips, scowling.

'You got a call!'

'Who from?'

'How the fuck should I know! He didn't give me his name!'

The rude awakening coupled with the t-shirt's attitude snapped something inside him.

'And you didn't bother to fucking ask?'

Travers' outburst knocked the man out of his stride and caused a stuttering reply.

'I fucking hate mornings at the best of times,' Harry began to rant, 'and you and this are not making them any easier!'

He was grateful to be clothed and strode over to the reception.

'Would you like me to connect the call to your room?'

Harry could have killed the t-shirt there and then, but stopped, took a deep breath, smiled, did an about turn and said very politely: 'That would be great.'

The old boy was enjoying the moment; let him have his small victory, he thought, and purposefully made no eye contact before returning to his room and softly closing the door: slamming it only reinforced his agitation and he was not about to concede anything.

Three minutes later the phone rang: it was Jeffries.

'Harry?'

'Anton.' He didn't care that his reply was far too formal.

'I've arranged for you to be taken on a trip.'

'Thank you, but-'

'And I've asked Tommy again to pilot you, is that okay?'

It most certainly was: 'Thank you, that'll be great.'

'Good. Tommy will pick you up around eleven at McMinn, and I'll see you later at my office. Have a good day.'

Before Harry could reply Jeffries hung up.

He looked over at the bedside clock: it read 09:15.

'Fuck, I hate mornings!' Harry blurted out before collapsing back on the bed, but at least this particular morning was tempered with another trip with the ever cheerful, garrulous Tommy; the one person Harry needed to talk to.

Harry was a lot of things, some good, some bad, others in between, but he was always punctual and he duly arrived in the terminal at McMinn airport, wearing a comfortable pair of sneakers, blue denim jeans and a banana yellow t-shirt, at ten minutes to eleven, just in time to see Tommy arrive in a Cessna 172 Skyhawk.

This trip was going to be an eye opener and he was ready for all and any surprises that fate deigned to throw his way: Tommy would hopefully shed more light on his uncle and maybe some on his business activities. Did he owe anybody money? Nobody had come forward yet, but it was still early days. Harry made up his mind after today to completely ignore Jeffries' advice. Who else had his uncle upset other than Sheriff Poulsen? But the Sheriff behaved in a courteous and reasonable manner. Yes, today would open a few more doors into the world of the late Jack Hennessey.

'Harry!' shouted Tommy, as he entered the terminal.

'Tommy.'

'You ready to go?'

Harry was more than ready.

'Let's not waste any more time.'

The two men rekindled their burgeoning friendship, and this was reflected in the constant chat between them as they crossed the apron to where the Cessna 172 was parked, so much so that by the time Tommy called for start-up he knew where Harry was staying, his true profession, which shocked him not, that he had met Jeffries and the Sheriff plus loves pizza.

'It should take us around twenty minutes,' Tommy stated over the intercom whilst the Cessna climbed through a thousand feet. Harry was enjoying the spectacular view and simply grunted: 'Okay.'

The view of the Tennessee countryside was truly breath-taking; yesterday he was too tired, too absorbed with the strange surroundings and everything going on to fully appreciate the full beauty of the Tennessee landscape.

'Beautiful isn't it?'

'It sure is,' Harry replied, not averting his gaze from outside the window.

'I never tire of it.'

'No, I don't suppose you ever would.' Harry began to centre his attention on Tommy who had levelled at two thousand feet, and set the cruising speed to one hundred knots.

'You're a lucky man Tommy. It's truly wonderful.'

'As pretty as anything you'll see anywhere in the world!'

'Explain this to me Tommy,' started Harry, searching for the answer to a question taking immediate priority over all others. 'How did my uncle get to be in a position to buy property over here, with him being a foreigner?'

'Dual nationality!'

'Dual nationality!' Harry repeated. 'How? Did he say?'

'When your uncle first acquired the property it kicked up a right hornet's nest in some quarters: "How come some Limey can buy our land?" What nobody knew was your uncle was born in the U.S.A.'

'Now that I didn't know!'

'Your ancestor, his father, was a banker in New York and that gave him the money and the right to apply for citizenship, which he did in later life.'

Harry took in this latest revelation as Tommy banked the Cessna to the left, heading east.

'Which naturally begs the question can I keep it?'

'Way above my pay grade,' answered Tommy swiftly. 'But if you decide to sell they'll be queuing around the block to take it off your hands.'

'How far?'

'Not long.'

Harry was in awe, admiring the panoramic view ahead and around with all the thoughts of selling the house, keeping the house, emigrating, what was it worth? Who would buy it? Could he even sell it? Was the property protected by some law or other?

* * *

Jeffries sat behind his desk with his head planted firmly in his hands: the Boyd brothers were, no matter how many times he told them to remain calm and let things run their natural course, on the phone badgering him relentlessly for information regarding Harry Travers. Discretion, he informed them, is the better part of valour, but he'd have been better off talking to the walls on Hennessey's house for all the good it did him: their attitude was for killing Harry there and then. All they required was a green light from this lawyer who he could see they regarded as nothing more than a hindrance, but Jeffries was still for caution.

* * *

Tommy slowed the Cessna to below flap limiting speed and extended the first stage of flap, followed smoothly by the second.

'Dead ahead!' he said pointing over the nose cone.

Harry craned his neck to get a better look, but the local terrain looked all the same to him. He smiled none the less at the spectacular beauty of the place, praising his uncle's sagacity for moving here.

Tommy banked the Cessna to the right.

Harry locked his sight on a section of dense foliage that bordered the western edge of the forest.

'Is this where he died?'

'They found some evidence that he'd been walking, trekking through this section of forest,' Tommy said, pointing.

Harry strained to see the section Tommy was alluding to.

'This ridge forms part of the Southeast border of McMinn County; any further east and it would have been outside the Sheriff's jurisdiction!'

Tommy gently descended the Cessna 172 to a safe, but legal altitude while Harry scoured the landscape.

It took a few minutes, during which time Harry castigated himself for being so inept, but finally he located the spot Tommy was referring to.

'Did he often venture out here?'

'Only when he wanted to be alone!'

'Was that often?' Harry suddenly felt an overwhelming feeling of animosity towards Jeffries; he was rapidly losing patience with the man. Here once again he was learning more about his late relative by what seems to be his only true friend.

'Didn't Jeffries tell you?'

'No!'

'I asked him once why he loved it out here so much. You know what he said?'

Harry said nothing.

'No, of course you wouldn't know: he said he loved the feeling of freedom it gave him to be able to fuck off whenever he felt like it!'

Now Harry could definitely relate to that, maybe just maybe he was more like his uncle than he gave himself credit for.

Tommy began to orbit the small section of forest that could lay claim to be Uncle Jack's final resting place.

'If it is Jeffries' responsibility to maintain my uncle's house until I inherit, and the Sheriff is no longer investigating his disappearance, then who is down there?' Harry said looking out of the passenger's side window.

'No idea!'

'Somebody down there is doing a very bad job of not being seen!'

Tommy banked the Cessna hard over to the left to tighten the turn and get a better look, but the figure realized the game was up and remained out of sight.

'You're sure there's somebody down there?'

'One hundred percent!'

'Could be anybody!'

'Then why hide?'

'Right!' The tone of Tommy's voice only hinted at his determination to discover this person's identity: 'Back to McMinn. We'll use your car. It's an hour or so drive.'

In no time at all the Cessna was accelerated, the flaps were bought in and they headed straight back towards the airport.

Harry felt the hairs on the back of his neck starting to rise: what initially shocked him was the excitement and the sudden adrenaline rush experienced now that danger lurked over the horizon. Who was this man? Was he friend or foe? Maybe it was the Sheriff trying to source new evidence to find his uncle's body, but why then hide under the canopy of the trees? He chastised himself in equal measure for being too easy in accepting the story of his uncle dying of a heart attack whilst on a jaunt in the woods.

Once Tommy had parked up the Cessna, they expeditiously made for the Scirocco and hit the road.

'About an hour or so you say?' Harry said pulling onto the main highway to head east.

'I reckon so!'

Harry sensed uncontrollable anger welling up inside him at the very thought of being taken for an idiot. Where would he be right now of it wasn't for Tommy? These thoughts fanned the flames of indignation and he instinctively put his foot down before being politely reminded of the speed limit on Tennessee roads. He liked the garrulous Tommy: he was honest, as far as he could tell, had liked his uncle enormously and clearly held authority in contempt, not a bad trait and one Harry respected. He steered the Volkswagen as per Tommy's exact instructions and an hour an twenty minutes later, after travelling in predominantly an East-Southeast direction, they turned right onto a two lane road bisecting an area of woodland. Harry sensed right away this was the place. He found himself examining, admiring every single tree lining the road: he had never seen such beautiful trees, but he appreciated his opinion was biased.

A narrow dust track slowly came into view off to the left, which quickly revealed itself within the surrounding lush foliage.

Harry slowed right down and turned onto the track. Immediately his inner alarm bell began to sound.

'A couple of hundred yards!' whispered Tommy.

'Why are you whispering?'

'I don't rightly know.'

'Looks as though we've got to park up, and walk the rest of the way.'

'I'm getting a bad feeling about this Harry!'

'You want to stay with the car?'

'Hell no: I haven't had this much fun in years!'

Harry parked the Scirocco off the track, facing the road in case they needed a quick getaway, before he and Tommy furtively made their way over to a small clearing. The wind in the trees gave the place an eerie feel.

Tommy placed a hand on his friend's shoulder and held his right index finger up to his mouth. The tension was almost tangible and the adrenaline rush sent their heartbeats racing.

At a range of fifty yards, off to the left, sat a dark coloured Dodge truck; carelessly parked to aid any would-be investigator.

'You recognise it?' Harry said softly.

'No, not seen it before, but it has Tennessee plates!'

They stealthily manoeuvred their way around the vehicle until they sat, crouched behind a large tree giving excellent views of its front and right side. And there they waited for what seemed like an eternity for any sign of movement. It was Harry who first displayed symptoms of impatience by shuffling forward until he was parallel with the tree affording them such great cover. He was halted by a well-timed hand on the shoulder: 'There's movement!'

Harry quickly dropped to his stomach.

A stocky bad tempered looking man appeared from behind a large tree without attempting to keep his whereabouts quiet, glanced over his shoulder, cussed and went to collect something from the back of the truck. Whatever it was he needed it wasn't there. Cussing again he promptly disappeared back into the forest.

'You know him?' asked Harry, eager to see what it was the stranger was up to.

'I'm afraid I do!'

This sounded ominous.

'Who is he?'

'Carl Boyd.'

'He doesn't look the most salubrious of characters!'

'He's a bad tempered, mean son of a bitch, but not as mean or as smart as his older brother Jake: he's got the temperament of a rattlesnake with the brains to back it up. Carl's a dumb shit!'

'Nice family.'

'There's a third brother Rudy and a sister Nancy.'

Harry got to his feet and in a flash was crouching by the front left side of the truck, straining to hear any discourse. Out of the corner of his left eye he could see Tommy waving violently. He was trying to mouth something, but any time spent attempting to decipher his silent language evaporated in an instant with a crushing blow to the back of the head. Harry tried to stand, but his head spun wildly; he only just managed to remain upright. Tommy rushed past him. His legs were jelly and he staggered backwards. Through the blinding pain enveloping his senses he witnessed Carl bear down on him.

"Bad tempered son of a bitch" was all he could think of and instinctively grabbed the first hard object his hand touched from the rear of the truck, and then swung the tyre iron with all the remaining energy his ailing body could muster.

Carl ducked and hit the floor.

Harry staggered back three paces to see Tommy engaged in a furious fight with another man.

The stranger roared at Carl, who was back on his feet facing Harry, to get the shotgun out of the truck and shoot this son of a bitch.

Man this stranger's got a weird, high pitched voice, thought Harry, and concentrated on attacking Carl a second time.

Carl managed to extract the shotgun from the same area of the truck that Harry retrieved the tyre iron, but before he could get the gun cocked Harry slammed the iron down onto his left arm and broke it. Carl dropped the gun.

Harry fell back against the truck and slipped onto his arse. Carl was now ahead of him dropping to his knees swearing oaths at him.

'I'll fucking kill you for this!'

This was red rag to a bull and any natural belligerence on receiving threats of that magnitude kicked in and his head cleared in an instant. Harry was on his feet in a second holding his weapon menacingly over the man's head.

'I think the phrase is "fuck you!"' he snarled.

Carl's eyes failed to hide the fear emanating from within the depths of his beleaguered soul and he sat down on his haunches awaiting the killing blow.

Tommy was getting the upper hand against the man with the squeaky voice, but in that split second it took him to take his eyes off

Carl, Travers felt his legs go from under him and he clattered to the floor. Carl, even with a broken arm, jumped to his feet and laid two or three brutally hard kicks into Harry, knocking the wind out of him.

'Let's move!' screamed Carl.

Rudy knew the fight was up and swung hard and fast at Tommy before running for the truck.

Tommy fatally paused on hearing Harry groan and caused valuable daylight to grow between him and the brothers and this brought an end to the conflict.

Carl wheel spun the truck out of the forest.

'You okay?' Tommy said, as he helped Harry to his feet.

'Been better, how you?'

'A few cuts and bruises, but I've had worse. You gave Carl something to remember you by!'

'Next time I'll be ready and waiting!'

'Next time you better be carrying some hardware.'

'It's top of my to-do list. Who was the guy that hit me?'

'Rudy, the younger brother I was telling you about.'

Harry felt the back of his head; it wasn't bleeding, but he was going to have a real peach of a headache.

'Let's get you to Doc Adams.'

'Yeah, I want a chat with him, but first let's have a good look around!'

The two men explored every inch of this small section of forest, but came away frustrated, disgruntled and none the wiser.

'Off to see Doc Adams,' Tommy said, as they made their way over to where the Volkswagen was hidden, 'and some running repairs.'

Harry was not for arguing: the headache he anticipated was starting to kick in.

'Fuck!' was all Tommy could utter as he opened the driver's door to reveal the vandalism the Boyd brothers had inflicted on the ignition-barrel. 'Oh well, it won't delay us too much.' Tommy hot-wired the car.

'A man of many talents,' Harry said admiringly.

'And master of none!'

Harry laughed at Tommy's quick response.

'Now there's a skill I need to learn,' Harry added, trying to get a better view of what his friend was up to. 'Back home you don't learn that in civilian life unless you operate on the other side of the law!'

'I used to work for a guy who ran a business repossessing cars for finance companies. He taught me everything I know, and I.......,' the car burst into life, '....will willingly teach you!'

'That's a deal,' Harry replied, rubbing his head, as he made his way round to the passenger side. 'You better drive.'

Tommy reversed the Scirocco smartly back onto the dirt track without too much bother and left for Doc Adams and those running repairs.

5

Jeffries couldn't quite believe what he was hearing: one they had totally ignored everything he had said regarding patience and biding their time until this Harry Travers was on his way home; secondly, to add insult to injury, two of them had got embroiled in a fight with the man and Tommy, which in the short term concerned him the more, and resulted in Carl gaining a serious injury; thirdly his car was vandalised. This was going to take some fast talking and persuasion to prevent Travers from spending most of his time investigating further. Either that, or say nothing and let the Englishman get bored with finding nothing of any interest and dodge bringing any suspicion upon himself.

'Don't tell me anymore!' he said between gritted teeth.

The request flew completely over Carl's head, who continued to jabber on.

'Don't say another word!' he repeated.

An indignant Carl finally got the message and threatened the lawyer with a visit from his older brother if he should ever speak that way to him again.

Jeffries couldn't give a damn: 'Shut up!'

Carl remained silent.

His back was up, his blood was boiling and why couldn't this family of boneheads obey the simplest of commands. 'I'll save you the bother of calling your brother.'

Carl remained mute.

'So where is the younger Boyd?'

Rudy came on the line.

'Silly question I know, but I've got to ask you two boneheads just the same,' Jeffries said, gripping the side of the desk in frustration. 'Did Tommy recognise you?'

The answer was in the affirmative and he swore under his breath.

'You'll need to take care of him!'

Rudy laughed.

'I'm glad you find it funny!'

'I've been waiting for this day!'

'Well congratulations to you now that you've managed to manufacture it, and would it be too much trouble to ask for Tommy's demise to be done quick, without much fuss, before anybody gets wind of this!'

Rudy assured him there was nothing for him to worry about, and the late Tommy Shearen would receive a great send off.

* * *

'Better watch our backs from now on!' Tommy said once they'd been on the road for a little over thirty minutes. 'You might want to consider leaving for home early.'

'No way!' Harry countered, while still rubbing the back of his head: it wasn't as painful as he first feared. 'I want to know what the hell is going on!'

'There's one thing for sure: if the Boyd family are involved it's illegal!'

'Should we tell Sheriff Poulsen? I only mention it to satisfy my conscience in having raised the topic and left it open for discussion.'

'Do you English always use twenty words when one will do? No!'

'So glad we cleared that one up.'

Tommy pulled up outside Doc Adams' surgery situated on the western end of Cook Drive.

Both looked the worse for wear as they entered the building.

From over the road Jake smiled: he was proud of himself for being one step ahead of them and having figured out their next port of call. 'They won't require Doc Adams' services next time,' he whispered. 'Nobody is going to get away taking liberties!' He glanced over his shoulder at an undertakers, situated no more than a hundred yards down the road: it always tickled him that a funeral director should be in such close proximity to a medical centre.

It took a little under thirty minutes to patch the two men up, prescribe pain killers and furnish Harry with another piece to the Jack Hennessey jigsaw: his uncle suffered a heart attack a few years prior, again Harry thought of the lawyer, and the good doctor prescribed medication in the aftermath of an operation to fit a couple of stents. Uncle Jack by all accounts was not the model patient: he point blankly refused to stop drinking, smoke expensive cigars, abhorred any form of exercise, which did beg the question as to why he was out on a jaunt in the forest, and continued to chase women like it was going out of fashion. It was no wonder he collapsed, Doc Adams had said, and what a waste of life.

'Waste of life,' Harry said boarding the Scirocco, 'sounds like he had a hell of a life!'

Tommy agreed: 'I'd be happy with half of what he got up to!'

After a brief conversation where Tommy enquired if he was happy to go back to the motel, they set off for the Oakridge.

Jake pulled hard out into the road with reckless abandonment to follow at what he perceived to be a respectable distance. He wanted revenge. Tommy was promised to Carl, but the Englishman was his; he couldn't have given a damn what the lawyer said, and after hearing of his attitude towards his brothers was hell bent on putting him in his place.

He parked across the road to witness Harry, and the soon to be late Tommy Shearen, slot the Scirocco into one of the motel's empty parking bays and head off for Travers' room. Then it suddenly dawned on him. 'Fuck!' he said with glee. So Tommy was spending the night here was he? How convenient for him to remove both these obstacles in one fell swoop and save a whole heap of trouble. It wouldn't take much to make it seem like the two men had a falling out and killed each other in a fierce argument. No, in fact it was far too convenient and would surely bring down too much heat on the place and delay their plans. Reluctantly Jake conceded luck had saved them today, and he unwillingly cooled his animosity for the time being and left to make a note of their room number. He was gone only a matter of a minutes and once back gunned his car into life and left to inspect the true extent of his brother's injury.

* * *

'So what mind boggling excuse you got this time?' Jake asked with a touch of menace, as his younger brother entered the family home.

'It's not my fault!' pleaded Carl, rubbing his arm.

'And whose fault is it then?'

'You should have warned us we'd be followed!' interposed Rudy.

'Rudy, what was the last thing I told you?'

'All was quiet.'

'After that!'

Rudy failed to answer.

'I still warned you to expect the unexpected.'

All three remained silent until Jake relaxed a little on seeing the distress the conversation was having on his brother.

'How bad is the break?'

'It's clean. Like the one I got when you pushed me out of the tree-house.'

Jake laughed and hugged Rudy and then Carl. It was the icebreaker, and the mood visibly softened.

'What we going do with Jeffries?' Carl said once they had separated.

'He's showing no respect,' added Rudy.

'I know, I know, but first things first. We got to prioritise,' replied Jake.

'I owe him!' growled Carl.

'You'll get your chance. We just need to be patient.'

Rudy went to the cool box and removed three beers. 'Do you think he told the Englishman?'

'No, he's not that stupid!' Jake said, hoping he was correct in his assumption.

'I'm gonna buy me the biggest truck you ever did see!' Carl said lightening the mood still further.

Rudy handed out the beers and they all graciously clinked bottles, each planning their own retribution.

'What you lot doing standing around, drinking beer?'

Jessie Boyd was a mean looking, stocky, six-footer who kept his grey hair short and spiky and was a no-nonsense guy who always expected, demanded to get his own way, and at nearly sixty years of age was too old in the tooth to live any other way. He went to the cooler and grabbed two beers; the first didn't even touch the sides and he threw the empty into a box, which acted as the trash can. Half the second quickly followed its cousin.

'Well, what you up to?' His piercing blue eyes interrogated each son in turn.

'Nothing,' answered Carl.

'What the hell happened to your arm? Please tell me you didn't jump out of a tree-house again?'

'That's what we were saying pa!' Rudy said, taking a step back to allow their father into the group.

'Pa, we haven't got any tree-houses!'

Carl paused for a second: he instantly realised that his position was now compromised and he'd left himself open for further investigation. Thankfully for him his father decided not to press it, and instead finished his second beer and went in search of a third.

Rudy kicked Carl in the leg while furiously tapping the side of his head.

Carl shook his, shrugged his shoulders and rubbed the pristine white plaster cast looking for sympathy that was not readily forthcoming.

'They found Hennessey yet?' Jessie barked, after taking two huge hits from his beer. He wiped any excess off his lips with the sleeve of his pale blue shirt.

'No,' answered Jake: he didn't want either of his siblings to let their father in on their business, not yet anyhow, not until the time was right.

'Just my luck to end up spending all that time and money trying to buy that son of a bitch's property and then he goes up and dies somewhere!'

'Too bad!'

'Yeah, too bad,' Jessie replied, belying the anger simmering just below the surface at his eldest son's flippant remark.

Jake could sense his father's mood swing: 'Surely the house will go to auction?'

'You know as well as I do his next of kin is here negotiating with that weasel Jeffries!'

'Yeah, weasel,' agreed Carl, still rubbing his arm.

Jessie drained the remainder of his beer.

His sons were ahead of him with theirs and the conversation turned, as it naturally did with the Boyd clan, to food.

'Where's your sister?'

'In town,' said Jake, taking responsibility to answer.

'Why is she not back?'

'I don't know, but if she bothered to carry that damn cell-phone we got her we'd know what time supper would be ready!'

Rudy backed off a couple of paces, turned and went to the window.

'Is that her?' Jessie rasped.

'No!'

'I'll kick her arse if she ain't here in half hour!'

Carl retreated into the kitchen and binned his beer bottle: he was not about to get in the firing line when his father's infamous temper exploded. Rudy saw what his twin was about and agreed that a few extra yards meant a few extra seconds to gauge the sudden change in Jessie's demeanour, plus it put them closer to the rear door.

Jessie began to pace the long, rectangular room running almost the entire length of the dwelling, and had access to all the rooms on the lower floor. He began to mutter that a man of his age should not be left waiting for his supper. Jake remained where he was. He for one was not about to cow-tow to his father's, sometime, unsavoury disposition: all the boys at some point or other had felt the force of his belt when either under the influence of alcohol, or his temper just got the better of him. His father suddenly stopped, spun round and confronted Jake: he being the eldest always got it first if they were all together.

His assault on his eldest child was aborted with the sound of an approaching vehicle. They each held station on hearing a door close, footsteps on the porch and the door to the entrance fling open to reveal the only person living who could quell a raging Jessie Boyd: Nancy Boyd.

'Where have you been?' growled her father.

'Pa, calm down, I got groceries,' Nancy said softly, walking past him into the kitchen and placing a brown paper bag on a large table in the room. 'You want your supper? Well, if any of you boys had bothered to use the brains that God gave you, you'd have looked in the oven and seen the Meatloaf!' she added without looking over her shoulder.

Jessie glared at each son in turn.

'You're as much to blame pa! You only had to follow your nose.' Nancy now stood in the kitchen doorway watching her father closely.

He could never stay angry with Nancy however hard he tried. She was the spitting image of his late wife, and named after her: both were strikingly beautiful with long black hair, piercing brown eyes with a full athletic figure and stood a shade over five feet three inches, but what they lost in height they sure as hell made up in personality: there wasn't anybody who wasn't or hadn't been charmed by a girl named Nancy Boyd.

* * *

Harry tossed a cold beer across his less than opulent motel room into Tommy's outstretched hand. Tonight was a night for the poor man's painkiller.

'I can't stand warm beer,' he said, cracking off the bottle top with the opener bolted to the side of the wall, 'and as I don't have a fridge you better drink up.'

Tommy watched the ice cold condensation run down the bottle and trickle over his fingers, and not being one to ever waste valuable drinking time standing on ceremony, downed the beer in all of ten seconds, once he'd freed the contents with the help of a bottle opener on his penknife.

Harry could sense a challenge and followed suit; all of a sudden he feared their provisions were not adequate enough. Tommy agreed and less than half an hour later, courtesy of a local taxi company Tommy knew, they were furnished with a further twenty-four beers and a Chinese take-out.

This is going to hurt real bad, mused Harry, but it was the stress buster he needed to take his mind off current events, and on these occasions he knew great friendships were forged.

Beer after bottled beer was consumed during which time any ravenous hunger was satiated with copious amounts of takeout; both men viewed the other with a growing respect which increased exponentially with their dwindling supply of bottled beer, but hit after hit could only leave them with one inevitable outcome and they attacked the bottle of Jack Daniels with equal vigour, their enthusiasm never waning for a second as the sweet brown liquid warmed their innards, sending their senses into ecstasy.

Tommy, because he missed his friend and here was his next of kin sitting before him matching him drink for drink, or he felt genuine affection and kinship with this visitor from a foreign land, felt the need to express himself.

'Harry, you're my best friend! The best friend anybody could want to have.'

Harry was choked.

'You're tops in my book Tommy, tops!'

It was the American's turn to get emotional, and the two intoxicated best friends drank well into the early hours to their continued good health and lifelong friendship.

* * *

Jake pulled up outside the motel, checked the safety on his stainless steel Smith and Wesson 4006 semi-automatic pistol then tucked it inside his belt. It was nigh on pitch black due to a couple of failed street lamps and he knew that a better opportunity to rid themselves of these two thorns in their side would not appear for a very long time; so what if there was a little heat, they would lie low until everything cooled off.

The car park was quiet with only one light shining from a solitary window like a beacon beckoning him forward and illuminating his path towards the successful fulfilment of his goal. He counted off the door numbers to be doubly sure he found room 217. Perfect, he thought, the only room lit was the one he sought and the familiar voices of his victims only confirmed it. He put his ear to the door.

'Fuck that Jake Boyd!' slurred Tommy.

'Yeah, fuck him!' agreed Harry.

The two would be dipsomaniacs laughed and giggled uncontrollably.

'You know what I'm going do the next time I see him?'

Jake strained to hear Tommy: he would like nothing better than to have a legitimate excuse to deal with him.

'What you going to do?' asked Harry. 'Give him both barrels?'

'Yeah, both barrels!'

Jake took a step back. Threats were nothing new to him; he dished them out all the time, but never until now had he been in a position to overhear the threat first-hand and it unnerved him. He returned to the door.

'You give him both barrels,' Harry went on, 'and I'll give him two more!'

Again Jake backed off from the door, but this time it was a sizeable step. It didn't take long for him to come to the conclusion that tonight was not the night to cross swords with this enemy armed only with a pistol when both of them were armed with shotguns and clearly been on the drink: a drunk would shoot indiscriminately without conscious thought or aim. No, he would have to wait for a second time.

Tommy slumped onto the bed and instantly fell asleep. Harry laughed, not because he viewed this as a victory, but his American friend had stolen the march on the bed, leaving him with the chair.

'Both barrels,' he muttered while making himself comfortable for the night. 'That'd be one piece of my mind he'd never forget!'

* * *

Morning announced its arrival by spearing shafts of sharp, golden sunlight through those parts of the window not covered by the pathetic excuse for a curtain, which was failing in its duty to bring feelings of well-being to those occupying room 217. And it was Harry who won the race back to consciousness by first opening one bleary eye to those golden rays filtering through the partially obscured window. His neck was the first to complain followed closely by his back and then inevitably his head: the throbbing was like a jackhammer pounding the inner rims of his skull.

'Fuck!' was all he could say, but it explained everything perfectly.

Harry finally managed to stagger to his feet and headed straight for the bathroom. He promptly threw up in the basin. It didn't improve anything and he dared not look in the mirror in case the face staring back at him was not recognisable from the one he shaved yesterday morning, but look he did.

'Good God!'

Any further exclamation was cut short by the arrival of his drinking buddy.

'Morning!' Harry said jovially.

Tommy chucked up down the toilet.

'You had a good night then?' Harry continued tongue-in-cheek.

'Ready for round two when you are!' Tommy replied standing upright and regretting it a split second later: the sudden rush of blood to his head was not what was needed and he fell backwards through the bathroom door into the main body of the room. His fall was thankfully cushioned by the double-bed, but it failed to prevent him bouncing off the mattress and onto the floor.

Harry collapsed onto the bed laughing hysterically and made a vain attempt to help the poor, prostrate Tommy up into the seated position.

'I think this day will be a day of limited excursion with much relaxation,' Tommy said before a second visit to the bathroom.

Harry felt surprisingly good after his brief visit.

'You aluminium tubing boys certainly know how to drink!'

'Thank you.'

'But what is needed here, as you English say, is "The hair of the dog!"'

'If you say so!'

Tommy re-appeared leaning against the bathroom door. From the look on his face Harry half expected a third expedition to the "John", but his friend was anything but predictable and wasted not a second cracking open the two remaining beers that had survived the night, which both men quaffed down in one go. Each stared at the other trying to gauge if either had need for the basin or the toilet.

'That went well,' Harry finally said.

The room phone, situated on the bedside table, rang and Harry subconsciously answered on the third ring. It was Jeffries. Harry mouthed his name.

'Hi!'

'How you feeling today?' enquired the lawyer.

Harry had to pause: did he know about their fight? It was best to err on the side of caution.

'Fine, how you?'

'Can you come by the office today?'

'Sure, I'll be there around eleven.'

Jeffries was more than happy with this arrangement and quickly hung up.

'Don't trust him!' said Tommy, 'I never really have.'

'I don't, but he knows the true content of the will.'

'Then just don't drop your guard, he's not a stupid man!'

'There is one obvious solution to uncovering the truth,' Harry said carefully cradling the receiver. 'Bring in a private detective.'

'You don't need one of those,' Tommy said enthusiastically, 'we'll do it!'

'And you've done some detective work in a past life?'

'Hell no! But I'd give it a go.'

Harry smiled at the thought of the two of them playing at private detectives: 'You need to teach me that hot wiring trick.'

'I'll teach you more than that Harry,' Tommy added gleefully. 'We'll fly up to my place where it's nice and peaceful with no prying eyes, and you can practice perfecting a few essential skills. What do you say?'

Harry was all for that.

* * *

Once showered and shaved, and wearing a fresh bright red t-shirt, nobody would have had an inkling that Harry Travers the night before was on the mother of all benders, but here he stood looking refreshed and ready for whatever bullshit Jeffries was going to try and spin his way.

'So tell me?' Harry decided on the way over with Tommy that attack was the best form of defence, and he was going to get his questions in first and put the mendacious Mister Jeffries on the back foot. 'What king of business was my uncle really into?'

Jeffries sat stone faced behind his desk before he began to rub the bridge of his nose and both eyes together: it was an old trick and a very poor time wasting tactic. It had the effect of getting Travers' back up. He was about to ask again when the man finally answered.

'He wasn't.'

'Then how did he live?'

'Very badly!'

What kind of answer is that, Harry thought, realising that he was not going to get the answers he desired. His anger intensified. The meeting was a waste of time.

'What news do you have regarding the will?' Harry asked trying to salvage something out of this.

'I took the liberty of having the contents of the house valued and along with the cash it comes to the tidy sum of one hundred and fifty thousand dollars. You can visit the house at any time, as it's now legally yours, and the money is at your disposal.'

Jeffries slid the house keys across his desk.

'I have been your uncle's lawyer, for better and for worse, these past five years: it was only five due to all the previous lawyers being fired!' Here he paused to allow time for his last statement to sink in.

'Why?'

'According to your uncle they stole from him.'

Which implies you have not, thought Harry. He picked up the keys.

Jeffries took the silence to mean his integrity was seriously in doubt: 'I never stole from your uncle, or ever would!'

Throughout this brief, intense, less than thorough, quick-fire confab Harry stood, but now took the time to adjust to his surroundings again. He felt more relaxed and in control, so he sat.

'Like I said before Harry, you would do well not to let people in these parts know why you're here!'

'I took your advice on board.' It was a blatant lie, but his conscience was clear.

'Glad to hear it. Are you going to sell?'

'Got no need for it!'

'That would be my recommendation.' Jeffries revealed a pernicious smile as he spoke. 'As for the house I would estimate a valuation of around four hundred thousand dollars.'

That was a tidy sum, but then again it was a fine house in Kensington Street. He rose to pour himself a cup of coffee: in truth it was now his turn to find time and use a delaying tactic. He poured two cups and handed Jeffries his along with sweetener and cream. He was taking his black today. Harry needed to choose his words carefully: the last thing he desired right now was to let it be known that the inheritance meant anything at all to him. Jeffries was eying him suspiciously. Best to say nothing and let people think you're an idiot rather than open your mouth and prove them right, and he wasn't left waiting long to be proved correct.

'I know that comes as a shock to discover such an inheritance is yours. It is a natural reaction.'

Harry paused before replying, repeating "choose your words carefully" over and over in his head, but now he became aware of the time and poor Tommy waiting in the car. Why hadn't he advised against it? Tommy said he didn't mind driving and could watch their backs. Harry for some reason, totally unbeknown to him, thought Tommy was in league with the lawyer, obviously not and it was having an unsatisfactory bearing on his attitude towards the man.

'I suppose it all depends if you are desperate for the money!'

'And you're not?'

'Take it or leave it, that's my motto.'

'I will be in touch as soon as I have a definitive figure for you.'

'When will that be roughly?'

'A couple of days should do it.' If Jeffries was rattled he hid it well.

'Good I'll have information before I leave then.'

'You can have access to the cash at any time, just call me.'

Jeffries volunteered nothing further, which only added to Travers' frustration.

Damn that Marvin. Harry tried hard not to show any concern: why hadn't he come back with that all important information? What was taking so long?'

'If there is nothing else Harry,' Jeffries said tapping his watch with his right index finger, 'I need to be in court in half an hour.'

There wasn't, and so he followed polite society by thanking the man for the coffee, and left with the appropriate good tidings coupled with a hollow promise to keep in touch.

Once in the car park Harry found to his annoyance that the man got right under his skin, and he paced the length of the parking bays in order to clear his head.

'You need a drink!' shouted Tommy.

'You're damn right, but I need to see my uncle's house first!'

'I know a place that stocks the best moonshine this side of Knoxville.'

A more inviting offer could not have been more welcome, and it had the desired effect of quelling his anger. He walked back to the car and climbed aboard.

* * *

His uncle's house failed to spread any light on the man's disappearance: it was brightly and tastefully decorated throughout, covered 3.400 square foot with an open plan kitchen-cum-diner, contained three bedrooms, two bathrooms, a sizeable rear garden and double garage, but no car. Harry loved it, and gave the idea of keeping it as a second home some serious thought.

The drive afterwards to the airport via the motel allowed him time to admire this part of Tennessee: the surrounding country was indeed beautiful; he loved nature and being outside enjoying the good Lord's omnipotent beauty. It was in stark contrast to his job and the associated pressures that went with it, but scattered amid the trees, set back at ranges of fifty to a hundred yards from the road, was the occasional small wooden construction. He could also envisage himself selling up one day and living the life of the hermit, but that would mean foregoing one of his favourite pastimes: chasing the fairer sex; and one in particular. Her name was Sheila Wallace, and she worked as a cabin manager for the same airline as Harry. Miss Wallace didn't just turn heads she practically snapped them off. Sheila was blonde, thirty-five, a five-foot five inch glam puss who had the body of a twenty-eight year old super model, and boy did she know how to use it. When she wore her favourite nine inch heels and swung her hips to a hypnotic beat, which guaranteed to mesmerise any onlooker, she oozed sex appeal. If ever there was a person for whom the phrase "sex on legs" was invented for it was Sheila Wallace.

Harry tried to find some logical reason, other than the obvious, as to why he should think of Sheila at this precise point in time. Maybe it was fate. The image of her became so overwhelming that he gave serious thought to texting a cheeky message: her number had only recently found its way into his phone after a long night flight when the first signs of a definite soft spot for him in that ample bosom surfaced.

'What you thinking about Harry?'

Tommy's innocent, straight forward enough question caught him off guard and he managed to stammer out: 'Nothing.' What a dick, he thought, then suddenly it became apparent that Sheila Wallace, albeit several thousand miles away, had aroused him beyond all measure. He fidgeted uncomfortably.

'You okay?'

'Yeah, fine!'

If only you knew the truth, he found himself thinking, and smiled. If only you could know Sheila Wallace then you too could sit in rising discomfort imagining her shapely curves swaying from side to side with a cleavage daring you to dive straight in, willing you to abandon all hope of salvation, for her to only walk over your back in those glorious nine inch heels.

Tommy drove with extreme caution, not wanting to draw any unwanted attention: the car's ignition barrel still needed to be fixed; a minor point currently overlooked by the car's owner, and he turned the Scirocco off the main highway from Athens. Next stop McMinn County Airport.

* * *

'Here already!' stuttered Harry, as they pulled into McMinn.

'You sound disappointed?'

'No, just lost track of time; lost in my own thoughts.'

'You got a lot on your plate right now.'

If only his friend knew the half of it. Eventually he would let Tommy in on everything, he owed him that much, but for now it was safer he didn't know. It also kept Tommy out of harm's way: if Jeffries had any involvement in his uncle's demise then the more he thought he was not going to share any information then the greater the chance of nobody coming looking for him. He still had to live here when all was said and done.

'Listen Tommy,' Harry blurted out, 'you and I both know I've got to get to the bottom of all this. It just seems to me to be all too convenient. I understand if you don't want to get involved, it's not your problem, but mine.'

Tommy parked the car, making sure he got smack bang in the middle of the bay, so to hide the ignition damage from any prying eyes. 'Harry, if you think for one goddamn minute that I'm going to let you have all the goddamn fun then you better take time to re-evaluate this situation!'

Harry burst out laughing: it was exactly what he wanted, needed to hear. Tommy said the right thing, at the right time, in just the right way and nothing more needed to be said. The two friends wasted no time prepping the Cessna for an immediate departure for the best moonshine this side of Knoxville.

6

Tommy's residence, which also seemed to pass for the main terminal on this private landing strip, resembled something out of the by-gone days of some gold rush, but Harry took an instant liking to it. To the left sat what he took to be the workshop and part-time barn, for outside were all kinds of machinery in various states of repair including the Seneca they had flown earlier.

'Home sweet home,' Tommy said jocularly, as he strode past Harry to enter the property.

'I see your security is top notch!' Harry tested one of the planks that made up what could be loosely described as a porch.

He could hear his friend's raucous laughter from within the dwelling and it wasn't long before he saw the root cause of it all: the roughest, meanest, mangiest looking bloodhound that you ever saw sauntered out into the late afternoon, early evening daylight and glared at the stranger who dared to have the temerity to invade his personal space and stand on his porch.

'Hi!' said Harry.

The dog remained mute without ever taking his eyes off the stranger.

'Nice doggy,' he continued before adding. 'Harry, you're an idiot!'

From inside Tommy invited him in, and not to mind the dog while rustling up some kind of surprise. Harry had his hands full with this four-legged security guard. He took a first tentative step towards whatever Tommy had in store. The dog let out a low, menacing growl. Harry retreated.

'Get a grip of yourself man! Look at him, he's a washed up old bloodhound seeing out his days in the peace and tranquillity of this beautiful Tennessee backwater!'

Again he took a tentative step and again the dog growled.

'Listen here you!'

This time a third more menacing, deep, throaty warning emanated from the hound, only now he followed it up with the sight of less than pearly white teeth.

Harry needed to take stock: what if the dog had rabies, his shots were way out of date and it was a long trek to the nearest hospital. No, he was going to meet this dog head on: enough people were trying to pull the wool over his eyes or attempting to beat the crap out of him, and as he only had a few days left they were going to be spent playing to his rules.

'Fuck you, dog!'

Harry strode purposefully onto the porch, which for a second or two seemed to take stock of his weight before agreeing to support his frame, and marched on.

The dog growled.

'Fuck you!'

He was now abeam the animal, bracing himself in anticipation of it lashing out at his right leg, but no, the dog simply rolled over onto its side, yawned and farted.

'Wonderful!' said a very relieved Harry, who gratefully accepted two ice cold beers from Tommy standing in the doorway.

'See you met Washington.'

'Great guard dog!'

'Don't be fooled, he's a damn smart dog: he watched you arrive with me, but he always tests the metal of any visitor by verbally challenging them. If you had failed and backed down he would have run you off my land.'

'Thanks for the warning!' Harry started the first of his two beers.

'He lives here, and has his ways just as much as I do.'

'Yeah, I suppose you're right.'

The two men took several hits of the smooth golden liquid and eventually slumped down into chairs Tommy had placed conveniently on the porch.

'Got to get your training started, Harry,' Tommy said polishing off his beer.

'What do you suggest first?' Harry replied and followed his friend's lead.

It was the opening his host was searching for and he produced the surprise from behind his back: a Glock 17.

'Where the hell did you get that?'

'I come across all kinds of things in my line of work!'

'Which is?' Harry was intrigued to learn more.

'I repair things for whoever, and for a great deal of money on occasions: airplanes, as you know, but cars, trucks, bikes and anything I can turn a buck to, but there are times when my customers are unable to settle their bill through normal channels, and so being a kind hearted soul, and not wishing to see my fellow man suffer at the cruel hands of fate, I willingly accept other forms of payment.'

'Including Glocks?'

'Or Berettas, I have an M9 at your disposal.' Tommy held onto a devilish smile.

'Essential private detective skills!'

'You got it!'

The two men downed more beer before restocking from a cool box, which Tommy collected from inside and expertly positioned behind them allowing his host the time to point out a target especially chosen for the Englishman to aim at, bearing in mind that he was a "gun virgin", to quote him: it was an old tree lying at a fifteen to twenty degree angle sitting in Travers' eleven o'clock at a range of thirty to forty yards.

Tommy handed him the Glock, pointing out how the safety worked, how to eject the clip, not to have too high a grip in case of slide bite and finally how to prepare the pistol for firing.

'Ready?'

'As I'll ever be!'

'Then take it away, Harry.'

Harry placed his beer on the porch then stood taking precise aim: the job as he saw it was not to look a complete arse. He took a deep breath and remembered all those films and TV series he'd watched over the years where the hero is taught how to use a gun for the first time and emptied his lungs in a long, slow deliberate breath. He squeezed the trigger. This action disengaged the safety and the Glock exploded into life letting out an ear piercing clap of thunder. The recoil, because he wasn't anticipating it, momentarily knocked him off balance.

The bullet ripped into the centre of the tree trunk, as the ejected shell casing hit the floor and bounced off the porch.

'Good shooting,' exclaimed Tommy. 'I never took you for a lefty!'

'Beginner's luck!' Harry replied focusing on the tree. 'Beginner's luck!'

'The ribbed grip is one of the advantages of the Glock and the grip force adapter helps prevent slide bite. Try again and see if your beginner's luck holds out.'

Harry again took careful aim and hit the centre of the tree a second time followed by a third, a fourth and finally a fifth.

'You're a regular Wyatt Earp.'

'It feels good,' Harry said, studying the Glock in greater detail.

'The preferred weapon for some law enforcement agencies,' Tommy was admiring Travers' spread on the trunk via binoculars. 'Yep, that is some mighty fine shooting.'

'Can I try your Beretta?'

'You're feeling confident?'

'While I'm on a roll!'

Tommy disappeared inside. Harry was convinced his luck would soon run out, and was pretty sure a few rounds with the Beretta would show his true worth and reveal the inevitable inadequacies in his technique.

'It's a real nice piece,' Tommy said affectionately, holding the gun in his right hand, as he walked back to where Harry was standing admiring his previous grouping before spending several minutes expounding the many virtues of the M9: how it felt solid in your hand, its reliability, how in the hands of an expert its accuracy was unrivalled and last, but not least, the sheer aesthetic beauty of it: how could something so beautiful be made purely to maim. It was the sort of weapon that lay at the root of the question: what is more beautiful, a gun or a poem?

Tommy handed Harry the Beretta butt first after demonstrating how to turn the safety on and off. Harry passed him the Glock.

It did indeed sit comfortably in the palm of his hand and instantly instil in the user confidence of never missing the intended target; it immediately felt to Harry as if it was a natural extension of his arm.

Harry slowly raised the Beretta in his left hand and took careful aim while supporting the wrist as before; the movement from standing at ease to ready to fire was smooth and effortless, as though he was born to do it.

Crack, crack, crack: three shots left the barrel of the M9 and deposited themselves into the centre of his previous spread.

Tommy let out a long, slow whistle and took a hit of beer. Harry picked up his and downed the remainder of the bottle in one go.

'You're definitely a goddamned natural Harry!'

Harry handed back the Beretta butt first, but not before checking that the safety was on.

'Sure you don't want to shoot some more?'

'These rounds are costing you money, Tommy!'

'There are plenty more where they came from,' Tommy replied with a wink and a cheeky smile.

Following more beer Harry emptied one final clip from the Glock into the tree, only this time his spread was as wide as his hand.

The two friends sat back down, but only after Tommy showed Harry again how to make the firearms safe, and they continued drinking until the early hours before nearly eating Tommy out of house and home while putting the world to rights. It was a good night: it was one of those nights where friendships are cemented for life and oaths sworn never to be broken. By the time the last of the beer was consumed it was clear to the other they had discovered a true kindred spirit.

* * *

Harry opened one watery eye followed by the other and tried in vain to focus. He attempted to reconcile his present position with events of the previous evening. Slowly the night became clear and lifted the veil of uncertainty that hovered menacingly over his faint recollection of yesterday's festivities. Why did he open his left eye first? Such inconsequential thoughts invaded the delicate balance his mind held over his current predicament. Somewhere in the background he could hear noises.

Shooting, he'd been shooting, but also had a meeting with Jeffries; part of him still wanted to give the man the benefit of the doubt: he chastised himself in the past for jumping far too quickly to conclusions over people. Curtis was a prime example, but here all his intuition told him Jeffries was behind the sad demise of his uncle.

How? His inexperience in these matters meant he couldn't fathom that one out and it annoyed him intensely. To indict any of the Boyd clan he required clean, hard evidence and then hand them over to the County Sheriff, leave it all to him and go home, but would they believe him? He was after all a foreigner in a foreign land. Yes, their countries were allies, but this was a crime, a murder without a body. He couldn't, wouldn't let it lie. It would fester inside him constantly, growing like a tumour until it either killed him or he killed it. No, there was no other alternative; he would have to solve this. It may turn out as Sheriff Poulsen had said, but then again it may not, either way Harry Travers would become Harry Travers Private Detective.

Tommy burst into the room after a cursory knock.

'Ham and eggs do?'

'What happened after the beer and guns?'

'Moonshine, moonshine and even more moonshine!'

The veil of uncertainty was hoisted clear and the sharp taste of Tommy's premium homemade liquor bit hard into his taste buds. He was right about one thing: it was good. Harry lifted his head off the pillow anticipating that jackhammer ready to split his cranium, but found to his pleasant surprise there was nothing except a fuzzy, heavy sensation he knew would subside once an adequate amount of water and orange juice was consumed. Suddenly the smell of ham and eggs hit his nostrils and he was up and out of bed. He had slept fully clothed again. Oh well, he thought, nothing new there. The sparseness of the room held no surprises; in fact it was in keeping with the rest of the dwelling.

Tommy laid out breakfast on a rickety old table in what substituted for a kitchen, but it sure looked as good as it smelt.

Harry took his seat and wasted no time tucking in. For a moment at least it took his mind off his uncle, Jeffries and the Boyd brothers, but he knew it was only a matter of time before it all retuned to haunt him.

'Tommy?'

Tommy grunted a reply in between mouthfuls.

'I am massively in your debt, and I hate to impose further-'

'I kind of figured.'

Harry ran over in his head the best way of putting in his request without sounding desperate.

'You can start after breakfast!' Tommy saved his blushes.

'Thank you.'

'Bed comfortable? I went out of my way to put fresh linen on just for you!' Tommy held onto a cheeky smile, as he finished off the last of his ham and eggs.

Harry said nothing and kept eating: he was not going to rise to any bait.

'You seem to have made up your mind to investigate this.'

'What else can I do? There isn't a part of me that is not afraid to uncover the truth.'

Tommy studied the Englishman closely, attempting to source any weakness in his character. None was forthcoming.

'I need to know all those tricks of the trade that you have so readily to hand.'

Both men sipped their coffee.

'You can shoot real fine, so I don't see a problem there bar practice-'

'I'll pay for the bullets!' butted in Harry.

'That's not a problem. When you flying back?'

'Day after tomorrow.'

'Then you'll get a good day's shooting and schooling in then!'

'I'm ready when you are!' Harry downed his coffee, saw Tommy still wasn't finished, so poured himself another.

Suddenly he felt that buzz, that thrill of excitement envelope him: he hadn't felt this invigorated, this much alive since he flew his first solo from the local flying club over twenty years ago in a small

Cessna 152; the buzz, the sheer adrenaline rush that day supplied bought with it one sad inevitability: he would never feel that way again. He didn't know if it was the danger, the love of flying, the achievement of taking a light aircraft into the air singlehanded and safely bringing it back down to earth or a mixture of all three, but right here, right now, that feeling was back with a vengeance.

* * *

'I looked Jake, I looked and I couldn't find nothing!' Rudy squeaked.

'That ageing bastard left it somewhere!'

'Relax will ya! We got all the time in the world,' exclaimed Carl, appearing from the kitchen of Jack Henessey's cold, brightly decorated, abandoned house. 'There ain't anybody here.'

'It's around here somewhere, I can feel it: he took the greatest of pleasure in goading me that we'd never find it, but I intend to, so I can dance on that son of a bitch's grave, waving at him from wherever he ended up!"

Jake stood resolutely hand on hips, eying the structure with disdain trying to figure out his adversaries last movements. 'Let's go over this place again.'

* * *

Hot wiring a car turned out to be piece of cake, as long as you accept the considerable damage to the steering column, but if your intention was to steal the car anyway who cares. Soon Harry became very efficient and was taking to these new found skills like a duck to water.

Tommy locked the car Harry was practicing on: it had been dumped on him by a client who couldn't pay and then subsequently got arrested for possession and incarcerated.

'Break in!' Tommy said, handing him a long, thin, flat piece of metal around two feet long with a hook on one end.

'How long have I got?'

'I'll give you ten minutes, as it's an old car.'

Harry set to work: he knew the theory, but that didn't stop it proving to be very difficult and after ten frustrating minutes the car was still locked.

'Time's up!'

'Fuck!' Harry hated failure.

'Watch and learn!'

Tommy took the thin metal tool off Harry, and with all the skill of a seasoned professional dextrously slid it down behind the window and popped the latch. The door was open in under a minute. 'See?'

'I got it!' Harry was keen to have another go, and with a renewed confidence attacked the door. In a little under four minutes it was open.

'You just need practice.'

For the rest of the day Harry practiced hot wiring a couple of cars before breaking into them. He was not fooling himself in what he was trying to achieve: this was not the real world and modern cars had far better security, but it was good grounding and where else was he going to learn such dark arts away from prying eyes.

It had not gone unnoticed that Marvin still had to make contact with that all important information and there was a time when he considered that maybe both he and Jeffries were in on some kind of scam to fleece him out of what was rightfully his, but this was dispelled shortly after he finished practice on the second day and his mobile sprang into life with Marvin's office number glaring back at him. For once the conversation was brief, and Harry joked it was the cost of the call that kept the confab to a minimum. The upshot was that four hundred thousand dollars was an accurate estimation. This once again led him to question why anybody would do away with his uncle when they couldn't possibly lay claim to the property, its contents, or the cash. He just needed to be patient and all would be revealed in good time.

'Bad news?' Tommy's polite enquiry snapped Harry back to the present.

'Just my lawyer back at home checking what day I'm due back.'

'Jeffries is going to start worrying if you don't show your face.'

'The thought has occurred to me.'

'We'll head back whenever you're ready.'

'You reckon he's that paranoid?'

'We're talking about a lawyer here,' Tommy said, heading back towards his house before suddenly coming to an abrupt halt. He turned and faced Harry. 'Whatever it is, they can't find it. Therefore it's not in the house!'

'No, it's not!'

'That would be far too obvious. And I don't doubt for a second that they have turned the place upside down by now.'

Tommy had clearly been giving this the same amount of thought and inevitably come to the same conclusion. 'It's in the forest!' They both said in unison.

'It's not the trees, that would be far too easy and anyway they're no different from all the others around these parts.'

Tommy nodded in agreement.

'Treasure,' Harry said jokingly, 'buried treasure.'

A smile slowly crept across Tommy's face: 'You think it's that simple?'

'My uncle: the mastermind criminal!'

'Wouldn't put it past him,' Tommy said. 'No offence meant.'

'None taken.'

The two would be treasure hunters ate a late lunch before prepping the Cessna for the return journey. Tommy decided it was best to stay out of sight, below the radar while Harry was in the United Kingdom and to keep in touch via e-mail. When it came time for Harry to return Jeffries would be given a date two to three days after his actual arrival giving them valuable time to follow any leads they might uncover.

The remainder of the day seemed to evaporate without trace with Harry managing to get in further practice, and it wasn't long before McMinn County Airport lay dead ahead. The two men kept the farewells to a minimum before Harry fired up the Scirocco, using his new found skills, for the drive back to the motel. Throughout the latter he constantly checked his mirrors lest one of the Boyd brothers should be lying in wait for him. Even when back in his room he moved around with great caution and trepidation.

* * *

The day of his departure for Atlanta came and frustratingly dragged on interminably. Jeffries was noticeable by his absence, but Harry could sense he was keeping a close eye on him. He took out his frustrations on TV commercials, the weather and anybody who appeared on the news on the wrong side of the law, for he now viewed himself as a peacekeeper, an avenging angel, a Righter of wrongs, a quiet man fighting for the underdog against the might of evil that infested society. He laughed out loud. 'Melodramatic, but true!' he said with conviction.

He checked his watch for an umpteenth time and cussed, but all his latent anger had one desired effect: it injected him with the courage to contact Jeffries to help vent his spleen. Before he could change his mind he rang the man. His call was answered on the second ring.

Harry lied through his teeth: he informed him that he'd dumped Tommy and driven to his uncle's house alone, and any locals he's spoken to seemed to like his uncle. The lie was to force Jeffries' hand. He didn't bite.

Now filled with growing confidence he lied more and more: the house was easy to find; it was a beautiful place, he paid particular attention to describe it in great detail so his adversary would have an element of doubt. He lied about going on a sightseeing tour of Tennessee; this was half a lie: Tennessee was a beautiful state and one day he intended to drive across it and admire the state in all its glory. He apologised for the damage to the car, stressing he had not yet contacted the police. Throughout it all Jeffries said nothing, queried nothing and made not a sound, so by the end of it all Harry was happy he had muddied the waters sufficiently to cast doubts as to where he had been. Lastly he enjoyed letting him know that once he was in possession of an up to date roster he could accurately give him dates for his next visit.

'You're returning then?'

Harry lined up an acerbic reply, but changed his mind at the last moment.

'Why wouldn't I?' he said.

'Okay.'

He could sense resentment returning with a vengeance: it was his personal shortcomings in not properly venting his anger that lay the foundation for his animosity.

'A couple of weeks should be good for me!'

'Sure, you just let me know. How are you going to get to Atlanta now that you've dumped Tommy?'

'I'll return your Scirocco and hire a car. You've got those repairs to pay for, and I want to see the state of Georgia before I go.'

It was a feasible answer and it turned out to be a good one.

'That's no problem Harry. Your flight's this afternoon, yes?'

Harry confirmed the time of departure.

'Then drop the car off when you're ready.'

Harry said he would in just over an hour, thanked the man for all his help, which grated him no end, and said he looked forward to his next visit.

As soon as the phone hit the cradle Harry dialled out and booked a hire car. He double checked drive times from Athens to Hartsfield-Jackson Atlanta International Airport: it was approximately 167 miles and a three hour drive, but that could vary depending on your route, and as the hire car had a built in satnav he could take one of a number.

Happy he could make the airport in good time Harry finished packing and arranged a farewell meal. He knew one thing: it wouldn't be pizza.

The long drive to Atlanta, after he'd dropped off the Scirocco and Jeffries inspected the damage, he never once asked how or where it happened like it was an everyday occurrence around these parts, was just what the doctor ordered: the car was comfortable, the drive was excellent and it matched the breath-taking scenery, so by the time Harry reached his destination he was relaxed and raring to get home and remove any shackles preventing the games from beginning.

7

It was raining when he landed back in the United Kingdom. 'What a surprise!' he said to an adjacent passenger, but was secretly happy to see and feel the welcoming and familiar arms of home embrace him. 'Welcome home! He added with a smile.

If Harry thought he was going to have it easy then any hopes were dashed the split second he checked his roster online via his phone.

'You're having a laugh!'

His new roster began with three consecutive flights over four days with each at least twelve hours long, and the first being an early morning start then the check in times gradually slipped back until the third was at 17:30 local time. This was followed by two mandatory days off then the same thing started again. Harry was just about to let fly a volley of expletives when he clocked the names of the other crew: to his immense delight the first block of four days contained one Sheila Wallace.

'God bless rostering!'

When he finally fell through his front door, Harry was utterly exhausted: it was harder on the body to travel west to east when compared with the other way round, and he hit the sack early to be refreshed enough for the first flight of three the next morning.

* * *

The sweet, heady smell of perfume was the initial indication she was in the building, but he had no idea what the name of it was or who made it, he just found the aroma intoxicating; the second sign was her infectious laugh that pervaded every corner of the crew room, so sexy was that laugh it turned every male head whenever it went off.

Harry thought about making some kind of entrance, but decided against the plan at the last minute in case she thought it pretentious, and anyway he knew most of the flight deck personally and they would latch onto his tactics in a heartbeat.

He casually dropped his flight bag next to one of the free terminals used to print off the flight-plan, briefing pack and send the voyage report when they finally checked back in. Harry exchanged greetings with a few of the guys already ahead of him sorting theirs before heading out or beginning the journey home. He went over to the vending machine in the far corner to grab a coffee: there was an ulterior motive to this for he would get a great view of the cabin crew briefing rooms and Sheila Wallace, but his attention was drawn to the thirty something first officer drifting in by the same door Harry used a few minutes prior: his name was Sydney Fuller.

'Wonderful!' Harry muttered.

Sydney was one of the good guys: he knew his job, was professional, could take a joke and crack one on any occasion, but most importantly, on this day especially, was utterly discreet. Harry nodded when the two men made eye contact and gesticulated towards the vending machine. Coffee was the reply.

'I see your Miss Wallace is in charge today,' Sydney said, sorting out the paperwork. Harry put the coffees on a nearby table.

'Is she? Can't say I really noticed,' laughed Harry. 'And what do you mean "Your Miss Wallace?"'

'Yeah, right!'

Sydney was cut short readying another jocular response when the source of the banter appeared behind Harry.

'Good morning, gentlemen.'

'Morning Sheila,' Sydney gave her a cheeky wink.

'Morning Harry.'

'Morning Sheila.' She made his heart race.

'Got any flight times for me?'

Sydney read them off the paperwork.

'I'll see you both out there,' she said softly. 'We're on gate twenty-three, and I'll make sure the kettle is on!' Sheila stroked Harry on the shoulder as she glided back to her crew.

'Luck is always disproportionately allocated.' The voice came from a fellow captain seated at a terminal.

'You either got it or you ain't, and you ain't Stevie boy!'

'Fuck you!' laughed Captain Stephen Lee.

'Must be my magnetic personality!'

'The side-stick's not going to be the only thing hard and erect on the flight deck today!' joked Sydney.

Before Harry could find a suitable response Sheila and the four other crew members floated past, leaving their collective perfumes hanging in the air. Through it all Harry could make out hers. He watched her leave while they drank their coffee.

Sydney prepped all the relevant paperwork and the two men clicked into professional mode: its validity was cross-checked, the block fuel was ordered for this outbound sector, taking into account all relevant variables such as taxi fuel, departure and arrival routings, en-route weather, and they set off for gate twenty-three, but not before Harry received a few more cheeky comments.

Sheila was good to her word and the kettle was indeed on once they finally arrived at the Airbus A320. She was dealing with the caterers and one of the younger crew members furnished them with drinks.

Harry was pilot flying on the outbound leg and wasted no time cracking into his duties: running all the pre-flight checks, programming the Flight Management Guidance Computer, liaising with the engineers, ensuring the aircraft technical log was up to date and the jet was serviceable.

Sydney departed for the pre-flight external check, the engineers soon after.

A sharp blast of that perfume was met with a soft hand on his right shoulder.

'Okay to start boarding?'

'Sure thing,' he replied, half turning to greet her, looking straight into her bright, beautiful, blue eyes. He could have sat there admiring her all day. 'Fuelling has finished.'

She winked and left without saying another word.

He felt like a silly schoolboy experiencing their first crush.

Thankfully for all concerned the boarding went off without a hitch with no missing passengers and none of them drunk; all the pre-flight checks were completed, departure clearance was obtained and with ten minutes to spare, once the departure briefing was over, Sydney called Manchester Clearance Delivery again for their start clearance. Sydney was passed over to the Ground Controller to request permission to push back off stand. While he did this Harry made a quick PA welcoming the passengers on-board, introduced himself and the crew, informing them of the flight time and the weather at their destination.

A little over five minutes later with both engines started and the push back tug, tow-bar and towing pin disconnected they ran the after start checks before requesting taxi clearance.

Today was a Monday, and if it was a Monday during their summer season then their destination was Dalaman in Turkey. Harry for once was happy at having two four hour plus flight times to talk to her: on the shorter flights there simply wasn't enough time to complete all the services, feed and water the passengers and take a break for a chat. He chose to fly the outbound leg on purpose so to spend as much time as possible laying some ground work during the turnaround.

It was a busy day at Manchester Airport, and the departure runway was 23 Left with dual runway operation: 23 Right was for landing traffic. By the time they had safely crossed 23 Right and parked themselves at the holding point they were number four for departure. The two of them completed all the pre-takeoff checks before Harry gave the passengers another PA to make them aware of the reason for the slight delay.

Eventually they were cleared to line up and takeoff, and ran through the remainder of the pre-takeoff checks and mentally prepared themselves for the actual takeoff, each comfortable with their duties in the event of any emergency.

Harry smoothly advanced both thrust levers until the engines were stable at 50% N1 then eased them further forward to set takeoff thrust. He called out the indication that thrust was indeed set off the Flight Mode Annunciator. Sydney confirmed it. The Airbus A320 slowly gathered speed, thundering its way down the runway, accelerating though one hundred knots.

'One hundred knots!' Sydney called out.

'Check!' Harry replied.

The A320 steadily accelerated, increasing its forward speed until it reached V1 or the speed of no return, and sometimes referred to as the "stop, go speed": the speed from which they must continue with the takeoff regardless of what happens.

'Vee one!' Sydney called out loud and clear.

'Rotate!' he added less than a second later.

Harry smoothly eased back on the side-stick to rotate the jet at the required rate of three degrees per second, and they launched into the air.

'Positive climb!' Sydney's said, referring to the aircraft's climb rate.

'Gear up!' Harry replied.

Sydney raised the landing gear.

In time they safely accelerated, retracted the slats and flaps, turned off the landing lights and stowed the speed brake lever, which was armed before the takeoff roll in case they had to abort therefore guaranteeing the ground spoilers would deploy and aid their deceleration, and followed their designated departure routing; this was busy airspace around Manchester and the climb to cruise altitude would take in excess of thirty minutes, but this was always going to be a long day and they were carrying a heavy load of fuel and passengers.

Thirty-six minutes later they levelled off at thirty-three thousand feet and immediately set about their respective duties. It didn't take long for Harry to surrender to his desire to see her, coupled with a need for a hot, refreshing drink and he called back to the forward cabin.

Sheila's soft, sweet dulcet tones came over the intercom. Harry thought for a second about a cheeky reply, but decided to save it, so he simply placed their order for drinks and sat back awaiting her arrival. Five minutes elapsed before a series of high pitched beeps signified a request to enter the flight deck. A quick check of the video screen and Sheila entered balancing two hot beverages, one on top of the other.

She handed him his tea with another delicate squeeze of the right shoulder. The touch of her fingers made him tingle. Sydney joked that you had to be a captain to receive such preferential treatment.

'It's those stripes Sydney. They just do it for me!'

'Better improve my sim scores then.'

'You just think of me next time you're in the "Box".'

'Oh yeah, that's definitely going to keep the mind focused!'

Sheila squeezed his shoulder a second time whilst smiling innocently at Sydney.

Sydney shook his head in mock disapproval and replied to a call from the radar controller. Harry followed the instruction giving them a direct route to a waypoint further down the track, shaving a minute off their flight time.

'Seen the menu?' Sheila said softly to Harry.

'Are you on it?' he whispered back: it was a cheesy reply and he instantly regretted it.

'If you want!'

'Will you two behave!' Sydney interposed.

She was teasing him and loving it.

'I'll see what I can do captain, but in the meantime I'm afraid you'll have to make do with the crew food,' she added with a provocative smile.

'Wonderful!' Harry replied.

'I've heard it called many things, but that's a new one.'

She checked what both had selected off the menu, when they wanted to eat, what time they were due to land and was gone.

'I ain't saying a word!' Sydney finally said.

'You either got it or you ain't!'

'And you're a real stud with such an exciting, dangerous, devil may care lifestyle!'

If only you knew the truth, thought Harry.

The radar controller called again to pass them over to the next sector and this, along with regular fuel checks and collecting the weather for all the available alternate airports, became the norm.

Harry was content he'd made the desired connection, but knew this would not do: there must be acceptable boundaries between work and play and he was a professional. The decision was inevitable not to waste any more time thinking of her: it would lead him to distraction. Harry could and would wait until they were on the ground.

The remainder of the outbound flight proved to be blissfully uneventful and four hours later Harry taxied the A320 slowly and precisely onto their designated stand, parked it, shut down both engines and called for the parking checklist. He was happier and calm and would wait his moment before striking like a cobra, going for the kill. You're an idiot, he thought, striking like a cobra. He looked over to Sydney once all the checks were completed, who was studiously activating the return flight plan.

'How much fuel again?' he asked.

'You're getting far too old Harry!' Sydney joked, trying to get a playful rise out of his friend. 'We discussed this less than an hour a go and you've forgotten it already!'

'It must have been your soft, southern, shite accent. I couldn't understand a single, damn word you said!'

Sydney slowly read back the required fuel figure over pronouncing every syllable, so slowly in fact that Harry could have been watching everything in slow motion.

'Is that the best you got?'

'Good enough for you!'

'You need to get out more!'

'Oh, and so says super stud!'

'You're just jealous.'

Harry rose to leave and supervise the refuelling. 'You ain't getting much are ya?' he said leaving the flight deck before Sydney could make a repost.

He laughed as he descended the steps leading down to the apron from the air-bridge. Once at ground level he donned his ear protectors, straightened his high visibility vest and set to work.

Fifteen minutes elapsed before Harry re-boarded, checked his watch and mentally prepared himself; he didn't have much time, but it seemed like he needn't have worried.

'Milk, no sugar.'

He took the cup from her smooth, slender, well-manicured hand. The nails rubbed over the top of his knuckles. How he would love to have those nails scratch the length of his back.

'Well?' Sheila said when they had a brief moment with nobody in earshot.

'Hot and wet, just the way I like it!'

'Very funny, Captain Travers,' she replied

Sheila studied the hand written menu, which she had conveniently left near one of the brewers in the forward galley.

'Well I'm partial to the chicken penne pasta, how about you have me with that next time!'

'With added sauce?' he added without thinking.

'Is there any other way?'

He was beginning to lose control: she only had to smile or scratch the top of his hand to send him into raptures, and they both knew it. He had to play this cool.

Before Harry could respond with a witty reply, Sheila took one step closer. He paused. It would prove fatal. Sydney appeared from the flight desk. He panicked.

'You know I've always liked you!'

'Harry!' Sydney said mockingly

Cool, thought Harry, you were supposed to play it cool. What did you do there? You played that like a bozo, you bonehead!

During the return sector he was going to have to fight his corner against Sydney's onslaught, but he was ready for anything. What an idiot he had been. There she was ready and willing; a golden opportunity landed square in his lap, and he blew it.

Harry sat back in his seat and began the pre-flight checks for the return home. He was glad for the distraction and slipped effortlessly back into professional mode.

The fight home was quiet, smooth and untroubled, just the way he liked all his sectors to be, and Sydney for once sensed his discomfort and kept a respectable silence only limiting the conversation to general topics regarding the airline, but Harry throughout wasn't convinced and constantly kept his guard up.

The seven crew members, once all the passengers had disembarked, began the long walk back to the crew-room as a group, and if there was an occasion for witty banter at his expense this was it, but no nothing was said bar the usual post-flight chat.

Harry had to say something lest she get the wrong impression that he was angry, which was as about as far removed from the truth as you could get. The fault was all his, and the ideal time would be once all the post-flight paperwork was completed, sent to operations and then, when appropriate, have a discreet word to get the definitive answer, for even though he had crashed and burned he still got the distinct impression the day was not lost.

The voyage report was submitted without a hitch and through the corner of his eye he made out the crew finalising the banking of the flight's takings. Surreptitiously he manoeuvred himself via the vending machine to be in the perfect position to intercept her as she departed, without bringing too much attention upon either of them. It seemed like an eternity before there was any movement in his direction, let alone leave, and he began to ask himself the obvious, inevitable question, but eventually yes, they all had homes to go to and Sheila finally collected her things and placed them in her crew bag.

The crew of five girls glided gracefully towards Harry, smiling serenely as they passed, as if they knew exactly what was coming, which caused him to burst out into a cold, clammy sweat.

Sheila was now only a yard or two away texting on her mobile. He moved off the wall he'd been leaning against in a vain attempt to look cool and steadied his fraying nerves; this was worse than being at school trying to catch a glimpse of your favourite girl during break time.

She looked up to see an awkward Harry half-blocking her path and in that instant he knew he was doomed to failure by the smile on her face.

'Good news?' he asked.

'I got a date tonight.'

'Great, that's great. Anybody I know?'

'You don't know this guy.'

'Should I be jealous?' he joked.

'Oh yes, he's one in a million.'

Harry was completely devastated, but tried valiantly, under the circumstances, to hide it. 'Hope you have a great night.' It was a blatant lie, but what could he do.

'Thank you, and you too.'

And with that she was gone.

Harry looked over to see Sydney staring at him.

'Get it over and done with!'

'The great Harry Travers has been blown out! If I hadn't seen it with my own eyes.....'

Harry had to laugh: he felt such an idiot. Yes, he liked her, he would never deny that, but he had behaved like a pre-pubescent teenager.

The two men said farewell and exited the crew room to go their respective ways, and during the ten minute drive to Baslow Drive from the staff car park all he could think of was her date and how perfect he would surely be.

Once inside the house his train of thought turned to Tommy and an e-mail was dispatched forthwith to establish the line of communication promised, then he remembered. Searching through his dirty washing he found what he was looking for and removed the folded piece of white paper Tommy had carefully slipped into the back pocket of his chinos. He had Tommy's cell-phone number.

It was time for food and Harry studied the list of all the fast food establishments who could benefit from his hard earned cash on this fine evening. As Harry was a self-confessed curry nut it didn't take long for him to ring out for a hot chicken curry, and coupled with two bottles of beer sat down thirty minutes later to an evening of football.

It had been a long day and Harry failed to appreciate how tired he was, especially after having a week off, and was asleep before the final whistle blew, not that it mattered much as the game as a spectacle was long since over.

Stiff necked and sore, a worn out Harry collapsed into bed full of eager anticipation of reading Tommy's reply: the excitement was almost tangible at the very thought of Harry Travers Private Detective solving the most baffling of cases and he slipped into the deepest of sleeps with the broadest of grins on his face.

Morning found him refreshed and raring to discover the latest news from across the pond, even if it was only to discover that his co-investigator had just been keeping his head below the parapet.

As he thought, Tommy was indeed managing to keep a low profile until his return, but it didn't stop a visit from Sheriff Poulsen, and that begged the question to when he would be free to return. A quick look at his roster revealed nothing but disappointment on that front for only a five day block, nine days away, offered any real hope. Oh, well that will have to do. Harry fired back a reply including those dates and then booked corresponding flights.

This brief, but essential business was a welcome respite from his trials and tribulations with Sheila Wallace.

* * *

Harry began to feel like his old self; Sydney would be his first officer again and he resolved to put yesterday's debacle behind him. The check in time for the Bodrum flight was slightly later than the previous one at 14:25 local, and a few hours' sleep would be the order of the day before he left the house at 13:25: this was a particular bug bear to him, as the drive from his home to the airport was ten to fifteen minutes at best, but if you mistimed your arrival at the car park, the bus taking you to the terminal beside the crew room could take just as long. He grabbed a late breakfast, watched some sport and hit the sack.

The alarm on his mobile phone burst into life, rudely awakening him from a refreshingly sound sleep. Harry let out a few well timed oaths, turned off the phone and rolled over to take an extra few minutes. It didn't last long though for as soon as he was back in the real world he was eager to get up and get going.

A check of his e-mails revealed Tommy's prompt reply. Harry made coffee then sat at the kitchen table to read it: Tommy had another visit, this time from one of the Boyd clan carrying a shotgun. Luckily for him he had been working studiously away and wasn't in the house. The first he knew of his less than welcome guest was a low growl from Washington. The two of them slid out the back way, or more to the point, thought Harry, he dragged a muzzled Washington with him into the woods. Whichever Boyd it was Tommy failed to get a good look at them and only realised their presence by catching a glimpse of their truck.

Harry felt a cold, sharp shiver descend the length of his spine. He should be there with his friend, and not have left: the company could have survived without him for a few more weeks, and he would never forgive himself if anything should happen to Tommy. He had been foolhardy to ask this man for his help knowing full well that he would get the brunt of any backlash in his absence. He typed another e-mail, for all the good it could do, imploring him to stay safe and wait his return.

Closing his laptop, the anger immediately welled up inside to near breaking point. Any thought of Sheila Wallace was pushed to the back of his mind as he contemplated the next move: should he get into contact with Jeffries and attempt to divert attention his way. It was an option, or should he negotiate some more leave with the company. Harry finished his coffee and took a hot shower: they always relaxed him and helped free the shackles torturing his mind.

Standing stock still with his head bowed, allowing the water to cascaded down his back, he ran over and over all possible scenarios: if he asked at such a late stage for unpaid leave it would plunge crewing into a mini crisis and beg the question as to why he never asked earlier. No, he wouldn't do that and bring unwanted attention down upon him; there was that call to Jeffries, that was still a viable option; or he could do nothing, sometimes doing nothing was exactly the right thing to do even when all your senses screamed out it was not. As difficult as it was, he chose the latter. The e-mail expressed his concern and being so far away Harry had no control over what Tommy did, but if there was any further sign of the Boyd brothers he would contact Jeffries and give the man something serious to think about.

* * *

Harry parked the Porsche and sauntered over to the nearest bus-stop and began his wait for a bus. The drive to work was laborious and tedious when compared to the day before: yesterday most of the traffic was travelling in the same direction, but today some were grateful to be on their way home while he was not.

He casually leaned against one of the circular metal posts that supported the plastic walls and roof of the bus-stop, and seemed on first reflection to be a touch over the top and checked his e-mails via his phone. Tommy's was there. Looking around to make sure nobody was watching him, which only had the effect of making him look guilty, he read the e-mail: Tommy had received a phone call from Jeffries asking about Harry: where did he go? Was he looking for anything in particular? Who did he talk to? And when was he due to return? Tommy told him next to nothing. Harry needed to trust him that what he was being told was true and even if Tommy did let anything slip it would be a blatant lie. Harry replied more to let his friend know the messages were being read regularly and to keep Tommy onside lest his head be turned.

A bus entered the car park and he paused for reflection after sending the e-mail; so caught up was he fighting inner demons daring to question the loyalty of his American friend that it took a blast on the horn by the bus driver to snap him out of it.

The crew-room was a welcome place of sanctuary allowing Harry to banish all thoughts of betrayal, murder, Tommy, the Boyd family and his uncle and slip effortlessly back into professional mode. It was his turn to arrive second; unlike yesterday Sydney had cracked on and printed everything off ready for their perusal. Harry never once looked over to where the rest of the crew were briefing, his mind was totally occupied with the job at hand, but if had given it free rein to wander on its own free will the net result would have helped alleviate his troubled soul.

The two men checked and cross-checked all the figures, studied the route, the weather for departure and destination and ordered the fuel. Sheila appeared enquiring about flight times and Harry noticed something subtly different today. It wasn't her; she was still as beautiful and as desirable as ever, but he who had changed.

She smiled that wonderful smile, which guaranteed to warm any room and then the whole crew appeared to march out to the aircraft as one. The stand was the same as before.

Ten minutes later Harry and Sydney followed suit.

Sydney politely kept mute regarding the previous day's events, instead he was more intent on informing Harry of Nina, the new love of his life, a girl he had known for all of three days: that was the thing about Sydney, he fell for any pretty girl that paid him attention, so by the time Harry reached gate twenty-three he had the complete lowdown on twenty-two year old Nina from Warsaw. Poor old Sydney was hopelessly head over heels in love.

From the outset it was one of those glorious days where everything went smoothly, so smoothly in fact that you waited for something, anything, no matter how small or insignificant to go wrong and pull it down around your ears and everything to collapse like a pack of cards, but even so Harry visibly relaxed and began to enjoy the day. Sydney, for his part, was the model professional and a joy to work with; obviously Nina was having a positive effect on him. Harry tried to dismiss any and all thoughts of the previous flight, and they were well over an hour into the four hour flight before he gave his disastrous attempt to get a date with Sheila any serious thought, and only then when she brought in two drinks. Prior to that any discourse between the two had been jovial, but kept on a professional footing.

Sheila carefully lent over his left shoulder, brushing him gently in the process, and placed the hot drink in the cup holder molded into the pilot's DV, Direct Vision, window. She serviced Sydney first, and it didn't go unnoticed.

'How was your date?' he asked, more out of something to say rather than actually wanting to show any genuine interest.

'Okay.'

The reply was not what he was expecting; if Sheila was anything, and her reputation more than backed it up, was that she was very picky about the men she dated. She was not one to waste any valuable and unnecessary time of no-hopers.

'Only okay?' he said, turning in his chair to get a better look at her.

She nodded slowly.

He could see the worry in her eyes, a worry that ran deep and probably kept her up all night; his new detective powers told him all this in an instant. He tried hard not to smile.

'Did he hurt you?' It was a logical question for a guy who has just heard that the girl he desires had a bad date.

'No!'

'Was he rude then? What did he say to you? Did he insult you? I'll kill him!' Harry had spurted it all out before he had given himself chance to engage the brain, and now sat there feeling like he was naked and all were laughing at him.

Sheila kissed him on the forehead.

'Wow!' exclaimed Sydney. 'Do I get one?'

'You've got Nina! Or have you forgotten?' she replied jokingly with a smile. 'He was neither rude, offensive and never tried it on, as I'm not really his type, and if he had I'm sure our uncle would have had a few choice words to say to him!'

The penny dropped and Harry let a huge smile erupt across his worn features.

'You thought I blew you out didn't you?'

'Oh, no!' he said, shaking his head, trying desperately hard to bluff it out.

'You know Harry all you have to do is to ask me when I'm free next!'

'When are you free next?' he blurted back.

Sheila laughed, blew him a kiss, told them she must be getting back to her passengers and she'd check her diary.

'Good on you H!' Sydney said quietly over their intercom, once Sheila had left.

'Women,' Harry muttered slowly, 'I love 'em!'

'You got a new problem now!' started Sydney, firmly planting the inevitable seed of doubt into the sagacity of any valiant attempt to woo Sheila Wallace.

'What's that?'

'Where are you going to take her? She's a classy lady!'

Bang on cue those first seeds of self-doubt began to raise their ugly heads, but luckily for him the job once again came to his rescue and concentrated the mind until turnaround.

Harry had been the monitoring pilot on the outbound sector, so it was now Sydney's responsibility to carry out the visual inspection prior to the return flight, while Harry loaded the return route into the aircraft's Flight Management Guidance Computer. He was keen to grab a few quiet minutes with Sheila and attempt to glean any information regarding her culinary likes and dislikes.

No sooner had he activated the return route into the FMGC than her warm hand gently caressed his right shoulder.

'Hope I'm not interrupting?'

'Not at all!'

Like him she did not hide her feelings well.

'What's up?'

'My date!' she said slightly tongue-in-cheek, but it did nothing to fool her onlooker.

Suddenly Harry had an epiphany and instantly ran with it: 'Who does your brother owe money to?'

'Are you psychic by any chance?'

'No, I'm just a good reader of people, except when it comes to asking you on a date!' The opportunity had showed itself mid-sentence and he pounced on it.

'Just ask me then!'

'Friday night, and before you ask it'll be my surprise.'

'Okay,' she said smiling, his request momentarily making her forget all her worries.

'I'll pick you up at seven thirty.'

'Remind me to give you my address.'

'No need!'

'You been spying on me?'

'Would I do that?'

He got out of his seat and the cramped conditions of the flight deck brought them closer together.

'What's your brother been up to?' he said, trying not to look too flustered.

'Enough!' she said locking those beautiful blue eyes on him.

Her breath flicked the side of his face as she spoke, and that mixed with the intoxicating smell of her perfume was a huge turn on. He was conscious not to make it look too obvious.

Sheila started to laugh.

'Harry,' she whispered. 'I never knew you cared that much!'

'Stop it!' he joked, secretly loving every minute.

'I can't wait to see me my surprise.'

'You'll just have to be patient,' he managed to muster.

'That'll be hard,' she cooed, her eyes momentarily darting downwards.

He was saved any further embarrassment by Sydney's arrival.

'Talk later,' she said softly, but the worry that previously etched itself across her fine features returned.

Sydney handed over a signed fuel receipt, as the first of the pre-boarders arrived at the air-bridge. Sheila left to supervise boarding and the two men slickly finished off any paperwork, checked and cross-checked the take-off performance before calling for and receiving their departure clearance. Harry gave Sydney his pre-flight brief. Then with near immaculate timing the female ground agent appeared, informing them that boarding was complete, and Harry handed her all the necessary paperwork. No sooner had she departed that Sheila arrived with the news that they all longed to hear: to confirm that boarding was indeed complete, to ratify the correct passenger figure with the load sheet and could she close and arm the doors for departure. Harry agreed with her on both accounts, giving her a cheeky wink as she backed out of the flight deck.

'See you boys up there!' she said the split second before closing the door.

She got the last word in again.

It didn't take long for them to push back, start engines, taxi, run through all the pre-takeoff checks, receive their takeoff clearance and launch off into the night sky and head home.

The return flight was quiet and smooth, which pleased both men no end, as each had a bumpy ride home on a previous Bodrum. Sheila came in on a couple of occasions, but he could tell instantly she was not in a mood to talk and he didn't want to push it, as it was only a matter of time before the opportunity would reveal itself to allow him to reveal his true feelings. Whatever her brother had done to cause the family so much heartache would come out in its own good time.

While sitting in the cruise sipping a hot cup of coffee, he was a sucker at these times of the day for the drink, Harry pulled down all the blinds to shield his eyes from the blinding golden light that marked the dawn of a new day. Sydney quickly followed suit. He had mixed views on sunrises: first it was indeed a beautiful sight and one he was privileged to witness, but secondly his eyes would burn and water like mad until they had re-adjusted themselves to the increased light levels; the forecast for the day was for clear skies with prolonged sunny spells and a temperature in the twenties. He would struggle to get some sleep before checking-in later in the day for the next deep night flight.

An hour and a half later they taxied onto stand at Manchester.

'Well, that was painless!' exclaimed Sydney, completing the parking checklist and starting on the voyage report.

'Thankfully,' Harry replied filling in the aircraft's technical log.

'So glad I'm off tomorrow and not operating that dreadful night Zakinthos!'

Harry did not deign to reply.

'That would be a brute, eh?'

'You can go off people you know!'

This last statement fell on the deaf ears of the younger man, who simply laughed the laugh of someone with three wonderful days off in order to chase after his beloved Nina.

'So where have you decided to take Sheila?' Sydney finally said once his responsibilities were over and was packing up his flight bag.

'Why? You want to make up a foursome?'

'Now there's a thought!'

'Beat it kiddo! You haven't won Nina yet!'

'It's only a matter of time!'

Sydney's confidence was infectious, but for all his cynicism Harry was not the type of guy to tempt fate, least of all when the prize was someone he held very dear.

'Does Nina know how lucky she is?' he replied mockingly.

'She soon will be!'

An engineer arrived and Harry passed on any defects that needed rectifying, which in truth were next to nothing: she was a good ship. He packed up his things and followed the ever optimistic Sydney out into the cabin. Sheila and her crew were not going to be long, and so he exited onto the air-bridge to meet the next crew waiting to take over. Harry didn't recognize the captain, so presumed he must be new. The conversation was short, but polite and he passed on any and all relevant information.

Out of the corner of his eye he saw Sheila and the rest of the crew pass by and wait for him. He made his farewells and departed.

Harry and Sheila lagged behind the crew by three or four paces.

'Stephen's gone and got himself into hock to a Debt Collection Agency!' Sheila muttered quietly, all the time not breaking stride or looking up at him.

'Oh!' was all Harry could muster.

'They want their money!'

'How did he end up owing them?'

'He won't tell me. I'm being spoon fed information, as and when he thinks it's appropriate.'

'Some creditors will pass on accounts that fall behind on payments or those who simply can't pay up over to debt collectors. It's cheaper than chasing the money themselves,'

'I told him not to buy that bloody car!'

'Why doesn't he just hand it back?'

'He's sold it!'

'Ah!'

'What? Oh, please don't tell me he's dug an even bigger hole for himself!'

The crew navigated their way through immigration and arrivals with all the hustle and bustle of coming and goings drowning out their conversation, which gave the two more freedom to talk.

'He can't sell it!'

'Why?'

'Not if he still owes money on it! They can still repossess the car at any time regardless of the fact that he's sold it on.'

'God knows what he's done with the money!'

'Do you know how much is outstanding?'

'He wouldn't tell!'

On reaching the crew-room the confab was put on hold, each promising to pick it up as soon as it was convenient.

The two pilots were eager to be on their way and neither procrastinated in any way shape or form, and it was only after Harry had watched Sydney leave with an extravagant wave of the hand that he gave her brother any extra thought. He couldn't help but feel contempt for the man: he was the reason his master plan had failed, he told himself, not because it was poorly planned and executed, oh no, not that, but due to her brother's incompetence with money. It was a good try to blame a man he hadn't heard of until today, but it was doomed to failure: the only person to blame for his abject failure was himself. Her brother did though give him the ideal opportunity to put that all behind him.

The time it took for the crew to complete any outstanding paperwork seemed to take an age, and in those last remaining minutes he fidgeted uncomfortably while rocking from one foot to another trying to look busy. Thoughts and images of his teenage years involving schoolboy crushes flashed across his mind. He was saved from the ghosts of loves lost by Sheila's imminent departure, and so quietly slipped out of the westerly of the two exits.

The crisp morning air filled his lungs and he began to feel at peace with the world before he would once again lay siege to that impregnable fortress that was Sheila Wallace.

With the roads busy with taxis, and to be seen waiting somewhat impatiently outside the crew-room easily proving an embarrassment too far, he sauntered casually over to the bus stop hoping that his arrival there would coincide with hers.

'Have I ever said what a great arse you have, Harry!'

Joy instantly filled his every pore, the chase was on.

He spun round to be met by the smiling countenance of Tania Leighton, a twenty three-year old, tennis loving hostess who had worked a summer season for the company last year, but who now worked for a rival airline. He failed to hide the shock of her not being Sheila.

'I never knew you cared!' he said trying to buy time for a witty repost.

'You never asked.'

Someone else he had failed to pay attention to.

'How's tricks?'

'Same dog, different leg!'

Harry laughed at the precise moment Sheila appeared from the crew-room running a quizzical eye over the two of them. He waved pathetically; he was going to lose a second opportunity if he didn't act fast.

'Great to see you again Tania, but I got a date.'

He wasted not a second and, smiling as he did so, retraced his steps. That smile soon evaporated when a large silver saloon pulled up alongside Sheila and one of the passengers vacated to confront her. She shot Harry a look that meant only one thing.

Harry quickened his pace and broke into a run, but by the time he reached her the man had re-boarded the saloon car and pulled away.

'You okay?'

'Guess who!' she said angrily, visibly shaking with a mixture of fury and fear.

Harry didn't need to be a genius to understand this was about more than an unpaid loan. He placed a protective arm around her and immediately had a flood of inappropriate thoughts.

'I'll walk you to your car,' he said guiding her gently towards the bus-stop.

His timing was perfect for the courtesy bus appeared from around the side of the multi-story car park that housed many of the car hire offices.

This was going to be awkward, he thought, and prayed that Tania wouldn't put a spanner in his collective works by saying anything untoward because he was acutely aware she had not taken her eyes off him.

The ride to the staff car park was one of those surreal moments in life that enrich its great tapestry: here he was comforting this beautiful woman whom he desperately wanted to get into bed, and opposite him was this stunner, twelve years his junior, as fit as you could wish, making all the eyes under the sun at him. It was a minor miracle that Sheila failed to spot her, but under the present circumstances had far more important issues troubling her soul. Suddenly the thought flashed across his mind followed by an all too visual image. Tania must have read his for the look in her eyes spelt it out all too clearly.

Harry blocked it out. So absorbed was he in trying to alleviate his own mental torture that he missed what Sheila had been saying to him, a cardinal sin for the would be suitor, but luckily for him he managed to get the gist of the conversation straight off.

The bus pulled into the first stop in the staff car park and to his dismay all three of them disembarked. How had Sheila not seen Tania looking at him? The question was beginning to torture his soul. Did she really not care? He was now starting to feel a little aggrieved that she hadn't fought his corner. A blind man could have seen Tania's intentions plus to add insult to injury all three had parked their cars on the same row and his car was the first.

'Where you parked?' he asked then panicked in case the wrong one should answer.

'The black BMW.' Sheila replied, pointing to a car six places further up the row.

'I'll wait,' he just managed to say before Tania grabbed his behind. Sheila thankfully had her back to them.

Tania never stopped walking; she simply made a beeline for her car, boarded and left. Even as she drove past there was no acknowledgement of any kind. Harry breathed a huge sigh of relief.

Sheila made her car, unlocked it on the remote, placed her bag on the back seat and turned to face him. She was close to tears. Now was the time: her brother may be causing her serious heartache, but faint heart never won fair lady.

'Here's my mobile number,' he said handing over a white slip of paper. 'Call me when you get in, so I know you're safe.'

'I'll be fine, don't fret!'

'I'll be expecting your call,' he added.

The two then boarded their respective vehicles without another word. Harry made a point of following her out of the car park.

8

The anticipated drive home was short, but not of a length to prevent him wishing that he'd offered to follow her back to her place and make doubly sure she was safe; it also would have given him the ideal opportunity to see firsthand how she lived, but so caught up was he with Sheila and then Tania he failed to notice the silver saloon keeping pace with him about four car lengths back.

Harry pulled into his drive, parked the 924, grabbed his stuff and was inside within a matter of seconds.

The silver saloon pulled into the side of the road three doors up. Inside were three men: a dark haired man in his late twenties sitting in the front passenger seat, who stood a little under six foot and was the one that confronted Sheila; an older, shifty looking man of about fifty who was driving; and a third, a fair haired man who was roughly the same age as the front seat passenger, but although smaller in height was stockier in build and spoke with a permanent sneer.

'How long?' said the front seat passenger.

'A few more minutes,' replied the driver, 'otherwise we'll start to run the risk of attracting some unwanted attention.'

The third man remained mute.

The driver was as good as his word, for once those few minutes had lapsed he ordered the two men out of the car.

They split up on reaching the parked Porsche; the front seat passenger tried to find a way round the back of the terraced town house while his comrade knocked on the door after discovering pressing the bell was useless.

Nobody answered, so he knocked a second time albeit louder.

Still nobody answered.

'Fuck him!' he whispered, failing to hide the menace within; the sneer returned with a vengeance. He called his friend back round to the front of the house via his mobile.

'He's not answering,' he said when his colleague arrived.

'In the shower?'

'I reckon so!'

'Good!'

The third man pulled a leather pouch from his jacket, unzipped it to reveal a lock pickers essential tool kit, and then wasted no time gaining entry into the house. He then slipped the pouch carefully back into his jacket pocket.

Once inside the sound of running water emanating from upstairs confirmed all they needed to know, and a quick reconnoiter downstairs gave the two men the freedom required to investigate the next level.

The running water never ceased and they gravitated carefully towards the bathroom. The third man placed an ear to the door, his frown at not hearing any movement inside caused the other to remove a knife from his pocket and flick it open. Both now spoke using hand signals and motioned to each other to check all the rooms on this floor first before returning to the bathroom. This was achieved with the minimum of effort and after a brief but silent discussion about investigating the second floor, which neither thought would reveal their prey, they burst into the bathroom.

The third man led the mini charge after producing his knife, which he held firmly out in front of him via his right hand ready to strike at Harry at the earliest opportunity, but he was to be bitterly disappointed when they discovered their prey had unwittingly deceived them both. They expeditiously backed out of the bathroom and headed for the second unexplored floor. Three steps from the top Harry appeared totally oblivious to anything that had previously transpired. The sight of two men, both armed, steaming up his stairway momentarily froze him to the spot. A well timed kick to the chest of the third man sent him sprawling backwards down the stairs, but being off balance and only able to attack one assailant at a time left him vulnerable to attack from the second; he managed to avoid a slash from the man's knife, but not the force of a fierce right hook as it slammed against his jaw.

Now Harry never professed to be the greatest fighter in the world, but he could take a punch and the blow did not have the desired effect. Harry stumbled back, rocking on his haunches. The man was now at the top of the stairs about to slash at him again, and the other was slowly getting to his feet. He instinctively lashed out. It was a perfect punch; the man was not expecting Harry to retaliate so quickly and with such force. The blow did to him what he wanted to do to Harry: it halted him in his tracks and gave Harry valuable seconds of breathing and thinking time. A volley of punches followed, raining down on the man badly dazing and knocking the wind out of him. Harry pushed him down the stairs.

The third man was four stairs up to them when his colleague smashed into him sending them both crashing onto the landing.

Harry had to show no mercy: there was no way round it other than to make the decisive move and take his chances with the law. He quickly darted into a side room and grabbed an old putter he knew stood against the wall then ran down the stairs before they could recoup.

The front seat passenger took a thunderous blow to the side of the head and blood began to seep instantly from the wound, the other man saw this and vainly tried to retreat, but it was to no avail, several sharp blows thudded into the rear of his head and back. Both men were now in rapid retreat.

Harry needed to keep up the intensity of the attack, but couldn't help thinking he'd left the shower running and his gas bill for that quarter would be horrendous.

The front seat passenger was starting to feel the force of the blow that nearly rendered him unconscious plus blood was starting to run into his eyes from the wound atop his forehead. Harry noticed the red, bold spots on his carpet.

'You fucking prick!' he shouted. 'That carpet's new!'

To the wounded intruders it brought on another furious onslaught and the end of their fight. They noticeably quickened their pace out of the house. Once at the lower level Harry could see his front door was open. He swung the putter violently down on the back of the man who had confronted Sheila, and took great pleasure in reaping more misery upon him.

Seconds later the two men fell out of the house and onto the drive before making a beeline for their car. Harry stopped short by his front door, the last thing he wanted or needed was a bunch of nosey neighbors peeping out from behind their curtains, gossiping to all and sundry about affairs that had fuck all to do with them, but he did want to clock the face of the man driving the car.

The silver saloon raced away, but not before Harry and the driver shared a moment: each looking straight into the eyes of the other firing off a look of pure hate.

Fuck the law, fuck prison, fuck porridge and fuck them, he thought. This stirred a passion so deep within him that in that second Harry answered one fundamental question: could he kill given the right circumstances? The answer was a resounding yes.

Once the car was out of sight and he very watchfully backed into his house, it dawned on him the shower was still running: 'Fuck!'

'That'll be no hot water then!' he muttered after turning off the shower and walking back downstairs to the kitchen to turn the hot water on for an hour or so.

The rest of the day was quiet bar having the locks changed. He counted his blessings for being able to grab a few zeds, but he wasn't foolish enough to let his guard drop completely.

The flight to Zakinthos passed without incident other than Harry arranging a dinner date for the following night with Sheila. He now had two days off and was going to shoot off another e-mail to Tommy and go see Marvin Schuler.

* * *

Harry politely knocked on Marvin's door and waited for his dulcet tones to beckon him to enter. It never took long, even when he hadn't made an appointment, and today was no different. He found him dictating to Elizabeth who hit him immediately with her come to bed eyes. It held no substance for him; one of the offshoots of the events of the last couple of weeks was a slow, but perceptible shift in his thinking and attitude to life: where before he had always meandered through his existence not really giving a damn one way or the other where it took him, except when he made a complete tit of himself over women, now he had a purpose: to solve his uncle's disappearance, win Sheila and discover who this man was pressurizing her brother.

'Harry Travers; it's always good to see my number one client!'

'And it's always good to see my number one lawyer!'

Marvin laughed, waived a casual hand to him to sit down whilst finishing giving Elizabeth the last of the dictation.

Harry still could not help but admire her curves, which were shown off to the full in a figure hugging dress. He sat down opposite Marvin.

'Tea, Harry?' Elizabeth asked, rising out her chair notepad in hand.

'Coffee, please.'

'Coming right up.'

He kept his line of sight straight ahead and instead watched Marvin follow her out of the office.

'I hate you Harry you know that!'

'Join the queue!'

Marvin smiled that "I'm going to sue your ass off" smile: 'She wants to fuck your brains out!'

'Really!'

'Yes, really, and don't be so blasé about it. My gorgeous secretary, who blew me out, wants to fuck YOUR brains out!'

'Can't blame her for that!'

'Who have you upset?' inquired Marvin.

The question was not what he was expecting. 'Probably some people my late uncle pissed off. Why?'

'Would it have anything to do with four hundred thousand dollars of real estate?'

'That would be too easy!' Harry was extremely reluctant to volunteer any information even to his own lawyer such was his new found skepticism.

'Cagey, very cagey: you just make sure you stay that way until this is resolved!'

His natural born cynicism kicked in and he immediately began to suspect Marvin. Only a severe bout of common sense, and the return of Elizabeth with refreshments, prevented him from ruining a good friendship.

Elizabeth floated past, and he found himself unable to resist: he was a slave to her wonderful rounded hips. Fuck, I love women, he thought, they truly are God's greatest creation. His eyes never left her and the flirtatiously wicked smile she gave him on the way out told him she had seen him watch her.

Marvin had, by the time Harry managed to get his head back in the real world, begun to discuss his uncle's estate and the amount of inheritance tax payable on it. Harry soon got his head in order.

'How much?'

Marvin repeated his previous statement.

'Fuck me! Those greedy bastards!'

'We voted them in!'

'Well, I fucking didn't! You should wave your fee as a sign of penance for inflicting such an outrageous hardship on the poor, conscientious, hard-working man!'

'Well, you qualify for one out of those three!'

His back was up, just like the time he paid twice to leave a multi-storey car park because there was a ten minute time limit on the ticket, which wasn't openly displayed anywhere, and he was delayed whilst he took a phone call. The fact that on this particular day, a Sunday, it was the same fee for all day meant nothing as the attendant couldn't let him leave without him having to pay again. He vowed never to use that chain of car parks again, and he hadn't.

'A hard working man comes into a little money and what happens?'

'You can offset some, and I know just the guy to help you. I'll give you his number: his name's Eddie.'

'Fuck all that!'

Marvin slowly shook his head as Harry ranted on.

'Does your books does he?' he finally said, cooling down.

'Sure does and he's as straight as they come, but he'll save you money!'

Harry took the number.

Marvin was a top lawyer and in great demand, so because of this Harry took him on his word and bade him farewell. Just as he was about to leave Marvin burst out laughing.

'You bastard!'

'There is no tax to pay this time round.'

'I'll keep the number just in case.'

The early morning temperature promised a fine, dry day, and as he entered the street from Marvin's office it did not disappoint. Glancing down at his mobile screen, before nestling it comfortably into his chinos, he saw he had a new e-mail in his inbox.

He slowly and deliberately read the message, for it was long and he was overcome by a dreadful feeling of foreboding: Tommy had received a few more unwanted visits from the Boyd brothers, and wisely realizing they were not there to try his fine moonshine left to go live in the woods; this was not such a hardship for him as he regularly camped out when going hunting, plus it kept him out of their way and one step ahead. Anytime he wanted to keep in touch now he would simply visit one of the Internet Cafés in town.

Harry needed to get back to Tennessee, but his hands were tied by a busy roster: there were these two days off followed by four more on duty before he could leave. Six days to prepare.

He strode purposefully back to his car. A thought had planted a seed during the night and he began to give the idea serious consideration: those three men had been sent to teach him a lesson, and it was not going to be such a lottery if they came a second time. One of his regular drinking buddies was a black belt in jujitsu and once tried and failed to recruit him as a new member; it was time to take his friend up on his invitation and as luck would have it a class was scheduled for tonight. A private detective should know how to defend himself at all times.

The drive home was over quickly and he was very cagey as he approached home: he knew most cars on the street and so was placated to an extent at the sight of no unusual vehicles in his road. Regular checks of his mirrors had revealed nothing.

He parked up and then with extreme caution approached his own front door. This made his blood boil: why should he have to tentatively enter his own house, any fear and trepidation should be for those who had the audacity to break in.

The house was how Harry left it. He knew this by the primitive security measure set before leaving: the door leading into his front room was closed with a single strand of hair stuck across the door frame at ankle level. The hair was intact and in its original position. Any intruder would need to open the door to access this part of his living quarters plus the kitchen.

Suddenly the house phone sprang into life.

'Hello?' he said way too sharply.

'Harry?'

His heart skipped a beat, it was her.

'Hi!'

'Can you talk?'

'I'm all yours,' Harry said softly, and slumped down on the settee.

'Hope you don't mind me calling, I got your number off Sydney!'

That's right, he thought, he forgot to give out his home number. Now this didn't upset him initially, but how come she has Sydney's?

'It's your brother?'

'Who else!'

'I wish!' he whispered. 'What's he gone and done now?'

'They came back to see him again. He's in hospital!'

'Sheila?'

'Yes?'

'This is about more than just repayments on a car!'

'I've been telling myself that ever since I went to see him.'

'Is he okay?'

'He'll live!'

'Have you asked him?'

'He won't tell me, and I can't blame him for that because I wouldn't either!'

The thought raised its head, winked at him and he knew there and then what was required in a crystal clear moment of clarity.

'I know a private detective who can make a few discreet enquires for you if you like? He's a good friend of mine and utterly professional.'

'You have a P.I. as a friend?'

'He's good, real good!' He didn't feel any guilt blowing his own trumpet, even though this effectively would be his second case and hadn't a clue where to start.

'Are you sure he can be trusted?' she went on.

'Absolutely. He'll take the case as a favor to me.'

He was pushing the boundaries of believability and he knew it, but viewed any less than truthful claims as acceptable advertising: how else was he going to get experience unless he promoted himself, and if he successfully resolved whatever trouble her brother had managed to get himself embroiled in then it could only lead to more work and Sheila.

'Okay, if you can vouch for him then that's good enough for me because at the end of the day I wouldn't have a clue where to begin looking, and even if I did I don't know whether I would have the courage to follow my convictions!'

'Consider it done. Now stop worrying.'

'If you say so.'

'I'll get my friend to have a word with him. We'll say he's a representative of a finance company or something.'

'He may clam up, as he does with me.'

'You just let me know when it's convenient and I'll send him round.'

He could tell from the tone of her voice that his idea was going down well, and after a few minutes of minor small talk where she gave him her full postal address, so his "friend" could find the house more easily, she made her excuses and hung up.

The silence that echoed around the room afterwards would normally have seemed morose, but not today; for today he had another way into her affections.

9

Harry slept well, all things considered, and awoke feeling refreshed. At the bottom of the first set of stairs he saw the flashing red light indicating a message that would signal him taking those first tentative steps.

The phone message was short, sharp and to the point: Stephen was out of hospital and going to be staying with her for couple of days, which meant they were going to have to put any dinner date on hold for now, and if the private investigator wanted to pay him a visit then anytime in the afternoon would be ideal, as she was working and wouldn't be back until the early hours.

Here was the perfect opportunity to gather all the relevant information without her suspecting him, albeit tinged with sadness at having to delay their getting to know each other better. He chose two o'clock as a time to arrive, figuring that he would not be the invalid's only visitor today.

* * *

At two o'clock precisely Harry stood outside Sheila's front door and knocked before waiting impatiently for him to answer. For a split second he feared Sheila might have swapped off her flight, but the hobbling figure he espied, painstakingly shuffling his way to the front door instantly allayed any anxieties.

'You must be the P.I?' Stephen said once he'd negotiated the door lock and swung it open.

The contempt in the man's voice was all too obvious, but it did allow him to drop the representative of the finance company angle.

Fuck you. You're the asshole who nearly ruined everything.

He tried to exude as much confidence as possible and stepped purposefully into the aromatic hallway with the tasteful flowery decor. She had good taste, shame about the prick of a brother.

Stephen turned and shuffled back into the rear leaving him to shut the door.

He was already beginning to paint a picture of this young man: of someone taking liberties with the goodwill and generosity of an older sister, who viewed all the problems and shortcomings in his life as someone else's fault and not his.

Once in the kitchen Stephen took a seat at a wooden table and sipped a coffee made earlier. Harry sat opposite. No drink was offered.

During the drive to Sheila's he played out all the possible scenarios over and over in his head until he had exhausted them all. There was nothing Stephen could say to which he couldn't respond to.

'They gave you a doing then?'

'I wanted to call the police, but Sheila talked me out of it!'

'Is that so?' It was a stupid lie and he knew it.

'What are you implying?'

'Don't kid a kidder!'

'I think you better leave!'

'I'm here as a favor to a friend-'

'No friend of mine!'

'No, yours were nowhere to be seen when you got turned over!'

'Fuck you! I thought you were supposed to be helping me?'

'I'm helping you now am I? But it's hard with a throat as dry as mine!'

'I'm an invalid. You'll find all you need behind me.'

For once he was content to make his own, for it allowed him the opportunity to explore Sheila's kitchen. She was tidy, tidier than him, and he convinced himself that their two opposites were a perfect match: the neatness and orderly way everything was arranged smacked of OCD and the hint of the perfectionist.

'So what did you do to deserve such a kicking?' Harry opened with as he sat back at the table with a steamy hot cup of tea.

'Nothing!'

'Of course, you were just the innocent victim of an unprovoked attack.'

'Yes, yes I was!'

Stephen spoke with such passion and conviction that he was convincing for all of a second.

'Bollocks!'

'You should really leave........now!'

'Fine, if that's the way you want play it. I'll drink this, as you couldn't be fucking bothered to make it then leave you to the retribution of your friendly neighbor-hood loan shark!'

The uncomfortable silence that followed his outburst only spurred him on: 'You owe a lot of money to people who don't like outstanding debts, and you have little or no hope of paying it back!'

Stephen stared blankly back at him.

'As for calling the police,' Harry said before pausing to allow his words to have the maximum effect. 'No doubt you were politely informed that any interference by the law would result in your knee caps being removed. Am I right?'

'Fingers!'

'You lost at cards then?'

'Poker.'

'There are easier ways to make a living!'

'They cheated me,' Stephen said before suddenly bursting into tears. 'They cheated me!'

'I do hope for your continued recuperation you kept such a statement to yourself.'

Stephen nodded and got his emotions back in check.

Harry was no longer a regular poker player, but any well drilled team could pick apart an unsuspecting victim. He didn't have to wait long for Stephen to describe everything in great detail.

'The whole table was in on it! Each of them won a big hand against me with nobody winning more than two in a row. Even when I had good cards, which on any given day were spectacular, they bested me. Nobody has the cards I was dealt and fails to win a hand, nobody! My only crime was to keep going hoping that my luck might change.'

'But why you?'

'I won big there a few weeks ago.'

'Where's there?'

'Nero's!'

Harry knew the casino only by its reputation. Sheila's brother was in trouble. He now faced his own dilemma: should he help or cut and run for an easier second case, but who was to say this wasn't the norm, and if he could find a way out for her brother then any experienced gained was nigh on priceless.

'What can you do?'

'You won't get that money back, write it off!'

'Already been done!'

'Give me a couple of days then we'll talk again.'

'Okay.'

'What's your mobile number?'

Harry removed a notebook and pen from his jacket pocket and took down the number. 'What I also need are the names, if you know them, and the descriptions of all those who at the table that night.'

'Okay.' Stephen furnished Harry with all the requested information.

Harry finished his tea, re-pocketed his notebook and pen and rose to leave.

'You have an idea already?' asked Stephen.

'Yeah, but it's going to be tricky. How much I've yet to figure out!'

'Thank you.'

'Don't thank me just yet!'

It was the first time her brother had smiled or been polite and he half-smiled back. Harry left after promising again to call.

Once outside he walked around the corner to where he parked his car, deciding the first thing he needed to do was buy a pay as you go mobile: it struck him when he asked for Stephen's mobile number that Sheila was bound to recognize his. Secondly, he needed to re-learn how to play poker.

The drive home was a drag: the traffic around this part of town had risen to unacceptable levels, in his humble opinion, and it took all his powers of self-control not to let forth a volley of oaths towards a number of drivers whose prowess behind the wheel left much to be desired

Back in the house, with all the safety checks completed, he settled down to watch one of the many televised poker games on one of the sports channels armed with a mug of coffee and a large triple-decker sandwich. This was all part of his private investigator education: a good detective must easily be able to move in all circles of society, to blend into the background and become part of the scenery. For over two hours he watched and learned all the names, rules, intricate moves and betting patterns regarded as the norm in Texas Holdem poker; and he began to re-appreciate the advantages of being the big and little blind, the flop, the turn, the river cards, how to begin to read your opponent, the advantages and disadvantages of a physical tell, how to bluff, why it is sometimes important to play a bad hand and not just your good ones, the need to practice your "poker face" and what the best hands are. It was a steep learning curve, but he found it exhilarating; this he could do, of that he had no doubt, and so without any hesitation he checked future programming and recorded as many on poker as possible. He decided for an early night and further viewing in bed.

* * *

The next five days dragged on interminably, but finally the morning of his departure for Tennessee arrived and the alarm from his mobile phone woke him. He swung his hand for the phone and knocked it headlong down the room: 'Bollocks!'

The alarm continued on for some time while he dragged his tired old body out of bed to begin the search for its final resting place. He only just managed to turn it off before it sprung once again into life, only this time it was Sheila, and at this time of day. He answered on the fourth ring: desperate he wasn't.

'Hi Sheila,' he said, not wanting to appear too concerned.

She apologized for the hour of the call. It was regarding her brother. During those preceding five days when time allowed between working and trying to source information on his uncle's affairs, which proved hopeless, Harry had been mildly successful. He parked outside the casino and recognized all the antagonists by the descriptions given to him by Stephen. There were four of them in total and he made a mental note of each of their faces. He was becoming good at that: every day he ventured out he played a game with himself by trying to remember a stranger's face. He carefully made mental notes then tried to draw it over again in his head. At first he was useless, but over a very short space of time became very efficient. Now here he was putting all that practice into fruition.

'It's a team of four alright,' he replied boastfully. 'I got a phone call yesterday,' Harry quickly added to Sheila's enquiry as to how he came by the information. 'I told him I'd be the go between for you both, that way if there's any nastiness you're protected.'

She thanked him profusely and he felt no guilt by lying. Any danger would be on his shoulders. Then Sheila dropped the mini bombshell: she invited him to lunch.

'I can't I'm afraid, I need to sort out my late uncle's estate.'

Fuck, just his luck. They'd be others he told himself, but he knew it was probably a lie. 'How are you fixed for next Saturday?' he asked tentatively.

'I'm free,' she replied.

An hour and a half later he was on his way to the airport.

The journey to Athens, Tennessee left him tipping on the verge of complete boredom. Only the thought of seeing Tommy and resuming their run in with the Boyd clan held any interest.

* * *

It tasted good, real good, and the first of many ice cold refreshing gin and tonics slipped down with all too much ease; it wasn't that Harry was a nervous flyer or anything remotely resembling a back seat pilot, he was just of the mind that it was a busman's holiday and therefore it would be nothing short of criminal not to exploit it to the full.

A little under ten hours later Harry touched down in Atlanta, Georgia and two more after that Tommy collected him. This time by car: a silver Nissan Sentra.

He was secretly overjoyed to see his friend healthy and in good spirits. The Boyd brothers had been at it constantly during his absence leaving poor Tommy to deal with all their shenanigans: not only was Tommy's place ransacked and emptied of anything remotely of any use to the brothers, but old Washington went missing. Tommy for the only time during this period was on the verge of marching straight round Jessie's place to seek retribution when the stupid dog finally deigned to turn up after a prolonged hunting expedition.

'Damn stupid, dumb ass dog!' exclaimed Tommy, taking a hit from a soda.

'Did you call the law?' asked Harry, cracking open a can.

'You kiddin' me!'

Harry knew it was a stupid question.

'I wasn't going to waste my time with any Sheriff! There were no witnesses and anyway half the stuff was illegal!' Tommy added.

The drive to Tommy's new residence took a little over three hours: he had decided against living in the woods, as it failed to live up to the extremely high standards of his previous abode. The new headquarters was in fact his grandmother's old place, about a twenty minute drive outside Athens, which made it ideal as a base to work from. She had passed away some years previous, and him not being the most garrulous of fellows regarding dead relatives, so nobody knew of it.

Harry immediately sensed a subtle shift in Tommy's demeanor; where on his previous visit he sensed that the man was helping him out of some kind of loyalty to his Uncle Jack or more realistically to protect the good name of Tennessee and the country he loved against any criticisms from a foreigner, here he was now chomping at the bit to get stuck into their investigations.

'I've been thinking!' Tommy said after a short pause in the conversation.

'Oh, yeah?'

'Sounds ominous don't it!'

'Only if I didn't know you better!'

'Maybe your uncle got dragged to a lair or something and if we go diggin' around in the forest we might discover some new evidence. What do you think?'

'Doubtful!'

'What about the Boyd brothers?'

'Yeah,' Harry said slowly. 'And your judgment is not clouded at all.'

'Good job I like you!'

'I like you too, and I have run over and over in my head about a thousand times every conceivable connotation and each and every time it keeps coming back to you know who!'

Tommy paused before replying: 'Then we have no option other than to try and force their hand!'

'Exactly!'

It was due to be a hot, humid day with clear skies and a few more sodas disappeared the way of their cousins by the time Tommy pulled up outside his grandma's old place in Etowah, and Harry could see in a second why Tommy liked it so much: the roof was in dire need of repair; the windows hadn't been cleaned in many a year; if the front door opened at all it was a minor miracle; the porch, containing a sleeping Washington, leaned over to one side; and the front yard was so overgrown one needed to mount an expedition to get from one fence to the next.

Tommy parked the car, taking great care not to leave any wheel tracks on the grass. Harry would have done the same.

The inside was in stark contrast to the exterior, and it was indeed the ideal base from which to spring their covert operation: no one would ever suspect they were there.

Tommy, as per his last visit, was the perfect host and after a sumptuous dinner the two men sat back to discuss what plan of action would best get their antagonists to show their hand.

Harry visibly relaxed, sipping on a large, straight Jack Daniels whilst studying their conundrum; he had deliberately been amiss in informing Jeffries of his arrival and, as was always the case with Harry, half a bottle later the idea struck him. They simply needed them to believe that Uncle Jack was still alive and release news of sightings of his dead uncle.

Tommy nearly fell out of his chair with excitement. He chastised himself for not coming up with the suggestion; it was so simple it was brilliant and he knew the perfect person to spread the news: he lived a couple of miles down the road and would swallow anything he told him, as he was that keen to inform anybody and everybody of any gossip.

Harry was intrigued.

'My cousin Macklin!'

'You know him well then?' Harry replied laughing.

'He grassed me up constantly with my folks: always Tommy did this and Tommy done that!'

'Ideal man for the job.'

'He'll tell the whole county if he could, but you got to stay hidden.'

'Anything you say.'

'Jeffries won't panic, but it will keep him off balance–'

'I hope so, but my gut feeling is he won't react the way we think.'

Tommy opened a bottle of beer and took a large hit. 'How do you think he'll react?'

Harry finished his drink: 'Of my short and distinctly disjointed meetings with him, he'll be unpredictable. I think we'll be left to wait a while until he can ascertain whether the stories are true, so your cousin needs to hear of a couple of sightings.'

Tommy nodded, contemplating where best to place his old friend.

Nothing else was scheduled, or arranged for the rest of the day, and the two drinking buddies with little reluctance saw out the day in much the same vain.

* * *

Harry was the first to rise, and his hangover this fine morning was not in the same league as before. Tommy remained asleep, snoring heavily.

He reached the door at the back of the house, unlocked it and swung it open to enjoy the dawn of a new day; he was changing like the day, slowly and inexplicably and the speed of transition was starting to drag for him: he was impatient to see positive results, to test his new found skills. His irritation to letting the natural course of events unfold as they will was a burden that hung around his neck, weighing him down and clouding his judgment.

'Coffee?' Tommy's question broke off his train of thought.

'Sure.'

'I'll call Macklin later.'

'He won't suspect?'

'Nope! I'll make the call and ask my uncle to go huntin'. Macklin can't help himself and forever asks me what I know. It'll be perfect you watch. By lunchtime the whole town will know.'

'I'll e-mail Jeffries later informing him of my imminent arrival, that'll give him a day or so to absorb this new found information and then we can gauge his reaction.'

'Perfect!'

Tommy made coffee.

Harry sipped the hot beverage, it was just the tonic: Tommy made great coffee. He savored the taste, allowing the caffeine to re-invigorate his sagging system, but also strengthening his resolve to get cracking into this new career then in a heartbeat he would ridicule himself with equal measure for being so childish to even consider Harry Travers worthy enough to be a gumshoe. His education, which only added to his consternation, was short by a wide margin of what he saw as the required level and in an effort to play catch up he visited a local second hand book shop before leaving home and bought a few well-chosen crime novels. Tommy's absence would allow him time to go back to school.

Breakfast was good, and along with the help of three further cups of coffee, was consumed in a mixture of impatience and boredom.

He flicked open the cover of a dog-eared paperback and tucked in.

Tommy was gone a little over four hours, but it was a good read and Harry never once checked the time.

'Glad to see you making yourself comfortable,' Tommy said, placing a large brown paper bag of groceries on the kitchen table.

Harry closed the book, it had provided him with more than enough food for thought; he was definitely not about to be the butt of any jokes or let anyone, even Tommy, in on his plans. To an outsider they were farcical, to him comical until he thought of his Uncle Jack; there were too many loose ends and certain individuals not being particularly forthcoming not to arouse suspicion and warrant a thorough investigation.

'It went just like clockwork', started Tommy. 'Macklin could tell instantly I had a secret to tell and followed me around like a little lost puppy, begging to be let in on the gossip. By the time I left he had made at least four calls that I know of.'

'Superb,' Harry replied slowly.

'All that's required now is to sit back, lie low and wait.'

Harry contemplated Jeffries' reaction to receiving his e-mail, which would be sent on its merry way in the early hours of the morning in order to give it an air of authenticity. He needed to keep the time gap between the U.S and the U.K. This left the rest of the day at their mercy, and the prospect of fighting off boredom. Tommy cracked open a couple of beers and instantly put paid to that. Harry prudently set his alarm to remind him to send the e-mail.

* * *

Jeffries' eyes focused on the offending correspondence and refused to let go; the day started off poorly and was on the verge of deteriorating before it had chance to begin.

His secretary neatly placed the morning post on his desk, swiveled and departed without their passing between them a single word; this was becoming the norm these days, she thought, ever since he lost that client, which wasn't even his biggest, or his most important, but the effect on him was seismic. In the four years since her arrival her employer proved to be an extremely funny and likeable boss. That was until Jack Hennessey died.

* * *

From across the room Harry could make out Tommy's lifeless shape in the aftermath of yet another monumental bender, but that e-mail had been sent, or so he thought. He racked his brains in a desperate attempt to remember anything about that part of the evening. It was painful to move, but move he must and after what seemed like half an hour stood beside his laptop computer. The lid was open, so he had opened it alright. He fired it up and waited impatiently. Finally he attempted to log on to the Internet and to his delight he gained access within a minute or two. For all of Tommy's rough edges and wild ways, he possessed all the mod-cons. Within another short space of time he stood, swaying, reading the message delivered to Anton Jeffries last night. 'Got to lie low until tonight,' he said quietly, and logged off. The battery level was dangerously low, so he tottered over to his hand luggage, retrieved the charger and plugged it in before shutting it down and returning to bed. He turned his cell-phone back on.

Harry was awoken from his enforced slumber by the strange sensation of his cell-phone vibrating in the small of his back: he had a voicemail.

'Was that him?' Tommy's throaty enquiry came from across the room.

'Don't know.'

'Smart to turn your phone off,' Tommy said stretching.

'It can only be one person!'

'He'd have read your e-mail by now.'

'I reckon so.'

Harry sat up and played the voicemail message. Sure enough it was Jeffries wishing him a safe journey and to contact him as soon as it was convenient.

'He'll check flight times, because that's exactly what I would do!'

A quick cross-check of all the relevant flights gave Harry the information required and he would simply tell the man that he preferred to drive and would hire a car for the purpose.

The hours ticked by interminably and no manner of his own self-styled schooling could possibly allay his growing frustration. Tommy had departed earlier to see his cousin again. This left Harry with no place to go bar pacing the length and breadth of the front room. The Boyd brothers weren't smart enough to foil his uncle, it needed to be an inside job, someone who could get close enough to kill him, make it look like a wild animal and convince the Sheriff of the same. Yes, the fake news was a start, and it would cause Jeffries some loss of sleep, but only for a while at least.

Harry stopped pacing and made coffee to keep alert.

Tommy arrived back and smiled, as he witnessed Harry call Jeffries, who in his absence thought it wise to have the conversation from inside Tommy's car. Harry swallowed the cost and dialed out on his mobile.

Jeffries gave nothing away, but he could sense him squirm whenever the question of the investigation into his uncle's disappearance arose. The call lasted all of five minutes. Jeffries never once queried the hire car

Back in the house Harry helped himself to some more freshly made coffee, making a mental note of the time for any future reference.

'Two hours!' he stated.

'Sure.'

'And this time you stay out of sight.'

Tommy nodded between sips of coffee.

'How old is your car?'

'Three years.'

'It should hopefully pass for a hire car,' he continued. 'Does anybody around here know you own it?'

'It's not mine!'

'Perfect! Does the owner need it back anytime soon?'

'I wouldn't have thought so, he's dead!'

'Perfect!' Harry replied without a second's hesitation.

His openly blasé attitude to driving a dead man's car shocked him momentarily, but he adjusted to his new role and carried on: 'How long dead?'

'Five days!'

'Excellent! Just as long as we get no tickets then nobody will be wise to the fact.'

'The guy was a speed freak and the cousin of a friend,' Tommy began, 'who unfortunately killed himself on a motorcycle, and because I'd expressed an interest in the car I was offered it.'

'Even better!' Harry finished his coffee.

Two hours later he pulled up outside Jeffries' office and found the man as he expected to find him: seated, leaning back in his leather chair with an arrogant air, and rocking from side to side with his eyes never leaving the door.

Wouldn't want to disappoint, he thought, as he strode purposefully, exuding confidence into the bright, well lit office. His secretary was out.

'You're late!'

'Didn't know I had an appointment.'

Jeffries stopped rocking.

'You heard the news?'

Harry tried his best to sound surprised. He knew he was being tested.

'What news? You got a lead on my uncle?'

'He's been spotted on several occasions roaming around the county.'

Jeffries' eyes never left him, as Harry pulled back the chair opposite his desk, interrogating Travers' every move, word, nuance, facial expression.

'Roaming?'

'Yes, roaming. That kind of had me puzzled too.'

Harry could see the burning question in the process of being loaded into the breach. He braced himself for impact.

'If he's alive then I'm afraid you fail to inherit his estate!'

He breathed a sigh of relief then just as quickly respected the need to keep his guard up.

'I don't care, just as long as he's safe. That's all that really matters, right?'

Jeffries broke off the eye contact and twisted his ball point pen into a blank piece of paper lying on the center of his desk. 'Yes, that is what's important.' His reply signaled the resumption of the eye contact.

It was now that Harry realized he was still standing and nonchalantly sat down. Jeffries once again stabbed the paper with his pen.

'What's up?' he said, feigning concern. He was growing tired of the mind games and laid it out there for Jeffries to trip himself up.

'Your uncle's dead!'

'How do you know?' Harry snapped back.

The sharpness of his reply knocked Jeffries out of the park, and he needed to go and pour himself a drink to calm down. He offered one to Harry, but he declined. Sitting back down Jeffries answered: 'Your uncle was dying!'

The abruptness failed to disturb Travers' state of mind.

'I knew he had a dodgy ticker, but what else did he have?'

'He confided in me that his heart was "shot to pieces"!'

'That's still no guarantee that he's dead.'

'Your uncle was a creature of habit in certain ways and hasn't been seen in a long time, so we are to assume he's dead.'

'Nobody's seen him in how long?'

'Long enough to be pronounced dead!'

'And what did the Sheriff's investigation turn up?'

'What I've always stated: nothing. Nobody's heard from him, nobody's seen him!'

Harry remained silent. It was time to speak to Sheriff Poulsen, alone.

'It's been a long day,' he said rising.

'Going already? Where you staying?'

'Need sleep. Same as before,' Harry added; he had been amiss not to book a room at the motel, but would rectify that on his way to see the Sheriff.

'We'll sell the house without too much trouble, so I reckon you'll have it all within the month,' Jeffries said politely.

'I can wait.'

'There won't be much need for you to return after this trip,'

'He was my family.'

'You'll be back then?'

'I like it here.'

'I'll take care of everything, and then you can be on your merry way as soon as it's convenient.'

Harry nodded: there was no point continuing this conversation, or the meeting for that matter, so said his goodbye, turned and left.

Once outside he ran the whole conversation over and over in his head and annoyingly came to the same conclusion as before.

10

After that essential detour to the motel, Harry made a beeline for the County Sheriff's Office on South White Street. The Sheriff was in and after a polite enquiry as to his availability was granted ten minutes of the man's valuable time.

His office was bright and airy, and clearly that of someone of a cheerful disposition. Sheriff Poulsen seemed genuinely pleased to see him, but any skepticism was his shortcoming and not the Sheriff's. He mustn't jump to conclusions.

'Mister Travers, it's good to see you again.' He held out his hand for Harry to take at his convenience. Harry accepted the handshake; any pause on his part would cause offence.

'I'm sorry I didn't come and see you during my last visit, I had a lot going on,' Harry said. He was trying to be sincere without sounding obsequious plus was eager to know the true extent of any further enquiry.

'We, I, rather got off on the wrong foot the last time we spoke.'

Harry recalled that fateful meeting.

'I think I'm afraid I kind of gave you the impression that your uncle's disappearance was not of any importance to me. Nothing could be further from the truth.'

Harry smiled: he didn't want the Sheriff to concern himself, he desired the man to keep talking.

'I may have not have seen eye to eye with your uncle on most things, as did quite a few people around these parts, but that doesn't mean I don't take his possible demise any less seriously!'

'Thank you.' The Sheriff had unwittingly answered one of his questions.

'I love my job very much Mister Travers, and I wear this badge with no small amount of pride, so this kind of thing troubles me more than most folk give credit.'

Harry could only nod; he admired the man's honesty.

'There have been apparent sightings of your uncle around the county, Mister Travers.'

'Call me Harry.'

'There have been apparent sightings of your uncle around the county, Harry,' the Sheriff repeated, 'but I'm not holding out much hope they're him.'

'Where or who did you hear that from?'

'That's not important, you just need to appreciate I don't hold out much hope.'

Harry couldn't help but feel the initial part of their plan going off without a hitch: he pictured a panicking Jeffries arrogantly storming into this office, demanding to know if Jack Hennessey had indeed been spotted and could he confirm if he was still alive. His contempt for the man was reaching biblical proportions.

'Why?'

'Call it a gut feeling.'

'People have been known to be wrong!'

The Sheriff seated himself behind his desk in a similar way to Jeffries.

Harry was beginning to get the feeling all his conversations would continue in this vein, and so found a suitable chair.

'Believe me Harry, he's dead! We carried out an extensive search for your uncle and turned up nothing.'

'Who reported him missing?'

'Jeffries.'

No surprise there, but Harry was conscious not to let his emotions show: 'Without a corpse or a grave there can only be one logical explanation.'

'Yep!'

'But there's no evidence to support even that theory?' Harry was clutching at straws and he knew it.

'If he died of a heart attack why would there be? Sufficient time was allowed to pass before he was officially announced dead, and hopefully within that time frame some evidence would have surfaced to prove one way or another, but it didn't.'

'What did Doc Adams say?'

'He added nothing we didn't already know or suspect.'

Harry was not going to get any new news, but he refused to give up hope.

'If there are any further developments then you'll be the first to know, Harry.'

Of course I will, he said to himself: his in-built cynicism, which was growing to become one of the private detective's greatest weapons, was exercised to its fullest extent here.

'I've had a long day Sheriff.'

'I'm sure you have.'

'Can I give you call you?'

'Just leave a message at the station and I'll return your call.'

Harry rose carefully. He offered and gave a firm handshake and studied the photographs plastered haphazardly on the Sheriff's office wall; they were of him posing with various celebrities and dignitaries. The Sheriff was popular. He wondered if his uncle realized how popular. After giving his cell-phone number he exited for some much needed fresh air.

He was tired of cat and mouse antics, and the long journey coupled with his self-inflicted lack of sleep suddenly hit him hard and his eyes stung in the bright sunlight.

* * *

Tommy woke him: it was nothing more worrying than dinner, and due to his somnolence the decision was made to order pizza. Clearly neither man excelled in the culinary arts.

'Fancy a drive after?' Tommy said between slices.

'Sure, could do with some fresh air after topping up my cholesterol!'

'Dig up any news?'

'Nope!'

'Didn't think you would.'

'Jeffries doesn't believe a damn word regarding my uncle; he didn't have to say, but it was all too obvious, as for the Sheriff he simply applied logic to come to the same conclusion.'

'Still it keeps them thinking, looking and off balance.'

The two men devoured the pizza and left for fresh air.

'There's a reason for us having this drive tonight?'

Tommy remained mute and kept his eyes on the road.

'You just love goading them?'

Tommy smiled.

'Jeffries will want to get to the bottom of the rumors, and so he'll have us tailed,' Harry continued. 'Go to the motel, park down the street and I'll enter via the reception under the proviso of collecting my room key. That will flush them out!'

Tommy needed no second invitation and took the next left.

Harry adjusted the wing mirror once he was again seated comfortably in the front passenger seat of Tommy's Sentra and consciously tried to limit his head movements. Tommy drove at a sedate pace around Athens on leaving the motel, stopping outside all the obvious shopping outlets and bars in an attempt to get spotted.

'We've been driving for over half an hour!' Harry said, now developing an annoying kind of Messerschmitt twitch by looking over his shoulder too often and peering through the rear window.

'Disappointing isn't it.'

'And boring!'

Tommy pulled the car onto the main road down to the airport. It was getting late and the lights from all the traffic now made it nigh on impossible to recognize anybody.

The road gently veered to the right and Tommy put his foot down once they hit open road. 'If we got a tail then we'll find out in the next few minutes.'

Harry turned sideways on and studied all the headlights closely; one by one they all tailed off until there were two bright, white orbs holding a relative position in the rear window. Tommy increased their speed, ignoring any restrictions. The car held station.

'Bingo!' said Harry slowly.

'Let's see what they got under the hood!'

Harry didn't need to ask the obvious question for the Nissan's acceleration pushed him back into his seat. The car still held station.

'They mean business,' he said.

'Yep!'

Tommy's driving was impressive: even at this speed he was smooth and professional in his application.

'Corvette!' Tommy said, as he kicked it down a gear and pushed the car through eighty. 'They'll have plenty in hand.'

The Corvette dropped back momentarily, but it soon loomed large and fast in their rear window.

They were now heading at high speed south out of Athens on the David W Lillard Memorial Highway, and up to this point Harry had not paid any heed to the thought of the police until he noticed the reminder on his right that the speed limit was fifty-five miles-an-hour. A quick glance over to Tommy reinforced his devil-may-care attitude to his current situation and the determination to push on.

The Corvette's headlights filled their rear view mirror. For the first time Tommy failed to match their acceleration.

'Glove compartment!'

Harry carefully open the passenger glove compartment fearing the surprise his friend had in store: it revealed the Beretta M9.

'If he comes down your side blow out one of his tires!'

Harry found himself accepting the opportunity of retribution with no small amount of glee and little hesitation. He removed the gun, took off the safety and cocked it. From his research since firing it he knew the effective range was fifty meters with little recoil, and he was confident he could take out a couple of tires.

Tommy slowed, positioning the Nissan in the center of the road.

Harry felt his heart begin to race, as the adrenaline pumped through his system, heightening his senses. He would empty the entire clip if required, in a heartbeat.

The lights disappeared from their rear window.

Harry kept his line of sight straight back and focused on the white lane markings emanating from under the center of the car: he didn't want their pursuers to have any idea as to the little surprise he had in store. The car failed to materialize. He shifted his balance and took aim over Tommy's right shoulder. Still nothing appeared.

'They've turned their lights off,' he said. 'The cheeky bastards are using ours!'

Tommy killed the lights.

'Hope you know these roads.'

'Like the back of your hand,' replied Tommy.

With their lights killed, the two men's eyes slowly adjusted to the conditions and Harry could make out the car three lengths back. They flashed past the turn off for the airport.

Tommy started to accelerate once again, but it was too late for they were approaching the junction with County Road 609, which caused him to slow. When he was satisfied no cars were going to emerge he pushed the Sentra past ninety.

The two cars continued heading South, holding station, each waiting for the other to make the first move. Ahead was a crossroads where County Road 525 emerging from their left became County Road 607. The street lights illuminated them perfectly.

'Lit up like a Christmas tree,' cursed Tommy.

Luck was on their side though and the traffic lights stayed green. Tommy failed to indicate and swung a hard right after the lights onto the 607

The Corvette followed hot on their heels, only now it accelerated up to a length behind and Harry instinctively knew they would pass on Tommy's side.

Suddenly a blast shook the car, rocking it violently. Tommy swerved, and a blast of air and glass fragments hit Harry square in the face. A second blast caused both men to duck, but it missed. Harry never returned fire: he held his nerve, he needed them to think they were unarmed, a sitting target. Tommy seemed to sense this and said nothing.

Their pursuers switched their lights on to light up their prey, and Tommy lit his to view the road. He floored the accelerator.

'Give it to them when I say,' Tommy said coldly.

'Sure thing,' Harry said slowly and deliberately.

He carefully monitored the metallic blue Corvette, now lit perfectly by the side glare of their front lights and the Corvette's own rebounding of their bodywork. The two cars were close, roaring down the road side by side. His hand gripped the barrel, with trigger finger suspended awaiting the signal to squeeze.

'Wait,' Tommy whispered, but still discernible over the car noise.

Harry could clearly make out the hardened features of the man in the front passenger seat while he pumped a Remington 870 twelve gauge shotgun in readiness for another blast at their car.

'Now!'

Harry let rip a volley of four shots in quick succession; he was not going to be found wanting when it came to retaliating to open hostilities; his conscience was clear on that front: this was dog eat dog, survival not of the fittest, but of those who refused to flinch, and flinch he did not.

The Corvette swung hard left as the first of the shells slammed into the fiberglass bodywork, then seemed to return for more before swinging hard left a second time. Harry thought about unloading another three or four rounds, but the Corvette continued on this zigzagging path along the road. Thankfully it was blissfully quiet this evening. Finally they stopped swerving and maintained station. Harry never hesitated to wonder when they would return fire, he simply unloaded four more rounds and watched through the dim light as the Corvette slowly veered left off the road, and embedded itself into a ditch before flipping onto its roof.

Tommy pulled over and turned off the lights, but kept the engine running.

'What do you want to do?' Tommy asked.

'Keep going and let's ditch your dead mate's car.'

'You'll never make a detective!'

'Why not?' Harry tried hard to hide his indignation.

'Because you've crossed that line!'

'Fuck that line!'

Tommy was right and he'd done it lacking any self-recrimination, but his friend was way wide of the mark regarding his skills as an upcoming detective. He was mentally ticking off boxes and here was another.

'Let's go ditch the car,' Harry said slowly.

'Sadly, you're right!'

Tommy switched on the lights and pulled out into the road leaving two white lights glowing in the ditch.

'I'm not wearing gloves!' Harry said looking down at his hands. Tommy was. He had been amiss not to spot that. That box was left un-ticked.

'Not a problem. I know a place where we can clean it up and dispose of it.'

Harry took a deep breath and began to relax a little; he was beginning to find that controlling his nerves was becoming easier with time and here this very night, following the first serious litmus test in his development, his nerves conquered all with flying colors.

'This isn't your ex-mate's car is it?'

'Stole it!

Ten minutes later Tommy pulled right onto a dirt track. A hundred yards further on the lights lit up another car, which belonged to his grandmother, and within the hour the Nissan was scrubbed clean of all prints and set alight.

* * *

Jeffries' face washed out any remaining trace of color, his eyes locked on a point on his desk; he couldn't and wouldn't believe the news filtering along the telephone line from none other than Jake Boyd. Two cousins of his were dead, found in their upturned Corvette. It was being treated as murder.

Jeffries knew the two miscreants all too well: he had represented them both on numerous occasions for minor offences over the years, but by the sounds of things had clearly met their match.

'That's a crying shame,' he finally said as a way of indicating he was still listening coupled with the need to show at least some semblance of sorrow. In truth the world was a better place for their not being in it, but good manners dictated this undeniable truth be kept quiet.

Jake continued on for many more minutes proclaiming oath after oath that someone should dare to take out a Boyd without fear of reprisal. Jeffries asked him if he had any clues to the perpetrators. More oaths ensued and he took that as a negative response.

By now he would have his day clearly mapped out, and be well on his way to achieving some of the goals and duties designated for the morning, but this Boyd was boring him immensely and he was itching to cut him off. The opportunity soon revealed itself and he hung up.

'Prick!' he snarled.

* * *

Tommy was as bright as a brand new pin: the previous night's excitement having left no aftereffects on his otherwise cheerful disposition. Harry on the other hand knew he would have to fight his inner demons if he was to accept this second life: death and all its machinations would now become inextricably linked to it and accepted as par for the course. Yes, he hadn't seen the bodies, but he knew they were dead; some of the rounds could not have failed to hit their intended target.

'Coffee?'

Coffee the great stimulator would now came to his rescue. Tommy placed a hot mug on the table in front of him now that he sat facing the television.

'How you coping?'

'Struggling, how you?'

'Don't let the guilt eat away at you, they deserved it. Don't forget who fired first!'

'Guilt's not the problem. You knew them?'

Tommy didn't answer.

'Who were they?'

'Cousins.'

Harry sipped his coffee, savoring the rich, aromatic taste. Tommy left for the kitchen. Why should he feel guilty? Tommy was right they had fired first. He ran his fingers over his face. He had not felt the need until now. There were no real marks, but a quick look in a mirror confirmed that he had no lingering scars from the shattered glass.

'You told them what car you were driving?' Harry said when Tommy returned.

Tommy held a vacuous expression then smiled a devilish smile.

'You're making a damn fine detective, detective.'

'We just killed two people!'

'Don't be losing any sleep over them, they wouldn't for you. Two shotgun blasts proved that!'

Breakfast was served.

* * *

The kitchen chair fared no better than its cousin and flew through the open window to lay splintered over the yard. The silence that followed was deafening.

'Who sent them?

Jake shook his head, shrugged his shoulders, and tried to placate his irate father before any more of the family furniture left the building. Rudy and Carl had earlier decided to keep out of Jessie's way and stood like statutes in the corner of the kitchen: this was big brother territory and Jake was more than welcome to it.

'Jeffries?' asked Jessie, trying desperately hard to keep some semblance of self-control.

'I don't know. I asked him if he knew of any reason why they'd be out that night and he was as shocked as we were!'

'Those damn fool kids. I always knew they'd go too far one day!'

'If we could get their cell-phones then we'd know the last number they called or received.'

'Rudy,' Jessie started, 'there are times when the son I knew you could be surfaces and brings joy to my heart, only for it to sadden when I realize it is only fleeting.'

Rudy smiled: 'Thanks Pa.'

The sound of an approaching car brought the conversation to a temporary halt.

'Let's hope your sister's got news.'

Jessie went outside to meet her.

'Police ain't saying nothing!' Nancy began once her father was in earshot.

'Didn't think they would.'

'But I spoke to Bradley's new girl and he got a phone call from some guy while out drinking with Shane at Rick's.'

'Yeah?'

'This guy was boasting that he was driving around town in Bruno's old car, and if they wanted it then they'd better come get it.'

'Dumb, just plain dumb!'

By now the brothers had all congregated on the porch.

'It was a set up!' proclaimed Jake.

'No shit, Sherlock!' said Jessie derogatorily.

Jake knew it was best to ignore the slight. These were after all two of his cousins, two of his father's god-children and justice would have to be seen to be done.

'Bruno's car was discovered burnt out about twenty miles south of Athens,' added Nancy.

'Who do we know in the police department?' Jessie looked straight at Nancy when asking the question.

'No!'

'It's for the family Nancy.'

'Fuck off Rudy!'

'You know it makes sense.' First up Rudy now Carl added his weight.

'The answer is still no!'

'Well, we can't make you if you really don't want to.' Jessie knew she took after her mother on this front, and to try and force her hand would only make her dig her heels in even more, but on occasions the old reverse psychology was known to reap benefits. He turned to go inside.

'Just this once!'

'You're a good girl,' he replied, stopping short of the doorway and spinning round to face her. 'Get everything you can, and you have your father's permission to use extreme prejudice!'

The object of Nancy's point blank refusal to involve herself with the local law enforcement was Deputy Wilbur Littlehorn. Now it was common knowledge that Wilbur had a soft spot for Nancy ever since their high school days, and was not shy in using what he saw as his position of authority to try and get whatever he wanted, and Nancy was top of his wish list. Nancy's repugnance of Wilbur was not without foundation: he was overweight, balding and suffered from the most appalling halitosis, which he did very little to alleviate, except around Nancy. In fact in certain circles he even went as far as to cultivate the affliction to gain any advantage he could.

Her hands trembled at the very thought of the man as they hovered over the push key numbers on the eighties style phone, and then waited with mounting trepidation after she asked the receptionist to be put through. She had been amiss with giving her name and his opening gambit showed why she held him in the utmost contempt.

'Yeah?' he snarled.

'It's Nancy,' she said softly, and as seductively as possible.

His tone instantly softened: 'Hi Nancy,'

'You busy?'

'No, what can I do for you? Is everything okay?' he said quickly. 'Sorry to hear about your cousins.'

This was the opening she wanted and sprung for the gap.

'Is there any news Wilbur? Their families are understandably devastated.' Her velvety voice caressed the line and sent the poor deputy into raptures.

'Not much Nancy.'

'You wouldn't keep anything from us now would you?'

'Now Nancy,' Wilbur joked, gaining confidence, 'would I do that!'

'I loved my two cousins and would do anything, anything Wilbur, to see whoever did this heinous crime brought to justice!'

There was a moment's pause as her words hit home.

'Anything?' Wilbur finally said quietly and deliberately.

'You heard me!'

Again there was another pause.

'Dinner at eight. I'll pick you up.'

She sensed he was willing to say something more, but voices entering the office in the background signified unwanted visitors, and he hung up.

'Well?' Jessie was impatient for news.

'I'm going to dinner at eight.'

'Good.'

'You're not the one going!'

'Just choose the most expensive item on the menu, you'll feel better for it!'

'Pa!'

'Extreme prejudice!' added Jake.

* * *

Harry was chomping at the bit to again pressurize Jeffries: the car accident had failed to provide them with any new leads, only two corpses.

Tommy frowned and Harry knew this was to be done flying solo. His friend realized too late that the crazy Englishman was serious, so much so that by the time he had come around to Travers' way of thinking he was out of the door.

Harry boarded a taxi ordered twenty minutes prior and gave his destination as a shopping mall walking distance from Jeffries' office.

The day was warm, dry, and he enjoyed what the walk did for his troubled constitution: he was flying without a safety net, unsure exactly what to do; he had also crossed that line, albeit in self-defense. The fact that Tommy knew them, called their bluff, and set them up was neither here nor there to him. He had killed and the fact worryingly weighed lightly on his shoulders. Every successful private detective must have the basic instinct to kill when asked, but only in defense of their person.

Tommy seemed to enjoy getting one over so violently on them. He liked the man, but this personality trait now meant he would keep close tabs on him. This last thought brought on a sense of overwhelming hypocrisy: Tommy was trying to help him, going out of his way to aid and abet, but his set up of the Boyd cousins was a personal vendetta. Why? Yes, they had trashed his property, and yes in some people's eyes that was reason enough.

He finally arrived at his destination. For all his arguments and counter-arguments he accepted the inevitable, undeniable fact to keep a close eye on Tommy. It was the sensible thing to do.

Jeffries was absent, but his secretary felt him no threat and so his request to wait in his office was accepted.

Harry sat back in the large sofa positioned on the left hand side of the spacious office, the desk sat at right angles to it and parallel to the rear wall. For the first time he examined the room in greater detail; it was neat and tidy, what you would expect from a professional man. Any files on previous cases must be stored in an adjacent room for there was no sign of them. Photographs of the owner were scarce, now that Harry found interesting. It was almost as if he didn't want anybody, any visitors to know what kind of a man he was or what he got up to in his spare time. Surely, he conjectured, that was nigh on impossible around here. Harry was trying hard to think and deduce like a private detective. He needed to master and fine tune these skills, to look at someone, study how they lived and at least get a feeling for the kind of person they were, or could be under their skin behind locked doors. He thought about rifling through his desk, but quickly abandoned that idea when he heard Jeffries arrive. From behind the closed door he could hear his secretary informing him of Travers' presence.

Jeffries entered in much the same way as a man would with his guard held high ready for the impending onslaught, but he appeared different in some way, cautious almost to the point of being paranoid and he hadn't even opened his mouth yet.

'Did my secretary offer you some coffee, Harry?'

He shook his head, but before he could answer that he wasn't really all that bothered, Jeffries ordered two.

'I can see you have made yourself comfortable. That's good!'

It was false and Harry sensed it: his being here was the last thing this man wanted or needed. Good, he thought, I'll make your day. He didn't get up or offer his hand, and Jeffries, by his body language, was not about to offer his.

'I went to see the Sheriff.'

'So I heard.' Jeffries made his way around the rear of his desk, but paused briefly before sitting to examine the drawers. Whatever security measures the lawyer had put in place were still intact.

His flippant reply infuriated Harry and he desperately wanted to look inside those drawers more than anything in the world right now, more than seeing Sheila Wallace naked.

The secretary arrived with two coffees, and Harry sat back to witness the brief exchange about a couple of clients, which amounted to nothing. She handed him his as she passed by. He thanked her.

Once they were alone again he sensed a subtle shift in the lawyer almost as if his brief confab with his employee had flicked a switch inside him and cleared any malfunction.

'What did the wonderful Sheriff Poulsen have to say?' he said sarcastically.

Harry held onto his reply until the full force of Jeffries' derisive tone hit him then he could use that to milk any animosity lurking just below the surface.

'My uncle has been seen,'

Jeffries laughed for all of a second.

'You think it's a joke?'

'Sheriff Poulsen is taking it seriously?'

'He's looking into it!'

'He thinks it rubbish then!'

Jeffries finally sat.

'You clearly do!'

'You're uncle did whatever he saw fit, but I don't think even he would have the temerity to be seen wondering around town without a care in the world, when the rest of it thought him dead having been eaten by some wild animal!'

It was the most Jeffries had ever said in his presence, but it showed that the sightings worried him.

'The Sheriff promised me a thorough investigation into the sightings, but it has had one advantage.'

'And that is?'

'It has kept the investigation into my uncle's death or murder, depending on your point of view, in the forefront of police investigations.'

Jeffries stared at him long and hard. Harry held firm, he was waiting for the response and he knew it was only a matter of time.

'You think it is murder?'

He nodded, and waited.

'On what evidence?'

'There's no body, but furthermore there's no concrete evidence that a wild animal took him either: there should be some bloody trail somewhere in the woods, and as you quite rightly pointed out my uncle did whatever took his fancy, but I believe would only venture into certain sections of the woods with those he was most comfortable with. That would explain the lack of evidence indicating a kind of struggle.'

'That's a very fancy-able idea.'

'Not if you apply logic!'

Harry fought an irresistible urge to rile him further.

'If the Sheriff fails in his promise to follow that line of enquiry, and I'll give him a little more time to finish his investigations, then I will!'

Jeffries sat stony-faced refusing to blink. He looked straight at Harry, or was it just over his shoulder, he could not tell.

'You have any suspects?'

'A few!'

'Care to name them.'

'Not at this time, but you'll be the first to get their names when I have found something concrete.' Harry looked at his watch: it was time to cut it short and leave Jeffries guessing as to his next move. 'Now, I'm afraid you'll have to excuse me I have another appointment.'

He rose exuding all the confidence he could muster, looking straight ahead at a print of a woodland painting; it was strangely familiar and it captured his imagination for a brief second, keeping him transfixed, forcing him to dissect the beautiful lines and brush strokes of an undoubted talent. The name in the bottom right hand corner was barely visible. He finished his coffee, placed the cup on Jeffries' desk. He just about made the door before Jeffries spoke.

'I would appreciate some prior warning next time you care for a talk.'

The tone was polite, but sharp in its delivery.

Harry turned to his left, looking sideways at the lawyer: 'Of course.'

A wall of dry heat struck him as he left behind the comfort of the air conditioned building. It snapped his mind into focus: his manner had been bordering on the offensive and it was a small miracle words remained relatively cordial. To his growing contentment his conscience could find nothing with which to chastise himself. Jeffries would find him no shrinking violet, and if he wanted to send the Boyd family or anybody else come to think of it then he was ready. This along with having to forcibly evict unknowns from his own home injected his confidence with bullish belligerence.

A passing car forced him to suspend momentarily his personal conversation. A quick glance confirmed it was no threat.

Once back at the car park, where his mini odyssey began, he scoured the surroundings and ordered a cab. It arrived within ten minutes and he was back at Tommy's in twenty.

* * *

Wilbur Littlehorn could not believe his luck that Nancy Boyd, the woman who invaded his boyhood dreams, torturing him throughout, was seated opposite, and in doing so wasted valuable time questioning her motives for the dinner date, then followed it with a wave of self-chastisement for wasting that time. His choice of eateries was a recent addition to the town's culinary delights called Charlie's, and he prayed the food was as good as its reputation suggested.

'Wine? Beer?' he asked politely, not wishing to sound pretentious.

'I'll take wine,' Nancy said softly.

'Any preference?' It was a stupid question and he immediately hated having asked it: here was the most beautiful woman he had ever known, who he had coveted for many years, but a wine expert she was not.

'I'll choose.'

'Sure,' she said again, just as softly.

The waitress arrived to take their order.

Wilbur was a model of good manners and chose a good wine before Nancy placed her order: she hesitated not and rattled off a starter and main course in quick fire style. Once a second or two had passed, and he was satisfied she was not going to alter it, he placed his. The waitress disappeared as expeditiously as she had first appeared with notepad flapping away in her hand.

'You must be busy at work with all this Jack Hennessey business?' Nancy opened with. She was determined not to waste any time with small talk.

'There are far more important cases to deal with,' he replied.

It was not what she wanted to hear.

'I thought the investigation had been put to bed?'

'Someone allegedly reported seeing the old man walking around town.'

'You believe him?'

'No, would you?'

'Suppose not.'

The waitress returned carrying a bottle of Chateau Neuf Du Pape, poured Wilbur a small glass to taste, which he did with as much aplomb as he could muster: he yearned to impress this girl, hence the wine in the first place, and any and all opportunities to promote his good breeding would be grasped firmly with both hands. The wine was indeed agreeable, and the waitress once more departed having poured two glasses.

Any pretentiousness Wilbur felt was ignored; at school she had not given him a second look, indeed it seemed at the time that she had gone out of her way to openly ignore and place him firmly in a position of ridicule, the very ridicule which latterly fuelled his desire to become a deputy. He was confident that it was only a matter of time before the post of sheriff was his, and then so would Nancy Boyd.

Nancy sipped her wine, allowing her lips to caress the glass and deposit her expensive lipstick seductively over the rim. Wilbur watched her every move, fascinated in her foreplay, he accepted he was not the sharpest pencil in the box, and his open admission allowed him the one big advantage over the self-absorbed: he knew his limitations and respected them.

She totally captivated him. Where she had dressed with utter contempt in her heart, here she was on the warpath, determined to glean all the information her father desired plus any extras, and to guarantee success she wore a stunning tight black dress that came to just above the knee with matching heels. Wilbur found himself unable to speak when he first laid eyes upon her. Her long dark hair draped majestically over her slim shoulders helping to accentuate her smooth complexion, sparkling brown eyes and high cheek bones. The rosy red lipstick was ideally suited to match the dark colors of her dress.

The starters arrived in less than fifteen minutes, and Wilbur was thankful for the opportunity of being relieved of something to say: he had played this scenario over in his head a million times, but now he was living out his dream. Nancy's striking beauty was scrambling his senses. Any loftiness or behavior in him other than what could be construed as the norm would burden him in his pursuit and so pitched proceedings accordingly: this was her choice and he welcomed it with open arms.

'If the police department thinks that Jack Hennessey is dead then why not just say so and use the county's valuable resources to try and trace the men responsible for my cousins' deaths!'

'I was wondering when you'd get round to that!'

The abruptness in his voice shocked her.

'They were family.'

He wiped his mouth with a napkin, swallowed his food, and in doing so gained valuable time to word his reply carefully. Out of the corner of his eye Wilbur could make out the lithe figure of Riley Ferguson enter the restaurant with a couple of his buddies who looked vaguely familiar; this he did not need. Ferguson had been his nemesis back in High School: at every turn he had been there in the background, shadowing him like a demon waiting to strike, to crush his ambition and he knew damn well how he felt about Nancy and so naturally dated her.

Riley sauntered over to their table, his eyes completely fixed on Nancy and ignoring the deputy.

Rage welled inside Wilbur blurring all logic and reason, ignoring its pleadings to maintain any semblance of dignity and good manners.

'Hi Nancy.'

'Evening Riley,' she replied with contempt dripping off every word.

'See you got yourself the envy of the town as your date tonight.'

Wilbur locked his eyes on that part of the table directly in front of him.

'We were having a good time!' Nancy replied curtly.

A wicked smile erupted across Wilbur's face; this was the opening he needed, prayed for, and rose to face his nemesis.

'That's your cue to leave!'

Riley stood a moment bemused trying to comprehend what he'd just heard: that this particular man, "Lard arse Littlehorn", dare to confront him, a deputy he may be, but he was Wilbur the school chump and always would be.

'I hear you chump!'

The sickening thud echoed through the restaurant. Nancy audibly gasped. Riley slammed into the wall, bounced up against a booth and slid down onto the floor. His buddies took one threatening step towards Wilbur.

'I know you!' he said to the first of the two.

The man stopped moving.

'And I'll find out who you are!' he said to the second.

The two men looked at each other and started to move on him.

'Anything wrong Deputy Littlehorn?' The manager's dulcet tones brought an immediate end to Riley's buddies' bravery.

Wilbur never unlocked his eyes from theirs: he wanted the animosity to be evident for all too see and he prayed for an opportunity to avenge years of hurt, embarrassment and humiliation. With a clenched fist, knuckles ashen, he gesticulated to them to carry their stricken friend away.

Riley erred on the side of caution and held his prostrate position, feigning an injury far worse than the one experienced, until his two comrades helped him to his feet then suddenly without warning laid a vicious left hook on the side of Wilbur's jaw. The deputy stumbled back half a step, but stayed upright. 'I think you better leave,' Littlehorn said slowly, his words dripping with menace.

It proved to be the final act in proceedings, and the four parted company with Riley and his two associates being escorted off the premises accompanied by the manager's warning of permanent disbarment.

Wilbur needed to vent some fury: his night was sabotaged. He turned to apologize to Nancy, knowing it was the end to their date.

'That was cool!" she said softly, now standing.

'That was a long time coming!'

'He was a jerk when we dated, and nothing's changed.'

'You want to stay?' He didn't want to ask unless the answer was not what he wished, but ask he did.

'Hell yes!'

Wilbur could not resist beaming back a huge smile and walked around the table to seat her.

'All I can say at this point in time,' he said quietly, 'is that the last message sent to one of their cell-phones, which clearly indicates their reason for being out that night, came from a burner phone, so it's proving untraceable. If I find out anymore I'll let you know,' he continued before seating himself, 'but please let's not discuss it anymore tonight.'

Nancy agreed.

11

His time had run out, but Harry was trying hard not to be bitter: the Sheriff was noticeable with his lack of information; any reaction from Jeffries came to the grand total of nil; his own investigation was stalling badly; and the investigation into the cousins' deaths was quiet. On the plus side the police were not searching for him or Tommy.

He thought it prudent to leave the same way he arrived and hired a car for the purpose. Tommy didn't argue the point. After making the usual provisions to keep in touch via e-mail, Harry started the drive to Atlanta.

The roads were quiet and the drive marked the beginning of a long journey home that thankfully proved to be not only relaxing, but calming to the point of bringing clarity: he would return one more time, knowing his latest visit had probably stirred up the hornets' nest he desired, but was yet to bear fruit. Any fear resulting from the unknown had evaporated with his less than subtle approach.

Harry deposited the hire car and wasted no time checking in at New International Terminal before negotiating airport security. Still in the back of his mind he could not shake the feeling of being watched. He tried to suppress any inner fear lest it raise any suspicion in the security staff. He needn't have worried, for all his years of training had prepared him for situations such as these and he remained calm and in control of his emotions at all times.

He browsed through a range of shops to stop himself from clock watching and in no time his flight was called and he boarded once duty free was behind him. The seat seemed to envelope him like a warm blanket, and the fatigue that until now hung ghost like in the background stormed forward to stake the claim to his consciousness. He soon fell into a deep sleep.

* * *

He opened one eye to view the cabin crew slowly making their way down the aisle toward him supplying valuable sustenance to those passengers accepting the fare. Suddenly he was ravenous, and gladly accepted a beef dinner after the crew member enquired whether he slept well. Harry devoured it. Normally he would have accepted any liquid refreshment with great relish, but today was different; he needed, wanted a clear head. His mind swirled back and forth in a vain hope that he may recognize any clue that may have slipped through the net and been bypassed. Sadly, he was to be bitterly disappointed. The crew member appeared right on cue and so he gave in and ordered a large scotch.

The hit he desired reinvigorated his senses: in three weeks his summer leave would be upon him, and the two weeks available would give him ample time. This time he was going to run solo: Tommy was a good friend, but his riling of Jeffries was going to make life very difficult for him; he had warned Tommy of this before he departed, but the man never seemed to mind and it was again going to be prudent of him to enter the country without alerting anybody to his presence; then and only then could he maneuver without the shackles of somebody always asking as to his whereabouts. In the interim, communications would once again be maintained via e-mail. This would leave him valuable time to concentrate resources on his other case.

His mind swung to Sheila and her brother. The poor lad's probably dead by now, and they better not have come anywhere near his house or they could join him. The scotch only added further stimulation to his rising anger. Harry had taken the precaution of asking his neighbor to look after the house and took a small crumb of comfort from the fact there had been no correspondence from that quarter.

The flight, considering they were flying west to east, was refreshing and he landed back into the U.K eager to hear any news. He sent a text informing of his arrival and enquired after her and Stephen. To his immense satisfaction she replied within minutes informing him she was looking forward to meeting up, asking whether the trip was an eventful one and that her brother had been the beneficiary of yet another visit, but this time she had lied, letting on he was out when all the time he was hiding upstairs. He never strayed outside after that. Harry text back without delay recalling the visit his private investigator friend made on Stephen with a promise to make sure he followed it up.

A little over four hours later he collapsed through his front door, dumped the bags on the floor and poured himself a rather large whiskey whilst sifting through the mail. It was mainly bills and junk. He sat down on the sofa and drained the whiskey. It felt good and the soothing liquid warmed his innards and gradually carried him off to the place where dreams are made of.

The ringing tone from his mobile woke him from a deep sleep and a few well-chosen oaths were vented in its direction. He chose to let the answer phone take it and slipped back, hoping against all reason to rejoin the beautiful dream, shattered by the outside world invading his quiet time. No message was left, and this fuelled any misanthropic tendencies slowly simmering below the surface. He checked on the time. It was 16:33.

In a flash he was up and out of the sofa grateful his alcohol intake was only one large scotch. Today was the day he would start an all-out assault on Sheila: she would shoot him down in flames or not, either way it was going to trouble him no more. After that it was the casino, and how best to expose their scam. It was the only feasible way to get them off Stephen's back.

Within the hour he made a call to meet up with her, showered, changed and ate a small bowl of soup: if there was any possibility of that dinner she promised and some quality time alone with Sheila then the last thing he needed was a ravenous hunger to interfere. She asked to meet at her house, and after rechecking on the address, and programming this into his satnav as a fail-safe, drove at a steady pace to the rendezvous. The few hours' sleep had the desired effect of recharging his batteries, and this along with the knowledge that his working roster began with a late standby followed by four flights, kept his spirits high.

The trepidation rose exponentially as he turned into her road and became almost unbearable with every step taken along the small path leading to her front door.

She answered immediately, as if waiting just out of sight with the direct intention of springing upon the unsuspecting caller. Harry took a visible step back, smiled then entered the house on her invitation. She looked good enough to eat with her tight designer jeans tucked inside her knee high black stiletto boots, he was partial to stiletto's; her top was a soft cerise colored jumper that hid her bosom just enough to make you want to see them, and this had the desired effect of making him fight the urge to jump her there and then. From downstairs Stephen could clearly be discerned making himself a nuisance.

'Stephen okay?' he said following her through the house into the kitchen.

'He's shaken up, but refuses to admit it. He walks around with this blasé attitude to it all.'

'I have information, but best not to share it with him, for now. The last thing we need is Stephen traipsing off on some vendetta.'

'What is it?'

'The game your brother played in was definitely rigged!'

'Oh!'

He knew what he was saying was nothing new and simply repeating what her brother had told him, but when she fed all this back to Stephen he would simply confirm it.

The kitchen was as he remembered it: of that popular, modern, minimalist style with granite black worktops coupled with oak colored cupboards. She stopped by the side of the kettle, and made preparations for tea.

'The other players simply bump up the bets happy in the knowledge of a big payday by whatever mug they're suckering that day.'

'They saw him coming?'

'He won big or more to the point was made to win big then set up for a bigger fall. Only thing was Stephen couldn't take losing and so borrowed more money!'

'Can we get these men off his back?'

'The only way I can see is for him to win it back. They are not going to let him off the hook without recouping their money: it will be seen as a sign of weakness.'

Sheila made the tea.

'I can't see how he can get hold of the stake money!'

'You let me deal with that.'

'No, you can't!'

'I know a guy who'll stand me a stake then we can play them at their own game. What do you say?'

She smiled that beautiful smile, and he felt a surge of self-satisfaction and confidence race through him.

'Trust me on this,' he said softly, stroking the side of her left arm.

'You can't risk your own money on my itinerant brother!'

'It's not a risk.'

'Of course it is, unless you're a closet card sharp.'

'I will not argue that nothing in the world of the gambler is guaranteed, but if we stack the odds as much as possible in your favor then we'll at least have a fighting chance.'

She handed him his tea.

'I don't like it!'

He sipped the hot brew whilst fixing his gaze directly upon her, examining the lines on her beautiful face, deducing she would not stand in the way of his plan even if the thought of it was anathema to her.

'You love your brother very much?'

'And it's not your problem! I promised my parents, before they died, that I would always take care of him.'

That was something new and he immediately felt emboldened at having her confidence on such a delicate matter.

'He had a history of this kind of behavior when they were alive?'

'All the time: gambling was his weakness.'

'Must have been hard?'

'Problem was he was good at it, and he would end up on these monstrous winning streaks making thousands upon thousands of pounds and then bam! It would all be over, gone, and the bad times then began until the next golden winning streak.'

Harry mulled over this new piece of intelligence; he considered helping him get back on another golden run. No, that was a bad idea: the inevitable outcome would be more debt owed to more unscrupulous people.

Stephen made his appearance and Harry immediately realized his schoolboy error.

'Hi!'

'Hi!'

Raised eyebrows, a knowing look of many a long, heated discussion behind closed doors greeted the elder sister. Stephen poured himself a mug of tea.

'We're off out to dinner,' Sheila said tersely.

Harry displayed no outward emotion: he was going to get Sheila alone without the interference of an annoying younger brother and he hadn't said a word, yet.

'You want to come?'

This he did not want.

Stephen read the scene to perfection: 'No, I wouldn't be good company. You two go and have a good time.'

Harry gave him a wink once Sheila had turned away from him to go and collect her things.

'I'm sure you both have many things to discuss in my absence.'

Sheila stopped abruptly in the kitchen doorway and swiveled through one hundred and eighty degrees: 'I wouldn't waste a fine meal on anything so trivial!'

Ouch, thought Harry, glad I live alone with my own triviality.

Five minutes later he was turning left at the end of her street. She had said nothing since.

'Sorry about that!'

'Don't be.'

'He's pigheaded at best, thinks he's done nothing wrong and why should all this be happening to him? What's he done to deserve this?'

Harry knew it was prudent to keep his own counsel and concentrate on the road. Any thoughts he had on the matter could wait until a better time.

'Where do you want to eat?' she asked.

Her tone was calm and he inwardly relaxed at the prospect of an improved Sheila Wallace before him.

'Marcello's in Wilmslow,' he replied without thinking, praying they had a spare table this night.

'The new Italian?'

'The very same!'

'How super,' she said laughing. 'That's almost as good as having this ride in your old car.'

'Hey! Enough of the "old", she's a classic.'

'I'm only kidding, I love classic cars.'

The decor of Marcello's typified many of the Italian restaurants in the area, but the big, and main difference, was Marcello himself: he personally met every single customer at his restaurant, greeted them with such a huge smile and grateful countenance, so that even before you sat down you knew you were going to enjoy the meal and re-book.

Tonight they were in luck and he dexterously led them to their table. Harry scoured the other guests, he was looking for any of the men who had followed him back to his house and been forcibly evicted. Part of him was calmed to find them absent whilst a tiny piece of him wanted to extract brutal revenge for having violated the sanctity of his private space.

He ordered a bottle of Valpolicella, on the recommendation of their waiter and looked straight across the table, clearly designed for the intimacy of two people wanting to eat in quiet consideration of each other. He was taken back, not for the first time, of how beautiful she was.

'Something wrong?' she asked, seeing him looking at her and not speaking.

'Nothing's wrong, nothing's wrong at all.'

She blushed.

'You look beautiful.'

She blushed more.

'Stop it!'

'You don't mean it.'

'Might do!'

The waiter brought over the wine and poured two glasses.

They toasted each other and both took a sip of the smooth red.

Harry smiled: he had the most gorgeous woman in the world at his table and he was happy.

'You know poker?' she asked, changing tack. 'I've never played!'

'Yes, I can play.'

'Good.'

'Then you're job on the night will be to look beautiful and utterly desirable, which you should find comes quite natural, and keep the other players occupied whilst we clean up!'

The crimson returned to her cheeks with a vengeance.

'We?' she finally said.

'Your brother and I: they will welcome him back with open arms if they thought for one moment he was going to drag himself even deeper into the mire. I will stand him his stake, which will cover his original debt.'

Harry sensed the return of Sheila's doubts and her tottering on the verge of vetoing the idea, but she veered off right at the death.

'Can you cover all that?'

'You bet I can!' He had an inheritance to play with, and was going to have some fun.

The waiter politely inquired if they were ready to order. They were.

The remainder of the evening was played out at a delightfully pleasant pace with little or no talk of work, work colleagues, or Stephen, instead they discussed topics and events neither thought the other had any knowledge of, let alone be an expert on, including the classic Porsche 924: he was impressed with her in-depth knowledge of the car, so that by the end of the evening it came as a complete shock to them both to discover there was plenty of common ground on which to base another date.

When it came time to leave he paid and left a sizeable tip, insisting it was his invitation to her and any idea of splitting the bill was anathema to him.

The evening drizzle was a welcome coolant to the two lovebirds and they sauntered off towards his car. Harry contemplated putting his arm around her shoulder, but resisted: he knew part of her detested the idea of dating flight-deck and being the subject of company gossip. A "flight deck floozy" she was not.

She smiled at him and took his left hand in hers. Just goes to show what you know about women, and he smiled back.

When they finally made the Porsche he had managed to stretch the short walk to a full ten minutes. She leant with her back to the passenger door and pulled him towards her.

'Kiss me.'

There was no second invitation needed; the kiss measured the walk in duration and surpassed it for passion: her lips were as sweet as wine, her tongue exploring every inch of his. His head began to spin, and the light-headedness threatened to sabotage all his hard work and bring them both crashing to the ground. She pulled away first and fixed her gaze upon him. He knew there and then that he loved her, would always love her, and be doomed to love her always. Harry kissed her again.

The two lovers were totally oblivious to all those around them, and had not an inkling as to how many passers-by witnessed their embrace, not that either really gave a damn.

Harry fished helplessly for his keys, but her hand beat him to the pocket containing the offending articles and she took the greatest of pleasure in taking her time extracting them. It was unbearable. He loved it.

'You're a naughty girl!'

'Am I?'

'Yeah, and I love it!'

'How naughty do you want?'

'As bad as you can be!'

She grabbed at him, massaging all the while, until he could take it no longer. Harry lifted her up against the side of the car. He was going to have her tonight and right here in the street if need be.

Just as that thought was consuming him, ramming itself deep into his consciousness, the silver saloon materialized, crawling past at a snail's pace, but it was clear they hadn't spotted or weren't looking for them. Out of the corner of his eye he saw it was the same driver, the other three he couldn't quite make out, but was sure the other two were there. There was only one thing for it, and he wasn't about to let this golden opportunity go to waste; he would have to find a quiet spot, as it was now impossible to go home. The car drove by a second time. It was definitely them. Harry held onto another long, moist kiss, but clocked them all.

'In the car!' he said quietly, but forcibly.

'Anything you say,' she replied submissively.

He grabbed her from behind whilst guiding her into her seat.

'Patience Harry, patience.'

'With you, never!'

Before he had chance to close the door, she took him in her hand, massaging him again. He gently pulled himself free, kissed her fully on the lips, sat her inside and closed the door. He was not going to run or be seen to from these people: he'd met them all head on before and would do again.

The drive back to his place should have taken less than fifteen minutes, but the silver saloon appeared in his rear view mirror and never left it. He wished that his glove compartment held another Beretta to dispatch these unwanted intruders. He remained calm. She would never suspect what was really lurking just below his tranquil exterior.

'How's the impatience?' Sheila's question broke his train of thought.

'Wicked!'

He studied his rear view mirror to gauge the saloon's forward speed; they were comfortably keeping pace with them.

'We have company,' Sheila said; the calmness in her voice was a joy to behold. He blew her a kiss.

'Keep buckled up.'

'Clunk, click!' She winked as she pulled at the clip.

Sheila knew what was coming, but still the acceleration along the Alderley Road took her breath away: it may be an ageing, standard two liter Porsche 924, but it pulled hard in every gear, forcing her back into the seat. Initially the chasing car fell back by three or four car lengths then disappeared from view as Harry took a left at a roundabout onto the Manchester Road and onwards towards the motorway. He knew the area around the airport like the back of his hand.

'Airport?' Sheila asked.

'Let's do it!' Harry replied.

Ahead now came two roundabouts. The road straight on towards Heald Green became the Wilmslow Road. Harry indicated right, but accelerated straight on; it was a minor deception and probably did nothing to delay the car behind, as it was a ways back and had plenty of time to adjust. He secretly admonished his own stupidity.

'They'll expect you to turn for home.'

'I know.'

This was the trigger for Harry to drop down a gear and boot the throttle: the Bosch K-Jetronic Fuel Injection System delivered right on cue and their forward speed was impressive to behold. Sheila gripped the passenger door handle and braced herself. Harry took a hard left along Finney Lane towards Heald Green after an annoying set of traffic lights. Next stop the airport. Luck was now to be on their side as the lights turned red, and a police patrol car coming the other way forced the silver saloon to wait.

Harry pulled left into Rosslyn Road.

'What you doing?'

'Cat and mouse. You up for it?'

If she was scared, she hid it well.

A few minutes later the silver saloon drove steadily past. For a split second he panicked in case one of the men should look in their direction: it wouldn't have been difficult to spot a blue Porsche 924, but none of them did and the threat passed.

Harry did a one-eighty degree turn and pulled out into the traffic moving steadily along Finney Lane and held station two cars back. Sheila wrote down the registration and read it out.

Slowly they navigated their way through Heald Green amidst the growing throng of traffic. Harry expected them to veer off at any moment towards his home. The high street drew to a close and the line of traffic never altered by the time they made the traffic lights crossing Styal Road.

'I want revenge!' Sheila said angrily.

'Hell hath no fury-'

'Damn right!'

'They gain strength from anonymity!'

The lights turned green and along with the two cars separating them they turned left onto Styal Road. Harry knew where they were going: the quickest way back to Stockport was east on the M56 motorway before connecting with the M60. Sure enough they drifted into the filter lane to turn right at the lights onto Ringway Road. One of the cars between them carried straight on leaving one remaining car to separate the "cat and mouse". Ringway Road took them north of the airport and Harry felt invigorated: here was another acid test. He would not be found wanting.

The saloon approached a major roundabout that would lead them to the M56 and Harry saw the lights guarding their entry to the roundabout were already green; if they remained as such there was a distinct possibility that they would find themselves flummoxed behind the changing lights. The lights changed to amber as his front wheels crossed the line indicating where to pull up. Harry was driving on instinct now; he knew the roads and his eyes scoured the car in front, watching the driver's head movement. The man checked and re-checked his rear view mirror.

'They have us!' Sheila stated, craning her head to confirm her statement.

'Don't know!'

The saloon never accelerated, but the wider dual carriageway leading onto the motorway allowed him to get a much clearer view of the occupants: they were all in a heated discussion. Excellent, they won't be looking for them and he dropped back another car length to allow a second car to hide their presence.

'They don't look too happy!' Sheila said still trying hard to get a better look.

'At least one of them wants to stake out my place. I would've done.'

'They may still do.'

'Maybe, but I think the driver is of the mind to continue back to base.'

'And crush their anonymity!'

'Precisely!'

The line of cars kept to the right hand lane and the M56 heading east to Stockport.

Here was an area, a skill, Harry needed to improve: it would be real easy to enroll in an advanced driving course without drawing any unwanted attention. Shooting practice was going to prove a lot more problematic, especially once he'd solved his uncle's disappearance: there would be no Tommy to allow him free reign to fire away in the secluded woodlands around his home.

The saloon pulled into the middle lane of the M56 and Harry did the same.

He began to try and second guess them, a dangerous pass time considering the tastes of the occupants and their liking for inflicting a particularly sadistic form of violence on their victims. This time though he was proved correct and the men kept on, eventually taking the M60 turn off. A few miles further down the motorway the saloon indicated left and took the exit heading for Cheadle.

There were now no cars between them and "Roscoe's Roundabout", which marked the end of the exit road and was named by the locals after a timber merchant who used to have a warehouse near-by. The roundabout looked busy; Harry prayed they would carry on across it regardless and then he could take his chances catching up, or that the level of traffic might reduce. The latter came to his rescue and they managed to enter the roundabout with a small white van now separating them. All three vehicles took the second exit along the A560 Stockport Road.

Harry was approaching unchartered territory: this was not a part of town he knew all that well, and it left him little capacity to concentrate on the car and the road. Luckily for him they all maintained station. Harry dropped well back. The saloon never deviated, but he anticipated a further turn. It came after a failure to indicate a left into Swythamley Road and eventually parking up outside a semi-detached house with an expensive Mercedes in the driveway. The van carried on. Harry pulled in on the left hand side and watched them enter the house.

'Funny, I never pictured them working from a semi!' Harry said quietly.

'Arrogance has been their undoing!' Sheila went to open her car door.

'You stay here while I take a look.'

'Not likely!'

Harry wasn't given any chance to reply. Sheila was out of the car and up the road in a flash. It was all he could do to lock the car and run after her before she made the drive of the large semi.

'You're being reckless!' Harry said through gritted teeth.

'You don't have to be here if you don't want to!'

He was incensed by the remark, but bit his lip. In future he was going to work alone and especially without any clients or family in tow.

Sheila slowed and began to study the semi-detached house in great detail; what she was expecting to find or more to the point do anything about, he had not a clue. He dropped back a pace or two. Harry needed the breathing space.

Nobody left the house.

Harry sauntered past with one eye on a gap in the curtains, allowing him invaluable access to one of the front rooms; he made out two of the men from the car in an argument, with a third man unknown to him acting as some kind of peacemaker.

Sheila stopped and remained out of sight.

'Well?' she asked once he'd caught up, the impatience for any kind of news clearly evident in her tone.

'Clocked two of them, but there is a third man.'

'He must be the ring leader!'

'We don't know that, but it does mean they are five not four.'

'Yes we do, they came here for him!' Sheila was getting agitated that their journey was going to be wasted.

'We just need to be patient and all will be revealed in good time.'

'Look Harry, I am not standing here like a complete cretin waiting for those fucking morons to make their move!'

'What are you going to do?'

She paused before letting rip with another onslaught.

'Patience,' Harry restated.

As if preordained one of the men exited the house, unlocked their vehicle with the remote, and began to rummage around in the back.

Harry pulled Sheila out of sight behind a hedge.

'If he goes back inside we'll have a few minutes to reach our car and make ready.'

The man found what he was looking for and returned inside. The door had no sooner closed and they were off.

'We shan't wait,' he said making his car, unlocking both doors and jumping inside. Sheila slid into the passenger seat.

'Why not?'

'Because I know where they're going!'

'Your place or mine?'

'I never thought you'd ask.'

She laughed and asked again.

'Mine! That man has a mark on his forehead courtesy of my putter.'

Harry pulled away, swinging the Porsche through a one-eighty degree turn. He didn't have to wait long for the saloon appeared shortly after in his mirrors carrying the original four occupants.

Harry thanked his luck when a small line of cars appeared between him and them. He took the third exit off the roundabout and continued on the A560 Stockport Road, accelerating hard. Sheila was about to ask why the turn, but a sign reading Heald Green put paid to that. Harry prayed they wouldn't think of taking this route; he regularly checked his mirrors, but after a few minutes of a no show he was content they had taken the motorway.

'What are you going to do when they turn up?'

'Still giving it some thought. I know one thing though, you won't be there.'

'Oh yes I will!' The agitated tone returned with a vengeance.

'It's too dangerous. We don't know what they are capable of.'

'I do!'

'Okay,' he replied. He knew it was pointless to try and argue. 'But you do what I say!'

'On this occasion I grant you that!'

'Thank you.'

'I'll say this Harry: a date with you is never boring!'

They made good time to Baslow Drive: the Porsche 924's superior handling making light work of the roads. He parked the car out of sight and entered leaving the lights off with no visible signs of life.

The time it took for the four men to pull up outside seemed like an eternity, but was in reality a little over ten minutes after their arrival, and in those valuable ten little minutes Harry composed himself sufficiently enough to see, in the crystal clear light, that here was the first step in the initial blooding of Harry Travers Private Detective on home soil; yes he had already got embroiled in one dust up, which meant they would be prepared for an all-out assault, but not in as much that it would attract the unwanted attention of the neighbors. Knives, as before: maximum damage with the least amount of noise.

He checked on Sheila, who was sitting pensively on the sofa, which ran parallel to the one of the main windows backing onto the road on the first floor. He had chosen his favorite armchair facing the television and preferred to listen to the passing traffic. It was uncanny how he could recognize every single vehicle passing by his window by the engine noise.

His mind focused on the ensuing battle. They would go for the throat: that the killing blow is to the left side of the neck due to the proximity of the heart. This is not to say that an injury to the right side won't prove fatal, it was just more fruitful to aim for that side. He surreptitiously got up and glided through to the kitchen, opened a large drawer and removed two medium sized knives then carefully placed them out of sight in the television room. If Sheila saw what he was up to or had any inkling to his train of thought, she kept it to herself.

A different engine noise stopped him in his tracks. It held his attention as the revs died down and finally stopped.

Sheila went to say something, but Harry lifted a finger to his lips and lithely positioned himself to the right side of the window.

'Is it them?' Sheila whispered.

Harry peered through a gap in the curtains that gave a restricted view of his driveway. Two of the men carelessly approached his front door; one he recognized, as the man knocked down his stairs. So they thought he was that easy? Harry pulled his head back and nodded once in anger. If it wasn't for the seriousness of the situation it would be almost comical.

'Where should I go?' asked Sheila.

'Stay here.'

Harry expeditiously went to the top of the stairs leading to the ground floor, running over in his head the mental security checklist: all was locked as tight as a drum and the game would indeed be played on his terms. He could defend his home within reasonable limits and a break-in would prove ideal if faced with a police investigation.

A scratching sound emanating from the rear of the house brought a smile to his face. They had abandoned the front door and were attempting to jimmy a window. The scratching ceased after a few minutes and the disappointment in their pathetic failure was almost tangible. Harry began to feel frustrated at their lack of success and he quietly made his way to check on Sheila, only to find her crouching by the window trying desperately hard to get a better view of proceedings. He knelt down beside her.

'We're still safe,' he whispered.

'I want them to enter; you haven't left a window open have you?'

'I don't think so.'

He ran over his mental checklist once more and it only confirmed what he already knew. The house was secure.

'Then open one!'

Sheila's last statement shocked him to his core; she was sincere in her wish for the two men to enter the house. What so she could kill them? He gave the request a good deal of thought and his lack of decisiveness angered his date.

'Open a window!' she said forcibly.

'No!' came the sharp reply.

'Why not?'

'Because you're not thinking straight; you want revenge for Stephen, I can understand that-'

'And?'

'And they need to break in!'

Whether it was this assertion or not he wasn't too sure, but she clearly cooled in her desire.

'If they get in under their own volition, then so be it, if not they'll be other days. Their anonymity is crushed and we can return fire at any time.'

Harry had no sooner finished talking than the scratching returned with a vengeance and he slipped off once more to keep tabs on the rear of the house. The thought of any repair bill floating its way towards him nearly forced him to run down the final few steps and confront the two men, but he calmed his rising vexation with the clear determination to use all experiences to the greater good of advancing his education. Once more the scratching stopped and their voices were heard in a heated discussion.

'Damn good double glazing!' he heard one of them say.

If you want their number you can have it. Harry laughed at his little joke.

The scratching returned a third time, and his inexperience in such matters told him this was going to be their Alamo: if the window held out it was going to be a quiet night, if not there would be a death in the family.

After a continued fruitless effort to break in they finally ceased and Harry let out a groan. How could they be so inept? If they were supposed to be these hardened criminals then why not try another window? But if they couldn't break this one then what chance a second? He had to remain focused until the men had definitely departed.

Sheila suddenly appeared behind him and whispered in his ear. They had left. Taking the gamble she was right he made for the front door, unlocked it and put himself in full view. Their car was nowhere to be seen.

12

The rest of the evening turned into an unmitigated disaster: Sheila was for going home there and then to check on her brother, as it had been amiss of her not to warn him of any impending danger, and why had Harry not taken into consideration the notion that both houses were to be hit simultaneously. It was his fault, he should have called the police the moment they had tried to break into his house and then this would all be a distant memory. Harry made a mental note to keep any future ideas on a need to know basis, but unfortunately dinner with a beautiful woman loosens the tongue faster than alcohol.

The return journey to Sheila's was silent, uncomfortable at best, and for the first time he couldn't wait to get away and back to his place for a stiff drink.

As luck would have it they found Stephen alone and he'd been that way all evening. In fact his own night's entertainment had been sorely interrupted by their return and he wasn't slow in coming forward in informing his sister.

Harry took a backward step, eyeing her front door and the outside world jealously; this fight was going to be more troublesome and problematic than with the two miscreants he envisaged doing battle with little under an hour ago.

'Thanks!' shouted Stephen.

'You're welcome!' was her reply.

Harry should have been paying more attention to the siblings and not his desire to be gone, for the look Sheila shot at him was the stuff of legend.

'I'll be going then,' he said, slinging his thumb in the direction of the door.

'You do that!' was the acerbic response from his date.

He left without saying another word.

Once home it didn't take him long to pour a large measure of Jack Daniels: he needed this sharpener more than anything and the smooth, sweet liquid chilled his agitated bones sufficiently to guarantee a good night's sleep.

* * *

The check-in time for the flight to Heraklion in Crete was 13:00, returning around 01:00. Looking down the names of his crew he discovered, to his delight, that Curtis Traherne was the first officer. He felt comfortable of a pleasant day's work.

That night he suspected his somnolence to be disturbed, after not being called off standby, but was more than pleasantly surprised to discover his awakening the result of a preset alarm clock. He had a burning desire for coffee and was up and out of bed in an instant.

It was still too early for today's post, but the previous day's deliveries were neatly piled by the phone on a table to the right of the television and he opened each one in turn while the kettle came to the boil. The grand total was nothing, but the usual bills and junk mail.

He knew his constitution well enough to appreciate that one cup of coffee would never satisfy him and two was just enough to wake him up without running to the bathroom every five minutes. Breakfast today was going to be his favorite: two soft boiled eggs, three slices of uncut bread and butter with the salt shaker handy, for when the moment took him, followed by yet another cup of coffee.

Standing with hands on hips, showered, dressed and fed, Harry delayed departing and instead watched with increased trepidation all the coming and goings down his street: he knew they must return, it was a matter of time, only now there was going to be no Sheila to spur him on to victory. Deep in his heart he had yearned for the two miscreants to break-in that night if only to show her in some foolishly, adolescent way how brave he was in defending her, and the disappointment of not being granted his wish slowly, but perceptibly, ate away inside him destroying now his will to fight when the time came. But time is a great healer, so his conscience subtly informed him, and time was most definitely on his side for when he finally did leave the house for the journey to the airport he was emboldened once again to protect his person and property. It came to a point, as he turned left at the bottom of his road that he positively wished for the silver saloon to ram his car off the road and the fight to begin.

* * *

'Hi Harry!' Curtis called out with the printer spewing out page after page off pre-flight brief. 'Been busy?'

Harry shook his head. 'Dead quiet!' He laughed at his unintended joke.

Curtis handed him the flight paperwork for his perusal.

'I'm working my ass off!' Curtis added. 'Not that I'm complaining, you understand, got a shiny new "boy's toy" to pay for!'

'What!' Harry ceased perusing in response to the boast. 'You got a porker?'

'Sure have: the latest nine-eleven straight of the production line.'

'How much overtime you been doing?'

'None, until now, but I am blissfully broke!'

The rest of the crew filtered past, offering salutations as they did so. Harry confirmed the gate number and passed on the flight times to the cabin manager.

'You won the lottery?'

'Inheritance!'

Harry immediately thought of his Uncle Jack.

'A lovely auntie left me a tasty little pile, so I thought what the hell, I've always wanted one, so I bought one,' Curtis said before adding gleefully. 'It's black with a black and red leather interior.'

'Fantastic!'

Curtis shrugged his shoulders and smiled.

Harry couldn't blame him for keeping that private.

'You're taking it out, so you choose the fuel. Just make sure you can justify it!' Like all captains he had a figure in his head of the acceptable minimum fuel that he wished to depart with.

Curtis rattled off his thinking behind the amount of fuel he wanted to carry, which towed the line perfectly with his and the fuel was ordered without any further delay along with the figures being forwarded to their ground handlers to print off the load-sheet.

The walk to the gate was now proving to be a drag due to improvements in passenger shopping, and now took a little over fifteen minutes with every step grating against his normally affable disposition; not that he was against passengers having a far greater choice with which to spend their money, as long as it didn't impact on the crew getting to the aircraft. Why? He said, until even he was sick and tired of hearing it, could there not be a dedicated crew channel which bypassed the terminal and cut down the time wasted between crew-room and gate, especially as time and departure slots, and the failure to make them, was now a serious issue.

Curtis chuckled to himself after yet another mini rant.

'What?'

'You!'

'Don't get me going!'

'You crack me up!'

'Don't, don't!'

Any further discourse was temporarily cut short by negotiating security, and the long, long drudge through the never ending shopping experience laid out before the eagle-eyed passenger just waiting for any excuse to dent the plastic and part with their hard earned holiday wad of notes.

The gate finally, and thankfully, loomed large in the distance, directing them to their salvation.

Again Curtis chuckled.

'What now?'

'You're right, you're dead right!'

Once on the air-bridge they expeditiously made their way onto the aircraft and the cheery countenances of the cabin manager and her crew; he was always so very grateful that they possessed such great crew who were a privilege to work with and made the personal torture behind them fade away almost instantly.

What precious time they managed to protect was eaten up with pre-flight business while boarding began. Harry watched after his walk-around the eager and not so eager faces of their passengers desperately wanting to be on their way to sun, sea and the one or two weeks that made the rest of the year remotely bearable. He envied them and thanked them in equal measure, for without their annual vacation in the sun he was out of a job.

With time to their departure slot evaporating like early morning mist, they closed all the doors, after Harry gave a welcome on board PA, pushed back and started engines. Once pushback was complete the tug was disconnected and he cleared the agent to remove the pin. Seconds later they showed him the bypass pin and Harry waved them off.

It was busy for a Wednesday afternoon and it took a few minutes to request taxi clearance for runway 23 left, but once attained they wasted no time getting under way.

The line of departing aircraft was four deep at the holding point, but both were comforted with the knowledge that Air Traffic Control would get them airborne as close to their departure slot as possible.

All the checks and briefs were completed once they'd crossed the landing runway 23 right, and almost immediately the controller cleared them to line up after a quick explanation to the other waiting departures they had an Air Traffic slot to make.

Curtis was flying the outbound sector, and once he'd lined up the Airbus A320 on the runway centerline, and heard Harry read back their takeoff clearance, he called out takeoff before standing the thrust levers up to about 50 percent N1. Harry replied with a call of stable, which signaled Curtis to the set takeoff thrust. Early in the career of the novice airline pilot the adrenalin rush is almost palpable, similar to that of a racing driver waiting for the flag to drop or lights to extinguish and the race to begin, but as flying experienced is gained, and hours accumulated, the mental powers grow with a clearly discernible ability to absorb all that is changing around you and keep valuable capacity in reserve while focusing on the job. The act of flying therefore becomes natural; there is no substitute to the physical act of flying, logging hour after hour, subconsciously absorbing the aircraft's behavior under all flying conditions, so that the pilot's responses to these swings in aircraft temperament is instinctive leaving them comforted in the knowledge that if the worst should happen then they are ready to act accordingly and follow the procedures practiced half-yearly in the simulator.

The Airbus A320 launched into the air after another blissfully uneventful departure and Harry moved the gear handle to the up position. Minutes later the flaps and slats were neatly tucked in and the wing was "clean". They accelerated following the Standard Instrument Departure designated for that runway and the direction they were flight-planned to follow.

Harry began to relax and enjoy the day: even after all these years, the sheer exhilaration of taking-off and landing fed his constitution, but it still required a few moments of self-reflection now that it had not been called upon to delve deep into the locker marked "For Emergencies Only".

As air travel expanded with the growing need, desire, of the general public to experience the exotic, hot climates of lands foreign, so the structure of the airspace above them equally grew to accommodate that need. The upshot was that more and more speed and altitude restrictions were imposed on airspace to allow the safe transition from Instrument Departure to the climb and cruise segments thus guaranteeing separation of the arriving and departing traffic. Whereas in days gone by a continuous climb to cruising altitude may take little under half an hour, now it wasn't uncommon to be climbing for nearly forty minutes with the resultant fuel burn to boot. This priceless commodity was all the more valuable when arriving at airports accommodating heavy traffic loads during rush hour, and then be asked to descend early, slow down sooner, and take up a hold at designated points before being given permission to make an approach to land. It never failed to make Harry laugh when the "green army", as he called them, started trumpeting on about the environment, noise pollution, greenhouse gases and the effect commercial flying had on it, and then as sure as eggs is eggs went on holiday. Never at any time had he heard someone stand up and publicly state, the indefatigable truth, that flying was the most fuel efficient, per mile travelled, mode of transport. He pictured these "greenies" driving their cars or more hypocritically ordering a taxi to the airport or train station, so they could transpose that guilt on the poor soul working all the hours God gave to make a living and therefore enjoy their vacation free from vexation. His quiet, rant aided and abetted the relaxation period.

The cabin manager, Rebecca Lawler, contacted them at the designated time, and offered the usual array of refreshments. Both men placed their order.

'Everything okay?' Harry asked a few minutes later after granting her access to the cockpit.

'Got a party of six boys giving it more than just a glancing blow!' Rebecca said, handing both men their respective drinks. Her weary tone was not lost on either of them. 'Had the same last week!'

'You happy to serve them drinks?'

'They're not causing any bother right now, but I'll keep you informed if the situation deteriorates. Why is it always Heraklion, and always on my flights!'

'You've got to deal with them, we don't.'

Rebecca made a polite enquiry if they needed anything else, and when the answer was in the negative, left without further delay.

'Why do some people always feel the need to treat this like a flying pub? Don't get me wrong, I'm all for having a good time and enjoying the flying experience, and if that means a few sharpeners then great, but don't get bloody wasted!'

Curtis grunted an approval, but before Harry could further wax lyrical on passenger decorum, he replied to the controller's instruction to change frequency, so that by the time he had checked in with the next sector the moment had passed.

Being a creature of habit Harry had his daily routine which he abided by no matter what. It was a pattern that he had fallen into subconsciously over the years, and with his disposition, gratefully accepted as an antidote to the stresses and strains the job placed on his body clock: first came the hot cup of tea, needed to accompany the sandwich chosen from the delicious fare presented to them by Rebecca during the pre-flight phase, which was inevitably doused in lashings of Tabasco sauce; then there was the low fat crisps, a small treat he allowed himself; another was to pamper to his weakness for

Jack Daniels whenever the opportunity arose: it was one of the drawbacks of old age to compensate his inability to consume the volume of beer that had enriched nights out in his younger days, so he counteracted this shortfall by drinking whiskey. It was a classic case of quality over quantity, but where possible, as his culinary skills were almost non-existent, he chose what he ate sensibly.

After a few sips of tea and the first nibbling of crisps, he took the initial bite of the recently prepared fiery sandwich. It made him remember the beer and pizza with Tommy. So much for the diet, he pondered between mouthfuls.

A further frequency change ensued and this became the pattern now for the cruise segment, only punctured by the regular thirty minute fuel checks, and the crew ringing in to find out if they were okay: both men took the advantage to order more tea and coffee, and ask for their outbound meals, which they were informed would be ready shortly. Harry enquired as to those passengers at risk of falling foul of Rebecca's wroth. So far, so good was the reply.

The flight was a little under three hours old when the inevitable occurred and Rebecca buzzed to come in.

'Here we go!' exclaimed Harry, unlocking the door once he ascertained who had buzzed to request entry.

Rebecca entered briskly with that look of someone who has seen it all before, but now seriously can't be arsed,

'Your boys kicking off?'

'Oh no, they're as good as gold. We've got three forty-something women obviously out for a good time causing mayhem, who we suspect of drinking their own alcohol. One of them is totally trashed, a second decided to sit on the legs of the man over the aisle from her, much to the annoyance of his wife, and a third feels the need to shout at everybody!'

'Lovely,' Harry said sarcastically. 'I take it they've been politely asked not to and warned about drinking their own alcohol?'

'Sure have, and been advised that they will not be served anymore!'

Curtis looked on with an air of resignation.

'Do you need me to make a PA?'

'No, not yet, just wanted to keep you informed.'

There wasn't much else to add at this juncture and following the obligatory raised eyebrows, plus a knowing look that it will only end one way, Rebecca went back into the cabin.

'What did you say earlier about a flying pub?' Curtis finally said once they were alone again.

'Good time girls,' was all Harry could muster.

During the next few minutes Harry sat awaiting the inescapable next installment: disruptive passengers were the bane of the cabin crew's existence, and most involved alcohol at some point, but so far the three ladies were only threat level one due to their disorderly behavior and the invasion of another passenger's personal space. The loud, garrulous one would be right up his street: it was a trait he abhorred in anyone intoxicated, nothing would give him greater pleasure than to put them firmly in their place.

The request to enter the cabin interrupted his thoughts; he was expecting it, had mentally prepared himself for the occasion and seeing Rebecca's face knew that the heavy handed approach was called for.

'We need the police to meet us in Heraklion, don't we?'

Rebecca nodded: 'The wife has just laid one of them out; the language would make a sailor blush.'

'You want me to make a PA now?'

With this physical abuse, albeit from the wife, meant the threat level had now escalated to level two with consideration given to a possible diversion to the nearest suitable airport, but as they were approaching Heraklion the logical course of action was to continue onwards to their planned destination.

'No, believe it or not that calmed everything down. Better get back.'

Once she was gone Harry gave the delivery of his possible announcement serious thought. He liked to deliver the kind of rebuking PA's that just hinted at the annoyance he felt at having to make them in the first place, but all thankfully remained quiet.

Just prior to top of descent Rebecca buzzed once again to enter the cockpit to be the bearer of even more bad news: the three friends were now mortal enemies, each blaming each other for the horrid beginning to their holiday and some of the crew had to keep them apart.

'Just do what you can, Rebecca,' Harry said shaking his head. 'We're starting our descent now.' He made the request with the controller, but was told to standby.

'Hopefully once we start going down and the seat belt signs goes on they'll shut the hell up!' smiled Rebecca. 'Well here's hoping! See you on the ground.' And with that she went back into the cabin.

Harry passed on responsibility for dealing with air traffic to Curtis and used the second radio to call ahead to their handling agent so they could request the police to meet the aircraft when parked on stand and advised them on how many wheelchair passengers needed assistance. Once back he resumed responsibility of the radios.

The descent into Heraklion requires anticipation and careful planning more than most with failure to do so invariably meaning you ended up several thousand feet high on the profile.

The controller finally came back to them clearing them down to a level only a few thousand feet below their current one due to another aircraft going to the same destination.

'Bugger!' snapped Harry on hearing the restricted clearance.

'I expected nothing less!' added Curtis, realizing there could be only one logical outcome to their predicament. He didn't have to wait long; the controller gave them a south-westerly heading to gain separation on the lower aircraft.

'Bugger!' Harry said again laughing.

The A320 majestically turned right with the two pilots monitoring the track of the other traffic; the major advantage of the heading change was the bonus of the extra miles needed to lose the height, the downside was the added minutes to their arrival and a possible reduced turnaround time.

Far off in the distance the street lights of Heraklion beckoned them on. Finally the controller turned them left direct to the waypoint signifying the beginning of the arrival onto the landing runway 27. The lower aircraft was now more than ten miles ahead and clearly heading for the same final approach fix.

The left turn instantly evaporated the miles-in-hand making them over three thousand feet high on the approach, but Curtis used the managed descent option to successfully bring the aircraft back on profile.

Below ten thousand feet the island began to reveal more of its illuminated contours and colors standing out against the calm Mediterranean Sea like a beacon.

Harry monitored the descent, Curtis was doing a fine job, and it allowed him time to enjoy this phase of the flight. Both men had been here many times and knew the pitfalls well. Once established inbound on the Non-Precision Instrument Approach with the PAPI lights visible, reading now only marginally high on the profile, which was expected, Curtis disengaged the autopilot and hand flew the rest of the way.

The controller cleared them to land.

Both men were aware, and in full anticipation, in the change of perspective that accompanies the final stages of the approach to runway 27 on this largest of the Greek Islands, as the landing lights illuminate the cliff face on short finals. It is one of the vagaries of landing on island runways when the airport is so close to the coast and added to this is the marked upslope on runway 27 in the first 500 meters. That alone has been the ruin of many a day.

Below a hundred feet Curtis mentally prepared for landing and listened for the radio altimeter call-outs. At the desired point he checked the rate of descent in order to obtain the required touch down; as a rule he flared slightly sooner at Heraklion, due to the rise in the runway increasing the effective rate of descent. The A320 kissed the runway and he gently lowered the nose before applying full reverse thrust. With the ground spoilers extended the auto-brake system kicked in and their forward speed rapidly reduced. At the required point the reversers were stowed, brakes reverted to manual and the spoilers disarmed before they taxied off. Both men began to relax on completion of the After Landing Checklist, but not fully as the apron was busy tonight and the two pairs of eyes worked overtime before Harry, as captain, took control to bring the jet safely onto stand with the help of a marshaller. Finally, he shut down the number two engine followed by the number one, once he was happy the auxiliary power unit was taking the electrical load.

Once it was confirmed between Harry and Rebecca that all the doors were disarmed, it was time to deal with the three contrary ladies: Rebecca had relayed to him they were still, in her words, kicking off.

Harry made a PA for all passengers to remain seated.

The arrival of the police had the effect of disconcerting most passengers: there were the few who panicked momentarily lest it was something they said or did, but secretly in the back of their minds were comforted by the fact that no words were exchanged between them and the crew; then there were those who loathed any and all kinds of confrontation; followed by the majority who saw it as nothing but an annoying inconvenience delaying them from basking in the delights there vacation offered and was being withheld by the belligerence of a minority.

Harry met two police officers by one door left. A hush descended over the cabin; if they couldn't be on their way to the terminal and vacation time then a ring side seat for the cabin's inhabitants was a good substitute.

The three ladies visibly sank into their seats when approached by the first Greek officer. The second remained by the forward galley. The three good time girls, followed by the wife, made their way forward when instructed to hand over their passports and boarding cards for records to be made. Not one volunteered a single word unless spoken to. The whole episode took a little over ten minutes, and throughout not a raised voice was to be heard, only abject apologize for any behavior that was clearly out of the norm for these normally law abiding citizens.

Rebecca and the officers accepted their contriteness along with the sincerity with which it was offered, and they were allowed to leave escorted by the police for a little heart to heart before being permitted to enter the country. This was the signal for the flood gates to open. The buses were waiting patiently outside for the rest of the passengers to be transported to the terminal.

Thankfully for all concerned the turnaround was swift and professionally handled, which meant they called for engine start ten minutes early, and coupled with the good flight time home would be back ahead of schedule.

The homeward sector was quiet: the passengers having checked out of their hotels earlier in the day slept most of the way home, and as expected in no time at all they were back on home soil and starting the long walk to the crew-room.

Harry, whenever a flight seemed to dissolve before his very eyes, began to wonder where the day had gone? Where was his life going? What about all the dreams and aspirations he had harbored as a child? Had he abandoned them that easily? Forsaken them for the mighty dollar? The shroud of melancholia enveloped him, blinding his view of the path his life had trod and would proceed along. He was one of the lucky ones: he had a job that was the envy of most; worked with some of the most beautiful women he had ever seen, bar working in show business there wasn't a vocation around that promised that; travelled the world; had plenty of spare time at his disposal; and was paid handsomely for the pleasure. What did he have to complain about? His childhood fantasy of becoming a formula one racing driver was never going to be a reality, but the excitement his job gave him more than made up for it, and now here was another opportunity to delve into the world of the adrenalin junky. He would only accept cases, he decided, that would fuel that need.

'You okay Harry?' asked Curtis.

'Yeah, fine. Was miles away!'

'You looked it.'

The rest of the crew failed to notice, and the team of seven passed through passport control without any hassle and arrived in the crew-room eager to be on their way home. Forty five minutes later with all the relevant paperwork submitted, including the Air Safety Report detailing the outbound incident, Harry and Curtis parted company before Harry said his goodbyes to the crew, leaving them to the final stages of their own post-flight paperwork.

For the first time that day since leaving the house he thought of Sheila, but now it was difficult, nigh on impossible to summon even the slightest hint of emotion. He chastised himself for allowing tiredness to dull his senses, but however hard he tried she was dead to him.

The car park bus arrived and he boarded. Sheila invaded his thoughts again when he recollected the men in the saloon and their night out. It had the effect of immediately placing him on guard lest they should have been smart enough to lie in wait for him knowing he was not at his place of residence. It wouldn't have taken much to ascertain how he made his living and sought the patience to set a trap, but there was no one around today. He buoyed his flagging spirits with the realization that he outwardly exhibited no fear instead he positively relished the thought of doing battle and experiencing the trauma of pain gained through combat. Was this the acceptable norm? Was he finally beginning the transformation into the private investigator he believed he should become? How far did he have to go? His impatience angered him: don't run before you can walk, he told himself. He was the only soul on the bus, and the driver was too busy listening to a discussion on the radio to be bothered with him. Tommy, he had to contact Tommy. Now he was pissed off. He had failed to make steady contact with his friend. That would soon be rectified.

13

He woke staring at the ceiling, imagining patterns, swirling, forming around the shadows reflected by the mid-morning light filtering though the blinds. It was three or four in the morning before he managed to get to sleep after sending Tommy an e-mail. Where in the past he was eager to read the reply, now his growing maturity in these matters was displaying its worth: there was nothing he could do right now even if there was a crisis.

He fell out of bed. Tonight he was off to Bodrum, again. Oh, joy of joys, the very delight of a working day: a night flight to Bodrum, Turkey. His lamentations were short lived when he checked his roster online: a change signaled an evening on standby followed by a day flight to Las Palmas. The day had begun well.

Harry made the obligatory coffee whilst breakfast boiled away and he read his e-mails. Sure enough Tommy had replied. All was quiet and had been since he departed. This left him feeling a little disgruntled, for if it remained a stalemate then any future disturbance from this norm would be placed firmly at his feet, deflecting any recriminations away from the guilty parties. He fired back a guarded e-mail, paying particular attention not to state the obvious lest any third parties should intercept it and use this evidence against him. He hoped his friend would get the general gist.

One aspect of private investigation that became immediately obvious and would require patience, were the 'dead' moments: long periods of time where it was plainly obvious nothing happened or was going to happen. No wonder most of the PI's drank too much, he thought, while munching on his egg covered toast, they were bored stupid more than half the time. It reminded him of his job: an old instructor once remarked that an hour's flying consisted of fifty minutes of boredom flanked on either side by five minutes of stark terror. He was going to love being a private investigator, he'd fit right in; any 'dead' moments would be spent usefully attempting to source further information to his uncle's business dealings although it did beg the question where to begin if he wasn't going to talk to Jeffries, but this after all was what investigating was all about.

Within the hour Tommy replied. He got it and concurred.

Harry lazed around the house watching television whilst constantly fighting with the idea of calling Sheila, who wasn't listed on his latest roster. There would be no opportunities in the near future to touch base with her. He was completely in the dark as to whether she liked him or ever liked him: had she played him just to get her brother out of a jam? Was he the sucker in all of this? For a split second he hated Stephen, but it was folly to blame that idiot, he had after all been the root cause of his getting the date in the first place, but the hatred still crept back, skulking in under the radar. Why? He couldn't tell you, but it was there niggling away at him. What if Stephen was the linchpin behind all of this? Why not stakeout Sheila's? They know he's there. The money, what about the money? He went and made another coffee, completely ignoring the film just about to start on the TV.

'The money!' he said quietly. Then almost as if a hammer blow had been struck inside his head along with the caveat to wake up and stop being so stupid.

He sipped the coffee, and it all became clear. The house phone rang and he answered straight away. It was crewing: he was back on the Bodrum with a standby duty to follow.

The drive to the airport reflected the rest of the day in that it became an all-consuming reflection on Stephen's case punctuated with trying to figure out how best to agitate the necessary parties. By the time the bus arrived to whisk him and the other workers to the airport he was happy that a plan of action was formulating in his head and he'd have it licked by the end of his working day. That, thankfully, went without any undue hindrance or complications, and he pulled into his drive, in the twilight hours, jaded and not in the mood for what awaited him lying on his doormat. It was a note from Stephen. How he knew he wasn't too sure, it was that gut feeling one gets when you're being dealt a duff hand and your opponent holds a full house.

Harry ascended the stairs, holding the letter between the index finger and thumb of his right hand. He furiously flicked it onto the kitchen table, once in the kitchen. He left his flight bag on the sofa along with his jacket.

'Fucking prick!' It hadn't taken long for the anger to rise to the point of exclamation. He made a coffee.

'Jumped up, fucking little prick!'

He prayed his outbursts would signal some deep remorse for thinking ill of the lad, but all his instincts were calling out to him, taking the greatest of pleasures in informing him that he was to be bitterly disappointed.

Harry opened the letter and his eyes immediately gravitated towards the signature at the bottom of the second page. It was from Stephen.

Composing himself he sipped his coffee and read the letter.

The first line was all it took before the much needed sanctuary of a breather and a brief moment to calm and remind himself that he was a professional.

Stephen wasted little or no time getting down to the point, which revolved around his not wanting, no almost demanding no more help from Harry or his detective friend. He paused a second time, should he call Sheila and try to ascertain whether she was behind this bullshit or not? He chose to read on. By the time this mini debacle was over it was plainly obvious she was not. This caused him another dilemma. He drained the cooler remnants of his coffee before taking one huge stride towards the drinks cabinet: he could feel a thirst of biblical proportions about to come over him. He stopped short. That would have to wait.

The five or so hours' sleep he managed was sufficient to allow any lingering fog in his head to clear and select the most acceptable course of action.

Harry showered, got dressed and ate a late lunch before leaving for his chosen destination. Five minutes down the road his mobile burst into life.

'Harry Travers,' he opened with, without feeling the need to even bother checking whose number was illuminated on the screen.

'Hello Harry!'

The voice was the one person subjecting his disposition to the utmost consternation. 'Hi Sheila, you okay?'

'Fine!'

'What can I do for you?' It was a formal reply, he was playing it cagey.

There was a short pause, which failed to shake his imperturbability.

'Have you received a letter from Stephen?'

'No!' He answered quickly and decisively, wanting to gauge her reaction.

'You will. He went through my things to get your address.'

'What does it say?' He put his mobile on hands free.

'It's a kiss off letter!'

'Oh, is it? How do you feel about it?'

'He's an idiot! But he's my brother.'

Harry smiled at her reply. He figured he'd heard that song somewhere.

'What do you want me to do with it if and when I get it?' He was not feeling any kind of remorse lying to her, she only saw her younger sibling in trouble and not the big picture, or she didn't want to admit that her brother was really that big an asshole.

'Ignore it!'

'Okay!'

He was approaching his destination and slowed to scour the road for an appropriate parking space.

'What are you up to?' she asked in that interrogating fashion people do when they suspect you're up to something, but for the life of them can't figure it out.

'Shopping!' It was a blatant lie, but he was beginning to enjoy pampering to his mendacious side.

'If you're not too busy maybe we could meet up later.'

'Sure.' He needed an opening to help him sign off. Sheila came to his aid.

'Well, I got to go. Give me a call when you're done.'

'I will.'

'Please do.' And she hung up.

Harry found a convenient parking space in the Q-Park Piazza in Central Manchester, and sat pondering his next move: no more than a ten minute walk away, sat the casino. He opened the glove compartment and removed a leather pouch, but not before he scouted the immediate vicinity to guarantee no-one was spying on him. He unzipped it and took out two thousand pounds in twenty pound notes. This was his emergency fund that had sat gathering dust for years and was now earmarked for the poker table, but if it came to it blackjack would do. He wanted to get a feel for the general ambience and the clientele without drawing attention to himself. Ten minutes later Harry stood at the entrance to Nero's, and without a second thought embarked on his self-made mission.

The casino foyer was dimly lit; he must acclimatize, he thought, and wondered aimlessly for a few minutes studying the décor: it was in fake nineteen-twenties Art Deco with a white ceiling accompanying gold and silver patterned walls; any appreciation for the interior designer's efforts were shamelessly cut short by the cold, icy stare of one of the doorman burying itself into his back. It was best to enter.

Harry used his driver's license as proof of identification then duly registered as a member; it was one of the quirks, he reluctantly accepted, that one needed to be a member here to gamble away your life savings. Once completed he fully expected to be accosted by the occupants of the silver saloon, but this he dispelled on the grounds of their not wanting to "Shit on their own doorstep". He chuckled at the expression his grandmother had first used, but this only brought him to the doorman's attention once again.

Expeditiously he entered the casino proper, studying it in every detail: it offered 24 hour gaming, dining and a late night bar. He approached the blackjack tables. Games were in progress, but he needed to act smart and not on a whim. Each of the tables had been color coded to signify which table required a higher minimum bet and therefore a higher maximum. Hedging this was a must along with avoiding the shoe tables, but at the same time don't be flash and draw attention onto oneself. He naturally gravitated over to one of the tables offering a twenty-five pound minimum bet with a hundred pound maximum. Harry waited for a game to finish, and attempted to display a keenness to participate. It did the trick and the doorman left to follow another.

Suspicious lot, he mused, and scoured the casino for the main poker table. It was not immediately obvious. He exchanged around five hundred pounds for chips in denominations of five, ten and twenty-five pounds, paying particular attention not to let it be known he had more and then studied the piles of chips of the other players. They were not faring well, but now was not a time to procrastinate.

His immediate hands were played conservatively, too conservatively for his liking resulting in his pile being a hundred lighter.

'This is ridiculous!' he said quietly.

The next few hands he played with reckless abandon; he lost a hundred to conservativeness, now for the opposite end of the spectrum. Four hands later he recouped his hundred and a hundred more. One of the other players made a beginner's luck crack, which he ignored.

Harry again searched the casino to see if he could discover the whereabouts of the poker table now that he was beginning to settle into his new environment; a private detective must be able to adapt, he surmised on previous occasions, and here he was in that very situation, in an unknown arena, playing at a style of life that was alien to him, but adapt he must and if the reckless streak served the purpose then so be it. The money was of secondary importance: you can't take it with you, he told himself, so enjoy it while you can.

Three more hands were played where he was successful on two and lost on the third, but his betting strategy had yielded a good return. Still nobody paid him much attention.

They're looking on me as a mug about to lose a mug's money, he thought. The next few hands Harry bet wildly, risking most of his pot on "double downs". To his astonishment he won each time. Even the other players shut up.

He scoured the casino a third time.

'Looking for someone?' asked the croupier.

'More action! No offence meant,' he replied.

Nosey bastard, he felt like saying, but he quickly adopted a stratagem never to get on talking terms with anybody in the casino: they were all out to get him, especially the croupiers and other players, and so it was better to keep everything and everyone at arm's length. The croupier must have read his mind for he never opened another conversation during any of the hands.

Harry bet heavily again and to his astonishment won again. He could feel the close circuit television cameras burning into his every move, studying his technique lest he should be counting cards, but his conscience and therefore his general demeanor were free from such restrictions of guilt and panic over a blatant act of cheating. He was winning fair and square. Even so the table was approached by a large, heavy set man with receding hair and dark piercing eyes. The man looked straight through Harry then whispered something in the croupier's ear. He looked straight back at him; he was not going to be overawed or feel threatened in any way.

The heavy set man left the table, but his imposing presence left an indelible mark on Harry and he promised himself to work hard on his self-defense: this is not the movies where the hero always wins, and he would defend his person today anyway he saw fit, legal or otherwise, but the heavy set man showed him a weakness in his make-up.

Hands continued as though nothing had happened, whatever the man said to the croupier he remained. Harry lost two hands, but the bets were of a moderate size and he was still ahead then he bet big again and won. He knew that to keep their attention, and continue to be noticed, he must stay ahead, well ahead.

Bet big, his intuition kept saying, bet big and scare the saps into showing their hand, but what hand? All he wanted was to case the joint, soak up the atmosphere and make Nero's feel as much a part of him as sitting in his beloved 924. He glanced over to where the heavy set man disappeared. Three sets of eyes met his: the heavy set man, and from their dress sense and body language his immediate bosses. These were two of the four men he knew duped Stephen: the man on the left was taller, around six three, thinner with brown hair graying over the temple. His dark brown eyes glowered and he wore the aspect of someone who was used to always getting his own way; the smaller came in around five ten with mousey colored hair and blue eyes. He kept his hands permanently in his pockets and gave the impression of having seen this all before, but wasn't about to tolerate much more.

He bet the maximum and won.

The three, dark suited men approached the table, but it was the lower ranking man who spoke first: 'You're having a good day today, sir!'

His patronizing tone of the word "sir" hung in the air for all to reach out and grab a piece of.

'Yes, I am, aren't I?'

Harry returned the compliment with a cherry on top.

An awkward silence descended like a death veil over the room, nobody was going to stand for that.

The taller of the two bosses leaned forward menacingly, placing both hands on the table. They were two slabs of meat wrapped around granite. The man had been a boxer in a past life. Harry thought of jujitsu.

'Reckless,' he sneered. 'You like being reckless.'

'You asking me or telling me?'

His reply stunned this ex-boxer into a glare that rocked the croupier, but not the player. Harry was relishing every minute of it.

'How reckless you want to be?'

He became aware that every game in the vicinity of his table had stopped playing, but he was not about to let them know that he knew.

Harry was determined to face them down and swept his right hand over the table, speaking slowly, but purposefully: 'You want to join me in a game?'

The smaller of the two walked forward and passed behind him out of view. Harry braced for impact. The man sat on his right.

'Sure,' he said slowly.

His partner took the seat on the Travers' left. The other players had already backed off, giving up their seats as if pre-empting the inevitable strike against his person.

'Deal!' barked the smaller man.

The croupier was the rabbit caught in the proverbial headlights, and stared dumb like at his employer before snapping back to reality and cracked the cellophane seal on a new pack of cards. Harry noticed the man's hands shaking; these two were clearly not to be messed with and he pictured them beating down on the poor, sad croupiers each and every night before they made for their tables.

Harry placed his bet of one hundred pounds, sliding the chips purposefully over the baize table. He was keeping control of his nerves admirably. His two new companions offered the same bet, but verbally.

The croupier dealt the cards.

The game was with cards face down with dealer having to stand on seventeen, and the three players studied their cards with the intensity of a down on his luck lawyer making his first big settlement.

Harry was the only one not paying too much attention to the other two, or the croupier.

The dealer engaged the smaller man first and he asked for another card; the subtle flicker, like a pilot light extinguishing in the man's eyes told Harry all he needed to know. Seconds later the latent animosity inherent in the man transformed into a callous sneer guaranteed to quake the boots of even the most resolute croupier, and he petulantly snapped his right wrist, sending the cards sprawling towards the dealer. Harry grinned inwardly to this reaction, and hit them hard with another "double down".

The croupier dealt him a third card, sliding it under the two hundred pound bet. Travers' vacuous expression said it all.

The taller man with the granite knuckles fidgeted constantly, he wore his anxiety like a coat of chain-mail: it was there to add a level of protection, but all it achieved at this blackjack table was to drag the owner down into his own personal black-hole.

He asked for another card then stayed put.

Finally the croupier played his hand to completion: he made twenty.

'Table pays twenty-ones!' he said, without any real conviction or authority, just in a matter of fact way guaranteed to hide any emotion or weakness in the speaker.

Without a second's hesitation the taller man revealed his three cards and a matching total of twenty.

Harry paused and took a deep breath, as if he was secretly regretting ever sitting at the table and indulging in this losing game of chance. The casino, for such a small game, was eerily quiet. Why pay so much attention to one game of blackjack that was never going to break the bank? The question now was how to extricate oneself from the mire. A bit late for that, he thought, and turned over all his cards: he made twenty-one.

The taller man got up and left the table without talking. The second leaned over to pass comment in Travers' ear: 'Back office!'

It was best not to argue, and he summoned all his available energy to leave the table after scooping up all his winnings. His legs felt like lead as he made the slow, laborious walk to the back office bypassing numerous tables; if he could just create a diversion, but the route to the exit was always partially blocked by patrons and doormen. There was nothing to do but take the beating.

A dark brown door to a brightly lit room sat ajar, and he braced himself for the inevitable. The heavy set man led the way and breezed into the office, brushing the door aside like he was swatting a fly. The other two had taken up the rear, to ride shotgun, leaving Harry the filling in the sandwich.

The office was airy and light with the faint whiff of primrose. Somebody's died in here, he thought, and they need the freshener to hide the evidence.

'Please take a seat!' The tall man said politely, but a little too politely for his taste.

Harry saw two expensive looking chairs facing a desk. 'If you're going to go, go in style!' He sat down, placing his chips directly in front of him on the desk.

'Going where?' The smaller man said in a very accommodating tone.

'Mister....,' the tall man sat behind the desk as he spoke. 'I'm afraid we don't know your name. That has been very amiss of us!'

'Travers! Harry Travers.'

'Well Mister Travers, you have us all wrong!'

'I do?'

The heavy set man stood by the door saying nothing. His exit was blocked, he was doomed. There was only one thing for it, just give it to them with both barrels.

'We are business men Mister Travers.'

The smaller man moved around behind him and cruised over to the drinks cabinet.

'I like your style,' Harry said cheekily. 'Whiskey's my poison!'

'Mine too,' replied the smaller man.

'We like yours. Style that is, your style!'

The taller man leaned back in the chair, placing his hands on his chest with fingers interlocked.

The smaller one gave him a healthy measure of whiskey. 'A proper drink, I think you'll agree.' Harry did. The man furnished all bar the heavy set man with drinks.

'What do you want?'

'A logical question Mister Travers,' started the taller one. 'We saw very quickly that you are a man who likes to gamble. I know that may sound a little on the ridiculous side considering our present surroundings, but not all who venture through our doors are genuine gambling type!'

'If you say so!'

'So we have decided,' it was the smaller one's turn to speak, 'to offer you the opportunity to gamble.'

'That's nice of you! Where? When? And how?'

'Straight to the point,' the taller man answered, leaning forward in his chair. 'I admire that!'

'You have the advantage over me!'

'We are terrible hosts Mister Travers!' said the seated man. 'I am Mister Willis, and this is Mister Moore!'

Mister Moore doffed the invisible cap on his head.

Playful, mused Harry, too playful. He studied both men in silence and drank his whiskey as all possible ramifications this unexpected situation could offer swirled in his head 'To gamble,' he finally said. 'How?'

'Poker!' Mister Moore said sharply.

Harry was struck dumb, not by the man's tone, but that all he had set out to achieve, plus these two gentlemen, were dumped right in his lap.

'We think you look like a poker player!' added Willis.

'Really!' was all Harry could come up with, and he knew it fell well short of the mark the conversation cried out for. 'That is very astute of you.'

'We noticed,' Willis stated, 'that you had a tendency to be distracted at the blackjack table, like you were looking for something else, something of a little more interest to you. That and you bet with the impetuosity of a poker player!'

'Thank you!'

'You're welcome!'

'The game,' butted in Moore, 'will be on a Wednesday of our choosing here in one of the private rooms, starting around nine or ten, depending on numbers. We play until the last man's standing!'

The last part was added for dramatic effect and Harry felt the need to play along with them.

'That's right up my street!'

'You'll only be given a few days' notice!'

Willis kept eye contact with him when he spoke, which Harry returned with interest before finally leaning forward to close the gap by a foot or so.

'I will amend my schedule.'

'Excellent!' barked out Moore making his way around the table in a show of solidarity to stand beside his co-recruiter.

Harry looked over his shoulder. The heavy set man had not budged an inch.

This was all executed very formally in an extreme matter of fact kind of way best suited to his temperament.

'I'll be here!' Harry said rising from the seat then turning sharply to gauge any reaction from the muscle blocking his exit. The muscle never flinched. 'What's the stake?'

'Again very amiss of us,' Willis said in monotone voice. 'Fifty thousand pounds buy in Mister Travers! Is that too heavy for you? Please tell me that it is not so!'

The reply was short, blunt and to the point; he was beginning to like these men, but he tempered his growing enthusiasm with the knowledge of their impending downfall lingering around his fingertips.

'No, it is more than acceptable.' He placed his glass on the desk before slickly collecting his chips, praying his hands would not begin to shake. 'If that is all gentlemen, I have a cold beer and a warm woman waiting.'

He was grinning inside like a Cheshire cat, as the muscle opened the door back into the salvation of the casino floor. It hadn't altered one iota in his absence, not that he expected it would, and exuded confidence while striding for the exit. A few of the patrons who had witnessed his removal dispatched open signs off shock on seeing his person appear without any signs of external damage, and not long afterwards he swapped their incredulity for the cool evening air after cashing his winnings. It was getting dark. He checked his watch. It was 21:30. Where had the time gone? He wasted no time making his car and heading home.

* * *

The thud of his front door closing behind him brought on another cranium splitting headache and he moved briskly to the kitchen cupboard given the responsibility for housing the required medication. He was eager for his head to stop throbbing and to think more clearly. He picked up the phone and ordered in food, it was too late to cook. He thought of Tommy.

A little over twenty-five minutes later Harry sat in his front room and tucked into a hot chicken curry, which he washed down with diet cola found from a previous night.

He was calmer now, more composed, more accepting of his fate; he was to play in a poker game with a fifty thousand pound buy in. He shook his head then openly chastised himself for being weak, but it was what he wanted, what he set out to achieve and here he was in the game. He needed to call her, but the time dictated that a call was out of the question. He sent her a text informing her of his being waylaid by his solicitor; it sounded feasible and a few minutes later she replied in a tone signifying she wasn't put out at all. Harry didn't know whether to be upset of not, so promised to call her tomorrow evening.

He hearkened back to the conversation in the casino: the money to his astonishment meant nothing to him, it was only money after all and he was now so firmly ensconced in his desire to fulfill his ambition to lead the double life of a professional airline pilot and a private detective that the thought of risking such a sizeable sum worried him not a jot. He pictured Sheila in evening dress standing beside him looking gorgeous, admiring his slick, professional card play.

The phone beside him on a small glassed topped table burst into life. Harry answered on the first ring.

'Hello!'

It was her.

Why did she always have the knack of calling me the very second I thought of her, he pondered, and composed himself for the next response: should he come clean? The answer was in the affirmative: 'I'm in the game!'

'Oh!'

The reply shocked, disappointed and annoyed him in equal measure, but he hid it. 'It's a fifty thousand pound buy in!'

'That's too much for you to risk!'

'How much did Stephen really lose?'

She remained mute.

'Twenty thousand!' she finally said, after the realization hit home Harry was not going to offer anything further.

'It'll be a long night then!' Harry said earnestly.

'Do you still want me there as your pleasant distraction?'

'What do you think?'

Her laugh broke the melancholy stranglehold on the conversation.

'Well do you?'

'Of course I bloody well do!'

Here was an opportunity and he went for it: 'I need you to be yourself, your best self and put the others off their game. You can do that!' Her dressing up was as much for him as it was for improving his chances of winning.

'Piece of cake!'

'After our previous chat I kind of figured you wanted space.'

Seconds passed before he heard what remotely sounded like a reply, and instinctively requested her to repeat it: she was on a guilt trip after their date, which she admitted was one of her better first date experiences, and rang to apologize for treating him in such a manner.

Harry thanked her, but calmed her agitation by saying that an apology was not necessary given the tremendous stress Stephen was putting her under.

'You're being too kind and incredibly understanding!' she said softly.

He accepted this went with the territory of being a private detective, before reiterating to her not to worry.

The confab was not the smooth, easy going exchange of words he wished it would be due to the concern and responsibility she felt for Stephen and for dragging a work colleague into her sibling's mess: anybody who ever came into contact with him seemed to end up getting embroiled in his disasters.

Harry brought the conversation to a logical conclusion. He knew it was best to cut it short before her melancholy won the day. He pressed the disconnect button on the hand held phone, and checked to make sure the line was clear before risking saying anything.

'Harry my boy, you got to get your head straight!'

It was all the remonstrance he was going to allow and he hauled his tired frame to bed for the following day's standby. Shortly before lights out he fired off an e-mail.

14

The sunlight spilled around the sides of the venetian blinds, filtering into his bedroom providing adequate light for him to navigate safely to the en-suite. He had woken early, cancelled the alarm, lay in until midday, fallen asleep again and now stumbled into the shower after nearly cutting his own throat shaving. Half an hour later refreshed, awake and raring to get stuck into what was left of the day he drank his first cup of coffee and checked his e-mails. Sure enough Tommy had replied. Thankfully all was still quiet, but the suggestions from his American friend for creating a stir were almost hysterical. Harry found his new found mirth much to his liking.

Further relief was almost tangible as his standby duty came and went without any form of contact from crewing, and the free day was most welcome: his batteries required recharging after the sojourn to the casino.

As promised he called Sheila, but when no answer was forthcoming left a message to call after the following day's Las Palmas.

* * *

The crew-room was a hive of activity when he arrived a full fifteen minutes early, a habit he cautiously reminded himself not to repeat too many times, or the management would be on his back expecting such a display of professionalism at every turn. There were four crews in transition: two about to make the envious journey home, after long un-envious night flights, and those about to replace them for the two day flights, both to the Canary Islands.

Harry tried to look casual as he sauntered over to a monitor without making eye contact with anybody in particular, logged in and sourced his briefing pack for the day. The printer sprung into life. Once happy this part of the day was running smoothly enough he collected the rest of the paperwork and went to introduce himself to the crew.

By the time he arrived back at the printer the first officer, Peter Reynolds, had arrived: he was a young lad of twenty-two, new to the company, and Harry followed protocol a second time. Due to the lad's relative inexperience he offered him the opportunity to fly the outbound leg, which he gratefully accepted. This set the routine for the day. Harry found himself in a pleasantly surprising semi-teaching role, and the day passed by most enjoyably.

* * *

He pulled the 924 smartly into his drive to be confronted by the quiet, foreboding windows of his empty house. It still unnerved him to a degree to come home to a cold, seemingly deserted home.

He kicked the front door firmly shut with his trailing leg and flicked on the hall lights before dimming them to their lowest setting. Littering the floor lay the day's post. One letter caught his eye. It was simply addressed to Mister Harry Travers in a plain white envelope. He carefully picked up all the post and ascended to the first floor. The rooms were only just beginning to warm and he threw his jacket onto the sofa followed by the post, bar the white envelope and placed his flight bag on the floor. He needed a whiskey before opening the letter.

Slumping down onto his sofa he sipped a large straight Jack Daniels and studied the letter in his right hand. It was definitely a man's handwriting. It was surely an apology. No, it had to be the casino wanting to make a point of just letting him know that they could touch him anytime they chose. He took a large hit of whiskey and opened it.

It was a formal invitation from Misters Willis and Moore. Funny that, he thought, growing instantly angry at their nerve to try and unnerve him, he had never given them his address then just as quickly remembered he had when he enrolled as a member: stupid, just plain stupid.

'Man, they must be keen!' He finished the whiskey.

* * *

He opened the good eye, the other being permanently cemented shut by heavy sleep, and he tried to focus on the letter lying at a rakish angle on the carpet ahead of him.

'Fuck!'

He was fully dressed lying half off, half on the sofa. Harry tried manfully to lift his head, but only managed to bring on a turn, which left him giddy and he returned to his original position.

'Fuck! You need to get your body clock back on track.'

There was only one thing for it. Stay put until the Travers' powers of recovery could kick in. Far off the house phone started to ring.

'I don't believe this! Who calls at this time of day?'

But what time of day was it? He checked his watch. The one operating eye told him it was 09:30.

The phone stopped ringing and went over to the answer machine: Marvin Schular's dulcet tones wrenched him off the sofa, head splitting, towards the phone. He managed to get within two strides before the message ended and he rung off.

Harry hit the play button.

It was a simple message for Harry to call round and see him.

'Is that it?' The earliest he could make it would be in the afternoon due to his need for some quality rest. He decided to return to the sofa. It put paid to the afternoon plans.

'Come on Harry!' he said rubbing the side of his head. 'Buck up.'

On the fridge door secured by a magnet was a number for a local taxi firm. He would ring later and see Marvin around midday. Harry made coffee.

The coffee tasted good, especially when washed down with scrambled egg and bacon with a side dollop of ketchup. He channel hopped until he hit the news: the newsreader was covering a story about joy-riders who'd killed an elderly woman while racing each other.

'Assholes!' he exclaimed.

His exclamation slammed home the memory of that tumultuous night in Tennessee; until that point his conscience had been quiet and not wasted a second on guilt for being directly responsible for their demise, or to the poor family left behind to mourn their passing. What was more the worrying, he never would and he knew it. This was not the Harry Travers of old, someone who in the past cared what people thought about him, was the kind of guy always choosing the path of least friction when it came to confrontation. Not now: antipathy ruled and any pampering to his growing misanthropic tendencies, in relation to those who chose to cross him, would be embraced, encouraged even to bring into sharp focus the job at hand, to prevent from clouding his judgment. He thought of Sheila. Yes, it was true he had strong feelings for her and the very thought of anybody else having her jarred him immensely, but the pull towards his new found destiny overrode any emotion that could possibly compromise his position. He would set himself adrift from all emotional contact and baggage with the opposite sex. A man is weak when what he cares for is threatened. He would not be weak, not from now or forever after.

* * *

Marvin Schular waved his right hand towards the chair sitting at a slant opposite him on the other side of his desk while talking on the phone.

Harry said nothing, and slumped down into the black leather chair. It was comfortable, and he swung a couple of three-sixties before coming to rest facing the furrowed brow of his friend and lawyer.

'I came as soon as I could,' Harry said once the telephone conversation had ended.

'You look like shit! Have a good night last night? Anybody I know?'

'Nope!'

There was a moment's awkward silence until Schular accepted his friend and client wasn't going to expound any further.

'It was very much a single-handed affair,' Harry finally said to help put his friend's curiosity out of its misery.

'Really.'

Harry could tell from the tone of reply that he was not being believed, but he didn't give a damn and asked the question: 'You've had an offer on the property?' He was shocked to get the news even with things as they were: 'When?'

'I got a phone call yesterday from Mister Jeffries, who asked me to convey it to you.'

Harry kept any misgivings about this man to himself and sat perfectly still bar the index finger and thumb of his right hand occasionally rubbing his chin.

'How much?'

'The asking price: four hundred thousand dollars!'

'Who?'

'A private buyer. You need time to think?'

'No!' His reply was abrupt, but Schular didn't seem to care.

'So the question is do you accept?'

This time the reply was softer and measured: 'No!'

If Schular was at all surprised at his refusal of such a generous offer it didn't show.

Harry felt an overwhelming desire to explain his steadfast refusal to sell up: 'My uncle's disappearance has not been fully explained to my satisfaction!'

'Jeffries mentioned something about your enquires into the police investigation, but it appears your uncle's disappearance has been laid to rest, so to speak, as an unfortunate accident while out in the woods.'

'Really.'

'I love your skepticism Harry; it fits your persona like a well-worn glove!'

Harry smiled.

'I will let Mister Jeffries know that you are considering the offer and will inform him of your decision in due course.'

Harry held onto the smile.

'When are you going over again?'

'Soon!'

Schular leant back in his chair, staring at a spot on the ceiling. 'We can easily stall them and make them aware that any acceptance of their offer will be made after your next visit,' he said nodding. 'Yes, that will do nicely!' He brought his line of sight down to Travers'. 'Yes?'

Harry nodded.

'But you're not going to tell them are you?'

Harry shook his head: 'You are! I will let you know when I've arrived safely.'

'Intrigue, I do love intrigue!'

The conversation, and therefore the meeting, reached its logical conclusion and the two friends parted company on good terms with each promising to keep the other informed at all times of any further developments.

Once out in the street Harry walked slowly, but purposefully, staring at the pavement directly in front of him as if he were looking for the firmest ground afoot. He halted abruptly and locked his gaze on an office block with a neon sign on its roof advertising a well-known insurance company. 'This will be explained to my satisfaction,' he muttered. Harry knew he needed to be professional at all times and not let his emotions take over.

A single taxi sat on the rank. Harry knocked lightly on the driver's window after seeing a man on his mobile phone. A nod told him he was free and Harry climbed in the back.

The driver apologized profusely for the phone call and asked for the destination. He answered coolly, trying hard to hide any ire in his voice. The taxi pulled smoothly away and Harry instantly longed to be home in the peace and quiet of his surroundings. The ride though seemed to take an age, but once he finally set foot over the threshold and the front door clicked shut he exhaled a long, slow breath before ascending to the first floor. He was ravenous: planning, bringing someone to justice had given him a hunger of biblical proportions.

He checked his messages. There were none.

Harry wasted no time with a late lunch and devoured a simple concoction of soup and sandwiches in a manner not remotely dissimilar from a castaway, and when fully satiated laid back on the sofa and contemplated channel hopping, but his head began to spin with all the ideas charging hell for leather through it on how best to deal with this man: should he remove him in one act of vengeance once his guilt was assured? This was surely not the way a true private investigator should behave? The doubts began to eat away within him, to question the malice rising to the fore forcing him to consider crossing that thin dividing line between good and evil and necessary retaliation, but it was there, always lurking in the background, orchestrating his every thought towards retribution and demanding satisfaction for the deeds done against one of his own.

Harry finally gave in and began to channel hop with his mind still racing at full tilt towards the planned destruction of another human being and only finally coming to rest with the opening credits of one his all-time favorite movies: Casablanca. He was exhausted and settled on hitting the record button.

Turning off the lights, after making sure the house was locked tighter than a drum, he started the long drudge to bed; the evening twilight brought home fresh memories of the fight here, the shooting in the car chase and his date with Jeffries' destiny. Even now, at this early stage he was aware that any inner peace would only be achieved with his demise and again crossing that line.

* * *

Harry stared intently again at the patterns sprawled across his bedroom ceiling in the early morning light; having slept well, and his mind now focused with great clarity, he lay calm and content with one leg in, one leg out of the duvet to remain cool. The radiators hissed lightly, releasing heat. He rubbed his fingers on the palms of his hands. They were dry. It perturbed him not. He closed his eyes and tried to sleep more.

The electric buzzer of his alarm clock woke him. He kicked off the duvet and jumped out of bed. Each day, he was determined, must bring on new horizons to steepen his learning curve and supply him with another layer of protection or knowledge to help achieve his goal, and once in the kitchen he wasted no time rustling up coffee and toast. Sitting at the breakfast bar sipping on a second mug of coffee Harry flipped open his laptop, fired it up and began his search: there were three jujitsu clubs including the one ran by his buddy, but it was not the nearest to him. He desired anonymity and chose the closest. He made a note of the number and called it on his mobile. A guy named Stuart ran the club and Harry left a message. This was going to be a boring day, he could sense it, and he tried not to let such a depressing thought affect him. If his job had just one advantage it released him from the mundane and made him appreciate all that life had to offer. The thought of Jeffries taking the life out of his uncle injected him with stinging indignation.

The day was indeed boring and he attempted to break it up with cleaning his kitchen cupboards and dealing with any outstanding correspondence, which only had the effect of boring him even more. The television this night was nothing short of woeful, but he was spared by Stuart returning his call: there was a beginner's class for adults tomorrow at seven. A quick check of his roster confirmed what he thought, that barring any delays he would be home before then and jokingly informed the guy he would begin his training with a vengeance tomorrow. All he needed now was to see the back of this most tedious of days.

Harry knew he had to accept the inevitable days where next to nothing or indeed nothing would transpire and on these he concluded training must take priority. To these ends a list was required detailing all his weaknesses and gaping holes in his knowledge and experience. This day his conscience was calmed with the thought of organizing the beginning of self-defense training.

The week disappeared without any kind of trace to help bring it back to the forefront of his memory, and for that he was eternally grateful; to anybody willing to listen, whenever he was questioned or criticized for his level of pay, he would simply state that if he ever was unfortunate enough to experience a truly bad day at work then they would have the pleasure, or not, of reading about it in the papers, and his pay reflected the responsibility his shoulders carried.

His introduction to jujitsu on the other hand was anything but uneventful: Harry sat expectantly on the obligatory hard wooden seats that circumnavigated the changing rooms of the local leisure center and felt a complete idiot in a t-shirt and tracksuit bottoms; other club members were decked out in their suits displaying an array of colored belts.

The lesson lasted an hour and afterward his back, shoulders and arms ached like hell from all the throws he administered or received, but the enjoyment he felt was immeasurable of finally having the doors to a world until now only a dream away opened to him. He booked the next lesson for three days' time.

With more free time looming just over the horizon he faced up to another barrage of boredom on his senses and seriously considered taking another crack at either Sheila or the blackjack table. Tennessee was still seven whole days away with all the flights now booked and the decision taken to inform Tommy of his arrival. What he needed was something, anything, to while away the time.

A simple breakfast geared up Harry for a brisk walk to the high street shops; an idea came to him and he was keen to explore it: all the people around these parts used the local papers to advertise, so if there was work in one for a private detective eager to learn his trade, even finding a missing cat, it was worth a look. Boredom would not be accepted.

He stood at the back of a small, local supermarket, licked his fingers and turned the pages to the classified section of a well-known newspaper. To his immense disappointment there was nothing. He closed it up, let out a deep sigh and checked another paper. He was disappointed and frustrated in equal measure. Surely somebody somewhere needed his services.

The shop was ideally situated to cater for all around and Harry took the opportunity to stock up on some provisions. Standing at the checkout his heart was lifted by a notice board beside the tills:

people had pinned white rectangular cards to the board advertising belongings for sale, but intermingled among them was a single card calling out to him, beckoning him forward: a woman's dog was missing. Perfect. He made a note of the number.

Harry almost skipped up the road and he played over and over the intended conversation with the poor, unfortunate owner of the pooch, now missing. It was simple, he would search for the dog, whether or not he was successful remained to be seen, and use the experience to interact with the general public.

No sooner had he entered his house, dropped the shopping on the kitchen floor, than he rang the number on the card from the house phone, but not before adding three numbers so his number would be withheld. It rang for eight or nine times with no answer. He hung up. Should he try again? He was strangely nervous. After about five minutes he rang the number a second time.

A double click signaled the opening gambit with a quiet, softly spoken voice, which Harry immediately sensed to be that of an elderly lady he pictured being the wrong side of seventy.

'I'm ringing about your dog.'

The softly spoken voice instantly picked up a few octaves: 'You found him?' she said before beginning a spiel about the dog's habits.

The dog's name off the card was Rusty, and from the lady he gleaned he was not the kind of animal to run off or leave his beloved creature comforts behind. Harry was saddened that his news was not what she wanted to hear.

'Oh,' the lady muttered, her voice dropping back to its original level.

'I want to help.'

'Thank you.'

He pictured her sitting beside the phone, head in hand after the short lived jubilation.

'Tell me everything about the day you lost Rusty.'

Hearing someone other than her speak Rusty's name sparked an outflow of emotion, and for the next few minutes it was a minor miracle she ever managed to pause for breath. Harry made notes.

After he pressed the disconnect button he looked at the digital clock on the oven door. The whole conversation from start to finish had taken six minutes. He made coffee whilst studying the notes; the first and most obvious thing to do was to visit the park where Rusty vanished. From the detailed description she had furnished him with it would not be difficult to recognize the dog.

* * *

The recreational park was not dissimilar from all the other parks dotted around the country. About half way down where a pathway surrounded the inner grassy section there sat a bench dedicated to a long lost husband who, ironically, loved to walk his dog here.

He sat down and took a moment to study those enjoying the day: nobody even remotely looked devious enough to commit dog-napping. This was not quite turning out the way he envisaged, but what honestly did he expect? That a complete stranger would approach him with vital clues or the villain would parade around the park wearing a sandwich board proclaiming their guilt. He walked over to the spot where he understood the old lady last saw her dog.

This area of the park contained a small playground with the obligatory roundabout, swings and climbing frame. He thought about having a crack at the swings when he noticed a dark haired, slim, middle-aged woman walking by with her young son, who was still wearing his school uniform, giving him a strange look. He returned it.

'Can I help you?' she said menacingly.

'Maybe,' he replied curtly.

His response made her approach Harry, curious to find out how.

'I lost my dog recently. I believe he was taken!' For the last part he tried to express as much emotion as humanely possible. It worked for the woman began to warm to him.

'I can only imagine how you must feel. I would be utterly devastated to lose Pickles!'

'Pickles?' Harry needed all his self-control to stop laughing. Then he noticed the boy: there was something about him that aroused suspicion. 'Do you know anything?'

The woman was about to get menacing again with this strange man confronting her son, when the boy replied.

'Dog fights!' The boy said without thinking, which was obvious by his now sheepish demeanor.

'What!' His mother was less than impressed by his possibly having any knowledge on the matter.

The young lad looked on Harry, pleading for aid. None was forthcoming.

'And what do you know about dog fighting?'

Her son took a visible step back: 'Nothing, only some of the older boys at school were talking about it!'

Harry needed to quiz the boy further without the mother being present, but under the present circumstances it was wise not to pursue this on its present course.

'Wait until I get you home!' The woman grabbed her son's arm, said her goodbye, as politely as she could, before spinning through one hundred and eighty degrees and set about frog-marching him home.

'If I describe my dog would you recognize him?' Harry asked looking at the back of them both.

'You need to speak to Katic!' said the boy.

'You know him?' demanded the mother.

The boy started to cry: 'No!'

'What do you know?' The mother asked with menace.

'He steals dogs!'

They stopped walking.

'Tell me of my dog!' Harry forced the issue before it was too late.

The boy turned to face him: 'Katic might have him!'

'And when did you start running with him?' snapped his mother.

'I don't!' said the tearful boy.

The mother took a deep breath and looked Harry straight in the eye: 'My son is a good boy, and not one of them!'

Harry nodded. He couldn't believe his luck.

She turned to her son and asked him straight: 'Now you tell this man where his dog is!'

'I don't know, but some of the boys at school say they're kept down by the river on the industrial estate.'

Harry knew it: half the estate was not under any ownership.

'Watch for Katic!' the mother warned, as if she was reading his mind.

'I will!'

And with that the mother and son left.

Harry walked briskly back to his car. Could it really be that simple to gain leads? He only wanted to scour the area to get a feel for the case, and any additional info would have been a bonus. Yes, he had grown instantly impatient, but this was way too good to be true. He sat in the car, laughed, and felt the rush of adrenaline surge through his veins with the thought of crossing this Katic.

* * *

The estate sat in a horseshoe shape and ran in an anti-clockwise direction beginning with two run down charity shops facing the road providing essentials for third world countries. Harry made a mental note to bring over any unwanted clothes. He slowed the Porsche to help navigate some speed bumps and examined in fine detail all the lock-ups under ownership until he was happy which of those could be used to house dogs or any animals. This led to his next conundrum: how to pick locks?

Bringing the 924 to a halt Harry considered at length using all the available daylight to investigate further, but that meant leaving himself open to any eagle-eyed employee or security guard, and his car stood out. No, he needed to return after dark following a visit to an old friend.

* * *

The house was in a serious state of disrepair when Harry pulled up outside: it cried out for some tender loving care. Its dilapidation only highlighted the length of time he had been amiss from paying his ailing friend a visit.

He slowly exited the car carefully carrying a plastic bag whilst keeping one eye on the road for any unwelcome guests. Approaching the front door with its flaking green paint he rang the bell twice and took a step back before looking over his shoulder.

From inside the faint sound of shuffling feet met his ears. The shuffling, shambling feet grew louder, coming to a halt with the unlatching of the door. It opened with a little effort. Harry instinctively leaned forward and gave the door a gentle push to reveal Patterson: no one ever used his first name and so he simply became known by his surname. At his full height he was on a par with Harry, but today stood with a slight stoop, his short dark hair graying at the sides, but those piercing brown eyes had lost none of the intensity as they focused on him. He was still wearing his pajamas under a purple dressing gown.

'Harry Travers!'

'Hello Patterson.'

'Come in, come in.' He took a step to one side and waved Harry in.

The hallway was poorly lit. Only a light filtering through the kitchen doorway at the far end gave any illumination for the purpose of safe navigation to the rear of the house. Harry made for the kitchen. Patterson closed the door with a thud.

'How you been keeping?' He asked without looking back.

'Some days good, some days...' His words trailed off and Harry was immediately overcome with guilt.

Harry stopped beside a cluttered breakfast bar in dire need of a good clean and waited patiently. In fact the whole house up to this point was crying out for the same.

Patterson filled the kettle and started to make tea.

'Sorry I haven't been in touch lately, Patterson,' Harry felt he needed to say something along those lines, but it was a genuine heartfelt apology.

'Oh, don't worry. You kind of expect it after a while. There's only so much illness people can handle!'

'What's the latest?'

'Got to keep taking these,' and he picked up a small white plastic bottle, rattling it several times.

Harry sat at the breakfast bar and placed the plastic bag for his friend to see.

'Milk, sugar?' asked Patterson.

'Just milk please.

Patterson made the tea and handed Harry his.

'What's in here?' Patterson asked jovially and peered inside. 'Bushmills! My favorite, you remembered.'

'Got to make up for being an absent friend.'

'No you don't! Now what brings you here?'

'One I genuinely wanted to see you, and two I need a favor.'

'Go on.'

'You once joked to me you could pick any lock known to man.'

Patterson sipped his tea pensively: 'I did.'

'Can you?'

'I can!'

Harry sipped his tea to prevent his throat from drying up: 'Teach me!'

Patterson took a second to let his friend's request sink in: 'You serious?'

'I am.'

'Why?'

'I have my reasons. And I'll pay you for your time.'

'No, you won't.'

Both men finished their drinks without another word being said.

'Okay,' Patterson was the first to speak. 'When do you want to start?'

'Now!'

'On one condition!'

'Name it!'

'You let me in on it, after the event.'

'Sure, and if you have any other hidden talents I'd like to know about them?'

'You learn a lot of things when you have the amount of spare time I do.' Harry didn't know what to say to that. 'But all in good time my friend, all in good time.'

'Well, I'm ready when you are.'

Patterson cracked open one of the two triple distilled bottles of Bushmills and poured himself a large one into a glass he had rinsed out under the tap. The mug was relegated to the sink.

'First things first,' he said amiably, downing the smooth brown liquid in one go before immediately poured another. 'You're driving,' he added.

'Yes, I am!' Harry replied jovially, secretly wishing he could polish off a large one. 'What about your drugs?'

Patterson said nothing. He simply beckoned Harry to follow, and he turned with a swish of his deep purple dressing gown and headed back to the front of the house. Harry saw his friend's life running full pelt into a cul-de-sac: they had joined the company on the same day, studied on the same ground-school course and been simulator partners, which made his absence all the more unforgivable. Then two years ago Patterson began to have severe headaches, migraines of near biblical proportions and the only drugs capable of suppressing the pain meant under Civil Aviation Authority rules, due to their side effects, your medical was pulled. Ultimately the headaches never receded and Patterson lost his license.

His friend led him into a dimly lit room with heavy draped curtains.

Patterson turned on the light. 'This is the only drug I need!' he said holding up the glass of whiskey.

Harry studied the room in close detail; it was a mess with nearly everything covered in a thick blanket of dust.

'Can't stand nosey bastards!' he exclaimed. 'Peeping, bloody Toms!'

Harry grunted in agreement.

'They come around here sticking their bloody noses into everyone's business under the guise of the neighbor-hood watch. I'll give them neighbor-hood fucking watch. I'll get me some high powered camera and stick it straight through their fucking front windows and then everybody can bloody watch that!' Patterson laughed.

The room now lit by a single bulb hanging from a pendant revealed amongst its shadows and recesses to be a veritable Aladdin's cave of hooky gear and contraband. Harry ran a finger over a pile of brown boxes and rubbed the collected dust between his right index finger and thumb.

'You come in here often then!' Harry said with more than a hint of sarcasm.

'Only to spy on those nosey bastards!'

Patterson pulled out from behind a raggedy collection of dilapidated boxes a hold-all carrying the strains and tears of its former owner's former career.

'Belong to you?'

'Afraid not.'

Patterson threw the bag over to his friend: 'Yours now!'

The bag was not on the light side and Harry let out a grunt more in surprise than anything else. The corners of his mouth began to turn down and he half-cocked his head to the right, as he watched Patterson rummage around some more. By the time his friend had found what it was he was looking for, the bag was still unopened.

'Any good to you?'

'Don't know yet!'

'Well, don't stand on ceremony!'

Harry looked inside the bag: to describe it as a burglar's essential tool kit would be an understatement. Every conceivable tool to aid breaking into someone's home was there.

'How on earth did you get this?'

Patterson took a second to reply: 'He needed money!'

'You mean they got themselves nicked, and needed to hock this stuff before he disappeared on an extended holiday at Her Majesty's pleasure!'

'Yeah, something like that,' Patterson said smiling, as he passed Harry carrying a scruffy brown box and headed back to the kitchen. 'Follow me!'

Harry turned out the light and followed his friend closely.

The rear of the house seemed somehow brighter now when compared to the Aladdin's cave and Patterson moved towards the conservatory where he placed his box of goodies on a table. Harry looked through the half-cleaned windows for any sign of the nosey neighbors. He needn't have worried; the windows even in their present state were a damn good defense against his friend's 'enemy'.

Patterson emptied the box onto a table. It was an array of padlocks and door locks. 'There you go! Consider it your apprenticeship. I'm going for a whiskey.'

Harry sat down on a dusty chair, placed the bag on the floor beside him, and began to examine the locks in fine detail hoping he would find out exactly what it was he was supposed to be looking for.

'Good. That's a start.' Patterson slumped down opposite.

'I haven't got a clue where it is I'm supposed to start!'

'Follow me through.' And his whiskey drinking buddy put a hand inside the bag and produced a leather pouch.

The pouch when unzipped revealed, on closer examination, what looked like a series of metallic tooth picks with ends of different shapes slanted off at various angles. Patterson then proceeded to insert two of the picks into one of the padlocks and within seconds it sprung open. You could not help but be impressed.

'Your go.'

Harry stared dumbly at the two picks handed him by Patterson.

'Take one of the padlocks and give it a go.'

He picked the largest lock. His thinking being, not without its merit, was that the biggest lock would have a larger slot for the key entry.

Tentatively he scratched and probed using the two picks, before being more forceful, with the end result that his only gain was soreness in his fingers.

'Bloody useless!' he said dejectedly.

Patterson drank another whiskey. 'Don't give up so easily.'

Harry attempted a second time until his fingertips gave out and he threw the padlock on the table.

'You're enjoying this!'

'Steady old boy,' Patterson said jestingly whilst pouring another shot. 'Watch this and follow me through.'

Harry tossed the two picks and the padlock over to him.

With much dexterity his old buddy probed, twisted and in a matter of seconds unlocked it.

'Got it?' Patterson asked cheerily, closing the padlock,

'No, but I've got to try again.' The first signs of reluctance began to rear its ugly head.

He tried to rub the soreness out of his fingers, collected the picks and padlock from Patterson, and set about his task with renewed vigor: from watching his friend he now had a better understanding of the sequence of events, which pick to place where, in what order and how to twist and turn whilst applying the correct amount of pressure. His previous efforts showed him subsequently what would not work. Three minutes later the padlock sprung open.

'I did it!' Harry was more astonished than anything else; there balancing in his sore fingers lay the large padlock which only moments before was the bane of his existence.

'Can't teach you anymore about padlocks my friend, it's now just practice, practice, practice because they're basically all the same.'

Harry nodded. The padlock still held his attention.

'Take the bag home and practice.'

Harry looked up and smiled.

'Now for some door-locks, and we shall start with the basics.'

Two hours vanished in an instant and Harry found himself sitting in his car studying the bag, which he surreptitiously laid on the floor out of sight from passers-by in the foot-well of the front passenger seat. The grin on his face could not begin to express the satisfaction he felt and he gunned the Porsche's engine into life. He now had some much needed homework to help wile away those inanely boring days that infuriated him no end, but would ultimately benefit his development.

15

Harry spent most of his free time practicing until he managed to bring his best time down to around thirty seconds. He was back on his roster for three days as of tomorrow then he was going to make an appointment with the industrial estate.

The days dragged: it wasn't the crews, they were great and it was a good day out on each occasion, it was something which he struggled to pinpoint or pigeonhole that ate away inside him pulling him towards a destiny he could only guess at, but secretly yearned to make acquaintances with. It unnerved him to think there was so much intrigue or crime just bubbling away just below the surface and he was only making the smallest of indentations into it. He found himself going about his everyday life studying people, making mental notes of how they behaved, what choice of words they used, their body language before asking simple, fundamental questions in an attempt to decipher what misdemeanor they were about. All persons were up to something, he had once been told by an aged family member. At first it was a chore chipping away at the very fabric of his life, but slowly and immeasurably he began to enjoy the task laid out before him, and his mental picture documenting all aspects of human behavior and endeavor grew perceptibly every day until he doubted his conclusions no more and instantly without question came to an assumption over complete strangers who may never cross his path again.

* * *

The evening of his appointment finally arrived and he vacated his house quietly confident.

Harry made the industrial estate in good time and parked the Porsche just over half a mile away where there were no CCTV cameras. His mini tool kit took pride of place in his jacket pocket. He put on a pair of gloves and strode off purposefully.

The occupied units were immediately obvious by being bathed in dim spot-lighting and Harry smiled at the ease he had investigated the first few unused units.

A startled fox scampered across his path causing two motion sensing lights to burst into life, illuminating the startled animal. Harry froze and studied the creature to gauge exactly where its movements had triggered the lights. When happy he knew how to stay clear he crept forward towards the next unit on his radar. To his astonishment the unit, even in this dim-light, was clearly unlocked, but to open it would create too much noise and attract any security. He placed his ear to the door and heard nothing. He made a note to return to this one before he left if nothing else transpired.

The next one under his suspicion was locked and had clearly not been disturbed for quite some time. The exterior of the third and fourth spoke of businesses only recently terminated and it saddened him to think of the hard working individuals who had tried to make a go of owning their own business and fallen short of the mark. He didn't dwell, the thought of Rusty forced him on.

Straight away the hairs on the back of Travers' neck rose and his own built-in warning system waived a red flag. He approached the shutter with increased apprehension, transmitted through his ever shortening stride: there were no motion detectors, no spotlights outside the unit, no name advertising the business, but the shutter, from its present state, was obviously in constant use.

He felt the side of his jacket pocket for the mini toolkit and the small crumb of comfort it gave him, and placed his ear to the shutter. There was no sound emitting from within and he felt severe disappointment coupled with a small tinge of relief. Should he move on and check out another unit? He was unsure and from his vantage point there weren't any that excited him the way this one did. Suddenly footsteps caused his heart to race and he backed off into the shelter of an emergency exit doorway.

The footsteps slowed, but never stopped. They weren't paying particular attention to any unit, he thought, and this boded well for his continued inconspicuousness. Without warning they grew progressively louder and his heart thumped progressively harder. He was grateful he now kept himself reasonably fit: one of the advantages of the jujitsu along with the other skills he was now learning would hopefully allow him to deal with situations like these, but in moments of introspection he cussed his own indolence for leaving the acquisition of such invaluable skills so late. The footsteps stopped by the unit he was so desperate to investigate, tried the shutter, checked the padlock securing it the floor then moved off. Harry froze, daring to breath. The steps belonged to a security guard, and he thankfully paid no further attention to anything else, as he made his way back to wherever he spent the night.

Once the guard was gone Harry slipped out of the doorway, let out a huge sigh of relief and smiled: of all the units here the only one to hold the man's attention was this one with no name outside or security lights of any kind. His inner alarm was working just fine and tuning itself to its new role.

He removed the toolkit and wasted not a second more undoing the padlock; to his intense delight the lock was picked in under two minutes and the shutter lifted and lowered within three.

As expected it was pitch black, and he flicked on a small, pencil size pocket light and saw that he was faced with double, blue framed glass doors. To his delight they were unlocked.

The doors opened with ease, backing up what all his senses were crying out to tell him that this was not the deserted, abandoned building they wanted you to believe. He caught a faint smell similar to one you would find at a butcher's. Harry knew that smell. He shone the light to illuminate the unit.

The floor was filthy, and he swung the beam at a measured pace over it. In certain sections there were dark stains, almost circular in shape, but arrayed in a pattern that concerned him: they were grouped in opposite corners. He approached the stains to his right, away in the farthest corner, and crouched down to give them a closer inspection. They seem to glisten when the light fell upon them and even with gloves on there was a clear tackiness to the touch. He looked over his left shoulder to the other corner; the symmetry was all too obvious: two separate groups standing milling around two arenas shouting, cursing, drinking, gambling over two separate dog fights before the winners faced off for one final hurrah. There was one clue that would clinch it and he scoured the floor surrounding the stains. His heart sank as the light revealed long scratch marks disappearing toward double-doors at the rear. Harry wasted no time and investigated. Behind the doors were two circular, metal frames standing approximately four to five feet high and around twelve to fifteen feet in diameter. There was nothing left to keep him here now.

Once outside in the fresh air Harry lowered the shutter, locked it and made for the doorway he'd used previously, expecting to be accosted at any moment. The sanctuary of the emergency exit was a welcome relief. He checked his watch; he would wait ten minutes to see if the security guard had been alerted.

Thirty minutes later he sat in his car saddened with his discovery, but at the same time happy and content with his investigation into Rusty's disappearance. It was another tick in the box for him albeit tinged with a sobering thought whenever he contemplated the poor dog's current circumstances.

* * *

'What does he have to say?' said a tall, dark haired man glaring, unblinkingly at the floor.

'He said, he checked it,' replied a slightly smaller, skittish man with mousy colored hair, which he constantly ran his fingers through whenever his nerves got the better of him.

'And I suppose the shutter moved itself did it!'

The skittish man shrugged his shoulders.

'Then go ask him, because if I do there won't be much left of him after!'

The man ran the obligatory fingers through his hair and departed to ask the fateful question.

While he was gone the tall, dark haired man crouched down and examined the padlock in finer detail, but the approaching footsteps of the returning messenger caused him to stand and half turn to his right. He waited impatiently for the answer. It was not what he wanted to hear.

There was only one thing for it and the shutter was pulled down to eclipse any daylight daring to invade the unit one more minute than was allowable. The electric light switch was flicked to provide the substitute.

Seven men occupied the space separated into two groups of three with the seventh, a solitary man, sitting strapped to a chair who flinched every time the tall man came anywhere near him.

One group of three stood in a line guarding the closed shutter, smiling, anticipating the inevitable.

The skittish man and his boss were two parts part of the other group; any interaction between them was shrouded by nervousness on one side and an innate hatred lingering menacingly just below and beyond any final remnants of benevolence on the other.

The seated man twitched incessantly.

'You checked it?' The boss said, standing over him with his hands on his hips.

The seated man nodded vigorously, grunting behind his taped over mouth.

'Sorry, I didn't quite hear that!'

The whole scene was repeated over again.

'No, I still can't quite grasp what you're trying to tell me.' And he violently removed the strip of sticky tape from over the man's mouth. The intense stinging pain took his breath away and a few short, sharp breaths were required to rebalance his senses before the next onslaught. The seated man was the security guard.

'Now, you tell me you checked everything?'

'I checked it, I checked everything over and over, and there was no sign of any entry, Mister Katic.'

'Then you explain to me why the padlock was found back to front!' Katic hissed.

'I don't know, I checked it, I swear!'

'Why don't I believe you?'

'I don't know.' And the seated man started to cry.

Neither of the other men made a sound.

Katic raised his line of sight to the ceiling contemplating his next move; he wanted to snap the man's neck to reinforce his position of authority, but that meant inheriting the awkward job of disposing of the body or he could show a small amount of leniency and let this schmuck off with just a slap. He pulled a switch blade from his trouser pocket and flicked it open.

'I don't know Mister Katic, I swear I don't!'

Katic stood stock still, poised, knife in hand, hovering it over his twitching victim then without any warning swiftly cut the binds holding his hands to the chair.

'They'll be back,' stated Katic, looking at the seated man, 'whoever they are, and when they do they need to see the same security guard on duty, that is the only reason why you're still breathing.'

The security guard nodded furiously.

'And you will not let them away with it next time!'

The guard again nodded furiously.

'Now get out of here before I change my mind!'

Within three minutes the security guard was nowhere to be seen.

'What about Saturday?' The skittish man asked.

'We still go ahead, but double the security.'

'Sure.'

'We can't risk anybody accusing us of sloppiness or unprofessionalism; our reputation, our foundation is built open us running the tightest ship around, more so than others, and if this gets out-'

'Based on a padlock?'

Katic turned to face them all. 'It's the simple measures that provide us with the greatest results: the padlock was placed in a certain way.' He moved his hands to signify the exact position. 'So that a quick examination can inform us if we've had visitors.'

'It's not him!' The skittish man said nervously, again running his hands through his mousy hair. 'He's been more than reliable.'

'I know. I took his past record into consideration.'

The three men standing quietly on guard by the shutter came forward on Katic's command to receive their orders, along with the other man who had remained mute throughout the episode, to prepare the place for Saturday's extravaganza while their boss made a few important phone calls to guarantee a more than respectable turn out.

* * *

Harry woke up and immediately thought of Rusty; the old lady had asked him for any news when he spoke to her yesterday. What could he tell her? He was off to Tennessee after a couple of standby duties for two weeks followed by trying to bail out Stephen with the casino, and on that point it had been worryingly quiet. Had he bit off more than he could chew? But the private investigator's life was one of feast and famine, so eat it up. Two days, he would give himself two days to get Rusty back or find out the truth about his demise, either way he would not charge this time. The thrill of the chase was more than sufficient to satisfy his needs. He prayed to be free of work to investigate that unit. He made a note of the number for the local dog warden and police station.

The day dragged on like a never-ending bad date or film with an explosive ending - one had to suffer to get to the final reel or the offer of coffee. Finally he parked his blue 924 in a different spot to last time, so as to not alert suspicion, checked again for cameras and took a different route to the industrial estate. He wore the same darkly colored, hooded jacket with black jeans, sneakers and gloves. Today was a Saturday and he figured, it being a weekend, they'd be punters with money to burn. Sure enough his sixth sense instantly alerted him that all was not the same and he made his way to a position to study the unit out of sight.

The unit's shutter was up, but the lights were mysteriously off with a mass of people milling around in the dark. Suddenly the light came on and they all entered in an orderly fashion. Harry looked around studying the surrounding area for the first time in detail to best ascertain the most expeditious route for a quick getaway. The unit was perfect for what was now its intended use: it didn't face the road, being situated well within the estate; a line of trees and a wire fence separated it from scrub land next to the river; any movement within could only be seen from an area illuminated immediately in front; and any noise was hardly discernible even from where he was crouching.

The crunch of gravel under foot caused his hand to reach for the Swiss army knife in his jacket pocket. He carefully removed it and opened the larger blade. The crunching stopped. His heart was thumping out of his chest; if whoever it was made a move on him he would stab a leg to gain a head start before their reinforcements turned up and stick to the shadows as best he could. The crunching became clearly discernible footsteps and the owner came into view. Even in the dim light Harry could see he was not to be messed with and displayed the body language of a man who knew of his previous visit. What clue had he left behind? He made sure his tracks were well covered and wore gloves all the time. Then it dawned on him. Had he been that stupid?

The stranger came into the light emitting from within the unit and Harry now saw a familiar face: it was the muscle from the casino, the one who said nothing during his brief conversation with Misters Willis and Moore. This put paid to his entering, but all was not lost when a large van turned into the estate. From inside the van a whining could be heard. He was not fooled and moved to an area by a large unkempt bush to espy the occupants exiting. Three handlers appeared pulling four dogs a piece and from their outward demeanor the twelve pooches clearly knew what fate awaited them. They all went inside.

Several minutes later two of the men returned with all their dogs.

Harry now had a conscience wrenching conundrum firmly on his hands: one he had no idea what Rusty actually looked like, the old lady described him as best she could so his mental picture was all he had to go on; second to release the eight meant sacrificing the four still inside.

The handlers loaded the dogs in the rear of the van, lowered the shutter, leaving it unlocked, and went inside with the muscle, pulling the unit shutter half way down before closing the door.

'Foolish!' Harry whispered.

The decision had been taken out of his hands, and he prayed for the four remaining dogs' suffering to be short lived.

Tommy's training proved invaluable and the van burst into life without too much trouble. He quickly selected reverse, gave himself room to maneuver, put it into first and crawled gently away keeping the engine revs low. Once out of sight of the unit he wasted no time increasing forward speed and exited the estate towards the river. He couldn't drive for long, as he was sure the van wouldn't be left unattended for great periods of time, so his thinking was to park the van on some waste land sitting beside a housing estate he knew was hidden from the road by a row of trees, let the dogs go before calling the council dog warden and police station complaining of a pack of dogs running riot and hopefully they would all get picked up. If any of the dogs matched his mental picture of Rusty he would inform the old lady that the council had her beloved dog.

It all went like clockwork and after replacing the public phone back in its cradle, he leant back against the door of the phone box before sauntering up the road happy with a good evening's work, and there was still time to get home and have a sharpener before retiring for the night. His joy was to be short lived when he thought of the four dogs left behind.

A car flashed past him straddling the center line, its speed reckless at best. Looking for the brake lights to illuminate he began to sweat and his heart rate increased tenfold. Less than a second later his question was answered.

The car reversed to within twenty yards of him and two men vacated.

'Where are you going?' The first man said ominously.

Harry knew to run meant an instant admission of guilt, but the man's tone infuriated him.

'What's it to do with you!'

The man took a step closer until his face was inches from Travers'. How easy, he thought, to cripple you with one swift upward jerk of my knee. Harry had positioned himself in a sideways on stance so any reciprocating movement would impact his thigh. The second man remained stationary midway between them and the car whose engine was ticking over sweetly.

Harry studied each man in turn; once the nearest man was disabled he would have to act fast to defend himself from the second.

'You better answer me!' snarled the nearest man.

It was him or them, and that meant all three being taken out with extreme prejudice: neither of the two had exited by the driver's door. His confidence level rose at this simple deduction under these intensely difficult circumstances.

The sharp, hard thud impacted his thigh, and it felt the most natural thing in the world to follow suit, only his hit the mark with deadly effect. The man exhaled under the pain and slumped to the floor. Man number two was only allowed three steps before a sharp kick to the solar plexus halted him; a quick step to the left with his right foot across the man's body coupled with his right hand over his shoulder and his left grabbing the man's right arm, and his adversary was thrown to the ground. Harry wasted no time following up the throw with two sharp punches to the face, breaking his nose. He turned sharply for the car, checking the two men were still on the floor as he did so, but it sped away.

Harry took a deep breath and three sharp steps backwards: this gave him some much needed breathing space. He was in the clear, for the time being, and expeditiously headed for his car.

His disposition fought at loggerheads with a desire for self-preservation. You are running away, it bellowed at him. Why? Why are you afraid of these? You should have stood your ground, they had nothing on you. He stood still car keys in hand, his right thumb rubbing the Porsche emblem on the key ring. He looked up the street waiting, yearning for them to appear, to help appease him from an enveloping, overwhelming feeling of cowardice.

He slowly placed the key back in his pocket. About ten yards from the end of the road he stopped and braced himself. Every car that drove past tensed his nerves ever tighter - he wanted them now. He needed to confront them, to crack their heads, to inflict immeasurable pain upon them: it was not only the dogs' suffering that stoked his anger, but the arrogance of these people to believe they could inflict pain on another living creature without fear of reprisal. 'Well here is your reprisal, I am your reprisal,' he said taking two further strides towards the junction, 'and I will gladly bear my pain long after you are gone!'

* * *

The house was warm and inviting. He checked his phone. There were no messages. He needed to hear from Sheila - not for any other reason than to begin the closure on his brother's case. Tomorrow he would find out when this card game will take place and if it somehow clashed with his visit to Tennessee. Even that was not a problem as there would be others.

He poured a large scotch and began to think of Tennessee and Tommy; the correspondence between the two was steady, about five messages a week, and with the day of departure imminent the excitement was almost tangible. This night's entertainment only stoked the flames of indignation: it was them or us, that's how it is, dog eat dog, survival of the fittest

The whiskey did its job admirably and Harry awoke stiff and still dressed. He was exhausted and wasted no time retiring for the night.

The day before his flight to Atlanta Harry had set aside, if he wasn't called off standby, as one of relaxation should the Rusty case be resolved, and after making a phone call to the old lady regarding sightings of a pack of dogs loose on a council estate, alongside a promise from her to call him if indeed Rusty was among those picked up, he sank into his sofa to watch a movie he'd taped weeks before and kept for when the time was right. That time was now. His phone rang. It was the old lady with good news.

* * *

Harry felt content, although there were no reported arrests over dog-fighting, which was disappointing. He packed his bags with the minimal of fuss. It was raining; he always liked to leave on a trip when the weather was bad: it made the traveling more acceptable. Tommy was alerted to his arrival and he had a date for the poker game: it was the end of the month, two days after his anticipated return. He could solve all three cases within one calendar month, and set off for Tennessee with a smile on his face and a decided spring in his step.

16

This third trip across the pond was the best yet and Harry touched down in Atlanta refreshed and raring to go: it is one of the beauties of having that precious knowledge before the fact which enables the ardent traveler to enjoy the experience to its utmost without the added vexation of wondering how the next stage of their journey will unfold.

He collected the dark blue Chevrolet Cruze hire car from the same firm as before with the same sales assistant as before, which meant he was on the road in double quick time regarded as the norm for valued returning customers. No time was wasted tuning the radio; he just turned it on, after a quick phone call to Tommy confirming his ETA: he had a change of heart over whether to let his friend know the exact time of his arrival, as it was decidedly to his advantage to have him watching his back. Harry was determined to enjoy the drive to Athens. The weather was fine with temperatures forecast to be in the high twenties and any clouds daring to challenge the day were dismissed accordingly. He set cruise control once on the interstate.

The scenery passing his window was awe inspiring and just the fillip needed to help harden his resolve to finally discover the truth regarding this man who felt compelled to leave his entire estate to him. The relative he couldn't barely have known and who would undoubtedly transform his life forever in a way he never could have envisaged; this uncle who Harry took very much to heart and whose death he felt personally to the point of adding names to a "kill list": a list only recently assembled as a way of never forgetting or becoming blasé over the demise of poor unfortunate souls daring to cross his path in search of the truth. His list currently held two entries: Bill and Bob. Athens held no fear for him: Tommy was still at large, free and single, so the police were as close to solving the incident as they were of finding the Loch Ness Monster and his conscience still held steadfast with not the slightest trace of guilt or sadness. He recognized in himself the hypocrisy inherent in mourning their passing because when if placed in the same position again he would surely repeat the exercise with probably an extra round discharged for good measure.

Harry smiled the smile of the contented man with a carefree disposition, happy in the knowledge that it would never change whatever the outcome.

The smooth roads never failed to impress him and over the airwaves came classic rock song after classic rock ballad. He was in heaven, and their hell awaited them - he would show no mercy to the originators of his pain and suffering. This agonizing void now ate away at his sense of injustice, deepening the sorrow for never having known or never will be allowed to know this man to who he held a deep respect. He took a cursory glance at the speedometer and slowly lifted his right foot to maintain a slim semblance of legality.

An image of Jeffries sprung up and his right foot naturally descended to previous levels. He was angry, livid, hell bent on revenge and knew his continued freedom depended on his channeling that hate towards the greater good of uncovering the truth.

A sign flashed past the window beckoning him onwards towards Athens, Tennessee. He backed off. Five minutes later his mobile phone rang. It was Tommy.

'Will be there a little after six!' he said before his friend could open any discourse.

Tommy said nothing.

'Tommy? Tommy?'

The phone went dead.

Harry checked the phone was indeed cut off then carefully placed it on the passenger seat. Was it Tommy? He mustn't presume anything.

Excellent, he thought, you know I'm here then just as quickly realized they didn't: the brief conversation had not given anything away. He couldn't have cared less. His heart rate increased and the adrenalin rush begun.

Hardware store, the thought flashed across his mind, he needed to find a hardware store. There's bound to be one close by in Athens. Go there first and buy adequate provisions, they will be waiting for you somewhere. Tommy's been compromised and they know everything.

The phone rang again, and he answered with hate dripping of every word.

'What you got to say that I want to hear?'

'What?' replied Tommy, knocked off kilter with the opening gambit by this clearly crazy Englishman.

'Tommy!'

'Who'd you think it was?'

'Them!'

'Why?'

Harry inspected his mirrors; he was not using hands-free.

'Why didn't you answer last time?'

'I could hear you, but you obviously couldn't hear me!'

'It occurred to me you, and your phone, were compromised!'

Tommy laughed a nervous laugh. Harry could tell from his tone during this brief exchange that his friend was aware of the seriousness the events were now being regarded.

'Everything's cool.'

'Glad to hear you're okay.'

Harry reiterated his expected ETA and then hung up. At least he and Tommy were now singing from the same hymn sheet.

On reflection the highlights of the day evaporated before his very eyes with even greater alacrity the older he became, as the familiar sights of Athens, Tennessee came into view inviting him on to fulfill his destiny. He slowed to allow himself one final look at the town from this perspective.

A right turn off the David W Lillard Memorial Highway followed by a left and Tommy's current residence on County Road 681, Etowah appeared before him. He parked in the road.

Harry took a second or two to scour its length and breadth. After two passes of the road nothing seemed out of the ordinary, and he vacated the hire car to walk over to Tommy's front door.

His friend's welcoming grin greeted his first steps on the porch.

'Saw you park. Everything okay?'

'Perfect. How's you?'

'Eager to get started. No bags?'

'In the car.'

'Leave them, we've got much to discuss.'

Tommy waved Harry ahead of him into the house before closing the door on the brightly lit interior.

The two men naturally gravitated towards the kitchen and icebox which was always filled with at least a couple of days' supply of beer.

'Help yourself,' said Tommy, 'I have emergency rations if needed.'

Harry removed two ice cold beers. The condensation ran down his fingers. He opened them on the bottle opener screwed to the kitchen work top and handed one to Tommy.

'What's the latest?'

'Jeffries has been conspicuous by his absence: he's out of town.'

Harry sipped his beer contemplating when to let the man know he was back.

'When are you going to see him?'

'When I'm good and ready.'

Harry disguised his anger and intense frustration at not being able to fire a broadside by quickly downing his beer and going in search for more. He retrieved two beers from the icebox.

'When did you find out he was away?' he asked.

'Yesterday: he left about ten in the morning, shortly after breakfast. I know that because I saw him pass me on the road.'

'You had breakfast together,' he said jokingly.

'Yeah, right.'

Travers' quizzical look called for more of an explanation.

'We share the same diner sometimes, but not since this kicked off,' Tommy answered mockingly.

Both men laughed that slightly awkward laugh needed to help clear the air before quickly falling back into the ways of their previous time together.

'Hungry?' enquired Tommy.

Harry was suddenly ravenous: 'Pizza?'

'You read my mind,' smiled the American and dialed out.

The alcohol continued to flow and the more they consumed the more the mutual appreciation society grew again between the two men.

* * *

Jake Boyd stood hands on hips staring incredulously at Jeffries' office door agitated at his not being there to answer some very important questions. He tried the door handle again. It was still locked. He gave it a sharp kick, muttered an obscenity under his breath, turned and stormed back to his car.

The black Corvette beeped twice to the interrogation from the key fob, and Jake bordered still seething. He picked up his cellphone from the center console, paused in order to run the opening line of the conversation over in his head, and rung out: Jake and his brothers had recently told their father everything regarding their run in with Jack Hennessey, and to their surprise he was not angry, but impressed that they should attempt anything off their own backs.

'The bastard's gone! What do you want to do?'

Jake braced himself. His father barked out a series of instructions for his eldest to follow.

'Someone's got to watch his office; he's gonna run!'

Boyd senior agreed, and it was decided to alternate the responsibility for Jeffries between the three boys.

'I'll take first watch on his house.' Jake was going to put his infamous short temper to good use if he ever found himself in the position to put this son of a bitch lawyer in his place. He hung up, looked around to ensure he wasn't being followed, gunned the Corvette into life and wheel spun out of the car park to begin the first of his father's chores.

Jake braked harder than he expected in order to obey the red light glaring at him from the cables suspended over the road. He cussed again and slammed his right hand on the steering wheel. This preoccupation with the light and its temerity to delay his forward progress distracted him from his mirrors and the dark blue Chevrolet sitting two cars back.

Harry double checked he wasn't being tailed. His tail was clear. The lights turned green and the train of cars gently rolled forward before progressively picking up speed until they all sat just under the speed limit. Harry found himself becoming bemused with his quarry: why is he not utilizing his car to the utmost?

One of the cars between the two men turned left. Harry instinctively dropped back hoping somebody would take their place.

The gap remained unfilled. Harry closed it once he was satisfied Jake hadn't clocked him.

The day was going to be a hot one, according to the man on the radio, and the haze already began to form. Although it was sunny with clear skies it was not an ideal day to fly. This was usually a good month with near perfect visibility in these parts.

Jake hung a left into Howard Street, the final car between them carried on. Harry had to follow. To his dismay Jake parked up only thirty yards into the road directly outside a pale blue house, and to make matters worse vacated the vehicle just as he drove by. Harry held his nerve, made a mental note of the house number and stared straight ahead. From the corner of his eye he knew Jake never looked his way.

He parked up and surreptitiously positioned himself in such a way as to get the best view and the undoubted fireworks that were going to erupt.

The elder Boyd stopped on the sidewalk for no more than a second, removed a slip of paper from his back pocket, read it once, returned it and entered the house with a determined, forceful look on his face.

Ten minutes went by and all was quiet.

A passing motorist jerked his head violently to the right and gave Harry the once over, their eyes examining his every detail. He hated to surrender this prime position.

The Chevy's engine burst into life at the third time of asking, but only after a few well-chosen words and phrases; his anger turned to impatience, but he paid particular mind to be careful not to draw any unwanted attention and this desire was transmitted in his driving. At the end of the road he turned right onto Cook Drive followed by a further right on Westside Street via Frye Street. Harry just had to keep turning right in order to return to Howard Street. Cleveland Avenue came into view and he took it.

A patrol car passed him going the other way, but his vehicle clearly was not their concern.

The house once again came into view, as he re-entered Howard Street and he immediately sought out Jake's car. It was still parked as before. He pulled in by the side of the road, but further up. He needed to be invisible, thought about reclining the seat, abolished that idea and opened the glove compartment. Inside was an old copy of a motoring magazine. He removed the crumpled, dog eared copy and pretended as best he could to feign interest and read. He was spared the contents beyond page three by the emergence of Jake carrying a malicious grin guaranteed to bring his blood to the boil, but he calmed himself with the knowledge that he had this address and would return as soon as practicable to source the cause of his quarry's amusement.

Jake made straight for the Corvette, fired her up and aggressively pulled out into the road. Harry followed at a sedate pace.

The approaching junction came into view again and he witnessed Jake slowing momentarily, make no visible indication, turn right onto Cook Drive and accelerate. Harry followed, entering the flow of traffic three cars behind.

He instinctively pulled on his inertia seat belt - this had all the potential to get messy.

Jake mirrored him and there was a moment when he thought his cover was blown, but the Corvette showed no signs of trying to outrun him. At the end of Cook Drive the Corvette turned right onto West Madison Avenue. Shortly after a quick right then left put them both on Rocky Mountain Road, which linked up with Congress Parkway South.

Harry was now lost, but cared not. He contemplated digging around in the bag deposited in the passenger seat foot-well and charging up the satnav, but this would ultimately mean having to take one's eye of the target and he was loath to do that.

Jake accelerated just as Harry got the notion to call Tommy: he had deliberately kept his intentions quiet and left the house before his friend was up. Tommy was a heavy sleeper, as testified by his snoring, so it was easy to slip away unnoticed. He called the house number.

For someone left in the lurch Tommy was surprisingly unperturbed at the change of events and proceeded to try and answer Travers' queries to his exact whereabouts: his best guess was he was heading north along the Decatur Pike. He wasn't far out. Jake turned left and north onto that exact road.

'Are you sure it's him?' he finally asked Harry.

'I've met the other two, and there's a distinct family resemblance.'

'He's alone then?'

'Sure is.'

'Be careful: Jake Boyd is as mean as they come!'

Harry then rattled off the address he needed Tommy to investigate, adding the obvious caveat to tread carefully.

Tommy licked his lips: this was more like it, he couldn't be bothered tailing people or doing any of the good old fashioned leg work this mad Englishman seemingly loved to do, but breaking and entering with full justification was more his forte.

Harry hung up and looked ahead just in time to witness his quarry double the gap. Like that was it? Was he testing him to see whether Harry was a tail? He'd find out soon enough and reduced the gap to three car lengths. He didn't have to wait long to get the answer.

Again Jake increased his forward speed, pulling out a gap of six car lengths, only this time he clearly made out the tell-tale head movement of someone carefully checking their rearview mirror.

A road sign flashed past his right side indicating the miles to run to the I-75.

Harry was already losing patience and increased his forward speed sufficiently to maintain a slightly smaller four car lengths. It was enough to spur the Corvette into action and if it wasn't for Travers' anticipation it would have been almost impossible to catch, but the Cruze, so far, was a match for the sports car.

He had taken the precaution before arriving at Jeffries' to fill the tank, and this was now a cause for concern: the extra weight, which the Corvette to the best of his knowledge had the advantage of not having to carry, was going to slow him down. He felt easy with every passing mile at the thought of a reducing fuel load. The gap, after all the fun and games, was a little over two car lengths.

Suddenly Jake, no longer wanting to be the stalked, decided to be the stalker with an aggressive application of the brakes. Only a near violent pull on the steering wheel allowed Harry to avoid rear-ending the Corvette. Jake pulled in behind him. Harry was now the prey.

He craned his neck to get a better view. If Jake was prepared to risk a near fatal accident to get the upper hand then he'd better do the same. A road sign appeared alerting drivers to the upcoming exit and the I-75 northbound to Knoxville. Harry stayed away from the inside lane. Jake filled his rear view mirror flaunting his new found position of authority, and his returning to Tommy's with him in tow was now not an option. He was backed up into a corner and both knew it.

Harry veered hard right across the inside lane judging his entry into the exit to perfection. Jake braked hard, but overshot it and was forced to carry on. Harry now faced with a new dilemma: how was he going to exit the interstate, chase down and find Jake amongst the throng of traffic? It didn't take a genius to realize today's sport was over. He would continue on for a few miles then take the next convenient exit for Athens. Harry wasted little time in making himself comfortable, plugged in his satellite navigation and programmed the way home before tuning in a local radio station playing mainly tunes from the seventies and eighties. Regular checks in his mirrors satisfied his demand for self-preservation.

A popular rock song burst over the radio waves and he sang along reliving his youth, remembering a time long gone when he watched this band live with his first serious girlfriend. It made him wonder whatever happened to her: their relationship ended when she made him force his hand and choose between flying and continuing being a couple, which under the circumstances was unfair in his eyes when you took into account the considerable amount of money already invested in attaining his commercial pilot's license. The song ended and he again checked his mirrors. All was clear.

The exit for the John J Duncan Parkway was advertised and he knew taking it meant he could connect with the Congress Parkway and head back to Athens.

The road was relatively quiet and Harry was beginning to calm significantly when the dark colored Corvette filled the space bordered by the confines of his rearview mirror. He smiled, but he shouldn't: it was not the reaction he would have expected from himself before all this kicked off, but it was the recognition of new breeding, a new beginning as Harry Travers Private Detective.

Jake pulled in closer. Harry waved then gave him 'the bird'.

He needed a gun, any gun: it was a foregone conclusion that Jake was packing some kind of firearm, but in his haste to be free of the house without alerting Tommy he was amiss not to cover all eventualities and secure one.

Oh well, he thought, if this is the way it has to be.

Both cars continued along the road, holding station for a couple of miles, although their speed was reckless on certain sections of the road drawing audible complaints from fellow motorists.

Harry was becoming irritable with this pathetic excuse for a game of cat and mouse and slammed on his brakes, returning Jake's gift with pleasure. Jake was not him and careered head long into the back of the Cruze smashing the Corvette's immaculate fiberglass bodywork. The impact was severe, but his air bag failed to deploy. Harry laughed.

It was best to keep the Chevy's two liter engine running because he figured the elder Boyd would make a run for it and sure enough Harry had but taken two steps out of the car, keeping his right hand in his pocket in an attempt to fool him that he was indeed armed, when the Corvette rapidly reversed, swung through one hundred and eighty degrees and was off back the way they came. Harry gave chase.

His growing confidence in reading situations allowed him to truly appreciate Jake's skill in the maneuver, for when he next espied the American he was well up the road.

For the first time that day he openly cussed the Cruze: its acceleration was not the Corvette's from a standing start, even though it was a stick shift, and hired for that direct purpose

The road ahead looked different, was different, and he was at a marked disadvantage: his quarry would know the surrounding countryside, be ready to brake, corner, accelerate and be cautious when Harry would not, but it was this cautiousness that led to the reduction in space and time between the two cars. Harry took the road as fast as the car could take it, nearly landing the vehicle in a roadside tree at least twice.

'Let's see what you got!' he called out before lowering his window to allow cooling air in.

The Corvette drew inextricably closer. He relaxed his shoulders, took a deep breath and took full notice of the brake lights illuminating on his prey's car as the road began to bear to the right. He would not brake and use the man's inability to drive to place himself on the Corvette's tailpipe, but his confidence was stupidity wrapped up in arrogance and the Chevy complained bitterly at what it was being ordered to do and carried straight on into a small ditch, through the other side and only a hard right turn avoided an impact with a tree. Harry kept the revs high in second gear forcing the car to drive one wheel in the ditch the other clipping bushes growing near the base of the trees. At a level section he rejoined the road ahead of a small truck that had up to that point been a spectator. The air turned blue with a few well-chosen words. The spectator blew his horn.

'You are not my problem today!' Harry was aware that Jake was now out of sight, and if he didn't make any kind of visual contact within the next five minutes then the game was up. The spectator was soon dispatched off his tail.

The road disappeared beneath the bonnet of the Chevy in a blur as he ate up the miles, his frustration and anger rising with every passing property. Ego and vanity raised their ugly heads to bring about his undoing, and he simply waved them on, accepting their kind words of encouragement and support onwards and upwards to doomed failure and the ditch of despair. He thumped the steering wheel three times hard and screamed. He was going to kill that scheming, lying, murderous son of a bitch; afraid of Jake Boyd, you kidding me, afraid of a man who runs from a "Johnny Foreigner" driving a Chevy Cruze. He banged the wheel a fourth time. The road ahead was empty.

Harry floored the accelerator, watching the speedometer needle cruise past ninety. Screw the police, screw the speeding ticket. His speed was over a hundred by the time the car came into view and the Corvette attempted to retaliate in kind by holding station for a few miles, but inevitably it failed: the damaged bodywork hampering any forward progress. Harry closed to four or five car lengths - he had his prey and there was going to be no reprieve this time.

Travers' anger was replaced by calmness and clarity of vision. He saw Jake's head twitch every second awaiting his move. He daren't risk the Corvette in another brake test and Harry knew this as well as he knew the Chevy was built to withstand punishment. He floored the accelerator again and rammed the Corvette.

'What you gonna do now, eh?' he shouted, and rammed it again.

The Corvette swerved violently first left then right under the driver induced oscillation. Harry waited with eager anticipation for the inevitable accident. To his bitter disappointment it never came, so he tried a third time to remove the car and Jake from the road. Any fear trying to explain all this to the hire company dissipated with Jake's original impact: the car was going to get stolen.

Jake, to his mild astonishment, began to pull away. 'Good boy!' Harry was impressed and pleased that his day's sport was going to be prolonged. He was totally lost now, caught up in this man's total destruction to worry about fear of reprisals or attacks of conscience.

The long, sweeping road headed north through the beautiful Tennessee countryside and it meant nothing to him anymore. They were well passed the interstate, his only desire was to witness the destruction of his enemy and if any locals wished to witness it then let it be his pleasure to provide some much needed entertainment at this Boyd's expense - have a gift from a "Johnny Foreigner".

Something now appeared different; there was a definite sense within him of a subtle shift in the balance of power, and it crept over him as he tried to digest all the available information. Jake's body language backed up what his innermost alarm bells were alerting him to, intimating, suggesting Jake's arrogance and an air of confidence. Was he now the prey? The cocky shoulder movement, the raised head searching the mirror was not for him. It was to gauge the arrival of reinforcements. Harry studied the road left behind them in their wake and sure enough he was being closed in on. Jake began to slow, and he nearly collected the Corvette.

'So that's how it is! You want to play that game?'

This game was new, and he accepted the challenge with open arms and a gratitude only appreciated by those willing to embrace victory and defeat in equal measure.

Jake passed a tight left hand bend. Harry braked hard and took it, turning left onto County Road 207, his satellite navigation system began to recalculate his position to guide him home, but he ignored it. Jake vanished from sight to be replaced by rows of tall, statuesque trees lining the narrow road like soldiers on parade awaiting inspection.

The freedom from the road gave him free reign to test the torque of the Chevy and gain as much breathing space as humanly possible. His taking the turn was a gamble: one he knew even less of this piece of Tennessee; and two Jake was obviously in two way communication with the other car, which had to be a sibling, and he could be, as he spoke, speeding towards a self-made trap, but these were mute points he saw daring to raise their heads above the parapet guarding the bigger picture incorporating the greater scheme of things.

The second car emerged from the main road taking a faultless line, giving chase. Even from this distance it was a brute of a machine guaranteed to eat up the yards separating the two combatants. Harry had the Chevy on the limit of his and the car's ability, readily accepting his fate, but their attempted seizure had unwittingly played into his hands: Jake would be waiting, breath bated for him to appear ahead of his brother in hot pursuit. After a right hand turn the road became the 213 and Harry accelerated hard once again before coming abruptly to a stop, parking the car, and hightailing behind some trees. Once out of sight he removed his Swiss army knife, opening the longest blade.

A dark red Mustang made the turn and following an aggressive application of the brakes parked up by the side of the road behind the Cruze.

Foolish, thought Harry, who was already on the move by the time Carl had come to a halt. He paid careful attention to avoid being seen in the Mustang's mirrors. Silence prevailed. Carl would ring out. Harry didn't hesitate and yanked open the driver's side door.

The pin sharp tip of the larger Swiss army knife blade impacted his throat and cut short the trace of Carl's fingers over his cell-phone. Harry said nothing, only pointing to the phone before running an index finger in a cutting motion across his throat. Carl never made the call.

'Put your hands on the wheel!'

Carl obeyed.

'I will kill you.....in a heartbeat, if you force my hand. Do you understand?'

Carl nodded, never taking his eyes off Harry.

Harry searched him and removed Carl's firearm and cell-phone.

'Now talk! Who killed my uncle?'

'We didn't!'

'Who did then?'

'Jeffries!'

'How convenient........why?'

Carl remained mute.

'Hoping your brother will save you? You'll be dead the moment I hear any car! Why?'

'I don't know!'

'Wrong answer, think again!'

Harry was on the verge of inserting the smallish blade into the side of the middle Boyd's neck. Two small beads of sweat began their slow laborious trek from Carl's forehead to his chin, as the first distinctive growls of the Corvette winding its way toward them could clearly be discerned. Harry moved his face to within an inch of Carl's.

'I neither have the time, patience or inclination to deal with people who do nothing but show me the true value of pampering to my misanthropic side!'

Carl blinked in quick succession: 'Money,' he uttered, 'and lots of it!'

'How much?'

'Millions!'

Jake's Corvette was imminent.

'You don't have very long.' He inserted the blade a millimeter into Carl's neck.

'I don't know it all, I swear I don't. All I know is your uncle discovered the whereabouts of a large sum of money stolen over thirty years ago and buried somewhere.'

Carl paused to swallow in a vain attempt to lubricate his throat: fear and panic at impending doom was drying him up.

'Go on.'

The Corvette was now only seconds away, but Harry never took his eyes off the younger brother.

'He told Jeffries where it was buried, and he killed him for it!'

Harry moved swiftly back to the Chevy, training Carl's gun on the Mustang. He threw the cell-phone across the road.

The Chevy started first time and he was out of sight by the time Jake came to rest by the side of the Mustang containing one shaken younger sibling, rocked to the very core of his own existence.

The previous highway was a welcoming sight to him, embracing in eager anticipation his agitation, willing to allay any rising concerns in the short term and beckoning him back with open arms to his temporary home to help restock, recharge and finalize the delivery of the appropriate justice.

17

Tommy was ready and waiting on his return, as if his arrival had been preordained. Suspicions arose and were quelled in equal measure. He parked the car, shut her down and from the corner of his eye monitored his friend: this uneasiness, this distrust was exhausting, draining what reserves were needed to be allocated for the lawyer.

'We got a problem!' Tommy said gravely, as he vacated the hire car.

'Why?'

'The man you saw Jake visit today is dead!'

The news failed to have the impact on his nerves one would expect; he half expected it and smiled sardonically.

'Heart attack,' Tommy added, knowing what the next question would be.

Harry grunted: he cared not to supply anything remotely resembling a response and backed it up with a labored shrug of the shoulders. He was utterly drained and this fatigue, rather than creep furtively up from behind, sparing the recipient any unwanted anguish in the anticipation, sprang full bore, overwhelming his senses.

'You'll have fun explaining that away!' Tommy said admiring the Cruze's bodywork.

He led his worn-out friend into the house and back into the open plan kitchen-cum-diner-cum TV room, and immediately started to prepare them both a drink from a homemade bar standing in the corner of the room.

'You've been busy in my absence,' Harry said on inspecting the new addition.

'I thought you might feel more at home with a place to rest those elbows of yours!'

Harry smiled and felt himself perk up at the first signs of friendly banter.

Tommy disappeared to be replaced with the clinking of glasses and the telltale resonance of full and half empty liquor bottles impacting. Harry stood patiently, fiddling with his car keys. Tommy still hadn't appeared after nearly two minutes.

'For fuck's sake, come on!' he finally said with rising frustration adding to the dryness building exponentially in his mouth with each passing second without a drink.

'Patience!' shouted the barman, still clinking bottles and glasses.

Harry took to tapping his feet in an attempt to give his drink the hurry up.

Tommy eventually appeared glasses in his right hand, Smith and Wesson M&P Bodyguard 38 in the other. A sudden chill descended over the room and straight down Travers' spine. His pathetic pocket knife was not going to help him here, and Carl's gun was in the car. His eyes darted carefully around the room trying desperately hard not to draw attention to any scheme that may aid his defense.

He clenched his right hand into a fist and the moistness of his palm made maintaining it nigh on impossible. Should he make a run for it? No, that would be pointless and a complete waste of energy needed for a sounder getaway. How about charging the man? No, his only possible salvation lay in persuasion and using their growing friendship as some sort of leverage to extricate himself from this mire. His mind now began searching for any common ground to use as a possible defense before an opening could be negotiated and an onslaught initiated.

'I'm impressed Harry, really impressed!' Tommy's booming voice snapped his train of thought in two. Tommy lowered the gun.

'You bastard!'

His so called friend burst into a fit of raucous laughter, almost to the point where he found it nigh on impossible to remain standing. 'My little joke,' he managed to get out between breaths. 'I wanted to see your reaction!'

Harry stood stock still, hands by his side, rooted to the spot, relieved, and smiling awaiting the inevitable return to normality. If there could ever be that in his world again.

Tommy straightened his back, put the gun on the bar beside the two empty glasses and collected a bottle of clear liquid from underneath. He poured two drinks, picked up the gun again before coming round the side of the mini bar.

He handed the firearm to Harry butt first: 'I saw it and thought of you!'

Harry stared dumbfounded at the revolver deposited in his hand and took a minute to get his head round the extraordinary gift presented him just minutes after he was contemplating killing his friend. The Smith and Wesson was lightweight, fitted with a Crimson Trace Laser Sight, had a synthetic grip, felt good in the hand and the chamber held five rounds of .38 S&W Special with a concealed hammer. He fell in love with it instantly.

'You'll need it more than you care to know!' Tommy said gravely.

Next came a half filled glass of the clear liquid, which he never hesitated to drink. The slow burning sensation trickled down his innards, as all good hard liquor does, and he felt himself relax under its effect. 'I was figuring out a way-'

'I know!'

Tommy once again erupted into laughter and it perfectly defused the potentially awkward situation.

The rest of the day was spent sharing information, conjecturing on the turn of events and where they were likely to go; the old man in the house had a history of heart disease, but Jake's unannounced visit didn't help, and what was his connection to the Boyd family? Jeffries must be due back tomorrow and it was agreed to tail him. Harry decided it was wise not to keep anything back regarding his interesting experience with the two Boyd brothers and the buried booty.

Tommy fell silent.

'What's up?'

'I know the job Carl referred to!'

'That's convenient.'

'What's that supposed to mean?' Tommy's back rose just as much and just as fast as Travers' suspicions had earlier.

Harry needed to tread carefully: 'Only they seem to have been trying to rub you up the wrong way since the first day we met. I have to wonder if they know too, or more to the point do they know that you know!'

Tommy poured himself and Harry another shot.

'How much are we talking about? Carl said it was millions.'

'Half a million to a million,' Tommy replied between sips.

'That'll buy you a whole heap of trouble!'

'It was a heist: a gang of four held up a security van. The year was 1967.'

Tommy paused for further lubrication.

'One was my father. He was clever enough to cover his tracks, even from the others who clearly were not, but who none the less never ratted on him. My father made sure to his dying day their families never wanted for anything.'

'Honor among thieves.'

'Damn right!'

'But do they know about your father?'

'The money was buried by a fifth man: the idea being that the four would drop of the cash, each knowing a separate clue to where the money would be buried, so not to be in a position to inform the police if questioned.'

'There are obvious flaws in that plan, which we shan't go into,' Harry interposed, 'but it does beg the question, who was the fifth man?'

'Don't know, but he didn't keep it for himself.'

'Jeffries found out. That would explain a lot: his reticence, wanting a quick sale with no interference and not wishing for any investigation to linger on for too long.'

Harry strode pensively over to a back window. 'We got to search my uncle's house again. Turn it inside out this time!'

'You have justification, not that you ever needed it,' Tommy uttered.

'I was trying to avoid the need-'

'This has got nothing and everything to do with me!' Tommy said. The last thing he needed or wished was to come under any form of suspicion considering Jeffries was the one who asked him to help out.

'It would be so easy to keep an eye on the both of us, with the help of the Boyd brothers, while he figured out where it was buried!' Harry said softly, belying his true feelings.

'And it's far too easy or convenient for a stranger with a history of heart disease to be the fifth member, far too easy.'

'He thinks you know where it is!' Harry said.

'My father, when he did finally admit to me his role in the whole affair, was not bitter about it, he never was. Whether he saw his continued freedom as payment enough I don't know.'

'What if the fifth man died?' Travers' eyes lit up.

'And Jeffries was the lawyer handling the estate.' Tommy was on his wavelength.

'Discovering hidden away in his personal papers information pertinent to the heist and where the money might be buried.'

'But in a cruel twist of fate your uncle had beaten him to it?'

Harry took a step into the center of the room. His eyes alight with the fire of indignation: 'As we speak the lawyer is digging.' He started to laugh.

'There's nothing we can do about it right now, but tomorrow we'll take the Cessna and partake of a little R&R.'

'One more for the road, I got to keep a clear head,' Harry said smiling. The two friends downed a large one.

* * *

The day began as the two men prayed it would with clear skies and the promise of more of the same for the next few days, but Harry had not slept well. His conscience, normally so reliable and steadfastly chilled when it came to anything remotely resembling guilt, had plagued him all night. The cause of his troubles: his treatment of Carl. He was not a killer per se or a man of intrinsic violence, he saw it only as a necessary action to be used in circumstances of extreme self-preservation, but Carl was different; killing him felt the most natural thing in the world to do. Harry tried to brush any misgivings under the proverbial table knowing that if the same scenario was played out all over again the result would be no different. His mood failed to improve much during the morning. If this was the life of the investigator he wished to be, he finally growled, then get used to it. This brief, sharp self-chastisement seemed to do the trick and he ate breakfast wearing a forced smile for his friend's benefit.

The drive to the airport was pleasant enough to perk him up sufficiently to discuss the day's events. Tommy had done the smart thing and fuelled up the Cessna in advance.

Tommy was confident that any digging work would be clearly evident from the air and to this effect asked Harry to do the flying.

Harry was instantly his former self and agreed whole heartedly. He loved the low flying: it fuelled his adrenaline habit, gave him a real buzz and it snapped him firmly back in line as they arrived at McMinn County Airport.

* * *

Carl's face stung with an intensity he'd long since forgotten when his wilder, younger days haunted his every move. His father had not hit him in many a year.

'I didn't raise you to act dumb!' Jessie growled.

'What was I supposed to do, pa? Let him knife me!'

'Now you're acting dumb!'

'Go easy on him!' Jake knew that his younger brother was taking the rap and sparing him the indignity of having to explain himself away.

'Do you honestly think,' Jessie went on, 'that this goddamn Limey would ever actually have the fucking balls to do it?' Jessie paused, allowing his words to have the desired effect. 'If you did then you are dumber fuck than you already look.'

'What's our next move?' squeaked Rudy, who was standing behind his father trying not to bring too much attention onto himself, but realizing that he needed to add something to the proceedings.

'Kill him!'

The three sons said nothing, leaving their father to repeat the threat: 'We got to kill him now that he knows everything, before we deal with that two-timing bastard lawyer, who as we speak has probably dug it up and re-hid it, plus there's the small matter of the Corvette to fix!'

'We should never have trusted him!' Jake said what they all were thinking.

'Your Uncle Remus,' Jessie started in a more softer, reverential tone, 'was as secretive as they come; he kept the secret of where that money was buried all these years and never once told a soul, not even to his own kin.'

'Nobody knew he was involved; if we had known Jeffries wouldn't have got within a thousand miles of it!' For once Rudy's natural squeak abandoned him for a more polished, confident inflexion. 'We started with the dirty work, so let's finish it with the dirty work. Kill 'em all!'

Jessie nodded then slowly studied each of his sons in turn for any telltale signs of weakness or dissension. 'No loose ends!' he said once satisfied.

* * *

The Cessna left the tarmac and climbed majestically, but methodically, up to three thousand feet on track to his uncle's supposed final resting place.

Harry was right at home: whenever life got him down or the stresses of everyday existence felt like they were starting to make inroads into his sanity, he would take to the air and remind himself of his luck and great good fortune to be paid to see the world from God's own perspective. Today was no different: Tennessee in all its glory lay before them, the Volunteer State beckoning them on, inviting those privileged enough to see her panoramic beauty as the omnipotent one intended.

Tommy made all the radio calls leaving both men alone in their thoughts.

'What do you expect to see?' asked Harry, starting the slow descent on Tommy's command.

'We'll know when we see it!'

They were now flying along the western edge of the large ridge that was Starr Mountain and to aid in each other's search he slowed the Cessna right down, extended some flaps to maintain a safety margin over the stall speed and lowered the nose to improve their forward visibility.

The two men agreed it was prudent to begin in one section and orbit using a fixed point on the ground as reference then once that section was clear move on to the next, this way they would be able to cover all the land in a reasonable time without the risk of missing something vital due to their impatience.

The first pass gave up nothing, but the second and third produced some interesting results in the shape of hunters out searching for sport. There were a couple of moments when it occurred to the intrepid flyers that they may be fired upon, but it passed without incident.

Tommy pointed to a clump of trees standing on slightly raised ground for their next reference marker. Harry made a beeline for it, descending to three hundred feet before eventually leveling at a hundred feet above the treetops.

Suddenly the Cessna shook violently under a fearful thud. Both men looked at each other then began the thorough examination of the aircraft and its instruments. Then it happened again.

'We're being shot at!' exclaimed Harry incredulously. He was furious at their effrontery, but reluctantly admired the skill of the shooter at being able to hit such a moving target. 'I have the 38 in my bag,' he added. Harry had brought a small bag in which he carried a bottle of water, a small first aid kit, his Swiss Army knife and the gun.

Tommy leant over the back of his chair and fished feverishly in it for the firearm.

'Fat lot of good it will do us!' he grumbled on righting himself.

The Cessna was rocked a third time.

'Stuff this!' Harry banked the aircraft hard over to the left to get the best view immediately beneath them to search the forest for gun flashes.

A piercing white flash appeared in his ten o'clock followed by the tell-tale puff of smoke. They were not hit.

'Got him!' Harry said with glee.

'Careful Harry, he's a damn good shot!'

'Trust me, I'm a captain!'

Harry locked onto the spot on the ground where he initially espied the gun flash, and circled.

'I don't feel comfortable with this,' Tommy finally said after ten minutes of orbiting. 'He's long gone. They would have fired a volley of shots by now.'

Harry hated to admit it, but he was right and began the climb away to relative safety. McMinn Airport would only take twenty minutes. He knew that to continue this futile exercise was only going to drag him before the authorities, if any complaints were logged about his low flying. He leveled off at two thousand feet.

Tommy placed the 38 back in the bag. 'The man is away on business, as far as we know. He does hunt, although I wouldn't have put him in this league as a shot, plus he now has the motive!'

'We'll come back tomorrow once we've checked everything out.'

Harry cross-checked the fuel gauges and the underside of the wings for any signs of vapor indicating a leak. Thankfully the gauges remained steady and happy that no emergency forced landing was imminent turned the Cessna 172 west and headed for home.

On Tommy's instruction he parked the aircraft away from prying eyes on a section of the apron that gave them the best chance of inspecting the damage without drawing any attention. The damage turned out to be nothing too serious: there were three holes the size of a small coin in the underside and topside of the fuselage about two thirds of the way up. Luckily all had missed the rudder cables.

'That was too close for comfort!' Tommy said running his hand over the bullet holes.

'I'll go alone tomorrow!' insisted Harry.

'You want to go again?'

'Yep!'

Tommy didn't argue.

* * *

Jeffries was sweating profusely: one he had ran as fast as his unfit legs would carry him to get to his office this morning before the inevitable calls rained in; and two he was nervous, more nervous than he had been for many a year. He unlocked his office door just in time to answer the first call of the day. Luckily for him his secretary was late today. It was Jessie Boyd.

'Calm yourself!' Jeffries said straight off, his nerves being replaced with the first signs of contempt. 'I'm not screwing any of you. It wasn't there!'

Boyd senior was not going to be placated that easily.

'And how do you possibly think I'm going to move that amount of money without bringing any attention upon myself?' Jeffries said to his recent partner in crime's accusation that he would never be able to get away with cutting them out.

Jessie calmed a little.

'You forget I need you as much as you need me, but I am taking more of a risk. If they discover the truth it leads straight back to me not you or your kin!'

Jessie calmed enough to suggest methods for the removal of the two thorns in their side.

'As soon as possible!' was all Jeffries offered.

'We know where they are,' Jessie said slowly, 'we've always known, and what they're doing, so it will be done by tomorrow's end!'

'I will clean up here, as for the money I've figured out where it is!' Jeffries said in a more reassured tone.

Jessie said nothing.

'As a show of faith you can retrieve it once the thorns are gone!'

Twenty seconds later Jeffries sat behind his desk with his head in his hands rubbing his tired eyes determined to put an end to this. He was exhausted. Why should he shoulder all the responsibility for everybody getting paid, let them take the risk for a change. He had never intended to have a partner or partners: this was always his idea to be played out to his timetable, but they had discovered he was also looking for the money and so their collaboration unfortunately became unavoidable, but here they were now fucking it up. Today was going to be one dictated to by a troubled mind racing with possible solutions to the deadly conundrum of disposing of a dead body; the killing was easy, the removal of any damning evidence not so, and letting loose a volley of shots at Tommy's Cessna, knowing full well that the chances of hitting the thing were slim to none, was really only an exercise in overcoming the self-imposed mental barrier protecting one's inner peace from such a heinous crime. The shots worked, he was ready to kill now once the form of disposal was agreed upon.

* * *

Harry was eager to be on his way this bright, sunny morning, but was forced to wait on the hire car firm to come out and check over the remains of the Chevy: he had lied through his teeth, loving every minute of it, telling the young woman on the other end of the phone that the car had been rammed both ends whilst parked, and as there were no witnesses he hadn't bothered to inform the police. It was a complete and utter waste of their time, he argued, but she had insisted on him being there to pass on all the relevant details, even though he had passed them to her over the phone. From the delay between passages he knew rightly she was taking notes.

He paced impatiently the length and breadth of the forward facing room, stopping each time a car passed by, growing increasingly more frustrated and angry every time a car failed to stop.

Finally the representative from the hire company arrived and the whole conversation was concluded in less than ten minutes: a second hire car would be at his disposal, and personally delivered by them within the hour; the police may want a statement off him, so Harry would need to make himself available for when that time came; and a tow truck was on its way to remove the damaged vehicle. After a quick explanation regarding his not being in the property during various times of the day, a time was arranged for his convenience. He and Tommy departed soon after.

The journey to the airport was executed in quiet contemplation for Harry while Tommy talked incessantly about what he might find, albeit tainted with the caveat that Jeffries would more than likely have been and gone and covered his tracks expertly by the time his amateur sleuth friend was circling high above hoping to catch him in the act. Harry grunted in agreement, still lost in his own thoughts: his life now bore no possible relation to that of only a short time ago and the worry again was that he was not worried; he should feel some kind of melancholy for times gone by, but did not. This here before him was now a part of his life forever and he was going to embrace it. Tommy pulled into the airport road and within the hour he was airborne.

From the car park the owner of a Ford Mustang witnessed his departure.

Harry loved the attitude to general aviation in America: that you could be airborne within minutes, and still maintain all aspects of safety. It didn't seem to take as long to reach that section of the ridge and he began to circle it by starting in the Northeast corner and move in a clockwise direction until all the points of the compass were covered.

Every second was a joy: it brought back special memories for him when he was learning to fly and acquiring all the skill sets required to begin the long haul to becoming a commercial airline pilot. The first two sections revealed nothing, and he pinpointed a group of trees to use as an anchor point for the wide orbit of the next and so descended to around three hundred feet to get a better look. The orbit again revealed nothing. Harry rolled the wings level. Immediately the windscreen of the Cessna was filled with the underbelly of another light aircraft. He instinctively ducked, and instantly fell back on his years of experience. Harry searched the sky. Height, he needed height as a safety net and initiated a climb. Harry could sense the stranger bear down upon him and seconds later the low wing aircraft screamed past his windscreen a second time, only now he got a much better look at it: it was a Piper Arrow Mk3. He knew the make well and thus its superiority to his Cessna in performance due to its two hundred horse power engine, retractable undercarriage and variable pitch prop. Harry turned and gave chase as best he could with all the one hundred and sixty horse power the Lycoming engine and two bladed fixed pitch prop could supply him.

All his instincts yelled the glaringly obvious to him: to cut and run; he was in a dogfight and laughed at the ridiculousness of such a statement, but the prospect invigorated him.

For the first time he cursed the Cessna's inability to keep pace, but his frustration was short lived when he espied the Arrow bank right on a one-eighty-degree turn, rolling wings level on a direct track towards him. Fool, he thought, relishing the game of chicken. Harry backed off the throttle: he was not about to gift this pilot a free victory due to his incompetence. He rolled slightly right and made a beeline for the Piper.

It was now all or nothing; self-preservation be-damned, his back was up: how dare they have the audacity to attempt to bully him out of the sky. If they honestly expected this Englishman to run for home then they had seriously miscalculated. He held his nerve, refusing to blink and arrowed in on the Piper. Right at the last the Arrow's pilot bailed out and rolled left. Harry immediately banked right, but again he fell behind due to lack of horsepower. He watched in astonishment, intermingled with delight, as the Arrow turned for another pass. There was only one thing for it, he had to lose height and continue this duel among the treetops. The car chase and his conscience regarding the two previous deaths reared its ugly head the split second he reached his decision. It was wasted, he wanted revenge and his weapon of choice today was the Cessna 172 Skyhawk.

The Piper Arrow followed suit.

He steadied his nerve, steeling it against the eventual outcome of death and destruction. This was not some game of valor played out over trenches on an active warfront or in the defense of one's homeland, this was a dog eat dog confrontation of the pure and basic kind: to kill or be killed, to hold the bragging rights of having the honor of watching yet another sunrise. Harry ticked off the point of no return in his head, the point beyond which now only a violent pulling back on the control column would guarantee salvation. He eased the throttle forward and checked his speed: the air speed indicator read one hundred and twenty knots.

From the left hand seat he could clearly discern the silhouette of the Arrow's pilot. He wanted to extract revenge, the ultimate revenge, their destruction at the hands of the treetops and yanked hard back at the right time, applying full power as he did so. Right at the last he witnessed the Piper do the same and flash past his right hand side before disappearing behind his wing.

He had failed and was livid. Harry executed a climbing left turn to put them back into his line of sight. When he finally caught sight they were high-tailing it out of this theatre of war. Harry tried to close the gap, but he knew it was hopeless and ten minutes later he throttled back to protect his engine. In all the excitement he had lost his bearings. They quickly returned once he climbed up to two thousand feet and scanned the horizon. His immediate concern now was to nurse his aircraft home: with all the excitement, and total disregard for his own safety, this poor Cessna had taken some abuse.

Harry taxied slowly onto the general aviation apron. Nobody paid him any mind, he was grateful for that, and he shut the Cessna down before briskly making his way through the terminal. Once outside he didn't stop walking and called Tommy. Finding his phone engaged he rang for a taxi from a local firm. Only at a safe distance from the terminal did his stride shorten and his breathing slow. His taxi appeared, settling his nerves and signaling a return of his anger. He gave the taxi driver directions and slumped down in the back, resting his head against the top of the seat. How stupid was he? Jeffries held a pilot's license. That was his incompetence, but he'd never thought of it. Why not? Was it arrogance on his behalf to think that nobody else would be lucky enough to fly? Tommy did. Just because the man kept his private life and hobbies secret that was no excuse for a private detective to be lapse and lazy in his application. Never again, he promised, for the time will surely come when such a schoolboy error will prove fatal. This had been a lesson learnt the hard way, along with the need to control his rising temper, which was threatening to be the undoing of him.

18

The key to the new Chevrolet Cruze was ceremoniously dropped into his left hand by the hire car's representative. The taxi fare to Tommy's had been reasonable and so he required just a small top up of funds from his stash before leaving for an unscheduled rendezvous with Jeffries.

The drive to the lawyer's office did little or nothing to quell any contempt he felt for the man or dampen any desire for vengeance. He called Tommy in a vain hope of venting his spleen, as well as to touch base; the idea being it would put him in a much calmer frame of mind, but instead it turned into a complete waste of time, as Tommy's rang out and went over to his answer machine.

Harry pulled up down the road from Jeffries' office on West Madison Avenue just in time to witness him get in his car and leave. Any choices he may have made regarding any confrontation were blown clean out of the water. He followed at a discreet distance, thanking his own prudence for once again packing the satnav. This second hire car came without one. Wherever this may lead, he accepted, it was the beginning of the end and he settled comfortably into the long drive where patience was a requirement at every turn; an acceptance that events were unfolding outside his control, and to embrace their outcome with all the sagacity and fervor of an avenging angel. Harry smiled.

It was mid-afternoon and the outside temperature reflected what the car's air conditioning was trying desperately hard to counterbalance. Harry looked at his watch, all the while tracking Jeffries three cars in arrears. He would not recognize the new hire car and Harry had to make that count when the time came: he may only have a small time window in which to use that advantage, but he promised himself a steely nerve when the time came.

The small train of cars drove at a steady pace in a Southwesterly direction by his reckoning. He tried to keep track of the road names and signs, but it was proving a disaster and admitted defeat after passing South Matlock Avenue. His cell-phone burst into life. It was Tommy.

'I'm on the lawyer's tail, where are you?'

'You not hanging around are you? But hallelujah for that! I'm following old man Boyd, so we seem to have something in common.'

'Sure does.'

'Seems our corpse was not the God fearing, law abiding citizen he wanted people to believe, according to his sister, who by the way was more than willing to talk to this newspaper man writing articles on the doyens of local townsfolk!'

'Go on!'

'The elder sister was more than a little upset at the prospect of losing what she saw as her rightful inheritance to a cousin, and couldn't talk fast enough: the corpse's real name was Tanner; he changed it to Kennedy and prior to his period of continued piousness ran with a real bad crowd, which culminated with Tanner becoming incarcerated.'

'Sounds too good to be true,' Harry said before checking his mirrors for any tail.

'So I quickly ran over to the house to cross-check some of my father's old papers, and sure enough a Tanner is mentioned.'

'What kind of man did your father reckon he was?'

'An asshole!'

'One less in the world to worry about!'

'His sister went on to say that Tanner or Kennedy, take your pick, was a mean minded son of a bitch in real life, and never stopped looking for some money he was owed. He was totally obsessed by it.'

'I kind of feel sorry for the guy: he wasted all those days, weeks, months helping to plan the operation, spent all that time in prison, as far as we know, and then sat back watching the man responsible for hiding it, keeping it a secret until the day he died!' Jeffries indicated right, but failed to take the turn. 'Tommy I'll call you when I know what this guy's up to.' Harry hung up before Tommy could answer.

He examined each mirror in turn. A dark blue car kept station with him and he fought to maintain a steady lead until the situation became one approaching the norm. Jeffries had pulled one on him and sent a wingman to keep tabs. Harry changed lanes. Jeffries stayed where he was. The dark blue car copied him. Surely they couldn't be that obvious and he returned back to his original lane. Yes, they were, and Harry laughed disdainfully as they mirrored his actions.

The three cars maintained the status quo and Harry found himself chuckling with the list of excuses he would have to think up if he took a second car back to the hire company carrying exactly the same pattern of damage. His first forays into this style of life elevated the adrenalin rushes to a whole new level: attacked in his home, which still needed to be revenged properly to his satisfaction; he'd investigated a dog fighting ring; been involved in one car chase already; was going to be one of the major players in a high stake poker game, and he wasn't kidding himself over any self-importance regarding his seat at that particular table - they saw him only as another sucker who needed to be fleeced; and now here he was in a possible three way car chase with a band of thieving murderers. Does life get any better than this? Yes, it probably did, but all he could think about right now was retribution.

Jeffries signaled to exit via Nipper Road. It was pointless Harry making any notes on where they were going. The dark blue car brought up the rear. They all re-entered a new road by making a right turn, Harry knew he was probably heading straight into a trap, but was powerless to do anything about it. His number may be up, but blood will be spilt before he waved this final goodbye.

His phone rang. He let it ring out then regretted it instantly.

All three crossed the Congress Parkway and joined Coile Road, which became County Road 114. About a mile or so further on Jeffries took a left into a domestic dwelling. Harry carried on, giving the house the once over. Now the dark blue car got his full attention. His disappointment was almost tangible when they too turned into the dwelling. No blood spilt, yet.

'Well, well, well!' Harry pulled into the side of the road and checked his phone. It was Tommy's number. He rang back.

'Tommy where are you?'

He tried hard not to sound too desperate, but in fact did the exact opposite.

Tommy described a building, as best he could from his vantage point, on which he was now keeping close tabs. It housed Jessie Boyd. From the description it bore a remarkable similarity to the one Harry had just passed.

'I've just passed you heading north,' started Harry calmly. 'I'll check my exact position using the satnav.'

All was confirmed when Tommy reported Jeffries pulling up in front of the house.

'Take it easy, and don't do anything rash!' Travers' calm tone impressed even him, and he removed the 38, checked it then holstered the firearm. 'I'll be right there.'

After hanging up he pocketed his cell and swung the Chevy round and headed back up the road. At about a hundred yards a small dirt track roughly twenty yards before the right into the building occupying the elder Boyd and the lawyer appeared, and he took it, parking the Chevy behind a row of trees so as to hide it from any passing traffic. From here on in he was on foot.

Luckily for him the terrain was not as rough as he expected and he calculated the building coming into view without too much investment in effort. His phone vibrated in his pocket. He answered Tommy's call with a whisper then placed it on silent.

'We're in trouble!'

This is not what he wished to hear at this juncture: 'Why?'

'A second car's turned up.'

'They were tailing me as I did Jeffries, but took the turn when I failed to. Who is it?' Harry hated to be wrong about anything and to completely miss the mark was going to grate.

'Poulsen's deputy, Littlehorn!'

'Shit!'

'Didn't see that coming!'

'You and me both.'

If the police were involved then any cover up went far deeper than he gave it credit. Had he got this so wrong? Had his sixth sense, his trusted gut feeling, let him down at the most vital of moments leaving him high and dry?

The house came into view and Harry crouched down behind an old rickety fence. He sent a text to Tommy detailing his position. The building had been renovated quite recently and whoever spent the money on its refurbishment clearly desired to live in it for a while to come: all the front windows had been replaced along with the proverbial lick of new paint in a creamy beige; the roof, porch decking and front door were new along with the small path guiding any guests to its entrance. Harry could make out the two cars belonging to Jeffries and Littlehorn, but there were two more parked down the left hand side. Tommy replied; he was crouched behind a tree near these two cars. Harry held off replying and made his way around the left perimeter.

From the outside there didn't seem to be anything untoward about this rather nondescript looking house, but may be that was the thing: not to bring any unwanted attention onto the owner or owners. Harry paused to take stock and listened for any movement. All was quiet.

Finally he reached a point from where he could study the land occupied by Tommy without giving up his position. He decided to text again. The reply was instant and Harry furtively crept around some trees and to his delight espied the man keeping a low profile with one eye on the house.

'You took your time!' Tommy said in a jocular tone that failed to relieve the tension.

'Good to see you too!'

'Nobody's left since the police turned up.'

'We've got to give everybody the benefit of the doubt.'

'Are you serious?' Tommy said incredulously. 'Is this the British sense of fair play coming to the party?'

'It's nothing of the kind; with the obvious exception being a certain lawyer!'

'And the Boyd family!'

'We don't know if the police are involved, because this might just be one of those coincidences.'

Tommy nodded begrudgingly. 'Would be something if they were; Poulsen would have some explaining to do!'

'How long do you think we should leave it?' Harry was eager to get a good look inside and dish out his own brand of retribution, but was mindful of his lack of firsthand experience in these matters, and this slammed home to him how much of a novice he still was. He may have come a long way in such a short space of time, but he was a greenhorn none the less.

'Hell, I don't know!'

Tommy's stark admission made him feel a whole lot better. Harry decided enough time had lapsed: 'We can use two of the cars as cover to reach the rear of the house.'

'And from there?'

'Play it by ear.'

'Is that what you English do, play everything by ear?'

'Works for me!'

Harry, stealthily or as stealthily as he could muster given the circumstances, slid off making a beeline for the left hand car. He really had no idea what he was going to do if they were rumbled attempting to sneak up on the house, but sitting, waiting, doing nothing was not an option. He reached the car and paused to take stock. Tommy appeared seconds later.

'So far, so good.'

'Your Englishman's ear is playing a good game!'

'It's talking to me just fine!'

Harry moved off without waiting for a reply and positioned himself to get a better look at the back of the house. From his new vantage point he could see no movement.

'We just can't kick the door in, 'cos what are we gonna do afterwards?' Tommy said highlighting the blatantly obvious once he'd caught up. 'Without any sort of clue as to the goings on inside we could be walking straight into a trap, a well contrived, custom made trap.'

'You wait here.'

Harry knew any responsibility was his to shoulder and felt no compunction to behave any differently. Tommy pulled him firmly back by his right arm.

'Stop being a bloody hero!'

Tommy swiftly overtook him leaving Harry to ride shotgun.

Ten feet from the white painted rear door, situated to the right of a porch running half the length of the house and protected by a hand rail, they heard the first voices. Harry recognized Jeffries, Carl and Rudy Boyd, but not the others, especially the girl's. Tommy held up his left hand to signal a full stop: 'Sounds like the entire Boyd clan is here, even Nancy.'

One question answered anyhow, thought Harry, and he strained to pick up the thread of the conversation, but it was muffled with each exclamation being followed by voices much lower, as if the whole confabulation was being conducted under some idea that they were indeed being eavesdropped on.

The American eased himself gently onto the porch until he eventually sat crouching, menacingly, directly beneath one of the windows. The voices continued again in much the same vein. From their tone Harry began to sense a subtle shift in the mood, which was reflected in the stern expression slowly creeping over his friend's normally calm exterior. The hairs on the back of his neck began to rise. Tommy, with pursed lips, slowly shook his head without making eye contact.

Harry instinctively locked his eyes on the back door and positioned himself in readiness. He felt inside his jacket, removed the 38 then carefully returned it to the pocket, but in a way to make it more accessible. Tommy's look of bewilderment disconcerted him. Harry shrugged his shoulders to ask the question, and a finger slid across the throat was the reply. Harry removed the revolver a second time.

As if preordained by some higher power pushing them on, the voices grew steadily louder, but now their precise clarity rammed home the significance of the previous few minutes. A cold, clammy sweat broke out all over him and Harry writhed under the sensation. The entire Boyd family exchanged threats in a heated argument with Jeffries over the disposal of a body. But which body? He gripped the butt of the firearm, his knuckles whitening under the pressure. Should he make a dash for the door and catch them off guard? There was no way in his mind of taking a backward step and retreating tail between his legs.

Tommy answered the way he would choose and surreptitiously crept to the left hand side of the door. Harry tapped his watch then opened his hand and spread his fingers to signify five minutes. Tommy shook his head, replying with the two fingered salute. Harry agreed.

Jessie's voice boomed with violent intent over the silence that descended between exchanges: he was for the killing there and then. The penny dropped and Travers' hand speared for the door handle. In a split second the decision was made, his mind was clear, the handle twisted and he burst into the house in a maelstrom of verbal and physical abuse.

Jake was the first to react to the unwanted and unexpected intrusion, and received for his effort the initial brunt of Travers' anger: a swift, sharp kick to the solar plexus disabling the elder son, and then followed it up with a skull splitting blow on the side of his head with the butt of the gun.

Jeffries stood shocked, frozen to the spot unable to comprehend what he was witnessing, and powerless to aid his co-conspirators in any way.

Boyd senior, normally one not to hold back airing his opinions and dislikes in a volley of four-letter words, remained mute and held that station until Harry slammed a right cross straight into the center of his face: Harry up to this point had never met the man, but gut instinct and a feeling for knowing the righteousness in the human spirit fed the compunction to lay into him. Carl, Rudy and to his surprise a stunning looking woman in her twenties looked on without in anyway attempting to intervene.

Tommy was now in close attendance and wailing into to all and sundry with a volley of oaths and threats.

Jessie Boyd hit the floor with a thud. It had the impact on events which the two men wished it hadn't.

Nancy sprang to her father's defense like a cornered cat: her lithe, athletic body closing the gap between her and Harry in the blink of an eye. The ferocity and speed of the attack was frightening and he fell back under the impact, hitting his head on a cupboard before it impacted with the floor. This part of the house was open plan leading into the kitchen, and Jeffries' mind was made up: he was off. Tommy saw him move, but his attempt to restrain the fleeing lawyer was intercepted by Carl's body-check sending him crashing into the opposite wall, taking out one of the window panes either side of the door then sliding down the wall onto the wooden floor. Shattered glass lay all around. Rudy, not wanting to be the odd one out and face the full force of his father's fearsome temper, ran over and kicked first Harry then Tommy before they could haul themselves back to their feet.

'Leave him!' screamed Jake, now that he had caught his breath, and kicked Harry in the back of the head.

Tommy finally got to his feet in time to block another of Rudy's kicks before countering with a one-two combination to the man's solar plexus then the bridge of his nose. The blood streaked across the floor.

Harry pushed back hard against the wall and scrambled upright, knowing the rules of fair play were not going to be enforced this day, and as Nancy attempted to dig her fingernails into the side of his face threw her over his shoulder, and into that part of the building that housed the kitchen. He was free to launch a second onslaught on Jake Boyd.

The elder sibling was not about to stand and take it and threw a volley of punches: some hit home, but the majority were successfully blocked on the arms. Harry took the blows, waiting patiently to keep his promise of extreme vengeance, but his retribution was thwarted by the father taking the wind out of him with a thundering blow to the stomach. Harry fell back again, crashing against the wall. Only a last ditch, desperate slide of his left foot to get a better grip prevented him from falling a second time and being at their mercy. Jessie threw a hard, right roundhouse punch, but a telegram would have arrived sooner and Harry ducked to avoid it before slamming home a straight right to the man's nose. It stopped Jessie in his tracks. Jake now took the full force of his righteous indignation. He rocked and rolled, but failed to drop. Harry was now faced with the dilemma of who to cover. A quick glance over his shoulder informed him that he and Tommy had a bigger problem: Nancy with a pump action shotgun.

'Tommy!' he only just managed to get the words out before the blast of the first cartridge ripped into the wall behind him.

The two men ducked in unison. Jake screamed at his sister to kill the motherfuckers.

Harry took aim with the 38 and emptied a round directly over Nancy's head. It was the warning shot that saved him for she cowered to miss the bullet, and this forced the shotgun's barrel upwards. She fired and missed.

Tommy drew his gun and let off one round from a Glock 17 at Nancy then two more at Jessie and Jake. All missed. Rudy wasn't for allowing Tommy to get his aim right and bolted out the door followed closely by Carl.

Nancy regained her composure after Tommy's onslaught to fire again with deadly accuracy, only now anticipating any head movement. She hit Tommy in the right shoulder, sending him flying. He was now a sitting duck. Harry knew it was now or never for his friend and before she reloaded shot her in the right leg without remorse.

A full range of obscenities exploded at him.

Harry swung the gun round on Jessie and then Jake - he wanted blood, their blood. But in the back of his mind there nagged the problem of the gun itself: there would be residue on him as evidence of use. And how should he deal with these witnesses? He couldn't rightly kill them, they deserved a fair trial.

Tommy groaned. The pain was searing.

'Your friend needs the hospital!'

'No shit, Sherlock !' His reply caused all present to take stock.

Nancy reloaded the shotgun.

'Better tell that bitch of a sister of yours-'

Harry never had time to finish his sentence before Nancy let off another cartridge, but missed wildly as both Harry and Tommy fired over her head.

'The next one takes your fucking head off!' Harry snarled.

Nancy laid down the shotgun. Travers' tone and body language spelt only death, whether it be his or hers.

Harry found himself fighting an overwhelming urge to shoot them all with extreme prejudice. His train of thought was disturbed only by Jake beginning to shuffle to his right: behind him stood a battered old kitchen table, which was totally out of keeping with the internal decor. At either end of the wooden table there was a tired looking drawer and he didn't need to be Einstein to figure out what his aim was. Should he let him try? That would give him reason enough to kill him or being a professional man should he give him due warning? Jessie ended the debate.

'So what you gonna do, Limey?'

Harry kept his counsel, but the urge to empty the chambers was growing by the second.

Nancy eventually sat due to the pain in her leg becoming unbearable: 'I need a doctor!' she cried.

Jake's right hand was now hovering with eager anticipation by the furthest drawer. 'Do it!' Harry now gave the elder sibling his utmost attention. 'Go on do it!'

His eyes now darted between Harry and his father, who refused to budge an inch since all the fun and games had temporarily ceased.

'I'll give you a fighting chance, which is more than your cousins gave us!'

Harry awaited Tommy's intervention, but he said nothing. Harry slowly placed the Smith and Wesson in his jean pocket.

'You call that fair?' Jake's voice was tremulous, and this emboldened him to push his luck.

Harry carefully removed the revolver and placed it on the floor about a foot from his left shoe then stood up. 'How's that for you?'

He felt his entire being buzz with excitement and became acutely aware, as if viewing proceedings as a third party, of all that surrounded him: this heightened state of perception meant he never allowed himself to focus on any one person in the room, but was more than capable of digesting all the information presented and breaking it down into easily discernible pieces. It was in these first few precious moments that he consciously picked up on those persons occupying the adjacent room; there were clearly more than one, and of those Jeffries' smiling, pernicious face sprung out at him egging him on to certain doom along with the treacherous Littlehorn keeping just below the radar in order to sneak up on the unsuspecting and save his wretched skin.

Nancy twitched: her leg was beginning to complain bitterly and she pleaded with her father to finish off the English, so she could get to the hospital.

Jake did not present any immediate threat and with Tommy now quiet Harry slowly took a step backwards, turning half to the left to check on his condition. One eye never left the party of three. Tommy was conscious, but in some distress. Jessie never moved or made a sound. This was a Mexican standoff that any Mexican would have been proud of and to add, as an extra, Carl and Rudy would be waiting outside to trap them both, picking them off from behind the trees.

A voice now came crystal clear from an adjacent room. Harry said nothing, waiting for the voice to speak again. When it came it held a mixture of distress and indignation.

'No honor among thieves then?' Harry said smiling.

'I wouldn't know about that English!' said Jessie contemptuously, gaining confidence with each passing minute of Travers' inactivity. 'You tell me? You come over here laying claim to something you have no right to own!'

'I don't want it, never wanted it! And my uncle became a citizen of your fine country in order to buy this something in a country he loved and you killed him for it!' Harry could feel his shoulders tense. 'For a crime committed over forty years ago!' His knowing about the money was not something any of them had taken into consideration.

'All this so you could be a good fucking Samaritan?' Nancy added between groans.

'He was my uncle. I thought you at least would have appreciated that!'

Harry could sense a mellowing of the atmosphere; it was not the reaction he sought and he needed to get everything onto a more comfortable level.

The voice spoke again, calling for assistance.

'Deputy Littlehorn not your idea of good husband material, Nancy?' asked a jocular Tommy.

Harry was pleased his friend felt up to joining in.

'Fuck you Shearen! You're just jealous you never hit the mark.'

Tommy laughed, but it was a laugh failing to hide that little bit of history between the two.

'Him!' hissed Jake, moving his hand away from the drawer.

All this was music to Travers' ears: it gave him valuable breathing space to pick his next move. Shooting Jake first was too obvious, but he needed to prevent Nancy with the shotgun from becoming inflamed plus Jessie was ominously quiet, too quiet for his liking. He pounced on his gun without warning. It caught Jake completely unawares, and Harry trained the gun first on Nancy, to stop her getting any ideas about letting loose another round, and then swung right to face Papa Boyd. His assessment of the situation was proved correct: Jessie as quick as you like whipped out a snub nosed .357 Magnum revolver from behind his back. Harry instantly recognized the weapon as one guaranteed to cause maximum damage at short range. Jesse fired a second later, aiming directly at Travers' midriff. He launched his frame to the right. The bullet ripped past, catching his clothing, but thankfully missing its target. Harry never fired. His own sense of self-preservation kicked him hard in the gut: he was carrying that unlicensed gun and had already shot and wounded one person in self-defense and was not about to shoot a second with an excellent chance of a kill.

'Drop it!' he said menacingly.

Jessie contemplated calling his bluff.

'Drop it or I'll drop you!'

That did it for the old man and he threw the Magnum on the floor. Tommy struggled to get to his feet to collect the piece.

'You can tell your man next door to show himself.'

None of the present Boyd clan deigned to answer.

'Well, if you're not going to play ball, you better warn those two that had the sense to make a run for it not to try and be smart because I'll cap you three before I go!'

Harry consciously reigned himself in.

'Cover them!'

'Sure.' The tiredness in Tommy's voice was worrying, but he seemed to be bearing up as he leaned against the wall with his left hand clutching his right shoulder.

Travers' sharp, staccato footsteps crunched over glass until he strode past the prostrate Nancy. Their eyes never met. Harry held the Smith and Wesson out in front of him; he was agitated with the frustration of having talked himself out of blasting a hole in the old man, and quietly cursed the weapon now acting as a barrier.

The open plan kitchen led onto a hallway from which there were two doors, one on either side. The right hand door was shut, the left half open, but from his initial standpoint a pair of feet could be seen belonging to someone who was obviously seated. Harry eased the door open with his right hand whilst keeping the gun trained dead ahead with his left. Slowly the person came into view: he was aged somewhere between early to mid-twenties and was tied to the chair. Harry couldn't rightly tell at first due to the beating he had suffered, and considering the time gap from when he heard from Tommy they must have set about him almost immediately.

He took the gamble on his being a friendly and untied him after pocketing the gun. The man slumped forward.

'Who are you?' asked Harry in a monotone, deadpan voice. He already knew the answer and was just following protocol.

'Deputy Littlehorn.'

So much for your stupid police conspiracy theory, he thought, as he eased Littlehorn back into the chair.

'They worked you over pretty good!'

'Took me for a sucker,' gasped Littlehorn, 'and I proved them right!'

Harry couldn't argue with that.

'Where are they?'

Littlehorn was beginning to slide into the role, displaying all the traits of the wounded, vengeful victim.

'We got Jessie, Jake and Nancy in the back, but Nancy needs a doctor.'

Harry could not avoid the inevitable, and seeing Littlehorn's head snap left in interrogation, answered before he opened his mouth: 'I shot her; it was kind of a Nancy or me situation and she drew the short straw!'

Littlehorn's subdued reaction with just a hint of malice to his admission answered a whole heap of questions just begging to be answered when better times arrived. 'You had it bad then?'

The deputy's eyes failed to hide the pain racking his tortured soul.

Harry could sense all was not well. He'd been gone too long.

He put his hand inside his pocket and tickled the barrel of the Smith and Wesson. 'Whenever you're ready,' he said and left for the back of the house, never asking whether there was anybody else hanging around because he already knew that answer. When he finally returned in the kitchen his heart sank. Tommy lay prostrate on the floor unconscious. The other three were gone. He checked his friend's pulse. Thankfully it was steady as was his breathing. Any retribution was going to have to wait. Littlehorn arrived and dialed 911 from a mobile phone left on one of the kitchen worktops. Harry concluded it belonged to the man.

'Tommy looks as I feel!'

Harry heard the words, but that's all they were to him just words. He could only think of one thing.

'An ambulance is on its way.'

'When did Jeffries leave?' Harry asked.

'Shortly after you turned up.'

'Alone?'

'I think so.'

Travers' head began to flood with theories and conjectures and they all came colliding back to one obvious conclusion.

He needed to get away before the never ending series of questions began.

Harry rose, looked down at his friend, quelling his anger with clenched fists. The time to gamble was now: 'Take care of Tommy for me and tell the Sheriff I'll be in touch.'

Deputy Littlehorn read it perfectly: 'Sure, but don't leave it too long.'

Harry never said another word and left.

19

He managed to keep a good pace while maintaining a vigil for anybody having the temerity to try and get the jump on him. More fool them if they tried. The journey back to his car took a third of the time it took on arrival and he hit the open road running on autopilot, relying on satellite navigation to give all the appropriate directions to a pre-programmed destination; it was a necessity borne out of inadequacy, an inadequacy forcing him reluctantly onto the back foot, but now technology was placing him firmly onto the front.

Harry kept himself firmly under control at all times by driving at a constant speed, not wishing to draw any unwanted attention from the law. He checked and re-checked his mirrors praying they would attack between now and his destination, but any odds on a successful outcome there were severely stacked against him; he had missed the mark by a wide margin in the past, but this time a life could be lost if he screwed up.

The first doubts began to creep into his head encroaching on what had been until now, bearing in mind any self-chastisement for inexperience and schoolboy errors, an almost impenetrable belief in what he was doing. Yes, he was only ever going to do this on a part time basis, but that was never going to detract from his dedication to the task, and yet here driving to the undoubted climax of a case that was not the hardest or most convoluted to solve he doubted the wisdom of setting forth on such a venture.

A county police car flashed past him followed in quick succession by an ambulance.

Harry was content, for happy didn't quite seem like the right word to use in the present circumstances, that his friend, who he had doubted on occasions and was prepared to help him, putting his own personal safety on the line for a stranger, was now being placed in good hands. He suddenly felt an overriding love for America and its people, bar a few notable exceptions.

The length of this drive was the perfect tonic to allow his anger to abate and his natural self-confidence to rise up and quash the negativity now receding back where it belonged. How could he have known? The police from what he was aware didn't, and if they did Sheriff Poulsen was one damn fine law enforcement officer. No, there was nothing he could have done differently in light of what he knew then and now.

Littlehorn invaded his thoughts: he could only have been there for Nancy, but why on this day at that time? Poulsen suspected, he knew, he always knew. Harry started to speed up. No wonder he let him leave. Poulsen was going to beat him to the punch and prevent him from seeking what he most strived for. He checked the satellite navigation for the estimated time of arrival: he had twenty minutes to go.

Harry examined the Smith and Wesson, balancing it in his right hand judging its weight; he was happy there were more than enough rounds left to get the job done before the law intervened and then he would dispose of the incriminating evidence to the satisfaction of all concerned parties, namely him. He carefully stowed it away in his left pocket.

Parking the car Harry vacated with a serenity savored only by the pious. He was on the final leg of a journey, but the first of a transformation he recognized as now being essential, almost ordained. He felt the army knife digging into him via his right pocket. He would need that - his little surprise for the lawyer.

Harry came to an abrupt halt roughly ten paces from his late uncle's front door. There parked at an acute angle to the front entrance, clearly brought to a standstill in a hurry stood Jeffries' car. What is required now, he calmly conjectured, is a clear, precise, sang-froid intensity of thought and action. He removed the knife and extended the longer blade before carefully returning it to his pocket with the blade facing rearwards.

His next step was labored, and he felt it grate against his own sense of righteous retribution. The one after that was leaden. These final few moments, before fulfilling what destiny had always intended, became a battle of wills between good and evil: this is not the behavior, good screamed, of anyone with the best interests of their client at heart, but I am the client, countered evil, and this is how I choose my repayment; you are a professional, a professional man with morals, good tried desperately to pamper to Travers' benevolent side but was cut off mid-stream by evil, and as a professional this will be quick, clean and executed with extreme prejudice. Harry took another step and suddenly felt the fingers of his left hand tickle the synthetic grip of the Smith and Wesson. It seemed to take an age, an eternity, to reach the door, the entrance into that other world which would signify his arrival and closure of his first case.

Where was Poulsen? Why was he not here to prevent this? The only logical reason why the Sheriff should be absent settled any future arguments. He was the one person who contained the power to nullify all his efforts and deny him what was rightly his. Evil once again came forward urging Harry to pull the revolver and enter the building gun ablaze and be damned to all who dared to stand in his way. He physically paused for the first time. No, that was not the way to go. This was not clear, precise, sang-froid action of thought and mind. Stealth, stealth was called for here. He re-checked the surrounding area realizing he was a sitting duck stuck out in the open for all to see and dispose of. Quick as he could he found cover and waited.

Crouching out of sight behind a large tree with foliage surrounding its base he waited a good ten minutes. The street was quiet today; he would easily hear his arrival. Nobody came out of the building, or made any sound. He pulled the gun and held it firm whilst steadying his left hand. If he was going to make a move then that move needed to be now; if the building was empty then he would have the advantage of surprise when they returned, if not then his entrance would provide surprise enough to catch Jeffries off guard, who clearly was more of a novice than he was for not spotting such an idiot approach in broad daylight.

Harry heard voices and lowered himself further behind the foliage. He bent his ear to catch as many words as possible. One was Jeffries'. The other was a stranger to him.

He was tottering on the edge of oblivion, and loved and hated it in equal measure: he despised the feeling of not being in total control, of being at the mercy to unwanted surprises, but the excitement, the adrenaline rush invigorated and elevated him to an unparalleled high. The 38 felt heavy in his hand now; there was no friend or colleague here to watch his back, to bail him out or countenance against anything rash, which failed to fall under clear, precise or sang-froid.

The voices grew louder, but now he had the added advantage of discerning the direction. His eyes gravitated towards the backyard, and slowly but surely two figures appeared walking one in front of the other. Jeffries took the rear with the stranger hobbling, shuffling ahead towards the rear of the house. Harry waited for them both to enter.

His first initial movement was overly cautious, tentative even, annoyingly tentative for his adventurous spirit, and his legs once again felt heavy and labored under their orders to advance. He cursed his body's reluctance to close the gap on the house. The mind was keen, but the body was not so sure.

By the time he finally reached the back porch the two men had been in the house a few minutes, a valuable few minutes enabling any plan to be formulated in defense against his onslaught.

Harry was itching to see an end to this, but restraint won the day and he stopped a few full strides short of the rear door. From his vantage point he could clearly make out their voices deep inside the building.

The feeling of déjà vu hit home hard, but the alarm bells were not ringing or sounding to a different tune. He tried the door handle and it moved smoothly in his hand not making a sound. He opened it fully and instinctively followed Jeffries' voice, by now the only one talking. His navigation through the house was smooth and untroubled with the voice of the man he wished to dispose of acting as a beacon, guiding him.

Jeffries stopped talking and Harry stopped walking. The time delay seemed like an eternity, but he was in the mind to be patient.

'I will not be denied!' exclaimed Jeffries.

All the pieces of the jigsaw finally fell into place.

Harry knew his annoying ability to judge people before finding out the full truth was a terrible weakness, but now a smile appeared: there was an acceptance that he may or may not pre-judge, and if he was guilty of such a crime then he was prepared to accept it as long as he recognized his shortcomings.

Jeffries spoke again with venom in his voice.

Moving stealthily to the door, behind which contained the room housing the scene being played out to his captive audience, Harry mentally prepared for the inevitable violence, but then suddenly without warning all fell silent, which caused him to take stock. Again he began to analyze his motives: these were not the true and honest actions of a private detective rather than the flimsy set of excuses of a wannabe killer searching for some lame justification to take a life. Harry pulled himself together: if he really, truly believed he had it within to become a useful addition to the profession then he was going to have to curb these blood lust desires. The voices started up again.

The other man mumbled an obscenity and received a thunderous blow to the face for his pleasure.

Harry took a step back, faced the door and raising his left leg delivered a straight kick to a point three inches to the right of the door handle. The door flew open with such a force that only a second smaller kick prevented the door from swinging shut.

Jeffries' face on seeing the last person on earth he wanted or expected said it all and for a split second Harry feared the whole situation would just become one damp squib and die a death, but Jeffries was not a man to lay down and accept defeat and in an instant produced a gun. Harry now faced the dilemma he always wanted, but now could no more follow it through than the guy sitting in front of him experiencing the lawyer's torture first hand. He raised his gun, aiming straight at Jeffries' forehead. The lawyer did the same.

'You couldn't leave it alone could you?' spat Jeffries.

'You're running out of time. The Sheriff will be here soon!'

Jeffries frowned, studying him with the air of a man who's convinced he's being bluffed.

'Poulsen has your number!'

'That idiot: he couldn't find a whore in a brothel.'

'Better make your mind up and decide what you want: your freedom or a bullet!'

'From you I suppose with one of your friend's discarded firearms.'

Harry said nothing.

'Probably hot anyway knowing him and a simple ballistic check will undoubtedly unearth some police file somewhere!'

The seated man now turned and studied Harry; his stare made him feel uncomfortable, but to acknowledge the look meant taking his eye of the real prize, so he froze the man out.

'Whatever you got figured out Jeffries it ain't going to work, we know everything.'

'"We", what's this "we"? You don't know shit! You don't even know what's happening right in front of your own goddamn face!'

Travers' knuckles turned white around the grip of the 38 and his trigger finger visibly twitched.

Jeffries was not a stupid man nor displayed any open tendencies to asininity, but he viewed the twitching finger with mild incredulity: this Englishman didn't strike him as being one possessing the required courage to shoot him or anybody. He trained his gun directly at Travers' forehead.

'What are you waiting for?'

This one simple question from the seated man stunned both combatants, and it was Jeffries who answered first signifying the enquiry was not aimed at him.

'Not you!' snarled Jeffries.

'Shoot him!' the seated man said softly to Harry, but with a conviction hinting at some hidden, suppressed desire.

The tension between the three tightened another notch. Any hope Harry harbored for the third man providing an easy fix evaporated at the sight of Jeffries' gun barrel.

The lawyer laughed.

Harry could sense his shoulders tighten and feel his face flush red with anger.

'You're more stupid than I gave you credit for!' mocked Jeffries.

'You like playing it loose Jeffries?' said the seated man still swiveling his head from side to side, splitting his attention between the two men.

'It fills me with inestimable amount of joy to see you two together at last!'

Hesitation is an infectious, dangerous habit like looking over one's shoulder with melancholy and a yearning to relive the past whilst awaiting the arrival of the fiend. Harry hesitated fatally. The shot rang out and Travers fell back, only managing to stay upright by a quick piece of self-preservation and grabbing the shoulder of the seated man. Smoke filled the air and his ears rang with the thunderous discharge of the hand gun.

Jeffries continued to stare straight back at him, pointing the gun at Travers' forehead. Slowly the firearm slid vertically down and the telltale signs of crimson began to spread outward across the lawyer's white shirt.

Harry looked at the barrel of his gun not one hundred percent sure if he fired instinctively or not, but he needed to know. He smelt the barrel then turned his head to the seated man literally holding the smoking gun.

Jeffries finally slumped to his knees holding a look of utter disbelief that he could have been outwitted. He went to speak, but the shock of being out-maneuvered seemed to steal the words right from out of his mouth.

'Takes his time to die don't he?'

Harry said nothing, finding himself unable to remove his eyes from the kneeling Jeffries.

Jeffries keeled over.

'Who's gun's that? Because it ain't yours!' the seated man said with a throaty cough and a rub of his chest.

'Do us a favor and check his pockets Harry: that son of bitch has my medication. Stupid, dumb fuck held it back from me thinking it would make me talk.'

Harry did as he was asked, and within a few minutes the seated man having swallowed it without the need of water began to feel a whole lot better. The elder man slipped a small Browning nine-millimeter back into his trouser pocket. 'Better give me that!' he said holding out his hand.

Harry gratefully handed over the Smith and Wesson, which the elder man wiped clean of fingerprints with a handkerchief.

'You care to tell Uncle Jack?' Harry asked.

The elder man stood, not without a little difficulty, and held out his right hand for Harry to take. 'How much do you know?'

Harry told him.

'I was left for dead in the woods and your man here came hunting treasure and found me, that's how I ended up with the pleasure of his company. All the money's gone! Only he, Jeffries, didn't believe it. I spent some buying this place!'

A simple raised eyebrow from Harry brought about the conclusion: 'I came across certain information pertaining to a heist that occurred quite a few years ago, and which you undoubtedly know about, and by simple deduction, mingled with a whole lot of luck, figured everything out. With the money I purchased this prime piece of real estate when it came up for sale to cover my tracks because I knew that someday someone would come a looking.'

'How did you hide the gun?'

'Our dead lawyer friend here was so hell bent on proving how smart he was, and forcing me to show him where the money was hid, that he took his eye off the ball for a split second and made a classic amateur's error.'

The two men studied the dead lawyer.

'I surreptitiously removed the piece from one of a number of hiding places around my house where I keep my protection against days like today. It's legal unlike yours!'

Uncle Jack waved the illegal firearm inches from Travers' face coupled with a broad grin: 'Tommy gave this to you didn't he?'

'Don't hold it against him!'

'Jeffries found out about his father's involvement, and figured he'd keep him close by in case he got too close to the truth and needed eliminating.'

'Does he know you know? Because Tommy is only really interested in not having his father's name sullied, even if he deserves it.'

'Tommy will be fine, unlike the lawyer; he was smart, but not smart enough to keep himself alive! You want a coffee?'

His uncle's unflappability in face of everything was admirable.

'Just to make you aware the Sheriff will be here soon,' Harry said following his relative into the kitchen. This was starting to get surreal: here he was about to drink coffee as if there wasn't a care in the world and they had a dead body in one of the back rooms.

'Poulsen!' Uncle Jack said with derision. 'He only paid lip service to an investigation. Jeffries thought the man a joke, which only prolonged the inevitable death of our lawyer friend!'

'You may be surprised.'

The old man had the coffee on the go with the swiftness all coffee lovers would envy, clearly unfazed by his having shot his abductor. Harry again experienced that eerie sensation of not giving a damn, feeling no guilt, embracing the sensation that just deserts were done and no one could prove otherwise. He felt a sudden affinity with his uncle.

The telltale crunching of tires on gravel sent the man over to the rear door and he heaved the illegal firearm with all his might into the wilderness, but only after a quick second wipe down. It wasn't a bad throw, thought Harry, for an ill man with a dodgy ticker.

Any questions he had lined up for his uncle were going to have to wait as two uniformed police officers entered the rear of the house with firearms at the ready. The coffee maker began to bubble.

'Glad you boys could join the party. The stiff's in the back!'

The flippancy amused Harry and shook off any encroaching intimidation.

'I would have called you myself,' he went on without openly displaying any signs of fear or trepidation, 'only my phone line has been disabled!'

The two officers slowly lowered their weapons, but not sufficiently enough to render them ineffective. Neither spoke, not even to each other.

'When's the Sheriff getting here?' asked Harry.

One officer went to investigate the back whilst the other informed both men that his arrival was imminent.

'You'll need this.' Travers' uncle produced the Browning, handing it over butt first. 'It's been fired once, by me, I killed him!'

The officer returned after a few minutes, his firearm still not yet holstered.

Harry watched his uncle closely: they don't know what to make of him, this is all too easy. I bet his heartbeat hasn't passed eighty. The old man made four coffees even though the question had yet to be posed. Sheriff Poulsen arrived with two deputies in tow followed by a forensic team from the Tennessee Bureau of investigation. The man was on a mission, and came to an abrupt halt three feet from the elderly coffee maker.

'Don't mind if I do!' Poulsen said taking a cup.

'Help yourself. Your two boys clearly aren't coffee lovers.'

'I never believed in ghosts until this point.'

'Well Sheriff,' the ghost began, handing the younger Harry his cup before helping himself to his own, 'us olden's tend to keep on re-surfacing when people least expect it!'

Poulsen received a quick rundown from the two officers who confirmed that Jeffries was dead in the back of the house and the old man had confessed to the killing with the Browning, which was bagged by forensics before they could stop talking.

'You're remarkably calm Mister Hennessey,' Poulsen said slowly, as if trying to invoke a reaction with that simple claim, 'for a man rising from the dead to extract revenge!'

'You don't know many zombies on a personal basis then? Shame really for they do like picking the bones out of a subject.'

'Self-defense Sheriff!' Harry interposed.

'And you witnessed it I presume?'

'With my own baby blues!'

'Forensics will have their say.'

'Keep it tidy!' The old man winked at his nephew.

Harry pictured the Bodyguard 38 lying snugly in long grass awaiting its inevitable discovery, but he would be long gone by then, and with no fingerprints on it his only explanation was going to be the gunpowder residue on his hands and as Littlehorn never witnessed his shooting Nancy, and if she was smart and not wanting to be found out herself, he was in the clear.

'You got here quick?' Hennessey said going on the offensive in order to divert any potential uncomfortable questions: he had full confidence in his nephew, but still needed get them singing from the same hymn sheet.

'We've been following Jeffries as part of our ongoing investigation into your unfortunate demise.'

Hennessey's back was up: 'You suspected that prick all this time and never pulled him on it? And all the while he's got me locked up on prison rations!'

'I needed him to make his move.'

Hennessey took several deep breaths and began to calm. His rising fury dissipating almost as quickly as it flared and Harry read the signs perfectly. 'Let me run this by myself,' he was in full flow now, but sat at the kitchen table to finish his speech. 'I get imprisoned, as previously stated, presumed dead, no doubt under the pretext of a bear attack or some such bullshit, in order my bent lawyer can get his hands on my property, don't worry you'll get all this repeated verbatim in a statement, and nobody thought it wise to tail him before now?'

Poulsen simply smiled and shrugged his shoulders stating that due to budgetary constraints, and several other ongoing cases including the deaths of two cousins in an automobile accident that bore all the hallmarks of a professional hit, he was experiencing serious man power issues.

'Shame!' said Hennessey.

Poulsen turned to Harry: 'I need to know your whereabouts on that night in question.'

'I'll check my diary!'

'Sass seems to run in your family.'

Harry was not for exhibiting any outward display of weakness, indeed he embraced, relished meeting everything head on, as anything else would surely signal his guilt, but at the same time there needed to be an element of shock and surprise that any allegations should be squared away firmly at him.

'We'll get you to a doctor,' Poulsen said to Hennessey, knowing that fighting a lost cause was a fight wasted, 'then copy your statement verbatim, but we'll take your relative's right now.' He stuck out a ringed finger in Travers' direction to emphasize the point.

'Sure thing,' Harry was starting to feel confident, but was mindful to temper any enthusiasm.

'Tell them the truth boy!' barked out his uncle, and looked the younger man firmly in the eye with pride and gratitude in equal measure.

Harry nodded: 'I always tell the truth uncle.'

He wasn't given any time to register the reaction, as he was immediately escorted to a waiting patrol car.

Once outside the panorama that greeted his eyes filled him with dread, as the local law enforcement scoured the area for vital evidence and for an instant it sent a shiver down his spine: they were searching the area around where his Smith and Wesson had landed. They would find it for sure, but they would never marry it up with him unless they discovered a reason to check for any gunpowder residue and could get a ballistics match on the bullet lodged firmly in Nancy's leg.

'I'll be real glad to see the back of this Sheriff!' Hennessey said, sipping his coffee. He was suddenly very tired.

'We'll all be glad to see the back of this little headache,' Poulsen said taking a seat, now resigned to the fact that he had to await the arrival of an ambulance. 'I should really arrest you for the suspected murder of your lawyer!'

'You think I'm going to make a run for it?'

'I'll grab your pills!'

'You wouldn't be the first.'

'Drink your coffee!'

'You rounding up anybody else?'

* * *

It was a surreal time for Harry: the case was over - he took comfort from the fact that he had been proved right - all the evidence was laid firmly at Jeffries' feet and was found guilty of various crimes ranging from kidnap, blackmail, fraud and attempted murder; the Boyd family bar Nancy disappeared, and Harry could see nothing coming from that line of enquiry; Tommy swore he never saw who shot him; the only man who could incriminate him in the crime was dead, but the law still dictated that his uncle had to answer for killing him; and the biggest shock of all was Littlehorn's admission that he was ambushed on entry into the house, the owner being out of town and his being there was following a tip-off of an illegal distillery, and he too never saw his assailant. Harry knew and sympathized: love is a many splendored thing and its boundaries are just figment of its own imagination. As the saying goes: "Love kills slowly", but that infatuation bore him his greatest worry: he had shot Nancy with Tommy's illegal handgun. Someone had to take the fall.

That fall, thankfully, never really materialized. Harry gave his statement and no forensic test was ever scheduled on him. It was a win, win, situation: Littlehorn kept his love interest available for him to pursue when she deigned to finally show her face after she recovered from her unfortunate hunting accident.

As soon as he could Harry went to visit Tommy in hospital.

* * *

His friend's broadly grinning countenance met his of grave concern the split second he entered the private room in the hospital.

'You're still enjoying your freedom I see,' Tommy said jocularly.

Harry placed a large bowl of fruit beside his bed. 'It must be love!'

'It must be!'

Harry sat back in a less than comfortable high backed chair seated on the left hand side of the bed situated by a large window, and immediately felt an overwhelming desire to sink into a deep sleep.

'How's your uncle?'

'In shockingly good spirits: you wouldn't believe by looking at the old sod that he'd been the victim of a kidnap and held hostage all this time!'

'He never told?' Tommy asked in a low tone.

'Never!'

Harry took the opportunity to explain how things stood: the police now believe his uncle's abduction was for the sole purpose of

Jeffries forcing him to change his will, which would have guaranteed his demise. As far as the money was concerned the less said the better, but his uncle now saw the whole episode as some kind of sign to use the ill-gotten gains for the greater good, and to that effect he informed Harry that he intended leave any money from the sale of the house to charitable causes.

'How do you feel about it?' asked Tommy.

'It's for the best. I couldn't have kept it. And if it makes him feel good.'

'Will you stay a while?'

'They can't hold me on anything, although I'm pretty damn sure they would if they could, but there's not a shred of evidence to prove any misdemeanor accountable to yours truly, so I'll be leaving for home in a couple of days once I know the two of you are okay. Of course I'll be back for the inquest.'

Those two days dragged on: not because Harry was overly desperate to make a run for home in case they should suddenly uncover some evidence to hold him, but now suddenly there was the yearning to return to familiar surroundings. He made the most of what time there was by visiting the hospital every day, and the one advantage of this was he got to know his uncle.

Finally the day to leave came and he stopped off at the hospital on the way back to Atlanta. His uncle was itching to be on his way home and sensed the same from Harry. The confab was short and sweet. Tommy on the other hand was quite obviously upset to lose a friend and made Harry promise to return as soon as possible. It was an easy promise to make.

Just as he was leaving Sheriff Poulsen made an appearance.

'Just thought I'd confirm you were actually leaving today!'

'Don't sound too pleased.'

'I'll be pleased when things turn back to normal, and talking of normal you wouldn't happen to know anything about two light aircraft being involved in a dogfight would you?'

'No, no can't say I do, Sheriff.' Harry suddenly remembered the bullet holes in the Cessna.

'Oh well, just thought I'd ask.'

He knew and Harry knew he knew, but who was the other pilot? Until now he hadn't given it any more thought. The Sheriff bid them both farewell and left holding a smile designed to disconcert the guilty.

'Dogfight!' Tommy said curiously.

'More of a dance!'

'You're still here, so I take it you were king of the dance floor?'

'Winning is not how you'd see it if you were there.'

'If I had been with you there'd have been no dogfight!'

Harry nodded slowly, but thoughtfully.

'You've no idea who they were?'

'No. I thought it must be him.'

'Afraid of flying, but Nancy isn't.'

Harry was suddenly glad he'd shot her.

Within the hour after saying farewell to his elderly relative, and confirming there was no need for him to stay, Harry fired up the hire car and hit the open road with melancholy as his companion.

20

Harry relaxed with a few well-earned drinks on the flight home and contemplated the conclusion to his one remaining case: he fully appreciated the need to feel positive regarding any future cases, and continually inform the darker recesses of his psyche that what he was doing was for a greater good. On far too many occasions when he least expected, and a few when he did, his annoying conscience, that was the bane of any self-respecting investigator, would raise its ugly head above the parapet and attempt to drag him down into a pit of despair with recrimination and guilt for bedfellows, but what really concerned him was the more these periods of dejection and gloom appeared on the horizon, the shorter was their stay; he was rejecting them now with an ever increasing ease and justification that any unsavory acts, for which he bore sole responsibility, were a necessity. It was him or them he argued, and as necessity is the mother of all invention, so he was reinvented with the killing instinct borne from self-preservation, and if anybody was fool enough to challenge his right to existence, an existence solely on his terms, then the only outcome would be their early removal from this world to the next. If indeed necessity is the mother of all invention then it was now the bitch that spawned his killer.

Harry woke from a deep sleep, comforted by the welcome ambience of an aircraft cabin rocking and rolling under the telltale signs of the onset of turbulence, which rippled through the aircraft arousing much consternation within certain groups. He had a lot of respect for those individuals who faced and conquered their fears simply to be able to take a vacation alone, with friends or family; their self-sacrifice was admirable and whenever the occasion arose he would go out of his way to allay their fears. Harry thought about it now, but other members of their group were doing more than an adequate job so he closed his eyes and dozed.

Sheila punctuated his thoughts, but not the way he intended: the absence of any contact whilst away had been a godsend; there was no outside interference, no time lost through distractions, and what was now plainly clear was her true feelings for him. She was using him, he accepted that; she had brought to him something personal, he respected that, but any future contact was going to be on a professional footing and no other.

* * *

Refreshed after the transatlantic crossing, Harry waited patiently for his connecting flight from London Heathrow to Manchester to be called; one of the advantages of flying from an out of base airport was the anonymity it afforded him, and he began to feel an inner peace that so far had alluded him ever since he'd set foot on this journey. How much of this journey was luck and not judgment? But judgment it could be argued is prevalent on experience and experience must be earned. He was doing just that surely, he was not sitting around doing nothing waiting for cases to fall in his lap. That was the domain of the television and literary private detective with the reputation to deserve such attention.

His mobile sprung into life. It was Sheila. He answered on the fourth ring.

Her voice sounded strange: it highlighted how accustomed his ears had become to the Tennessee dialect. She was worried about him, hadn't heard from him for a while. Had those men been back? She was convinced they were following her. When was the date set for the game? Oh yes, the poker game, the game on which his last assignment now hung. He informed her that it was dependent on him enquiring, which was a minor lie, but he promised he would ring to confirm dates as soon as he hung up. The vacation, he began to inform her, the nice relaxing vacation, then stopped mid-sentence and laughed at his own stupid joke; she wouldn't understand, so what hope was there of even beginning to attempt an explanation. He was cold to her expressions of concern: it wasn't her, she'd done nothing wrong, hadn't insulted him, behaved in a way at odds to his feelings for her, he simply knew, reluctantly at best, that any relationship was doomed. It was a no-hoper, a no-brainer. He would cut it off at source slowly, but methodically, and in a way not to cause offence or long lasting damage. Was he being arrogant to believe she cared for him in that way? He couldn't and wouldn't take the chance. She was a friend and a valued work colleague, but business, especially this kind of business, was business. If he kept her brother out of harm's way, and made his troubles disappear that would suffice. We all have to make our mark in this world, he mused, be it good, bad or indifferent, the difference lay in whether the choice is yours or not. The lady on the address system called his flight. It was time to begin making his choice. He hung up.

* * *

'What a depressing sight!' Harry said surveying the mound of post piled up on a small table by the front door.

However hard he tried Harry found it nigh on impossible to muster up any form of enthusiasm regarding anything remotely routine, and so slumped down on the sofa to watch some sport with a mug of hot, steamy coffee. His bag littered the kitchen, his coat ended up over the back of an armchair, the post took up new residence on the kitchen table and he didn't care; normally after trips gone by he wasted no time putting the mundane chores behind him before beginning the long drawn out wind-down that invariably followed a return to home. Only today was different, there was no wind-down: there was the next case to begin and the prospect of pushing Sheila to the back of his mind.

Harry had no idea how long he had been asleep. The first indication of the deep slumber he'd descended into was the panic that overwhelmed him when he remembered the mug of coffee. It was empty. He lay back against the backrest of the sofa and watched some cricket. England were playing and winning. He thought of his bag, the post and Sheila, but still couldn't bring himself to get up and sort it. Coffee, he needed another coffee then thanked his own sagacity for stocking long-life milk.

On his return to the sofa he picked up the post, channel surfed and ended back with the cricket. He enjoyed cricket, but life without football was almost as unbearable as life without alcohol. He missed the football season and he yearned for August. Harry opened the post then wished he hadn't. Bills, bills and more bills: the electricity firm was putting up its unit rates; the gas company was threatening to put up its rates and the less said about his credit card bills the better. Oh well, he sighed, no reason for doom and gloom on that score.

It was getting late, he was hungry and as a natural lifelong hater of diets he rang out for his favorite Indian take-out. What he had consumed over the past couple of weeks didn't make good reading, so he stopped making mental notes by the first Wednesday. When the food arrived his bag was empty, a wash was on and he even managed to find a DVD in his massive collection that he genuinely wanted to watch: it was a never ending source of frustration and amusement to him that if a film appeared on the box of which he owned a copy he watched it without fuss.

The phone rang the split second he'd dumped the dishes in the sink. He knew immediately whose voice would be on the other end before his hand reached out to answer the call.

'Hi Sheila!'

'How did you know it was me? Am I becoming that predictable?'

'How's Stephen?' he replied, avoiding answering the question.

'Gambling!'

'He hasn't learnt his lesson then?'

'No!'

'We've got our work cut out!'

'We're still a "we" then?'

Should he tell her now and get it out of the way or wait? Here was a golden opportunity to put himself out of his misery. No, now was not the time. This choice was an easy one, he'd wait, he needed to collect his thoughts, and not rush in. Anyway, he said to himself as a way of justification, all things come to those who wait.

'Of course we're still a "we"!'

There was an uneasy silence that Harry recognized as being the precursor to a "Dear John" moment.

'It should be me asking you the question, as I haven't heard from you for a while. I was beginning to think you weren't interested,' Harry continued.

'It's difficult.'

'Difficult?' he repeated without pause.

'Difficult, complicated, what's the difference?'

It was time to ask the question, the question to help put his troubled mind at rest: 'What do you want?'

Here was another prolonged silence, only this time Harry was not about to be the one to break it. The silence was interminable, and there was now in his head only one course of action left open to him, but he doubted whether he possessed the courage to take it. He pulled the phone away from his ear and stared at it as if he was expecting it to suddenly burst into life, sprout legs and run out of the room cursing him every inch of the way for answering this call. He placed the phone back to his ear. She was still there, he could hear her breathing. He hung up.

There it was, over, his last case concluded. Not to his satisfaction, it must be said, but finished just the same. He smiled and slid back into the sofa. Harry knew she would not ring, why would she? Sheila always needed to control things her way, you didn't need to be a genius to figure that out, and his hanging up meant the onus was on him to reopen proceedings, and he was loath to do that. Ten minutes later the phone rang again. He answered it confident in the knowledge it was anybody other than Sheila Wallace.

'I want to be difficult, complicated, but difficult and complicated with you!'

Harry was elated to hear her sweet, soft, caressing tones, but could not answer: he wanted so hard to say what he truly felt, how she made him feel, but the words simply dried up the instant they made his lips. It was difficult and complicated. He was difficult and complicated.

'Good!' was all he could muster. It was a pathetic response.

She laughed that sexy, seductive laugh he loved to hear and was a welcome fillip to his troubled soul. No matter how long the gap between correspondence he could not expunge the memory of her and nor, if he was brutally honest, did he wish to.

'I need to see you!' she said.

'Ditto.' His heart began to race,

'How about I come round tomorrow night and rustle us up some good, old fashioned home cooking?'

It was his turn to laugh.

'What do you fancy?' she said before realizing the most obvious response. 'No, you don't need to answer that one!'

'Surprise me.'

'Oh, don't you worry Captain Travers, I will definitely do that!'

Any worries still hanging over him evaporated the instant that cheeky, sexy giggle followed her promise. Harry was smart and respectful enough not to prolong a conversation restricted by the topic, and rang off with the date set for tomorrow night.

* * *

It was top of his to do list now that the case was back on after the briefest of cancellations. Mister Moore answered without a hint of subtlety, barking out what amounted to his excuse for a polite enquiry.

'It's Mister Travers.'

This still failed to register with Moore who continued to talk in gruff, disrespectful, irreverent tones clearly disgruntled at having this man call his personal line.

Harry was seething: this attitude stroked the flames of indignation to the extreme. 'It's regarding your personal invitation for the poker game.'

Moore's reaction to his last statement was in stark contrast to the previous few exchanges and this only added to the contempt Harry felt for him, Willis and the casino as a whole. Money talks with most people, and it damn near shouted with Moore.

'Of course Mister Travers, how are you? Please remind me again when we can expect the pleasure of your company?' Moore said exuding disdain with every word.

Patronizing little bastard, thought Harry, 'Is there still a game on?'

'Tomorrow, would you like to play?'

'Certainly!'

'Game starts promptly at ten.'

'I look forward to it!' Harry began with just a hint of scorn; he was determined to stand his ground against anything they threw at him and hold his own against individuals whom he had little or no respect for.

Moore rattled off a series of detailed instructions which Harry jotted down long hand. This was panning out perfectly; he and Sheila would hatch a plan tonight and then play the game the following evening while it was all still fresh in his head. He began to tingle with excitement at the thought of crossing swords with Willis and Moore - it fed his adrenalin rush.

'Are you comfortable with the buy in?' Moore added with glee.

'Want to separate the men from the boys, eh?' Harry was enjoying, reveling in having the last word with this patronizing, self-centered, little shit.

'Don't be late.'

'Setting my watch as we speak.'

Moore hung up. Harry cheered himself with the thought of the patronizing, self-centered, little shit eagerly informing his partner in crime of his imminent arrival for tomorrow's game. He was not a Stephen, he was nobody's fool and recent events had only emboldened his reserve to see this one through to his own satisfaction.

* * *

She looked stunning in a tight black dress that stopped inches short of her knees, just the way he liked, her shoes were a matching black adorned with seven inch heels, which shocked him to the core because he was a man that adored women in heels: he loved the way they changed a woman's posture, the way they walked, but this caused his heart to palpitate. Around her slender neck hung a beautifully understated silver necklace of a design matching a set of earrings. He was lost, mesmerized, she had him and he didn't give a damn.

'Surprised?' she cooed.

'You've made my day, week, month and year!'

There was that sexy, throaty laugh again.

'Hungry?' she asked, heading for the first floor and the kitchen.

Harry impatiently swung his foot and kicked the door shut with his trailing leg so he could get a good eyeful of her ascending the stairs; she gave it her all knowing full well he'd not be able to resist and the two climbed the stairs in tandem each with their own agenda, but ultimately the same objective.

* * *

'They're just required to make up the numbers,' Willis said sitting at his desk, drumming his fingers on the table, his mind focusing on the bigger picture. 'Don't lose sight-'

'Katic is history!' Moore said with confidence, pouring them both a drink.

'Not yet,' warned Willis.

'What about the other players? We got any plans for them?'

'None!'

'Excellent, because I got some plans of my own!'

Moore brought over two drinks.

'Travers, by any chance?' enquired Willis accepting his.

'Cocky bastard!'

'He's really got to you!'

'Never liked Mister Travers from the first time I set eyes on the man. I just have an insatiable urge to smash his face in!'

Moore drained his drink then went to pour another. Willis sipped his; the deliberateness of his actions mirroring deep contemplation. His colleague returned with a larger second glass and carried on where he left off, as if he'd never broken stride.

'His destruction, either by fair means or foul, will leave a delightfully sweet aftertaste for a long time to come!'

'You're taking this far too personally,' Willis said with no real conviction.

'You know I like to have a pet project: someone I can get my teeth into and keep my interest up while we hunt bigger game!'

'Katic is no fool!' The conviction was now clearly evident in Willis' voice.

'You worry too much!' Moore said, downing his second drink and going hunting for a third. 'The man's a has-been or soon will be!'

* * *

Beads of sweat cascaded off his forehead, down his cheeks and into the corners of his mouth: Harry was in heaven.

Sheila flipped Harry onto his back and jumped on top of him. He wanted to be ridden hard and dared her to treat him as her "fuck toy"; she burst out laughing and duly obliged by riding him hard and fast: he loved every second of it. Harry adored dirty women, the dirtier the better and he wasn't ashamed to share this secret with her. Sheila knew, but had been amiss in not sharing her true feelings for him: it was a love that started out with denial, a denial borne out of embarrassment and fear of being pigeonholed "a flight deck floozy", but there was no getting away from what her heart felt every time her head tried to use reason as an excuse not to contact him; she made a conscious decision during their prolonged absence not to indulge in any discourse with Harry during his vacation, but the temptation became overwhelming when she knew he was back in the country. Now here she was satisfying his every desire, and it shocked and excited her to discover how deep her feelings went. She rode him harder and harder feeling him throbbing inside. She was aching for Harry to take her and treat her in any way he wished.

Harry grabbed her hard from behind and squeezed, she groaned. He lifted her up and penetrated her hard and fast from underneath. Sheila kissed him passionately, thrusting her tongue deep inside his mouth before he flipped her onto her back. Now on top he thrust himself deep inside her until she groaned with pleasure.

'I love you!' he whispered. 'I always knew.'

A tear came to her eyes, and he gently wiped it away.

'I loved you from the first time I saw you!'

He began to slow down and was close to climax. He gently entered and withdrew for maximum sensitivity.

'That would be nearly ten years ago!' he said incredulously

She smiled.

'I've been dreaming of this moment and you've fancied me all this time?'

She smiled a second time and gently kissed him on the lips. 'Fuck me,' she said seductively, 'fuck me hard, fuck me like a dirty, little whore!'

He was aroused more than ever.

With every thrust she called him to fuck her harder. His head began to spin with the pleasure taking this woman gave him, and he penetrated her harder and faster until he exploded inside her.

He was panting, sucking up the air. She licked the sweat of his chest. Harry wanted her now, again, he needed her and could not and would not live without her for another second. He withdrew and she forcibly pushed him onto his back and took him in her mouth. He cried out uncontrollably. He loved her beyond all comprehension.

* * *

The early morning light filtered around the outer regions of the venetian blinds keeping Harry awake. Sheila was fast asleep, her head upon his chest, his left arm carefully caressing her shoulder. Her breathing was deep and rhythmical and he listened intently, relishing every second. Glancing over at his bedside clock, it read 08:30.

Sheila rolled over onto her left side, pulling his right arm as she did so. They now lay side by side, and he was aroused being so close to her. Now awake she began to massage him with her right hand, pushing him beyond the point of no return. He pulled her towards the center of the bed and rolled her onto her stomach, placing a pillow under her. Harry was not going to be subtle; he was not the subtle type.

'You're a bad boy!' she whispered.

He pulled Sheila until she was on all fours, wrapping his hands underneath her, cupping her breasts in the process, and made wild, passionate love. Harry pulled his right hand down and played with her before Sheila lifted herself up. He grabbed a handful of her beautifully, soft blonde hair, pulling her head back and never letting the intensity of his penetration drop for an instant. Harry wanted to own her, to own every inch. He let go of her hair and forcibly pushed her head down into the pillow, taking her ever faster with increasing desire and passion. She was close to climax and eventually exploded over him with a shriek of delight. The sensation sent them both into raptures.

She pushed him back onto the bed, taking his manhood in her mouth in one swift, erotic motion. Harry knew he couldn't hold out for long, and he groaned loud and long. He kissed her afterwards without a hint of reservation.

The rest of the day, until it was time to leave for the casino, proved to be an anticlimax for them both; they discussed at length what they expected and Harry owned up about his so called friend the private detective, and then found himself completely dumbfounded when Sheila admitted she knew all along; her biggest concern was him risking his personal wealth to save her wayward brother, her emotions now being torn between these two men, but Harry was adamant and without worry on the matter. Seeing the love in her eyes only hardened his resolve.

Finally the time came to leave and Harry impatiently paced the hallway by his front door dressed in a snappy, dark suit, pink silk shirt with no tie awaiting his love. The sight that met his eyes drew every ounce of breath from his body: Sheila wore a figure hugging red dress with matching stiletto's, under her left arm she carried a strapless red handbag, around her neck, which hours ago Harry had kissed with relish, hung a slender gold necklace, from her ears she wore long, slender gold earrings, bordered on either side by her shoulder length hair.

'Wow!' was all he could muster.

'Thought you'd like it.'

'Have I told you I love you lately?'

'Not for at least an hour,' she replied giggling.

'I love you.'

'I love you too.' she said, kissing him gently on the lips.

21

The casino was busy. Harry carefully parked his shiny blue Porsche 924 about fifty yards down the road from the casino's entrance. He had it washed, waxed with a full valet when he visited his bank to collect the money required for the buy in, and they now had a little luck on their side with finding this parking space now affording a quick getaway, if required.

Throngs of people mingled outside waiting to enter. Harry checked to see if Stephen was among them. He was not. Harry was proud to have his girl on his arm and expected her to turn a few heads: it was what they planned, to try and distract as many of the fellow players as possible; not all of them would be professionals, that was accepted, but those they could narrow down would help push the odds more in their favor.

'You look fantastic,' he whispered. They walked arm in arm towards the entrance.

'I'm not wearing any underwear!'

He needed every ounce of concentration simply to maintain focus.

Harry took everything in; the whole scene being played out before him, particularly the doormen clocking their arrival, especially Sheila's, and he tried to place where the two men would have seen him to know he was one of the players in tonight's main game. He could not and by the time they had been escorted into the casino, and the private function room, he still had not been able to remember, but it was of secondary importance to his making a mental model of the internal layout and the most expeditious route to the exits.

The room was half full, but before he had time to try and ascertain who his opponents were they were introduced to the other players and their entourage by a female staff member. His heart began to race and he felt that adrenalin rush overtake him: Katic was here, but he paid no attention to Harry, his eyes locked on Sheila instantly. This part of the plan was working a treat, and he felt her squeeze his hand in reassurance. He squeezed back.

As the room slowly began to fill Harry took a moment to count the chairs: there were eight amounting to a three hundred and fifty thousand pound killing. He re-familiarized himself with those he knew were playing. Two were missing: Willis and Moore were going to partake when they deigned to arrive, and play in tandem to break as many as possible, but he was small fry compared to some of these. There was a much grander plan being executed here which poor Stephen got caught up in, but it did beg the question why couldn't he have seen what to him was so obvious, and was now acting as a beacon lighting the way, guiding him onto the righteous path.

Harry kissed Sheila tenderly on the ear and explained his theory. She smiled and he saw that love again in her eyes, only now there was something else - a deep rooted respect.

The room was expensively furnished, and ideal for the purpose, with a red patterned carpet that was soft under foot, and a recent addition; the chairs were clearly bought to match the decor, their cushioned seats and backs ideal for those anticipating a long night; the wall paper was expensive, but not to his taste and he used this weakness in the room to stoke a feeling of contempt he knew he required to play a good game. Katic could not take his eyes off Sheila for a second: she did look amazing and with each passing minute he thanked his good fortune for having the love of this woman. He was going to win tonight for her. He felt it. It was a foregone conclusion. There was not a player here who could beat him, not even the professionals: they could bluff, use any intimidating tactics available, he was going to win and that was that.

The game was to be No-Limit Texas Hold'em. Harry was more than comfortable with this format.

At the stroke of ten precisely Misters Willis and Moore, made their appearance and the game began without delay after each player took their designated seat amid more introductions from the croupier. Harry locked eyes with Moore, held it, winked, relishing the head to head confrontations to come. Moore sat stoned faced, giving nothing away. Harry quickly became bored with the man, so studied each player attempting to gauge who were the professionals, the other victims and those in possible cohorts with the two men behind the game. Sheila placed a reassuring hand on his left shoulder. He stroked her slim, delicate fingers feeling the smoothness of her nails. Of the other players only Moore and Katic paid any attention.

The croupier slickly laid a large tray of chips on the plush green table, and on Willis' command they all produced their buy in money of fifty thousand pounds. Harry, as cool as you like, removed a fat envelope from inside his suit and flipped it nonchalantly towards the croupier: the money was from the sale of the family home that had sat gathering interest, and no small amount of dust, but it held no importance to him and he could think of no better way to spend it. The room was getting warm and Sheila slid the jacket off his shoulders and draped it over the back of his chair. He smiled a confident, cheeky smile at her. She was nervous and it showed. Harry winked; even her nervousness he would use to his advantage, and gamble on the whole room feeling her uncertainty. Sure enough, the whole table focused on Sheila. Travers' confidence was sky high, albeit with an enthusiasm carefully tempered.

Chips replaced the fat envelope and Harry watched intently as they were scooped up and stacked in pretty, neat piles, paying particular attention to all the quirky mannerisms, nervous ticks, the immediate constant fidgeting, the way players fiddled incessantly with a chosen chip or chips; he was searching for any kind of 'read' or 'tell': it was mostly an act and he accepted it as that, a way of annoying their competitors, of trying to wheedle their way into the player's psyche and color or cloud any judgment. Harry had seen it all before when poker was a major part of his life: he hadn't played seriously for a few years now, but the feel and experience of the poker table never leaves you, it becomes ingrained into all your conscious thoughts the split second you take a seat, feel the chips and rub your hands over the table.

The croupier for the first few hands was a dark haired male who obviously enjoyed his food. Harry put his age at mid to late thirties. The man was confident in his mannerisms, which was mirrored in his calm, reverential tones, as he explained the blinds - this was more for the benefit of the spectators than the players.

Harry felt the need to again lock horns with Moore; again nothing was said, no hand gestures made, but both men were eager to do battle and could see it in the other.

Willis had cannily placed himself in seat number six of eight players. To Travers' thinking he clearly didn't want to be first with the blinds. He on the other hand was the second player to the dealer's left and was the initial big blind.

With the blinds on the table: the smaller started at five-hundred pounds, the bigger at a thousand, two cards were dealt face down to all the players. Harry took his time to turn up the corner of his cards: the jack of clubs, and the ten of diamonds stared back at him. It was an excellent first hand, but still he checked any impulse to bet wildly and with abandon.

The player to his immediate left was a nervous looking, dark haired man in his fifties who went by the name of Bennett: he had a drink problem, for he polished off numerous shots of hard liquor before they sat down, and continued in the same vein once the game started. Harry just needed to bide his time with him and play cautiously until the inevitable effects of the alcohol kicked in. To his right sat a fair haired guy calling himself Wheeler: he was either a pro or a very bad actor, only time would tell, but one thing was immediately obvious, he was seriously overweight with a major body odor issue. Opposite sat Moore looking more pernicious with every passing second. He was followed by Katic. Harry now had the ideal opportunity to study the man in greater detail: he was tall at around six foot five inches and looked like the kind of person who was into dog-fighting and gambling in any sort of way. Even without knowing his name Harry could tell he was of Eastern European extraction with short, dark hair, piercing hazel eyes with a long pointed nose and robust chin. Katic was sandwiched on the other side by Willis. The seventh seat was occupied by the only female player tonight: a trim, glamorous, mid-thirties brunette named Miller; she was the dark horse and sat with the air of one who played recklessly, but he wasn't convinced. Finally there was Robshaw, who Harry figured was the pro: he was fair-haired, blue-eyed, clearly the youngest player at the table in his mid-twenties, was far too calm and casual for his own good, dressed like he didn't give a damn and behaved like he owned the table. We are all your victims are we? Well, count me out. Harry took a sip out of a bottle of mineral water. If Katic was indeed the target here then Robshaw was going to be the main beneficiary in terms of chips with Moore and Willis playing to his hands. It shocked him that none of the other players seemed to be aware of the perilous nature of their present predicament. For now though he needed to keep a close eye on the reverential dealer.

Harry jerked his head around looking for any telltale signs.

'Anything wrong?' asked Willis.

'Stiff neck!'

Sheila massaged it for him.

This gave Harry ample time to study the room; it may have taken a few scans of the interior, but he found them. Tucked away in the corners were tiny holes barely discernible unless one was looking for them. The sneaky bastards were using cameras.

'You can do mine when you've finished,' Katic leered.

'Thank you, but no thank you,' Sheila replied as politely as possible.

Harry pictured Sheila biting her lip, itching to put this man in his place.

Bennett folded, Moore upped the bet, as did Katic, Willis folded with Miller close behind him, Robshaw raised the bet further, Wheeler folded. Harry, Moore and Katic matched Robshaw and further cards were dealt.

The dealer now laid down the flop: the jack of diamonds, the two of hearts and the nine of spades.

Harry carefully pondered whether to go big and try to scare the other three off or play the percentages and make an educated guess on their hands, sacrificing funds in the process; it was a necessity he accepted in order to get the 'read' on them. He decided on the latter and added another thousand to the pot.

Moore was not fazed and increased it by a further five hundred. Katic must have a good hand for he never flinched or hesitated for a second and improved the bet by another five hundred. Robshaw matched him after much deliberation. He was paying special attention not to make any eye contact with either Willis or Moore. Harry needed, wanted to see the turn and called. Moore followed suit. The dealer dealt another jack, this time of hearts.

Up to this point Harry had only looked at his cards the once. What to do? He was sitting holding three of a kind. The cards had gone his way, a pair would make at least a full house, and the odds of four of a kind were for them drastically reduced; a straight was on, but he only had nine, ten, jack, and unless one them was holding a seven, eight, queen or king he was okay, but he could bluff a four of a kind. He bet two thousand over the minimum bet with a face made of stone.

'Feeling confident?' Moore sneered.

You're obviously not, thought Harry, trying hard to stop himself from cracking a smile: smiling was not good at a poker table, and the face of stone ruled.

Moore sat motionless, studiously contemplating his next move. Harry examined the actions and idiosyncrasies of the players: Robshaw looked at him for a second, it was the first time that evening; Katic's eyes never left the table; Moore now began to fidget, as if sitting on a bed of nails, the game clearly not his forte, which just reinforced his deduction that Robshaw was the man designated to win big tonight. Moore folded amidst mutterings of nobody could have played his hand better. Katic paused when it came his turn.

I know, you know you're going to see the next card, so stop procrastinating and place your bet, mused Harry, and looked at the man as if he'd asked a question verbally and still had not been given a satisfactory reply.

Katic matched the bet.

Robshaw was not in any kind of mood to hesitate or mix it up with rank amateurs and added a further five hundred to the pot. It was back with Harry and he naturally increased the bet by a small margin: it was the obvious thing to do. Katic called him, leaving Robshaw with little alternative but follow.

The dealer after a brief delay revealed the river card: the ten of spades.

Fuck your straight! Harry now looked upon the pro with utter disdain and contempt: not through disrespect, but in the honest belief this player was out to screw them all and line his own pockets with a couple of crooks who were after bigger fish to the detriment of the smaller ones. Five people at this table sat here in the genuine belief this game was fair. It occurred to him that Katic may have a full house: tens over jacks. It was time.

'All in!' he said pushing his chip stack into the middle of the table with an air of supreme confidence. From behind him Sheila's breathing became audible. There was silence everywhere else.

Katic studied him, but he chose not to lock horns. From the corner of his eye he detected the first signs of fear in Robshaw. He prayed the prick would follow suit. Katic folded with an animated toss of his cards: he did in fact hold a full house, but it was too early for him to gamble on an all in. Robshaw sat like he was set in stone with only a blink giving him away. Harry could feel his pulse racing. Katic had played a good hand; yes he may be ruing a possible bluff, but time would prove him correct. What he wanted was this pro to get too cocky for his boots and think this amateur was bluffing. Ten minutes later he got his answer: Robshaw went all in.

Willis and Moore immediately looked to their right at Harry for some sign of reassurance that Robshaw had played the hand to perfection. They were to be bitterly disappointed.

'Cards gentlemen, please,' announced the dealer.

Harry flipped over his cards in flamboyant fashion with a flick of the wrist, and the full house Katic expertly avoided lit up his face. Robshaw sat stony-faced.

'You clearly thought I was bluffing!' he said in a monotone voice. Robshaw failed to respond, finding it hard to comprehend he'd been outdone by one of the amateurs. 'Get it over with and show us the straight!' Harry added with more than a hint of disdain.

The dealer asked again to see Robshaw's cards, and his eyes never left the table as he reluctantly revealed the seven and eight of hearts.

A sizeable pile of chips slid Travers' way. It had taken only one hand to completely scupper Willis' and Moore's master plan, and now he did allow himself a smile and a locking of horns with Moore especially.

'Beginners luck!' Harry said mockingly, knowing it would guarantee the reaction he most sought.

'It's going to be a long night,' Miller interposed.

Her injection into affairs caught him off guard for a second, but he regained his composure quickly. 'As the song goes: "I have all the time in the world".'

Willis failed to hide his fury as Robshaw packed up and left for the night.

Over the next few hands Harry deliberately folded displaying little or no compunction to play: one or two he could have, but his instinct told him to fold. He spent the time carefully studying the remaining six.

Two cards slid their way across the green baize from the slick hands of the dealer, coming to rest lying at a forty-five degree angle to each other. Wheeler was first to bet now after the blinds; his luck was not yet in and he folded. Harry looked at his cards: the eight of clubs and the two of spades. A rubbish hand if there ever was one. He decided to play.

Bennett upped Travers' bet of twelve hundred pounds by only a meager one hundred, but it was enough to make him sense that the drinker was there for the taking if the cards came his way. Moore added to the pot. Katic folded. Willis followed him. Miller now sat looking at her cards, her inner alarm sounded and she too folded. It was back with him: a small increase would be seen as a sign of weakness and he bet big with five thousand. Bennett took a sharp intake of breath, but tried hard to hide it. Harry knew he was going to fold way before the man did. Moore was the only player left in and the flop wasn't even on the table yet. Moore called and the dealer dealt the cards: the ace of spades, the nine of hearts and the three of diamonds.

Travers' next move could be the one to set up the whole table for the night if he managed to bluff his way through this hand. Ten thousand pounds slid their way into the pot. He looked at Moore the entire time with a steely determination to push this man to the edge. Moore, after many minutes of contemplation, during which he talked constantly to Harry in a vain attempt to figure him out, matched the bet.

The dealer produced the eight of hearts. Harry at least had a pair.

It was now all or nothing for him, and he took special care to count all of Moore's chips before betting the exact amount. Moore now faced elimination. The calmest one in the room was Harry Travers, because deep in his heart he didn't care whether he won or lost: he would pay off Stephen's debt if he had to, and this game was only an added bonus. He had already won the one prize he sought the most, and the smell of her perfume brought a smile to his face. Moore misread this smile and folded. Harry won his second hand and made a show of throwing his cards face up so all present could see the bluff.

He began to play hands without emotion; they were more to take stock than anything else: he discovered quite early on when he first started to play cards that the come down after winning a big pot took a couple of hands before he was ready to take another swing at it. These evaporated before his very eyes and so inconsequential were they that he failed to remember them after, even the ones he lost.

The dealer casually looked at his watch forcing the others to do the same: they had been playing for nearly two hours and it was time for a break.

He turned to face Sheila. She looked even more beautiful than before, and the two of them walked arm in arm over to the bar at the far end of the room.

'What's your poison kid?' she said giggling.

'Something diet or non-alcoholic, I got to watch this figure of mine,' Harry answered patting his stomach. 'Is that my new pet name?' It was a bonus to see her in good humor.

'I thought "Kid Travers", "Captain Harry" or "Ace", the choice is yours!'

'Just "Yours" will do.'

She laughed that sexy laugh he loved: 'You're so cheesy!'

All manner of refreshments were beautifully laid out for all to enjoy at their leisure and Harry gave them the once over before taking Sheila's order when someone caught his eye: Robshaw was back in the game. He had purchased more chips and was stacking them carefully in front of his former seat.

'Looks like someone's back!' said Wheeler softly while passing towards the food and drink.

'I reckon so.'

'Our lady competitor says the hosts have financed him!' Wheeler had started a mini run prior to the break, and this emboldened him for the forthcoming battle: 'I'll take first crack at him!'

'Be my guest.'

Wheeler went off to stack his plate.

'You took him once and you can do it again,' Sheila said, kissing him on the cheek.

Harry wasn't afraid: in fact he positively relished the idea. It was the disappointment that some small part of him felt it needed to be proved wrong when his misanthropic side screamed out the truth.

Willis and Moore were conspicuous by their absence. Probably off looking at the video footage, he thought, and it was noticeable by their body language before the break that the old confidence was returning when they finally appeared. Harry looked around briefly at the other players; he wasn't too fussed how they felt about their hosts or whether they honestly believed they were already doomed to failure.

The game resumed shortly after with a smart, new, female dealer: she was a petite blonde, supremely confident and good at her job; it struck Harry that she was not the kind of person who could hide the knowledge within her that she was cheating the table, but it was a forlorn hope and he knew it. The small blind was now a thousand pounds with the big two thousand.

The first few hands finished with sizeable bets made by first Bennett then Miller followed by Wheeler and then Bennett again. Harry throughout all these folded; again there were at least two he should have taken a gamble on in hindsight, but his inner alarm bell rang hard and true, so he folded.

The dealer slickly slid second cards out to Miller, Robshaw and Wheeler. The pro had been quiet at the resumption, and now sat back awaiting the bets. Nobody folded. Harry was the small blind. He studied them all one by one until it came his turn to look at his cards: he held a couple of sevens. It was worth seeing the flop at the very least, the hand warranted that.

Moore initially bet big trying to ward people off, but it didn't work; Harry guessed a couple of aces. Katic matched it; king and another ace he figured. Willis upped the bet by another thousand; Miller added another five hundred; Robshaw carefully matched the last bet plus another thousand; Wheeler feeling confident matched Robshaw. Harry bet the minimum, as did Bennett and the rest of the table.

The dealer finally laid out the flop: two of clubs, five of hearts and the king of diamonds. Harry folded, but he was the only one. There was going to be casualties. He leaned back, saw her beautiful smile and took a swig from the bottle of mineral water. Bennett was beginning to sweat neat alcohol.

The hand proceeded along that well-worn path with one player trying hard to muscle the others off the pot, but now it was substantially different with the mass of chips on the table.

Three kings, Harry figured, was out there somewhere waiting to gobble up the unsuspecting. Maybe he should have continued to the turn, but he dismissed the idea after the last round of betting when the turn card turned out to be a jack. The bet now stood at ten thousand pounds. Wheeler wasted no time betting twelve.

Bennett and now Katic were sweating under the stress: one profusely, the other imperceptibly. This drunk should not be playing cards, and for his own good just quit, thought Harry, but the man bet fifteen thousand.

Moore now folded, Katic up the bet to sixteen, Willis folded: they had their man where they wanted him: it may or may not be their pro who takes him down, and quite frankly they didn't care. If he took him down then so be it, his main and only concern was Sheila.

Miller reluctantly folded with an overly audible tut, her chip pile drastically reduced: she had tried to bluff and it had failed to pay off. He had to question it: the first bet had been so high, so why prolong the inevitable. Robshaw bet eighteen thousand.

There was going to be an "All in!" call sooner or later. There was no other avenue for one of them, so Harry leant back in his chair to enjoy the show.

Slowly the pile of chips expanded to reach proportions guaranteeing elimination, and a hush descended over the room, that kind of hush reserved for the most solemn of occasions. The hosts had surpassed the point of no return: it was win or bust and one person was going to stand on top of the pile.

The river card's inclusion into events brought about the usual round of audible exclamations: it was the jack of hearts.

'Interesting!' Bennett muttered.

All eyes fell on the man sipping vodka and coke.

'Interesting doesn't win poker games!' whispered Robshaw.

What a prick, thought Harry, on hearing the supercilious little shit.

'If you can't say anything we all want to hear then shut the fuck up!' Katic snapped.

Robshaw knew better than to have the final word.

Harry would have liked Katic had he not known about the dog-fighting.

It was Wheeler's turn to bet and attempt to scare off the other players: it was unavoidable, he went all in. Any and all indecision was removed from the other players and slowly one by one they all pushed their remaining chips into the center of the table.

All eyes fell once again on Wheeler to kick-start affairs: he overturned a pair of twos

'A full house,' said the dealer, twos over jacks!'

Bennett wasted no time revealing a pair of fives. Wheeler dropped his head into his hands amid a solitary laugh from Bennett's partner.

'Another full house,' the dealer continued, 'fives over jacks!'

Bennett's joy was to be short lived, Katic turned over two jacks.

In a flash Harry looked over to a now panicked stricken Robshaw: he held nothing better than three kings, he was convinced of it.

All the blood drained from Willis' and Moore's faces as he was proved right. Katic jumped out of his seat punching the air to the delight of his followers now tens of thousands of pounds the richer.

Harry knew he could take Miller and Katic as long as he was patient; Willis and Moore were not card players, they may have a couple of lucky wins, may even take a sizeable pot or two, but not over an entire game. They had grossly miscalculated the level of expertise of their victim. Harry cleaned them both out in the next three hands: he knew Katic was going to take a few deals to get his head straight after the win, and Miller, although she folded, seemed to be in a state of shock.

It was kind of written after Katic's big win, and his somewhat smaller one in comparison earlier on, that the two of them would end up facing off. Miller tried too hard with a hand and was indeed reckless when caution was called for.

Harry castigated himself on his own stupidity: he could never become even remotely friendly with this dog-fighting man, even if he hadn't the slightest clue of his nocturnal activities. Katic's arrogance was infuriating: he behaved like he owned the place. Some would argue that he had won the privilege, but Harry wasn't about to sign up to that particular fan club, and his constant leering towards Sheila brought on an intensity which opened up a whole new range of emotions: he knew now what true love must feel like and yearned for more, he desired all the comforts relationships offered where before he wished only for solitude and this man's near obsessive lasciviousness towards the woman, who made him feel whole, required nipping in the bud.

Katic cheekily asked for an unscheduled break and got it. Harry was livid. He took several deep breaths and felt her soft hands on his shoulders. He wanted her and toyed with the idea of taking her off to a quiet room somewhere. The room emptied until only they and the dealer were left.

'How long is this break?' he said not bothering to hide his true feelings.

'I don't know Mister Travers, thirty minutes to an hour, it's an unscheduled one,' answered the dealer.

'Is there anywhere I can take a quiet thirty?'

'Of course, sir,' and she passed on detailed instructions for them to easily find one of the quieter rooms reserved for gold card members.

Harry politely thanked her and took Sheila's hand. Looking back at her beautiful blue eyes, soft mouth and blonde hair draped seductively over her shoulders, he knew at once she wanted the same.

They found the room without too much bother. Harry pushed the door open, kicked it shut and kissed her passionately. The door was closed but a second before he had her dress over her hips.

Sheila unclipped his belt, unzipped his trousers, brutally yanking everything down and forcibly took him in hand: she was going to take control, never relinquishing it for a second. Harry pushed her back against the wall, lifted her up before she pulled him into her. She groaned loud and long with every thrust, every penetrating stroke. She bit his ear hard and dug her heels into his legs and buttocks until they started to bleed. Harry loved it, grabbed a hand full of hair and ordered her to dig them in harder. The turn on was immense. The more he was aroused the harder he wanted to take her over and over again. Sheila held him in with her left hand whilst grabbing his hair with her right. All thoughts of the other guests, players, dealers evaporated when in each other's arms. Sheila then pushed him back violently onto the floor and jumped on top of him before he could move and made good her promise.

* * *

Harry felt the whole dynamic of the poker table had changed yet somehow remained the same: the dealer was still there sitting serenely in her seat; Willis and Moore continued to exude menace, unhappy that their man was eliminated; and Katic still behaved like he owned the place. Most eyes were on Sheila, tinged with that hint of longing, except Katic that is: his displayed an unwelcome and uncomfortable carnal desire that his present circumstance would never be able to satisfy. Harry had seen that look before.

Winning this poker game was now of secondary importance to both men, and they played it that way. Harry always had the upper hand and struck for the jugular whenever possible: he despised himself for putting Sheila in such a position and the man sitting opposite for his temerity in thinking she was there for the taking by someone other than him. Katic was oblivious to his predicament for he had a new purpose and his dwindling chip count worried him none until it was too late. His eyes never left Sheila; he wanted her and was going to have her tonight. Harry finished the game off with an "All in" call that stunned the man. The aftershock was unavoidable.

For the first time that night Moore broke into that pernicious, odious smile, the smile of satisfaction of mission complete. Katic had lost, not to Robshaw, but lost just the same and clearly his pride was hurting. He would return again and try to recoup his losses.

Harry called it quits for the night, counted his chips, collected his jacket, took Sheila by the arm and headed for safety.

'How would you like your winnings Mister Travers? And may I be the first to say well played,' Willis said, intercepting them and walking by their side.

Harry wanted out of the room as soon as, but needed to conclude his business.

'Thank you. My stake in cash and a check for the rest will do just fine,' he said, content that to hand over such a large amount would gall them no end.

'Whatever suits you Mister Travers,' Willis said obsequiously. 'I'll get it now. Nothing wrong I hope?'

'Sheila's not feeling well!'

'I'm sorry to hear that. Is there anything I can do?'

'No, and thank you. I just need to get her home!'

They entered the main entrance of the casino and Willis bade them farewell to collect his winnings. Twenty minutes later, three hundred and fifty thousand pounds richer, they both disappeared into the night.

Travers' eyes darted here, there and everywhere, as he scoured the street for any sign of Katic's men: he remembered the mother's warning in the park and was not about to give the man a free shot. The coast was clear, but now he deeply regretted his decision to ask for some of his winnings in cash and that stupidity infuriated him. They made the Porsche and jumped in. He threw the bag on the back seat, fired her up and pulled smartly out into the road. Harry breathed a huge sigh of relief.

Sheila's silence worried him. He looked over to her. She smiled a reassuring smile and placed her hand on his knee. Harry loved her, would give everything up if it made her happy even for the briefest of moments. Halfway down George Street in Central Manchester Harry took a left onto Princess Street. Headlights filled his rear view mirror, but he checked increasing their forward speed.

'I love you, Harry,' she said ominously.

'I love you too. Everything will be fine.'

Words can only clutter emotions and undermine those few precious, fleeting moments when true love transcends all around; he needed to protect her and would at any and all personal cost.

The headlights were blinding, but failed to overtake even with him slowing to give them ample opportunity to do so. There was only one thing for it: Harry braked hard and the headlights disappeared underneath his boot. He floored the accelerator.

'Brace!' was all he could get out before their forward motion pushed them both back into their seats. The Porsche growled and they hit sixty within seconds.

'You sure know how to show a girl a good time!'

'I've had better ideas,' Harry replied checking his wing mirror to gauge the gap between them and Katic.

Harry decided to take a sharp right turn at the next junction. He turned onto Portland Street with careful consideration for his passenger.

Not another fucking car chase, he thought suppressing a smile; been down this road before and alone the decision would have been a no-brainer, but he was carrying valuable cargo now and these miscreants needed an alternative method of removal. Portland Street crossed Oxford Street to become Chepstow Street. Luckily for him the lead up to it was free of obstructions and he made good progress. They were still being followed. Harry no longer wanted or desired the life the previous few weeks had brought him: all his Christmases had come at once the day Sheila became part of his life and the alternative method he agreed upon was to return all Katic's money bar what was needed to bail out Stephen. Any nagging doubts regarding Katic and Sheila were dismissed with the knowledge that the man obviously loved his money. Harry pulled over as the road began to bear right. The trailing car did the same.

'You wait here, this won't take long.' He leaned over kissing her tenderly on the cheek, smiled and unbuckled his seat belt. He could sense her apprehension. 'Everything will be cool.'

'Don't trust them!'

'Did I ever tell you I love you?'

Her smile stayed with him, flooding his every thought, as he approached the dark blue BMW five series, anticipating Katic's next move. There was no way he was going to outrun that with Sheila next to him and seeing the man's car made him feel a whole lot better about his decision.

A dark, heavyset man with mean looking eyes exited the front passenger seat; the way he carried himself left nothing to the imagination or caused him to lower his guard. He looked back at Sheila. She was smiling at him through the rear windscreen. Harry kept on walking. In the rear seat he could make out the man he needed to speak to. Now the driver exited the car and stood, arms folded, awaiting him. The two men could have been brothers. The driver looked vaguely familiar. From behind he heard Sheila vacate the Porsche. He turned and held up a hand to pacify her, then closed in on the BMW. The rear door opened and Moore vacated. Harry froze to the spot and immediately ran through all possible scenarios. He gesticulated to Sheila to get back in the car.

'You were lucky tonight!' Moore called out.

'Lucky?' Harry desperately needed to stall them until he could formulate a sensible escape plan. It was all about Sheila now. 'You mistake luck for skill!' The thought did occur to him to take the beating and then be on their way, it was a scenario that involved Sheila not getting hurt.

'You've over played your hand, Travers!'

Harry heard Sheila imploring him to return back to the car, but he knew it would be fatal to even consider it: he wouldn't get ten yards. Harry studied the three men; the only pussy among them was Moore. Sheila called again.

'You got yourself a nice little bitch there Harry!' It was the driver, but the author of the insult was irrelevant to him.

Without any command from Moore the driver unfolded his arms and strode menacingly towards Sheila, but Harry was ahead of the game and positioned himself in such a way as to easily to cut him off, but at the same time be able to block off any further attacks. Man is weak when what he cares for is threatened: Harry now truly appreciated the truth behind that statement. Then he clocked him, he was one of the men who exited the van the night of the dogfight. The man's body language fuelled the flames of indignation and Harry speared a right hand punch towards his face. The driver anticipated this and easily blocked it, but Harry was not about single blows and a sharp left uppercut struck the man squarely just below the ribs. He yelled in pain and doubled up at the exact point that Harry brought up the underside of his elbow to smash into his nose. Blood splattered the driver's face, oozing through his fingers, as he tried in vain to stem the flow.

He could see out of the corner of his eye the heavyset man make his move: this man was quicker with his hands and it was his turn to defend; any rudimentary understanding of Jujitsu came into its own as an avalanche blows rained down upon him, which he managed mostly to block, but one or two broke through and sent him reeling.

Sheila screamed and he made out the sound of her heels over the road.

The man went for the kill, but he was premature in his belief that Harry was finished. A sharp left-right-left combination to the solar plexus and face stunned the man and stopped him in his tracks. Moore was on the move, but he was powerless to stop him, as he ran past during his retaliation. Sheila screamed. Harry turned and ran at Moore. He didn't get two paces before he was tripped up. His face thudded into the road and he felt blood ooze from a cut above his left eye. He tried to get to his feet, but a hard, fierce kick winded him badly. Sheila screamed again and he saw her fight furiously to get free of Moore. A second kick struck him, but this time he was anticipating it and grabbed the foot, twisted, leaning all his weight onto the inside of his right leg and brought the man down then wasted no time in getting to his feet and kicking the stranger senseless with a fury unparalleled.

Harry leapt over the prostrate body of the heavyset man and made a beeline for Moore. Sheila bit the hand holding her. Moore let out a scream and threw Sheila across the road. She stumbled to regain her balance. All he could remember was her face: that beautiful face with blue eyes to die for and flowing blonde hair, as the taxi cab slammed into her launching her helpless body up the road.

He screamed out her name fearing the worst, while sprinting to the spot where she came to rest. The taxi cab screeched to a halt.

By the time Harry reached her he could see from the wide open, cold, lifeless blue eyes that she was already dead, and he sobbed uncontrollably. Collapsing beside her still warm body he cradled her head in his hands and talked softly, lovingly, in one last desperate attempt to inject life.

* * *

The police openly displayed no shortage of skepticism: refusing to believe how Harry could not possibly remember a single identifying feature of any of the three men who attacked them, but his temporary amnesia never lessened their fervor for unearthing the truth. The taxi driver was no less helpful in that regard, as by the time he'd brought the cab to a halt the three assailants had vanished. Harry could only give the briefest of descriptions, and his lack of clarity was put down to the trauma of losing a loved one. In time he was offered the usual counseling if he should so need it, but refused on the grounds that the memories were still too raw. In reality he was already planning the most heinous forms of retribution for all three plus Willis, if he should dare to intervene. Collateral damage is how he viewed him.

On his return home he just managed to scrape together a modicum of self-control and informed work of his sad involvement in the tragedy. Harry was not too surprised to learn that they already knew via her bother. His immediate roster was cleared, marking him off on log days.

* * *

Harry waited a couple of days before starting out; he was mindful in case the police were monitoring his every move, but still half-expected Moore and his cronies to turn up on his doorstep. That was definitely too much to ask. It was late when he finally left the house, but Harry wasn't planning to seek revenge there and then, he simply wanted to lay the all-important ground work. Preparation is everything, he constantly told himself, plus he had his winnings from the poker game at his disposal. Parking the car outside the casino in exactly the same spot as before, his heart sank with the thought of her. Hate soon followed.

Harry sat waiting, waiting for one of them to show their face. It took most of the night, but the driver eventually appeared. He fired the Porsche into life. Tailing the man proved surprisingly simple: he was shocked at the ease with which he kept pace and still remained out of sight. Harry began to become incensed with the sheer effrontery of the man, imagining his blasé attitude without fear of any reprisal.

Harry eventually pulled in by the side of the road some fifty yards shy of the driver's final destination, got out of the car and walked up to a set of cast iron gates guarding an impressive five bedroom detached house off Clay Lane in Wilmslow. It was only a few miles up the road from where he lived and one of the more up market areas of Manchester where he knew a couple of the crew resided. He clocked a CCTV camera and stayed just out of sight. The house was plush looking from the outside and clearly out of the price range for a chauffeur. Moore or Willis had to be inside, and again the indignation rose rapidly within him that only a brief walk up the road away from the house managed to subside. He will wait here every night if need be until he witnessed Moore visit the house.

Patiently he sat for five consecutive, frustrating nights, plans drawn, starting around thirty minutes before the driver's estimated time of arrival and each night he was prepared: if he got just the driver and Moore then so be it, the third man would live in fear once he saw the fate that awaited him. On the sixth night Moore arrived.

His car was moved out of sight lest any eagle-eyed neighbor should finally make a connection with the night's events and his Porsche. He walked the half-a-mile to the house wearing a dark-hooded top along with gloved hands. The desire for retribution invaded his every thought and action; revenge took hold of his soul and ran with all its might through the night aboard the man hell-bent on inflicting pain and suffering on God's little children, the very offspring who had dealt him the cruelest of blows, denying him the happiness he sought. Harry put his hand inside his trouser pocket and once again felt for that reassuring Swiss army knife he always kept as back up and now a second knife with a long thin blade in a protective plastic cover.

The CCTV camera only covered about three-quarters of the actual gate and so it wasn't too difficult to circumnavigate and climb it without being seen. Once inside the grounds he quickly scanned ahead to pick up the other cameras. Happy with his route to the house the next few steps brought on the feeling of enlightenment and a journey which could only be categorized as karma.

He made the house without being detected and peered menacingly into one of the front rooms through a slit in a set of heavy looking curtains. The room was empty and so he moved onto the next portal into the private, undisturbed world of his victims. Again he was to be disappointed, but the third, around the left hand side of the house, brought him the satisfaction he desired.

Moore was sitting looking smug around an expensive looking pine table in a magnolia colored room. He was in a deep conversation with the stranger from the other night. The driver was nowhere to be seen. Harry checked he hadn't been spotted before continuing to monitor the two men closely. The white windows were of the modern double glazed design and locked from the inside; he may not be able to enter via this window, but he could certainly leave. He noticed a doorway off to the left of the room under observation and he naturally investigated in that direction.

From the aromas that hit his nostrils the door led towards the kitchen. After the briefest of considerations he found to his delight that the door connecting the kitchen to the rear garden was wide open. It was warm for the time of day and he should have anticipated as such; the anger that arose because of his lack of appreciation for the conditions subsided only when he took issue with his own state of mind. A man came to stand in the doorway and smoke a cigarette: it was the driver. Harry hugged the side of the wall, pulled the long, thin knife from inside his jacket pocket and slid off the protective cover; he was not stupid enough to enter the building in a rage, waking everybody up, alerting them all to his presence, even if his demand for revenge called for it. If the job was to be done effectively then stealth was the order of the day.

The driver stepped away from the door and out into the back yard, the light from the kitchen illuminating his back. Harry held his breath whilst slowly pocketing the cover. In the dim light only a rash act would give him away. The driver took another step, took one last drag on the cigarette and flicked it into the darkness, turned sharply to his left and felt the wind leave him. It took a second, but he recognized the cold, hard features ahead of him and tried to no avail to call out, as the life drained out of him and his legs became lead. Harry put his right hand under an armpit to take the dying man's weight and keep him upright. He hauled him over to a small tree. There he dumped the man to die in peace, but only after searching him and finding a handgun which he neatly tucked into his belt.

There was no case to solve here: if he hadn't been forced to pull over then Sheila would not have been in the road.

The bright, piercing light from the kitchen beckoned him forward. All reason was abandoned. He moved the gun to his trouser pocket: he wanted this to be personal and a gun to him was not personal. The inside of the house was warm and inviting, a good night to die, he surmised, and wasted not a second navigating his way out of the kitchen and into a small hallway that contained the doorway on the right leading to the two men. All was quiet, nobody was talking and he inched slowly to the doorway and listened for activity. It soon became apparent the room was empty, so he furtively moved deeper into the house. The next door was on the left, but was shut and emanating no sound. Ahead to the right was the staircase facing the front door, and to the left a second room with the door slightly ajar. He was now caught between a rock and a hard place if anybody came down the stairs or vacated the second room. Harry quickened his step and made the bottom of the stairs undetected. To climb the stairs increased the odds of detection: he only had to hit one creaky step. The element of surprise needed to be maintained.

The frustration ate away inside him like a cancer, but Harry by his professional training was a measured person and not naturally impulsive and so held his nerve and the justification for his patience was rewarded when the stranger appeared and nonchalantly skipped down the stairs. Harry quickly backed off, disappearing into the room with the closed door before the man made the ground floor. From inside the room he could make him out entering the kitchen and call out the name of the driver, first in the kitchen then secondly from the garden. He needed to act fast. Harry pulled out the gun, checked it and replaced back into his pocket. Still the stranger called out.

The kitchen now seemed warm and inviting to Harry as he furtively slipped out the front-door, dissolving into the night. He must not allow him to re-enter the house and this thought alone steeled his nerve, hardening his resolve to dispose of him quickly and efficiently.

The stranger continued to search for his friend and colleague in hushed, cautious tones. Harry ran round the side of the house, retracing his previous footsteps and positioned himself for the kill; not at any time did he pause for thought or try and reconcile his actions with a dwindling conscience overcome with hate and loathing. He stepped forward into the darkness, tightening his grip on his preferred weapon of choice. Ahead of him he could still make out the man's faint silhouette in the garden, hunting unsuccessfully for his colleague. You will soon be joining him, smiled Harry, easing his frame around a small tree in order to come up from behind; there was going to be no chivalry here, no willingness to allow this man to die with honor, he would extend swiftness of the kill, but even that rankled in its generosity. Sheila's face and cold blue eyes burned into his memory forcing forgiveness and compassion to the back of his mind, to the wilderness of forgotten dreams and promises. There was only one promise worthy of his consideration and he was about to see it two-thirds completed.

The man was now no more than four or five feet away and easily alerted to his presence if he'd bothered to stop and take stock. Harry wanted to see the man's eyes when he plunged the knife deep into his chest and so paid little heed to being discovered at such a late stage. He positioned the knife ready for the strike in expectation of a desire fulfilled, but the man turned away from him distracted by something then swung round to face him. He had pulled a gun. Harry lunged and went for the kill. The man fell back under his weight, as he thrust the blade forward while grabbing his gun hand, forcing the barrel downwards. A blinding light met his efforts. Harry took a second blow to the back of the head from the butt of a gun before slashing the knife at his unseen assailant. He remembered reading that a blow behind the left ear can prove fatal and grabbed his intended victim and swung him hard left; this did the trick and the stranger's limp body fell to the ground on receiving the fatal blow. He was now free to attack Moore. Harry slashed violently without thought or proper control and Moore miraculously escaped serious injury until he grew too confident in his own ability and caught a stinging blow across the left cheek. For the first time he saw, at close quarters, fear in Moore's eyes, as the crimson flow covered the lower part of his face and he smiled whilst pushing with all his might to drive the knife home into the man's chest, but Moore was not for rolling over and used Travers' own weight against him, pulling him forward and throwing Harry to the floor. Moore wasted no time fleeing to the house rather than finishing the fight outside.

'Careless,' Harry said quietly, furious with his impetuosity. He picked himself up, collected the stranger's gun and hightailed after Moore.

Moore made the house and looked over his shoulder the split second before he slammed the door shut. There wasn't time to lock it as his pursuer's heavy boot kicked it open.

Following Moore gave him instant pleasure, a pleasure now with a nice trail of red polka dots littering the floor, but he was a wounded animal and Harry needed to apply caution. He held the gun out in front: it was a Smith and Wesson 1911 semi-automatic pistol. It felt good. His only certainty was his quarry's inevitable phone call, in the short time allowed, would not be to the authorities. The window of opportunity would be small. He carefully stowed the knife for future use.

Cautiously re-entering the small hallway with the two rooms off to the left and the one to the right, he found all doors shut: it was a ruse to delay him while he lay-in-wait. Harry took the gamble, ignoring the rooms and made a beeline for the stairs. He wasn't going to be a complete fool and kept an ear out for a latch opening.

The stairs were fourteen in number with a right-angle turn to the right on the eleventh. He carefully tried the first step, there was no creak, neither from the second or third or fourth, and the door latches hadn't been released. The remainder of the stairs passed by without a sound and the upstairs loomed large with a landing in an 'L' shape. Four doors now faced him. With all the stealth he could muster he crept up to each door in turn ready to unload the SW1911 should the murderous Mister Moore burst out and try and catch him off guard. To his bitter disappointment not a sound emanated from any of the rooms. Eventually Harry found himself at the top of the stairs looking down at the door of the second room on the left. There was only one way he could see to catch his prey and he immediately marched on the spot. Fourteen steps later Harry stopped and waited for the reaction. He heard a shuffling like someone carrying a severe injury to their leg, then nothing. Harry bent his ear towards the lower floor and the shuffling sound began again only this time accompanied by a series of small bangs separated by a short pause. Harry was down the stairs in a flash. Three steps from the bottom Moore came bursting out the room nearest the front of the house and let loose three shots. Harry jumped the banister, rolled on the floor and returned fire. Both men missed.

He now found himself at a serious disadvantage having ended up flat on his back with Moore potentially able to stand over him and finish him off in quick fire fashion, so he wasted a second shot to give him some valuable breathing space in order to regain his feet. Moore fired two rounds in a panic from his automatic. All three shots missed their target, burying themselves into walls.

Harry needed to remain calm. He remembered his training and took a deep breath, steadied his frame and calmly fired a third shot at the largest part of his target, hitting the man squarely in the chest. Moore flew back crashing against the inside of the main door audibly exhaling, as if he'd been punched violently, and slid to the floor. Harry was banking on having at least six rounds left plus the gun in his belt. He pointed the barrel firmly at the prostrate Moore's head and strode forward for the kill.

'This doesn't end here!' wheezed Moore with blood beginning to trickle out of the corner of his mouth, and went to raise his gun, but Travers' swift right boot launched it out of his grip and into the room the dying man had recently vacated.

Harry said nothing and resolutely held his aim.

'Who the fuck do you think you are?' Moore continued in one last defiant gesture. 'We will have your balls for bookends!'

Harry continued to keep his counsel.

'The strong, silent, dumb type,' Moore went on, laughing.

He refused to bite and stood stock still, unblinking.

'Who are you, and what do you want?'

Harry chose his words carefully replying in clear, precise and quiet tones, while trying desperately hard to hide the emotions tearing his insides apart: 'I am the Captain, and this sweet revenge is no substitute for a broken heart.'

The split second after his left index finger squeezed firmly on the trigger the back of Moore's head departed from the remainder of his skull.

He never looked back, refusing to: Harry was scarred now, altered forever and out of the house and long gone by the time the police arrived. On reaching his car he was calm, collected and content in the knowledge that if Willis suspected him and came looking, seeking revenge, he'd be ready and waiting.

THE END

Captain Harry Travers will return in Sky High.

Printed in Great Britain
by Amazon